Theatre at War, 1914–18

Dr. Larry J. Collins enlisted in the Army as a Junior Leader in 1957 and served with the Royal Signals. He left the army in 1966 to train as a teacher of physical education and history at Madeley College where he graduated with a B.Ed. in 1970. In 1974, after gaining an M.A. from Leeds University, he taught at Worcester College of Higher Education. While in Worcester he joined the resident amateur theatre company at the Swan Theatre. In 1980, he left education and became a professional actor. Acting initially involved touring with small-scale companies, including a four-month tour doing revue in top security prisons. Further work included repertory in Manchester and other cities, touring with the Northumberland Theatre Company and work in television. While "resting" he taught drama. The military connection was resumed in 1986 when he was commissioned in the R.A.F.V.R. [T] where he served with the Air Training Corps. In 1991, he transferred to the Army Cadet Force. A return to academia resulted in a Ph.D. in theatre history being completed in 1994 at the Royal Holloway College, University of London. In 1996, Dr. Collins moved to Shropshire, where he writes, teaches and serves part-time in the Services. In June, 2000, he was awarded the MBE for services to the Army Cadet Force.

Previous publications:

Theatre at War, 1914–18
        [Macmillan]. First edition, hardback. 1998.
Cadets – The impact of war on the Cadet Movement.
        [Jade Publishing Limited]. Paperback. 2001.

Theatre at War, 1914–18

L. J. Collins

◆JADE◆

Jade Publishing Limited,

5, Leefields Close, Uppermill, Oldham, Lancashire, OL3 6LA.

This revised impression published in paperback by Jade Publishi
Limited 2004.

© L.J. Collins 2004
    All rights reserved.

ISBN 1 900734 28 1 Theatre at War, 1914–18. (Pbk).

Printed in Great Britain

Typeset by
Jade Publishing Limited, Oldham, Lancashire.

British Library Cataloguing in Publication Data
Collins, L.J., 1942–
  Theatre at War, 1914–18 – New Ed.
  Includes bibliography and index.
    1. World War, 1914–18 – Theatre and the war
    I. Title
    940.4'8

ISBN 1–900734–28–1

Dedicated
to the memory of
Monica Collins

Acknowledgements

It would have been difficult to complete this book without the he
and varying assistance of the following: Joseph Managhetti who ga
me initial encouragement; Captain Tony Furse of the Army Cad
Force for the use of his family album; the helpful staff at the Imperi
War Museum, particularly those in the Documents and Boo
departments, and the Licensing Officer from the photograph
archives; as well as those of the British Museum, National Newspap
Library, Westminster Library, Hertford Library and the YMC
Library in Walthamstow. Thanks, too, must go to the Society f
Theatre Research whose financial assistance towards the cos
involved in my first year of research was greatly appreciated. I a
especially grateful to Derek Forbes, formerly Hon. Secretary of t
STR, who was not only very supportive, but also provided invaluat
advice. Thanks, too, to Adrienne Forbes for her encourageme
Acknowledgments are due to Harper Collins Publishers for perm
sion to quote Edmund Blunden's poem, and to George T. Sassoon a
Penguin USA for Siegfried Sassoon's poem. I am also indebted
Professor J. S. Bratton of Royal Holloway, University of London f
her academic counsel and to Brian Prescott for his patience, diligen
and continuous support.

Larry J. Collins,
January, 2004.

Contents

The cover was executed by Baxter-Cox Design.

Illustrations

All copyrights are acknowledged and permission was sought, and granted, to reproduce the pictures shown in this work.

Introduction

In the decade prior to the First World War the entertainment profession experienced a period of considerable change, especially in the repertory theatre. There was a discernible move away from the dominance of the actor, and in particular the actor-manager, and the contents of the play assumed a greater importance. Commercial consideration was no longer the sole prerequisite for mounting a production. Barry Jackson, the director of the Birmingham Repertory Theatre, exercised his commitment to art by concentrating on plays by contemporary playwrights, for example Bernard Shaw and new dialect works by regional authors. Jackson did not, wrote the critic J.C. Kemp 'set out consciously to convert the Birmingham Philistines',[1] but he attempted to 'educate' them by concentrating on the aesthetics of production; this sense of obligation was shared by his manager John Drinkwater — a playwright and minor poet — who on the opening night of the city's purpose-built repertory theatre in 1913, recited a poem specially written by him for the occasion. The first verse reads:

> *In these walls*
> *Look not for that light trickery which falls*
> *To death at birth, bought piecemeal at the will*
> *Of apes who seek to ply their mimic skill;*
> *Here shall the Player work as work he may*
> *Yet shall he work in service to the play.*[2]

These words were indicative of the direction the major repertory theatres were moving artistically during the Edwardian and immediate pre-war years. Harley Granville Barker at the Court Theatre, in co-operation with J.E. Vedrenne, concentrated on psychological realism in his productions and was the most influential director of the Edwardian period.[3]

The movement towards art and local theatre was not confined to Birmingham and London. The Glasgow Citizen's Theatre in 1911 became the first British company to produce Chekhov. Liverpool, too, was experimenting with new works. In 1911, at Kelly's Theatre, Galsworthy's *Strife* was performed – a courageous choice considering there was serious unrest in the Liverpool docks.[4] At the Gaiety Theatre in Manchester new local acting and writing talent had, since 1907, been encouraged by the director Miss Horniman.[5] Other theatres, such as The Old Vic, London, the Theatre Royal, Bristol and the Abbey Theatre, Dublin, had an influential effect on the British stage in the Edwardian era: each company, in its own way, attempted to combine the twin aims of bringing new 'local drama' and established classics to their audiences. Prior to the war there was also discussion within the profession regarding the creation of a National Theatre. This artistic movement, however, came to an abrupt end in the summer of 1914. 'Art for its own sake' as envisaged by the Edwardian theatre pioneers was a peacetime 'luxury'. Drama during the war had much more mundane, although no less important, functions to perform within the world of theatrical entertainment.

The repertory theatres, for the most part, closed down during 1914–18. The established West End houses, on the other hand, after an initial hiatus and tentative period of readjustment continued working. There was, however, a change in fare and in style. The upper-middle class drawing-room play by, for example, Somerset Maugham, with its attendant fashion-conscious audience in dinner suits and long dresses was to become a thing of the past. The military uniform, particularly for the younger men and increasingly for some women, was *de rigueur*. People adjusted to the wartime conditions: restrictions on lighting, food, liquor and travel; its air raids and increase in working hours.[6] Despite these inconveniences and the concomitant decrease in leisure time there were more people at work; as Marwick points out, 'the balance was restored by the greater spending money accumulated by those in domestic employment, and the presence of soldiers on leave with little to do but sample the pleasures of civilian life'.[7]

To judge by the paucity of writing about the stage for the period 1914–18 it seems that theatre historians regard the war years as of little consequence. Phyllis Hartnoll[8] and Allardyce Nicoll[9] virtually ignore the war, although Hugh Hunt devotes a two-page chapter to the period in *The Revels History of Drama in English*.[10] Comments on the war and the stage are left to the critics such as J.C. Trewin,[11] Ernest Short[12] and W Macqueen-Pope.[13] This latter group, the critics, were naturally more interested in what was performed and by whom; the question of why and its effect was of secondary importance. One reason for the lack of retrospective interest may be, perhaps, that the recognized playwrights were strangely quiet, and that little new of universal note was produced. It is true that John Drinkwater wrote and Barry Jackson produced *Abraham Lincoln* at the Birmingham Repertory Theatre before bringing the play to London in 1918 – but as Lynton Hudson said, the play 'was a swallow that did not make a summer'.[14]

This book is, however, chiefly concerned with what lies outside the ambit of the dramatic critic. A great deal of what was performed in camps and hospitals was for a private audience. What the majority of audiences wanted was colour, an antidote to the dreariness of brown mud and khaki uniforms. The theatre was also, for both civilian and serviceman, a temporary release from the agonies of the war; and for this escape they looked, on the whole, to musical comedy and to the music hall with its songs, farcical one-act sketches and revues. Revues and pantomimes were especially popular as entertainment in the armed forces, for reasons which were both psychological and practical.

'Undoubtedly' wrote Arthur Marwick 'the intellectual content of almost all the theatrical productions... was minimal';[15] or as G.T. Watts writing in *The Englishwoman* in 1916 said 'The drama for the time being may be said scarcely to exist, having been replaced by a species of inanity'.[16] It may appear that entertainment, frivolous amusement, was all that was wanted from the theatre at this time: *Maid of the Mountains*, *A Little Bit of Fluff* and *Chu Chin Chow* all exceeded 1,000 performances. But the generally-held opinion that the theatre in 1914–18 was simply an antidote to war is not true. Theatre was much more than a diversionary and escapist tactic employed to provide temporary relief; indeed, the theatrical profession, in order to justify its existence, had to produce a theatre that was seen to be purposeful and relevant, and in order to do this specific functions were developed. An examination of different accounts and of over 400 plays in the Lord Chamberlain's collection shows that the theatre was employed as a recruiting and propaganda agent, and raiser of funds for war. Conversely – or some might argue, perversely – the theatre also served a useful medically-remedial function in hospitals, as well as collecting many millions of pounds for charity. To place the numerous references to sums of money in a relative context, the Retail Price Index can be employed as a rough guide (there appears no other really satisfactory means of comparison): thus the amounts quoted can be multiplied by 30 in order to give an approximation to today's values.[17]

The aim of this book is to fit together in a coherent form the myriad

of over-lapping and different types of theatre provision offered durir
the First World War, and add further pieces to the jigsaw of the perioc
cultural history – pieces which have not so far received significa
attention.

Recruitment and Employment

At the beginning of 1915 the Regular British Army totalled less than 250,000 men; many of whom were serving in other countries, thousands of miles away from the forthcoming war in Europe. In addition, there was a further quarter of a million serving part-time in the Territorials. All of these men, and also those in the Royal Navy, were volunteers. The continental countries operated a system of conscripted service and hence their armed forces were very much larger in number. Therefore, on 6 August, 1914, Parliament was obliged to authorize the initial recruiting appeal: the target was 100,000 men.

The recruiting campaign was strategically necessary in view of what was to befall the British Expeditionary Force of 90,000. The BEF, under the command of General Sir John French, battled hard during the fighting retreat with the French armies in August and September. This was the first of the battles known as the Marne, where both the British and French managed to halt the German advance on Paris, albeit at the cost of a quarter of a million casualties. Nevertheless, the BEF successfully refuted the Kaiser's derogatory remark referring, at the outbreak of hostilities, to the BEF as the contemptible little British Army'. Clearly, it was not large enough for the task but 'contemptible' it never was, and from then on, 'little' it never would be. Indeed, the authorities, via the press, made full propagandist use of the Kaiser's reputed phrase and as a result recruiting figures increased substantially.[1]

It soon became apparent to people such as Field-Marshal Lord Kitchener, the man in charge of recruiting, that the war was not going to be a short encounter, let alone be over by Christmas as many believed – and the retreat to Paris merely underlined this fact. The appeal launched just two days after the Declaration of War reached its target on 25 August, 1914. However, more than fifty per cent of the BEF were casualties; 'one in ten had been killed [three quarters of them at Ypres] ... the old army had gone past recall'.[2] At the end of the month another target of a further 100,000 was set, and by the end of September this increased to another 500,000. To accommodate the shortage and increase numbers the conditions of entry were altered: the age was raised to thirty-five – later to forty, then fifty – and the height restriction lowered. The requisite height of a volunteer at the beginning of the war was 5 feet 8 inches, by October it was 5 feet 5 inches, and on November 5 it was again lowered to 5 feet 3 inches.[3] Until this time recruitment was restricted to single men, but now efforts were being made to entreat the married man to enlist.

The necessity and resultant drive for military recruits had an immediate effect on most trades and professions, including the theatre industry. The result was felt both corporately and individually. In the corporate sense theatre companies lost a considerable number of male employees. Individually, artistes and musicians felt, like many other people, duty bound to respond to 'the call' and hence voluntarily enlist. The latter performers had the additional option of joining recruiting bands, and the former would at times combine with the musicians in concerts for the specific purpose of recruiting for the military. There was also coercive pressure to enlist which came from differing quarters: a man's peer group, the public, the young ladies, the government – and in the case of actors and artistes – from some theatre managers. The number of theatre employees joining the military was significant enough to worry the entertainment industry.

INDIVIDUAL EFFORTS AT RECRUITING

The effect of war, at its outbreak on 4 August, 1914, is impossible to judge with any accuracy; about half of the West End theatres were, by tradition, closed during the summer.[4] Many of the patrons disappeared to their country retreats, were away on holiday, or the events of Ascot and Henley took precedence in their social calendar. However, *The Era*'s editorial columnist was not slow to point out, on 5 August 1914, the theatre's role in the ensuing conflict, saying:

> *The recreation of the playhouse, the variety theatre, and the*
> *picture palace acts as a relief from the national stress.*[5]

The immediate problem confronted by the theatre managers was, how should they professionally react to the declaration of war? The same *Era* writer proclaimed that on Sunday managements were apparently sensitive enough not to include patriotic displays for fear of upsetting the foreign members of the audience, or presumably of inciting anything resembling recriminatory bad behaviour. This tentative feeling toward neutral reaction dissipated on the evening of the ensuing Bank Holiday Monday. At the London Opera House, for example, a young baritone sang *Long Live the King* and *Tommy Atkins*, and the matinee performance at the Palladium began with the National Anthem. The fervent feelings of patriotism became more obvious at the London Palladium as halfway through the programme the orchestra played the Russian National Anthem, and a few of the audience responded with vocal accompaniment, but when the *Marseillaise* was played the entire auditorium rose to its feet and gave voice; and *Rule Britannia*, as they say, 'brought the house down'. At the finale the curtain rose to reveal a huge Union Jack and the inevitable singing of *God Save the King*. A similar pattern was repeated at music halls and other theatres around the capital. The New Middlesex Theatre show incorporated a 'tableau representing France bearing the Triple Entente', and again the singing of the French anthem with a female figure holding a tricolor, and behind British and Russian flags formed the backcloth.[6] Thus started the move to stir the hitherto subdued nationalistic pride of the British and make it manifest upon the public stage of theatrical entertainment.

Leading actors took it upon themselves to join the recruiting drive. Apart from playing their parts in the forthcoming patriotic dramas, actors, such as Frank Benson, performed specially-written short pieces (entitled *Shakespeare's War Cry*) in the London and suburban theatres.[7] Benson included the speech 'O God of Battle steel my soldiers' hearts' (Act IV, Sc I) and, of course, the famous St Crispin's Day speech also from *Henry V* (Act IV, Sc III).[8] Benson was not alone in his crusade. Ion Swindley, another actor, would before the curtain went up recite *The Flag* by Rudyard Kipling as a patriotic gesture.[9] Lieutenant Philip Ridgway, after being invalided out of the army, toured the country delivering recruiting speeches in numerous theatres. Later, despite the introduction of conscription, various individuals still felt it incumbent upon themselves to urge the young men to volunteer; beside everyone wanted to be seen to be 'doing their bit'. Sir John Martin-Harvey, another notable leading actor, staged specialized evening war lectures with patriotic recitations and musical accompaniment in the theatres and towns he toured.[10] Martin-Harvey, like Benson, encouraged, not to say inveigled, the young men to enlist there and then, and in doing so earned the gratitude of the Prime Minister, Lloyd George.[11]

The recruiting drive was not confined to the enthusiasts of the legitimate stage. The Variety theatre had its 'agents' as well, none more enthusiastic than the famous music hall artiste Harry Lauder. In his autobiography, *A Minstrel in France*, Lauder recalls the time he visited his son, then a Lieutenant in the Argyll and Sutherland Highlands, at his training camp. In response to Lauder's question, 'What do you need most, Son?' The soldier replied, 'Men, Dad, Men!' The result was that Lauder assembled a pipe band with drummers to go on a recruiting drive of Scotland. The Scottish artiste combined concerts and speeches with the patriotic stirrings of the pipes and drums and, rather like the Pied Piper of Hamelyn, led the young men to the recruiting officer. Lauder extended his zeal for recruiting by giving speeches in theatres after shows, wherever in the British Isles he performed; even widening his sphere of influence to encompass a corner of the Empire, namely Canada. And as he recorded in his memoirs:

> *They tell me that I and my band together influenced more than twelve thousand men to join the Colours; they give me credit for that number, in one way or another I am proud of that.*[12]

To the name of Benson, Martin-Harvey and Lauder can be added: Will Evans, Harry Tate, Seymour Hicks, Sam Mayo, George Robey and a 'host of others.[13]

No section of the public was spared in the drive for recruits or in the attempts to propagate support for the war. At a Patriotic Rally at the Albert Hall organized by the Business Government League there paraded on the platform, 'wounded soldiers, sailors, members of the Sportsman's and Football Battalions, League of Frontiersman, Red Cross Nurses, Boy Scouts, special constables and Chelsea Pensioners'. The entertainment was supplied by the singing of patriotic songs by Charles Coborn and Mrs Leo Dryden, and recitations by the well-known actress Constance Collier. [14]

RECRUITING SONGS

By 1870, wrote MacKenzie, the content of the popular song sheet had become 'nationalistic, xenophobic, respectful of authority, glorifying military adventure, and revelling in the defeat of "inferior" peoples', and a perusal of the songs sung during the Boer Wars bears this analysis out.[15] Such messages and sentiments can be seen in Leslie Stuart's *Soldiers of the Queen*, and Kipling's *The Absent Minded Beggar*. The songs of 1914–18 had, by and large, become less jingoistic, although an examination of the evidence indicates that there existed two discernibly different types of song: one for home and civilian consumption, the other for military usage. Some critics, it was reported in *The Era*, deplored the superficiality of the music hall songs. To the purist they contained no musical merit, were over-sentimental and little more than a 'jingle of rhymes'.[16] The British soldier and sailor should, thought some high-minded critics, be singing *Rule Britannia*, *Men of Harlech*, *Scots wha hae* or *The Minstrel Boy* depending upon which part of the British Isles they hailed. The stirring melodies of Sir Charles Villiers Stanford's adaptation of John Newbolt's *The King's Highway* and *Drake's Drum* did, reported the lead writer in *The Era*, 'reach our great middle class and so do something to stir popular sentiment in the right direction and ring out the clarion call to the front, but they did not fill the soul of Mr Tommy Atkins'.[17] The same could be said of Begbie and Cowen's recruiting song *Fall In*. The songs of 1914–15 that were unequivocal in their message such as *Fighting for Their King and Sireland* by Frederick Day, *For King and Country* by Robert Harkness, and *Your King and Country Want You* written by Paul A. Rubens, fell on almost deaf ears. The latter was billed as 'A Woman's Recruiting Song'. It is probably best remembered because of its inclusion in Joan Littlewood's 1960s hit musical *Oh, What a Lovely War*, and the haunting message of the first line – 'Oh! We don't want to lose you but we think you ought to go'. The words, the message of these songs are too strident. The lyrics reflected the earnestness of the message and reminded a man of his sacrificial duty both to his country, and women. These sentiments are outlined in the chorus of Ruben's song *Your King and Country Want You*:

> *Your King and Country want you more than I do,*
> *So go and be a soldier and a man*
> *Now is the time when I and other mothers*
> *Must be as brave as English women can,*
> *And let them see you're of the Bulldog breed.*[18]

Tommy Atkins did not want to think of the strong woman at home. It was the romantic ideal he sought and would be willing to fight for; sentimentality was a more potent force than nationalistic pride. Another important factor was humour, as in the song *On Sunday I Walk Out With a Soldier*, sung by Gwendoline Brogden. The humour is evident in the sexually suggestive lines:

But on Saturday I'm willing
If you'll only take the shilling
To make a man of every one of you.

Patriotism, if sung about, had to be done with humour rather than with solemn seriousness. This was the way they did it in the music hall and this was where the common soldier went for his entertainment. And if it was not a woman he was missing then it was a town, or particular place. Thus the popularity of *It's a Long Way to Tipperary* rested not on the knowledge of where Tipperary is – most did not know, or indeed care – but it was, as Pulling points out, the line 'Good-bye Piccadilly; Farewell Leicester Square' which was its appeal[19]. The association would have been very strong considering that most troops passed through London on their way to the Front. London was by far the biggest 'transit camp' in Britain, and the soldier's very last night may well have been spent in the theatres, music halls or bars of Piccadilly and Leicester Square.

The War Office in acknowledgement of the music halls' effect wrote, in September 1914, to the managers of the major variety theatres asking them to including such songs as *Fall In!* in their repertoire, '... with a view to encourage enlistment'.[20] It is not known whether or not, or to what extent the managements complied with this request; it is assumed they did, but such blatant recruitment ballads could not compete with the popularity of Tipperary. Everyone was singing the latter and the song gained 'respectability' when it was rendered at the Albert Hall in October, 1914. The soloist was Charles Mott and the chorus was sung by the Royal Choral Society. The audience of several thousand added to the occasion by accompanying the singers in the final verse. Among those who sang the refrain 'with heart and voice' were Sir Frederick Cowen, Sir Frederick Bridge and Sir Henry J. Wood, three of the country's leading composers.[21]

Women in the popular songs were, for the most part, seen as objects of attraction or dependents at home. The one time when a woman did have an active role was when the song was sung by a male impersonator. Several female artistes dressed in military uniform and sang songs that either encouraged recruitment, or promoted a branch of the Services and regimental loyalty. The earliest of these male military impersonators was Bessie Bonehill, who sang *Here Stands a Post* and *The Tattered Flag*.[22] Bonehill performed in the latter third of the nineteenth century. The practice was continued into the

Edwardian era by amongst others, the actress Cicley Courtneidge and two well-known music hall artistes, namely, Vesta Tilley and Hetty King (*Figure 1*). The latter first sung the continuously popular *All the Nice Girls Love a Sailor* in 1909. The song also gained infamous popularity with a crude bastardized version sung by the troops. It has long been recognized that a well-cut uniform on a trim physique is attractive; and when the wearer is a shapely female the attractiveness for many men is multiplied. It has, writes MacKenzie, 'a curious inverted sexual appeal'.[23] The personification of this mode of apparel and appeal was Vesta Tilley, whose recruiting song *It's All Right in the Army* was still selling well in 1916. Apart from the overt sexual attraction of the male impersonator there was the covert function which, wrote Summerfield, 'allowed these women to step across the sexual divide of Edwardian society into the male preserve of militarism'.[24] And in so doing it permitted them, perhaps, to play a more identifiable role during the war years. The extent of the value of Vesta Tilley as recruiting agent is difficult to gauge, but it was reported in *The Era* that a platoon was formed in Hackney 'as a result of her song'.[25] It is

(Figure 1) Hettie King (left) and Vesta Tilley (right) two famous female music hall artistes, who donned military uniforms in their wartime acts.

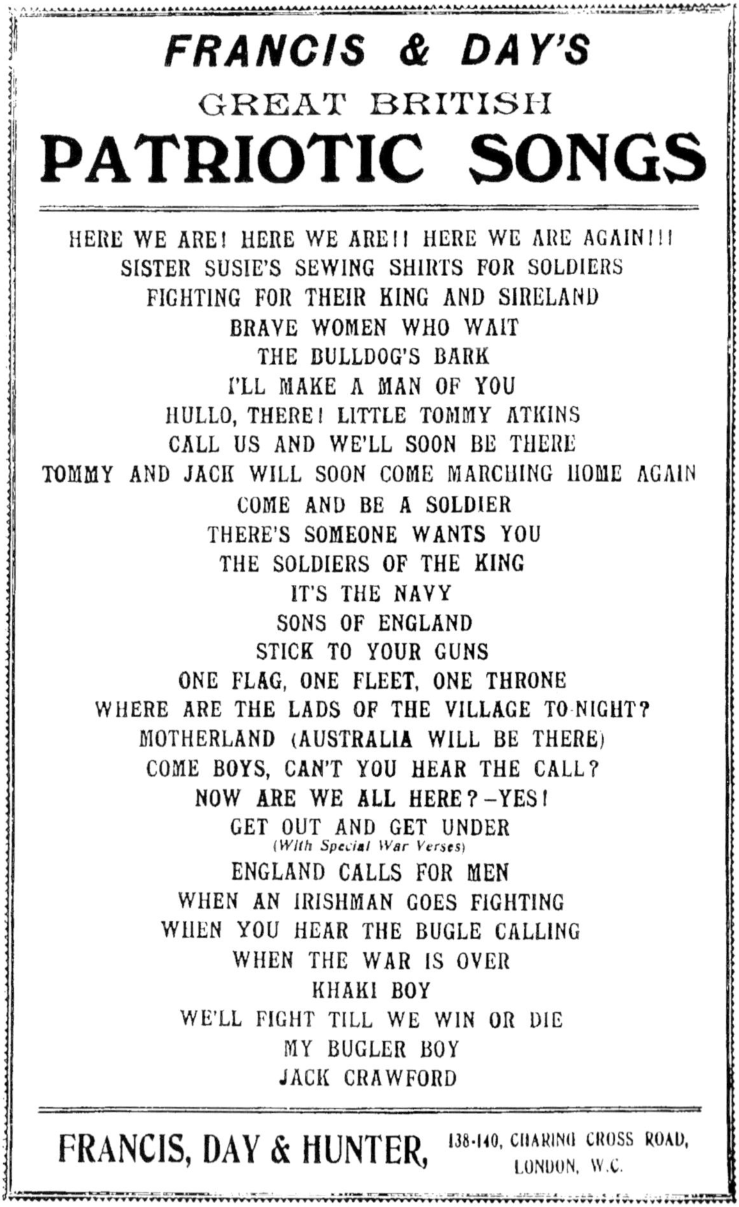

FRANCIS & DAY'S
GREAT BRITISH
PATRIOTIC SONGS

HERE WE ARE! HERE WE ARE!! HERE WE ARE AGAIN!!!
SISTER SUSIE'S SEWING SHIRTS FOR SOLDIERS
FIGHTING FOR THEIR KING AND SIRELAND
BRAVE WOMEN WHO WAIT
THE BULLDOG'S BARK
I'LL MAKE A MAN OF YOU
HULLO, THERE! LITTLE TOMMY ATKINS
CALL US AND WE'LL SOON BE THERE
TOMMY AND JACK WILL SOON COME MARCHING HOME AGAIN
COME AND BE A SOLDIER
THERE'S SOMEONE WANTS YOU
THE SOLDIERS OF THE KING
IT'S THE NAVY
SONS OF ENGLAND
STICK TO YOUR GUNS
ONE FLAG, ONE FLEET, ONE THRONE
WHERE ARE THE LADS OF THE VILLAGE TO-NIGHT?
MOTHERLAND (AUSTRALIA WILL BE THERE)
COME BOYS, CAN'T YOU HEAR THE CALL?
NOW ARE WE ALL HERE? –YES!
GET OUT AND GET UNDER
(With *Special War Verses*)
ENGLAND CALLS FOR MEN
WHEN AN IRISHMAN GOES FIGHTING
WHEN YOU HEAR THE BUGLE CALLING
WHEN THE WAR IS OVER
KHAKI BOY
WE'LL FIGHT TILL WE WIN OR DIE
MY BUGLER BOY
JACK CRAWFORD

FRANCIS, DAY & HUNTER,   138-140, CHARING CROSS ROAD, LONDON, W.C.

Figure 2. Advertisement for *Great British Patriotic Songs* 1915.
[Imperial War Museum]

attracted the recruits; the way she sang and the way she looked would, it is thought, have been more influential factors.

Efforts were made by Sir Charles Villiers Stanford to get bands to play old folk songs such as *Lillibulero* – a song made popular during the Marlborough Wars. The Oxford University Press published six patriotic *Songs of War* all of which, according to *The Times* 'ought to have a sure place in every camp repertory'.[26] A number of firms published sheet music of Patriotic songs such as those listed by Francis & Day (*Figure 2*).

Despite the efforts of publishers and pundits there was a difference between what they wanted the young men to sing, and what the men themselves preferred to sing. As *The Times* reporter commented in January 1915:

> *...there is a real distinction between the songs which men will listen to, enjoy, and perhaps take a part in at an entertainment arranged for their benefit... and the songs which they will break into by a sort of spontaneous combustion on the march.*[27]

Soldiers were relatively unimpressed, not to say fed-up with recruiting songs written by civilians. The soldiers by dint of sardonic and biting wit changed the words so that to the tune of *Your King and Country Need You* the revised first verse went:

> *For we don't want your loving,*
> *And we think you're awfully slow*
> *To see that we don't want you,*
> *So, please, won't you go.*
> *We don't like your sing-songs,*
> *And we loathe your refrain,*
> *So don't you dare to sing it*
> *Near us again.*[28]

There was also the better-known plagiaristic adaptation of *Come, My Lad, and be a Soldier* with these rewritten words:

> *I don't want to be a soldier,*
> *I don't want to go to war;*
> *I'd rather roam*
> *Here at home,*
> *And keep myself on the earnings of a lady typist.*

I don't want a bayonet in my stomach,
Nor my eye lids shot away,
  For I am quite happy
  With my mammy and my pappy –
So I wouldn't be a soldier any day.[29]

Even these rewritten words are censored. In a cruder version which is still sung in rugby clubs and the armed forces, the men are worried about losing their testicles rather than their eyelids, and the lady is not a typist but a prostitute.

Clearly, the men in uniform were not taken with the jingoistic sentiments of the songs penned by the civilian lyricists. A spell in a bombarded trench, the hardships of the military routine, and the precarious existence of life at the Front, or at sea, were bound to give the serviceman a different, more cynical view of war time reality. It is small wonder therefore that the fighting man, and in particular the entrenched soldier, soon felt alienated from the civilian at home. The stirring words of encouragement, sacrifice and honour of the patriotic songs only served to heighten that estrangement.

ENLISTMENT

Despite any cynicism on the part of the veteran soldiery the young and inexperienced flocked to the recruiting offices during the first year of the war. Some men and boys would lie about their age in order to enlist. One such was an actor, Lionel Mackinder, who, as reported in the obituary column of *The Era* in 1915, turned his professional knowledge of disguise to effect; the report reads:

The brave fellow had no light conception of his duty to his
country for though beyond the age limit he did not allow this
to turn him from his purpose, but ordering a new toupee, he
made himself look younger and got through.[30]

The seemingly euphoric patriotic enthusiasm and the rush to enlist was to abate later as the true reality of the war became universally understood.

Many actors enlisted voluntarily during the first year; by December, 1914, the total exceeded 800.[31] Indeed, the tradition of actors' part-time involvement in military service dates back to 1864, and the formation

Figure 3. Playbill for Artists' Rifles *Grand Recruiting Concert* 1915.
[L.J. Collins]

of a Corps of 'artistes' which consisted of 'painters, sculptors, engineers, musicians, architects and actors'.[32] They eventually became known as the 38th Middlesex (Artists) Rifle Volunteers. During the First World War the Artists' Rifles was basically a training corps. Eventually three battalions were raised in which actors and musicians formed a significant part. Two of the battalions' sole purpose was the initial training of officers. Part of their instruction included 'on the job training', which meant a short visit to the Front.[33] The home-based battalion's duties included guarding prisoners in the arena at the Olympia Exhibition Centre and carrying out traditional ceremonial duties at the Tower of London.[34] The Artists' Rifles used their expertise to good effect when recruiting by organizing variety concerts for that specific purpose (*Figure 3*). This was, as the playbill and accompanying blurb proclaim, for would-be officers.[35] By the end of the war in 1918 the Artists' Rifles had supplied ten thousand officers to other units;[36] and eight of those who graduated from this school of training were to gain the Victoria Cross, the highest award for bravery.

In 1914 another volunteer organization, the United Arts Force, was formed as a 'club for voluntary organized military training for Home Defence' which later, in 1915, became known as the United Arts Volunteer Rifles. Its chairman was the well-known playwright Sir Arthur Pinero. Other notable members included Sir Frank Benson, Arthur Bourchier, Allen Aynesworth, Godfrey Tearle and Nelson Keys.[37] As the title indicates, the UAF members came exclusively from the world of entertainment, and were initially nick-named 'The Unshrinkables' on account of the white pullovers they wore when training. At first they must have resembled something approaching an enthusiastic but rather elderly Boy Scout Troop. Training involved little more than marching, map reading and some first aid as weapons were hard to come by; they eventually managed to obtain .303 Martini carbines, which were either sold to members for two pounds ten shillings or hired out at a deposit of two guineas[38]. In time the white cardigans were discarded in favour of a green uniform. In 1916 the War Office finally took control of the Corps and khaki uniforms were issued. The title was eventually changed to the 1st Battalion (United Arts Rifles) County of London Volunteer Regiment, and was ultimately to become part of the Artists' Rifle Battalion.

Training for the UAF consisted, once under War Office control, of digging trenches in Epping Forest, drilling in Earl's Court exhibition

Figure 4. Playbill for concert in aid of *Artists' Rifles Concert Fund* 1918.
[L.J. Collins]

centre, anti-aircraft duties and exercises in Hyde Park which entailed 'defending or attacking the bridge over the Serpentine'.[39] A substantial number, following initial training, joined other regiments and served abroad. In 1917, due to the depletion of numbers, the unit was joined by a separate company of The Pharmacists Corps. Like any organization consisting of entertainers they employed their talents to raise funds. In March 1915, funds were being collected by the Corps through matinee concerts at the Haymarket Theatre. The 'All Star' cast included: Violet Vanburgh, Mari Lohr, Arthur Bourchier, Plunket Greene, Harry Tate, Harry Dearth, Courtice Pounds and many others. And in January 1918, the battalion produced a concert at the New Theatre in aid of the Artists' Rifles Comfort Fund *(Figure 4)*. The sum raised amounted to £200 (about £6,000 in today's currency). Some members of the Corps did see service abroad when a company was sent to France in 1917.

Many men preferred to serve in units that accommodated people of like interest, such as the UAF, others favoured regiments that had a family or local geographical link, such as the county or city regiments. The Central Recruiting Office offered mass enlistments as an incentive to sign-on, as evident at a preliminary recruiting meeting for actors held at *The Stage* newspaper offices. The recruiting officer stated:

> ... *that if those who were serious in joining enlisted in number of no fewer than 50 together they would be formed into companies... and would serve together.*[40]

The response was 'splendid' said *The Stage* reporter and some 'fifty or more actors are now drilling in B Company... at the White City' stadium.[41] This was in September 1914.

The 'inducements' to enlist came in different forms. In the case of Pals Battalions – where a whole town, village or work force enlisted – it would have been extremely difficult for an individual to disregard such enormous peer group pressure. In addition there was persuasive leverage in the form of social ostracism and ridicule from some women, made manifest in the presentation of the White Feather: the 'badge' of dishonour and cowardice. The feelings of a considerable proportion of people were best demonstrated in a letter to the press, quoted by the poet Robert Graves in his book *Goodbye to All That*. The missive was titled 'Letter of "a little Mother"'. The letter is an emphatic statement of what is expected of women at home and an

Have You a Relative Fighting in the Great War?

IF so you are entitled to wear this Badge. It is given only to women who have relatives serving.

Send 1/-

and the name of the relative serving for the Badge and a Certificate of Membership in the Women's Branch, National Service.

The Pendant of Service and Sacrifice.

Address all letters, Hon. Secs. Women's Branch, 64, Temple Chambers, London, E.C.

Cheques and Money Orders should be made payable to National Service, and crossed Coutts & Co.

Figure 5. Advertisement for *The Pendant of Sacrifice and Service* for women 1916. [YMCA Library]

unashamed cry for bloody sacrifice on the battlefields, as this extract shows:

> *To the man who pathetically calls himself a 'common soldier' may*
> *I say that we women, who demand to be heard, will tolerate no*
> *such cry as Peace! Peace!... There is only one temperature for the*
> *women of the British race, and that is white heat. With those who*
> *disgrace their sacred trust of motherhood we have nothing in*
> *common... We women pass on the human ammunition of 'only*
> *sons' to fill up the gaps, so that when the 'common soldier' looks*
> *back before going 'over the top' he may see the women of the*
> *British race on his heels, reliable, dependable, uncomplaining.*[42]

Besides such nationalistic, superior and overtly jingoistic sentimentalism printed in the national press and the White Feathers, there was the 'Medal of Sacrifice' worn by some women who had relatives serving in the armed forces (*Figure 5*). The medals were advertised for sale in *The British Empire YMCA Weekly* magazine. As the cheques were made payable to National Service it is assumed that the sale was government-inspired. The letter too, as there is no signatory, may have been similarly induced, but this is mere conjecture. Suffice to say that coercive means of recruitment took several forms.

The action taken against men who did not volunteer could be perverse as it was, in many cases, impossible to know all the reasons why a man did not enlist. No protection from the ignominious presentation of the White Feather was afforded the young man who was acting on stage in front of a large audience; most of whom were clad in uniform, the remainder being young women –'escorts to their warriors'. The actor Jack Buchanan felt the ominous threat of ridicule strongly. Leslie Henson, who was performing with him in a sketch called *In the Trenches* (1916) at the Coliseum, commented:

> *And there was an officer, played by a very charming modest and*
> *good-looking young actor, tall and with a fine figure. He went in*
> *dread of being handed the white feather, but the truth was that he*
> *was almost at death's door and would not have passed the doctor*
> *at any time. This was Jack Buchanan, who laboured heroically for*
> *many years against the handicap of physical disability.*[43]

The question of the White Feather was taken-up in the entertainment press. It was reported in *The Era* that the twenty-two-year-old leading actor in the play *The Flag Lieutenant*, Godfrey Tearle, was taunted by a lady brandishing a white feather. This prompted him to respond by giving an interview to the *Daily Chronicle*. The impression he gave, however, was that actors were both too sensitive and effete to even comprehend soldiering. Tearle argued that:

> *The actor is the least fitted man in the world to become a soldier...*
> *as the actor lives, almost constantly in the elements of make-believe,*
> *the martial spirit is practically non-existent.*[44]

The editors of *The Era* thought Tearle had gone too far in his assumptions, and did not agree 'that the actor is "feminine" by profession'. They pointed out that there was no reason why the actor should be deemed less fit than the office or factory worker, the literary man or student. The editorial writer points this consideration out, but in doing so makes some odd comparisons, saying:

> *There are few callings which lend themselves easily to war. Those*
> *of the pugilist, the professional football player and the slaughter*
> *house man may be quoted as instances.*

The writer, in order to make amends for the actor's comments, extends the hyperbole in the opposite direction by lauding actors as members of a profession who are 'more spirited, vivacious and energetic' than other people. And concluded by stating that actors had faculties that were ideally suited to soldiering.[46] Godfrey Tearle was able to verify the different suppositions regarding the actor's ability to fight as he was conscripted into the armed forces later in 1916, where he served until he was demobbed in 1919.

Partial blame for the vilification of actors was placed on the shoulders of theatre managers who did not make it apparent to the public exactly who, and how many, of the theatre's staff had enlisted; nor importantly, why those left behind were unfit for military service: the public, inevitably, suspected the worse and assumed the remainder were 'shirkers'. It was not enough, wrote an actor in the theatre press, to 'simply say that they [the managers] will not employ anyone fit for military service, which only puts the manager right with the public...'[47] A number of managers actively encouraged their theatre staff and actors to enlist; they did this by adopting a selective employment policy.

There were, argued a touring manager in *The Stage*, 'plenty of middle-aged actors out of work in addition to the medically unfit who should be given priority, thus releasing the able-bodied to join the armed forces'.[48]

The manager was, to some extent, in an impossible position, torn as he must have been by the desire to fulfil his patriotic duty, but at the same time keep the business going. One correspondent to the theatre press praised, albeit faintly, the profession for its patriotic efforts but then deduced, by the crudest method of analysis, that:

> *There must be scores of young men eligible for the Army working in various revues and musical comedies now running. To judge from the advertisements in your columns there might easily be a battalion.*[49]

The complainer's main criticism was levelled at the managers for ignoring the country's needs and being interested only in filling vacancies for 'consequent pecuniary gain to themselves'. There is no proof to show that the theatre vacancies were filled; indeed, evidence suggests that many of them were not.

Pressure in the form of an appeal to enlist came from the trenches. In a subsequently published letter to his mother in the summer of 1915, an actor wrote:

> *Has father noticed how many young men are still playing [acting] instead of fighting... We want everyone. The maimed, the halt and the blind must do work at home.*[50]

To what extent the actor-soldier's sentiments were governed by feelings of sheer patriotism or anger at the thought of others escaping the afflictions of war cannot be known, but such pleas must have helped to increase the pressure on those hitherto uncommitted. Captain Templer Powell, another actor, took a different approach. He related his 'personal experience of the asphyxiating gases, the latest weapon of Kultur' and thus, intended to incite feelings of horror and retaliatory action. *The Era* editorial applauded his frankness, adding:

> *We want this sort of realism driven into the minds of the audiences, and we are glad to hear that several who have been invalided home and have recovered are doing good work by addressing meetings in aid of recruiting.*[51]

At a meeting at His Majesty's Theatre in the latter days of 1915, the thespian Sir Herbert Tree paid tribute to the part his colleagues played in 'the common cause of the War'. Not only did they help raise money for the war effort, entertain the wounded, but also voluntarily supplied manpower for the armed forces. He estimated that, by the end of 1915, 1,500 men had joined the Colours – about 25 per cent of all actors.[52]

CONSCRIPTION

As the war progressed the daily casualty list in the press was growing inexorably longer. The heavy losses at Neuve-Chapelle, Festubert, Ypres and the failure of the Battle of Loos in 1915, plus the debacle on the Eastern Front at the Dardanelles meant more recruits were required. The idea of national conscription was not greeted with unanimous acceptance by the political parties. Indeed, the need for enforced military service, at least before 1916, was open to conjecture, writes Marwick.[53] Taylor, maintained, that the call for conscription was a response to a psychological need. 'There was' he wrote 'a general belief that thousands of "slackers" – some 650,000 was the figure usually given – were somehow evading their country's call'.[54] The political parties were certainly divided on the question. The Conservatives were in favour; the Liberals, but not Lloyd George were against it; and the Labour Party feared that the Government would apply a similar system to the labour market in general – thereby keeping the workers' wages low. In the event a compromise was reached.

In the winter of 1915 a limited form of persuasion know as the Derby scheme was introduced. Under the scheme the adult males were separated into groups and each group would be called for when required. In the interim men were asked to 'attest' – that is sign a document pledging their availability – the rider being that married men would not be called until the ranks of the unmarried had first reached depletion. Although unfair for the single male, it was a clever ploy as it appeased both the political left and the right-wing: a degree of voluntarism had been maintained, but if it failed, national conscription would be inevitable.

The Derby scheme posed many problems for actors, managers and theatrical agents. First, some agents became reluctant to book attested actors as they (the agents) feared that a loss of commission would result. Secondly, as one actor complained in the theatre press, a manager actually sacked all the men of his company who were eligible for enlistment in order 'to save himself the trouble of getting new men and rehearsing them when the others are called-up'.[55] This was unfair as under the conditions of the Scheme an artiste was obliged to give his manager two weeks' notice: the reverse did not apply. The actors, with some justification, proposed that the management should give preference to the attested man in consideration of the fact that such a man 'has offered his life to help protect the manager to whom he is applying for work until his group is called-up'. The Derby scheme was, considering the invidiousness of the priority system of selection, and the enormity of losses so far incurred, bound to be short-lived. And by May 1916, national conscription was introduced.

The theatre industry's greatest dread was not so much the inevitable reduction of numbers – the theatre with its over-abundance of unemployed could afford to lose a quantity of people – but rather the wholesale withdrawal of a particular section: namely, the younger men. The Leader article in *The Era* of January 1916, did not view the absence of young men as an insurmountable loss. It was suggested that 'a young man of eighteen is not a very deep or strong character in drama', although it was conceded that the 'freshness and ingenuousness which distinguishes youth should be suggested'.[57] The remedy for this shortfall could, it was concluded, be made good by the employment of women; after all, it was added, a great many male occupations are undertaken by women'. A peculiar analogy to make, seeing that in other professions the woman assumes the man's skills but not his sex! But as pointed out the disguise of sex on stage was no novelty, witness the 'breeches parts' of the Restoration actress. What was to be more worrying was the extension of conscription to the age of forty and beyond. To this regard *The Era* correspondent referred to the Shakespeare roles of Hamlet played by Henry Irving and Johnson Forbes-Robertson when both actors were in their forties. This narrow view took no account of the castings for revues, musical comedy and contemporary drama. The conclusion was that there existed no 'insuperable bar to sex'. Finally, the writer added, rather perfunctorily, that 'fortunately, face-hair is out of fashion at present, so women in beards will not be required'.[58]

The apparent flippancy displayed in the theatre press in January changed considerably by May when the Military Service Bill was made law. It was suggested in *The Stage* that the resultant casting problems could be solved, or at least relieved, by the importation of American vaudeville turns, actors and plays. Some movement had already been made in this direction and, not surprisingly, British artistes viewed the whole affair with considerable alarm. *The Stage* regarded the prospect of an 'American invasion' with an air of philosophical detachment, claiming that 'demand would regulate supply... and only a very small number of American artistes are likely to remain on the English stage permanently, and then only on their merits'.[59] An alternative view was expressed in the profession's other paper. The main concern was the threat to those working in *Variety*. Rumour had it that between fifty and one hundred acts had already been booked to tour the major towns and cities of Britain. No evidence had been found to support this rumour; nevertheless the perceived urgency of the situation prompted a special meeting of the Variety Artists' Federation to be called in May, 1916. As a result, a strongly-worded cablegram was sent to the White Rats Actors' Union warning American artistes:

> ... *not to accept engagements in England during the war period. Conditions here unfavourable. British performers strongly resent importations to take the place of performers serving in the Army, whilst sufficient remain to fill vacancies, and will adopt all possible means to prevent foreign artists playing.*[60]

In the event no such trans-Atlantic onrush occurred. Either the letter had the wished for effect or perhaps American artistes had no real desire to get involved in the war in Europe. Besides which, with prowling U-boats constantly on the outlook for allied shipping, crossing the Atlantic could be a hazardous experience.

Actors were resentful of any British artiste who looked as though he was evading the 'call' by going to work abroad. The feeling turned to anger following the Military Service Bill which introduced conscription; in fact, the Council of the Actors' Association drew-up a 'blacklist' of those assumed shirkers working overseas; and in May, 1916, the Council passed a resolution which said:

> ... *this Council... shall forthwith appoint a committee who shall endeavour to ascertain the names of those actors of military age who... have failed to respond to their country's call, that this Council shall then consider what steps, if any, shall be recommended for giving preferential treatment to those others of similar age who have not shirked their military duties.*[61]

The accumulated list must have been quite small in relation to the number of registered actors. In any event, no list has been located. It is presumed, however, that if an actor did incur employment penalties then it is likely that such 'sharp practices' would not be made public; in any case, it would be practically impossible to prove discrimination in such a precarious profession: reasons for not employing someone can be multifarious, and indeed in the majority of cases are not known by the auditionee.

The effects of the Military Service Bill were immediate. Sir Frank Benson's tour of Shakespeare plays had to be postponed until the spring, and reports in the press told of major operatic companies suspending operations. The absence of singers, particularly bass and tenors, also adversely affected musical comedies.[62] In an effort to ease the problem a call for more all-women companies was re-echoed in the *The Era*. Advocates of such a move harked back to the days of 1885 when the comic opera *An Adamless Eden* was produced for an entirely female cast, and with an all-female orchestra. Such a situation almost existed at the Lyceum Theatre, Ipswich. The manager, Eugene Stafford, engaged a female band and the staff, both front and back of house, were women. The only men, apart from himself, were the older actors.[63] It became not unusual to see Captain Absolutes and Young Marlowe being played by late middle-aged actors. Whatever expedient action was taken it nevertheless meant a weakening of casts in London and a 'rapid decrease of companies' in the provinces.[64]

The case for exemption of service was not felt to be acute by a significant number of managers. Correspondence in the press indicated that proprietors and managers were slow in coming forward to seek exemption from the Tribunals set up by the Government specifically for this purpose. Some like Alfred Butt, the producer of revues at the Palace Theatre, considered it unpatriotic to approach a Tribunal to claim exemption for a member of his staff.[65] Opinion regarding exemption was so diverse that no combined effort on the part of owners or managers was forthcoming. In Manchester, for example, most managers were over-age for conscription and there was a 'passive acceptance of the situation'. In the words of W Roberts-Maxwell, manager of the Gaiety Theatre, 'rates and taxation' were of 'more consequence'.[66] Roberts-Maxwell, it must be said, had two sons fighting and like any manager who had relatives at the Front would not be inclined to make an appeal on behalf of any of his male staff aged under forty. Oswald Stoll, the entrepreneurial owner and leader of one of the largest music hall circuits in Britain, sought exemption for the Manchester

Hippodrome's manager, although no such efforts were made on behalf of the remaining staff. The theatre had already lost twenty-five personnel and the remainder of the attested men were to follow when called. In the same city at the Queen's Theatre, Thomas Beecham's opera company was 'full of attested men' and the company had, due to military demands, to be disbanded at the end of the season.[67]

There were discrepancies regarding the exemptions. Findings show that managers stood a far better chance of gaining either a total or deferred exemption as compared with an actor, or member of the backstage crew. At Barrow-in-Furness and at the Marylebone Tribunals in London, for example, theatre managers were given exemption on the grounds of the 'tax-earning capacity' of the theatre under the terms of the Entertainment Tax, while at the same time a leading actor's application was refused.[68] It was clear to the Tribunals that for financial reasons managers were necessary, but seemingly beyond their comprehension that a production also depended on the cast. Other Tribunals insisted that theatre employees undertook some work of 'national utility', that meant enrolling for National Service.[69]

Performers were still regarded by a significant number of government agents as people not to be taken too seriously; their work was considered trivial and not germane to life at this time of hostilities. A classic example was the response by a magistrate at the North London Police Court in 1916, to a charge levelled at an actor for failing to report himself to the military authorities. The magistrate said of the defendant:

> *He fools about the country with a party of players who in sterner Puritan days would be regarded as rogues and vagabonds and placed in the stock on their appearance in any town.*[70]

In this case the defendant, an Irishman, was not eligible for call-up into the British army. The magistrate, with some reluctance, discharged him 'to continue his foolery'. Actors had not been subjected to the Vagrants Act since 1824, but the myth of them being rogues and vagabonds still persisted in some quarters.

The fact that the theatre business would provide its quota of evasionists or shirkers – as indeed did every other section of society – is not disputed, but the authorities went to inordinate lengths to weed them out. The police or army would regularly visit theatres in order to scrutinize the papers of all males in the company. Any member found guilty of not attesting or failing to report to the military was fined, an amount usually equivalent to one or two weeks' wages, before being marched-off under escort to the nearest barracks. At Croydon in 1916, the police visited various theatres. As a result Ferdinand Thomas Green, a 38-year-old actor appearing in the aptly named show, *We Can't Be as Bad as All That*, at the Hippodrome, was summoned to court for not registering. He produced discharge papers showing that he had already served twelve years in the army, and had fought in the Boer War. He thought his discharge exempted him from further military service, although he also stated that he had tried to attest whilst in pantomime in Manchester. In view of his previous service he was not fined. His manager then explained that the company was in Croydon for a week and there was no replacement, and asked if the actor could be spared until the end of the week. Green was referred directly to the military.[71] The managers were in an invidious position in that if they failed to report members of their company who did not register they themselves would be penalized with a fine.[72]

The number of reasons for claiming exemption were very varied. Many were genuine, but some appeared somewhat dubious. An example of the latter was witnessed at the Worcester Appeal Tribunal in 1917, where a 29-year-old acrobat artiste pleaded for dispensation on financial grounds. He claimed that 'military training would make his muscles stiff and unfit for acrobatic work'. The recruiting officer replied 'that however interesting the acrobatic business might be, it would not help us to win the war'. The appeal was, inevitably, dismissed.[73]

Theatres played a significant role in recruitment. They provided the platform where recruiting 'evangelists' like Harry Lauder and Frank Benson could deliver their stirring orations; the theatres themselves were seen and used as official recruiting posts. Recruiting meetings were held at various venues including, for example, the Tyne and Pavilion Theatres in Newcastle, at which Lord Haldane, Lord Curzon and Arthur Henderson, MP were in attendance in 1914, and the London Opera House.[74]

It must have been extremely difficult to evade the call-up but allegations were constantly made to the War Office stating that large numbers of young men were still escaping registration. In response the War Office, via the police and army, instigated a system of 'rounding-up' evasionists. The places to be particularly targeted for their operations were parks and theatres – indeed any place of public amusement: a seemingly illogical method of investigation considering the fact that any would-be shirker was more than likely not to be seen in public. 'All over the country', reported *The Times*, 'at theatres, railway stations, football fields, public parks... law-abiding citizens are liable to be suddenly surrounded by a posse of military and civil police'.[75] It was reminiscent of the modus operandi of the Naval press-gangs of an earlier century. The males apprehended had, in order to prove their innocence, to produce their registration cards, although they were 'expressly cautioned to keep those cards at home'.[76] This rounding-up must have resulted in publicly branding the innocent with suspicion, besides irritatingly interrupting his business or pleasure. The various reports in the press suggest that the methods employed were unproductive as the numbers detected were 'ludicrously small'.[77]

At times the raids bordered on the farcical. In September, 1916, a travelling circus at Camberley was raided by: the army, police, special constabulary and volunteers. Seventy names and address of those without the necessary papers were taken before all the lights went out. It was reported in *The Times* that, 'they were put out deliberately', and thus 4,000 people were literally left in the dark. Someone lit a stable lamp and a police sergeant, displaying a remarkable swiftness of mind, prevented a dangerous stampede for the exits by calling on the audience to stand and sing the National Anthem. This they dutifully did, but the raid and the show had to be abandoned. [78]

The pressure to do one's patriotic duty was increased from both sides of the footlights. Many artistes did, of their own volition, volunteer in the years prior to conscription, and by mid-1916 the remaining males were compelled to join the armed forces. By the end of 1915 several actors had, in military terms, acquitted themselves well. The most notable were Lieutenant Lambert who was awarded the Distinguished Service Order; Captain (later Wing-Commander RAF) Robert Loraine, an already well-known West End actor, received the Military Cross; and Lieutenant Wilbur Dartnell won the highest accolade, the Victoria Cross, whilst serving with the 25th Battalion Frontiersmen Fusiliers.[79] However, for some the agony of not being able to serve was acutely felt. The entertainer Frank Pettingell must have suffered considerably from innuendoes, direct taunts or 'presents' of white feathers (*Figure 6*). The pain of rejection, accusation and apparent humiliation prompted him to respond publicly by writing, publishing and performing a musical monologue that most poignantly states the dilemma faced by him and those who, for various reasons, were unable to serve in uniform. The monologue summed up in

MUSICAL MONOLOGUE.

WE CANNOT ALL BE SOLDIERS.

(MEN WHO ARE LEFT BEHIND.)

Words
by
Frank
Pettingell.

Music
by
Horace
Bernard.

Performed by

FRANK PETTINGELL.

COPYRIGHT   ©   PRICE 2/- NET.

The Music Hall Singing Rights of this Monologue are Reserved. Application for Theatre Singing Rights should be made to the publishers. All other Performing Rights are controlled by the Performing Right Society Limited.

LONDON:
FRANCIS. DAY & HUNTER.
138-140. CHARING CROSS ROAD. W.C.
NEW YORK;
T.B. HARMS & FRANCIS DAY & HUNTER, INC. 62-64, WEST 45TH STREET.

Copyright MCMXV, in the United States of America by Francis, Day & Hunter.

Figure 6. Songsheet cover for *We Cannot All Be Soldiers* 1914. [Imperial War Museum]

pathetic terms their feelings, and is worth quoting in full. It is called, *We Cannot All be Soldiers*:

You are young and strong and healthy, and you join the Khaki ranks'
Giving up your job and pleasure with your Country's love and thanks;
You are clad in martial costume and you stroll along the street,
And you get a glance of praise and pride from people that you meet;
You have proved your love of country, you have shown your manhood's worth,
And you're proud to think you'll do your bit for the land that gave you birth.
Or perhaps you're turned of fifty; there are wrinkles in your face,
And your grey-flecked head is showing many a blank and barren space;
Your waistcoat fits you tightly, and you can't run as you used;
But your blood still boils to hear of Treaties broken – peace abused.
And you see these gallant Khaki-boys go swinging on their way:
'If I could only go with them and fight' is what you say.
Then you'll heave a sigh regretfully as you think, 'Too old for that!
But I'll be a special constable and wear a special hat'.
So you sleep at nights in comfort knowing that you've done your best,
And your honest heart of English oak drums peacefully in your breast,
Now in the streets and in the shops and everywhere you'll see
A lot of men who'll look as fit as anyone can be,
And you'll say with bitter feeling, 'Why don't that fellow 'list
And make another one to smash the Kaiser's Iron Fist?'
And you'll dub him as a coward and you'll treat him with disdain,
As one who is afraid of drill of danger and of pain;
As one who loves his skin too much, who'll slight his Country's call;
But don't you judge too harshly – that is not the case with all.
There is many a single fellow who is snubbed by stronger folks
Who give him the white feather and play other well-meant jokes;
And the girls all turn their noses up and eye him with contempt,
For they don't Know that Nature has made that man exempt.
And he'll grit his teeth and suffer, and he'll feel a beastly pain
When he sees the Khaki uniform and hears the bugle's strain.
He'll turn his back and walk away clad in his civvy's clothes
And he'll droop his head and mutter 'I can ne'er be one of those!'
So he'll go to work as usual, and he'll stick it all day long;
He'll laugh and smoke and chatter, but underneath it all
Is the sorrow that he cannot be one brick in England's wall.

God bless you, gallant Tommies! you're lads of whom we're proud;
You chucked up all your comforts to join the Khaki crowd;
You are patriots, you are heroes, and many a British Lad
Would leave his job to-morrow to join you, and be glad;
But we cannot all be soldiers; we must wait, and work and long;
We must stand the taunts and gibings of luckier healthier friends;
So the poor civvy cowers, and his neck in silence bends.
O brave and gallant soldier, O patriotic maid,
O British dads and mothers, the civvy's not afraid.
Because he isn't strong enough to do his little bit, it doesn't say
he's wanting in honour or in grit.
Just think a little better, just be a little Kind,
And don't class a shirker every man who's left behind.[80]

To help assuage the problem facing the younger men who were involved in essential war work, but who could be subjected to harassment, a system of identification, via badges and arm bands, was introduced by some firms.[81] But, alas, no such protection existed for theatre employees. Some theatres did include, apart from the recruiting notices in the programmes, a declaration stating the availability-status of the company members. In the programme for the musical comedy *Vivien* at the Prince of Wales' Theatre, Birmingham in 1915, there appeared on the front cover an appeal for:

50 STRONG ABLE-BODIED MEN WANTED
for long engagement at Good Pay. Uniforms provided, with
Food, Lodging and Allowance to Families and Dependents.

And on the inside pages, included with the cast list, the additional notice proclaims that:

Every Male Member of the Company has either actually served at
the Front, or has attested or is ineligible for Active Service.[82]

Thus, at least inside that particular theatre, some protection was afforded the actor and backstage staff.

By 1916 the figure of theatre employees voluntarily in the armed services was considerably higher than the 25 per cent quoted in 1915, although the exact figure cannot be known as a man would usually enlist under his private as opposed to his professional name. The inception of compulsory service was seen as a devastating blow to the profession. It would not, many felt, have been unreasonable, considering the amount of essential war work the theatre was doing in recruiting, fund raising, entertaining the wounded and those in training, and generally helping to keep up public morale, for there to be some limited measure of relief. It was not forthcoming, except for a handful of managers and then only for economic reasons. To designate a small number of theatre people as part of the reserved occupation category would, as the critic Bernard Weller pointed out in 1917, have 'made no appreciable difference in a military sense'.[83]

Effects of War on Theatrical Production

The effects of war on industry, apart from the reduction of the workforce via conscription, were wide ranging as the Government sought to utilize all modes of industrial output and communication in an effort to secure victory. The Government's appropriation of the country's main means of transport, the railways, followed by the printing and paper restrictions caused the theatre industry instant and continued concern. The problems of mounting productions were further compounded by the coming of air raids and the ensuing lighting restrictions. Added to this was the inevitable raising of costs as commodities became scarce. That apart, the industry felt particularly hard done by with the implementation of an Amusement Tax. There was also the temporary problem caused by the call for National Service.

NATIONAL SERVICE

A year after the establishment of military conscription, in March, 1917, the Ministry of National Service was formed. Its stated aim was to make 'the best use of all persons... able to work in any industry, occupation or service'. The stage, like any other occupation, was to come under the scrutinous eye of its first Director-General, Neville Chamberlain. There was a definite need for co-ordination between the different agencies, the War Office and the Ministry of Munitions, but it is difficult to see exactly where the new ministry fitted in, particularly as the Ministry of Labour had recently been established. In consequence, all that remained for the Director-General to do was to run a campaign designed to recruit volunteers for a variety of civilian jobs in order to release more men for military service.

At the outset Neville Chamberlain brought pressure to bear on the stage by including theatre employees and musicians in the Restricted Occupation Order, 'which was a form of industrial conscription'.' The business of theatre was not 'Restricted' but it did mean that employees could be called upon to do other 'essential works'. It also meant that managers were prohibited from engaging any new staff in an industry already experiencing an acute shortage of male workers. The measures came as a surprise to the industry considering

Chamberlain's record when he was Lord Mayor of Birmingham. As mayor he installed himself as the director of the movement to provide entertainment for the sick and wounded in the city. In so doing he ensured that not only the theatres, but also the military depots and hospitals had recreative amusements. Chamberlain referred, when mayor, to the necessity of entertainment, insisting 'that the curing of the wounded was not merely an affair of drugs and dressing'.[2]

At a meeting in March, 1917, between Chamberlain and a cross-section of the theatre industry, the chairman Sir George Alexander reminded the Director-General of the important work the industry was already doing. Chamberlain re-iterated his earlier claims and stressed the stage's vital role, but then proceeded to dumbfound his critics by proposing that its operation be limited, saying:

> ... *I think that in War time amusements should be taken in moderation. And I am not sure that the sight of long queues of pleasure-seekers during the day in War time is calculated to conduce to the seriousness of spirit, that appreciation of a necessity for putting all our efforts into the struggle, which is what we want so much to impress upon the great mass of the people today.*[3]

He declined to go into details because, as he admitted, he was unfamiliar with the way in which the stage functioned. He did, in his ignorance, also suggest that men operating stage lighting and building scenery could be better employed 'upon work more directly conducive to the prosecution of the war'.[4] H.B. Irving, replying on behalf of actors and actresses, told the Director-General of the contribution the industry had already made regarding military service volunteers, and suggested that the raising of monies – via war loans and taxation – was tantamount to a form of National Service. The representative of the National Association of Theatre Employees added that many men had vacated the theatre for work in munition factories. Oswald Stoll was forthright in his attack on the National Service organization, claiming that 'The National Service Department' is a part of the Labour Exchange and 'ceased to be necessary... because there are no unemployed, and most people are working on the verge of breakdown'.'[5]

This seemingly invidious attack on one profession was keenly felt by its members, but the profession did not wish to be seen as being unpatriotic. Managers therefore encouraged their employees to register for National Service. They also, where possible, cut down their staff numbers and refrained from engaging any new men, although there must have been few male staff members left not directly involved in some form of part-time national service. At Birmingham Rep men already went to work at the Aluminium Casting Co. on Sunday mornings to make shell cases.[6] In London thirty to forty actors were mustering at Bow Street police station to don the Special Constable uniform to do the 2am to 6am shift, others drove ambulances.[7] 'Yet', wrote Weller in 1918, 'when the traffic had been thrown into confusion.... and an impoverished state... by the Director-General's requisitions and "rationed" amusements, the National Service Department could only find places for forty-one of the thousands of stage workers who come under the order'.[8] Neville Chamberlain's time as Director-General was short-lived, as he resigned after only a few months in office; for as J.A. Fairlie, commenting on the British Administration in 1919, said: 'he had nothing to do'.[9] Nevertheless, a National Service recruiting campaign continued within the theatres by means of publicity slides projected on a 'kinema sheet'.[10] In addition to this public appeal, the Joint Committee of Representative of the Entertainment Industry sent out 50,000 questionnaires to managers asking for details of their staffing. A similar letter went to male employees in which they were asked to declare their age, military history, nature of job in the theatre and their availability for National Service.[11] The paucity of theatre volunteers indicates that most men might well have been too old, already engaged in part-time national employment or invalided due to war service, and therefore unacceptable. Chamberlain's successor, Sir Auckland Geddes, scrapped the Restriction Order, and reorganized the department so that it became an integral part of the War Office.

TRANSPORT

The need to mobilize hundreds of thousands of men and the essential movement of supplies necessitated the take-over of the railways by the Government. In managerial terms there was very little change, since it merely meant that a committee of the railway managers ran the railways on behalf of the Board of Trade.[12] The effect on the entertainment industry was, however, immediate as 'theatrical traffic could not be afforded for the time being the usual facilities'.[13] Normal service was, at best, interrupted and, at worst, suspended; the theatre industry faced a further problem as the three-quarter fare concession enjoyed by the theatre companies, and the Music Hall Artists' Railway Association (M.H.A.R.A) ceased altogether. Touring managers in 1914 were presented with a dilemma; they were unsure whether to call in their companies and stop operations temporarily or carry on in the hope that it would be a short war. They realized that any form of stoppage would cause enormous economic hardship to the artistes and stage employees, and might also disrupt business to such an extent that any future resumption would be extremely difficult. The M.H.A.R.A Committee did, after negotiations with the railway management, manage to obtain the restoration of the three-quarter fare concessions.[14] Despite this there was a considerable amount of disorganization and disruption as the various railway companies were not well co-ordinated. It was not only theatre business that suffered from the ineptitude of the railway organizers. As late as the summer of 1916, for example, 'leave trains from France were stopped for five days so as not to interfere with holiday traffic'.[15] There is no record of what the servicemen thought of this imposition!

Transport difficulties arose again in December, 1916 when price increases amounted to 50 per cent; once more the three-quarter fare concession, first secured in 1896, came under threat. Theatrical companies were also concerned that the Sunday Specials would be withdrawn. The latter posed particular problems to the touring companies as Sunday was the major day for moving both personnel and scenery from one venue to another. It was the only day in the week that extra rolling stock could be provided; but, due to the combined efforts of the M.H.A.R.A and the Theatrical Touring Managers' Association, the disruptive consequences were kept to a minimum. In fact, in 1915 the Great Western Line showed an increase on pre-war traffic figures, but this was the exception rather than the rule.[16] The other railway lines showed a decrease in passengers and civilian freight.

In January, 1917 the Board of Trade raised the tariff on fares by a further 50 per cent, but, once again, due mainly to the efforts of the stage associations, the concession was retained. The proviso was that the three-quarter payment of the new fares was restricted to companies of not less than ten, and variety parties of not less than five.

Regarding the transportation of scenery, a free truck, when available, was to be provided for parties of ten or more and further trucks at 6d a mile.[17] The theatre people most inconvenienced were those engaged in speciality music hall acts that were reliant on heavy props as luggage was restricted by one third to one cwt. per person. Any luggage exceeding this limit had to go by parcel post at 1d per pound in weight.[18] Theatre companies made efforts to reduce costs by asking company members to cut down on personal luggage, but this proved impossible for a tour that lasted from, perhaps, May to September. Stage scenery had to be pared back to the minimum required. Various suggestions were proffered to help alleviate the transport difficulties. One method was the sectioning off of the country into areas. This meant a company would play a given locale before moving to another, thereby dispensing with the difficulty of traversing long distances across the country at the end of each engagement. Some managers considered this unworkable. George Dance, a manager, pointed out that 'In each area there would be, perhaps, two first-class theatres, four second-class and a number of smaller ones. A company suitable for first-class theatres might possibly, at a loss, play at the second one, but certainly not at anything smaller'.[19] One alternative was for theatre companies, most of which operated on the weekly repertory system, to extend their runs; but there was little co-operation among either the resident or touring managers. The number of touring companies had, inevitably, to be reduced and the Stage struggled on, coping with the increased expenditure and the reduction and unreliability of transport until normality was restored in 1919.

PRINTING AND PAPER

The decrease in unemployment – in effect its virtual disappearance – meant there was not, according to Taylor, a shortage of money with which to buy goods.[20] There was, however, a scarcity of purchasable imported commodities due to the acute shortage of shipping. Like the railways, ships were requisitioned for naval and military purposes. In the first twelve months of the war approximately twenty-five per cent of British shipping was removed from normal merchant trading. The loss could not be made up by the shipyards as they, like the major part of heavy industry, were primarily concerned with war production, and 'their output sank to a third of the pre-war figure'.[21] By April, 1917, as a result of submarine attacks, the monthly toll of Allied shipping had exceeded 975,000 tons.[22] The resultant reduction of goods was felt nationwide. One commodity that was in short supply was paper;

in fact the importation of paper was down by one third, and this had a direct effect on the theatre industry.

The limited supply of paper, combined with the rising costs of printing and posting, meant that theatre managers had to cut back on advertising. Some managers felt it expedient to co-operate with each other in order to reduce costs. In Sunderland a group of seventeen managements from theatres, music halls and picture houses formed an association for such a purpose. Their task was to tackle the problem of diminishing supply and the rising expenditure of advertising. The Association decided to curtail, from March, 1916, the purchase and distribution of day-bills, and to limit their advertising to hoardings and adverts in the local papers.[23] The Sunderland example was followed elsewhere, but it soon proved to be inadequate as the supply of paper became further restricted through official regulation.

It was the producers of melodrama that made the greatest use of pictorial printing. Sensational scenes were vividly displayed on large hoardings in the hope of filling a theatre, and as cities and larger towns contained more than one theatre an element of competition was inevitably present. Bigger and brighter posters were thus produced, 'sometimes', it was argued in *The Stage*'s editorial, 'whether the play [lent] itself to pictorial advertising or not',[24] The Paper Commission – a government department – in one way helped to confine this form of competition and thus reduce managers' costs by restricting the size of posters. The printing and paper difficulty continued throughout the war, and as late as May, 1918, a further restriction was imposed upon the theatre managers following a meeting with the Controller of Paper; programmes were henceforth to be limited in size to eight crown quarto pages or its equivalent. This reduction resulted, wrote Weller in 1919, in 'a considerable loss in advertisement revenue to managers'.[25]

AIR RAIDS AND LIGHTING RESTRICTIONS

The illusion that modern warfare only occurred in foreign fields was unequivocally dispelled when, on 16 December, 1914, a German naval force shelled the towns of Hartlepool, Whitby and Scarborough; a few days later, on Christmas Eve, the enemy dropped its first bomb from an aeroplane over Dover. The following day it was reported in *The Times* that the people of Sheerness had their Christmas celebrations interrupted by the 'exciting spectacle of a British aircraft chasing an enemy raider'.[26] In the new year the threat came not just from ships and aeroplanes but also from the giant Zeppelins. A raid on the east coast towns of Yarmouth and Shearing on 19 January killed four people. Subsequent air raids in 1915, whether by aeroplane or Zeppelin, caused considerable material damage, although comparatively little loss of life. The people, if, indeed, they needed telling, now realized that the war could affect everyone if only vicariously.

In 1916 the enemy air force widened the target area, venturing beyond the confines of the capital and towns of south-east England. On 31 June the enemy bombing raids reached the north midland counties of Staffordshire, Derbyshire, Leicestershire and Lincolnshire. The effect on places of entertainment was one of inconvenience. No theatre was completely out of action. Local authorities did, as an immediate precautionary measure, temporarily disconnect electricity and gas supplies, and theatres were unexpectedly plunged into darkness whether or not the raiding aircraft was in the vicinity.[27] The audiences had little choice but to struggle home in a blackout, though, ironically, they may well have been safer inside the structure of a theatre rather than fumbling about outside in darkened and crowded streets. Some performances did continue with the aid of makeshift lighting in the form of candles, cycle lamps and other improvised methods.[28]

In contrast to the provinces, the London theatres continued with what might be termed 'minimal interruptions'. No lights were extinguished inside the West End houses; although in order 'to mislead the Zeppelins the parks of London were brilliantly lit and the streets left in darkness'.[29] When the closeness of the major parks to the administrative and trading centre, and the docks of London – the presumed targets – is realized it would seem, in retrospect, that this ploy merely heightened the dangers of theatre-going whilst, at the same time, provided the marauding enemy aviators with additional navigation assistance. The Government, apart from the reason of air raids, decided in April, 1918 to enforce a 10.30pm closure of all places of entertainment in order to make savings by cutting the nation's fuel bills. The twice-nightly music halls were the most inconvenienced by this enactment. The halls coped by readjusting to the earlier start times of 6.45pm and 8pm. The public adapted to the changes, but with reduced train services, buses ceasing to run late and taxis limited in number 'it became necessary for central London houses to end their performances as soon after 10 pm as possible' reported Weller.[30] The problem of speeding up performances was not easy as theatre staffs, 'through the scarcity of labour', were pruned to the minimum.[31] Management was also required to reduce electrical consumption by one-sixth; an almost impossible requirement when producing a musical comedy or revue which had exterior scenes. This pressure remained until the Government lifted the Order in late December, 1918; three and a half weeks after the war ended.

Despite the fact that damage from air raids proved more imaginary than real, some managers debated the possibility of closing their theatres for the duration, others took evasive action in the form of matinee performances. C.B. Cochran, the Alhambra manager, substituted matinee shows in place of late night performances. This reduced the takings as much of the clientele was at work. At the Royalty Theatre the second performance began at 5.30pm, soon after the matinee; and Frederick Harrison, manager of the Haymarket, had only matinee performances – except on Saturdays. He outlined his fear in a letter to Sir George Alexander in 1915, saying: 'The more I think of the result of a bomb dropping on the audience, the more I dread the responsibility of having them there'.[32] However, it appears that the profit motive overcame his humanitarian spirit on a Saturday night!

On the advice of the police 'take cover' notices were posted in the theatres when an air raid was imminent. The notices were also accompanied by a verbal warning from the stage. The reaction to the danger signals varied in the extreme. Most people remained within the relative safety of the theatre, and totally ignored any approaching peril, whereas others took the completely opposite action. Horace Watson, the manager of the Haymarket Theatre in 1917, complained that 'A lot of them wanted to come outside skygazing, to see what was going on and I have had the greatest difficulty in restraining them. The women are as bad, if not worse than the men'.[33] Presumably the men, at least those in uniform, had seen enough bombing. The theatre building did, at least, provide protection against shrapnel, indeed some were deemed bomb-proof The London Opera House, for instance, had a double roof 'designed', wrote a *Stage* reporter, 'to check the descent of projectiles such as those which have been falling; while the Criterion advertises with truth that it is built entirely underground, and is thus immune to air attack'.[34]

Not all theatres paid heed to the possible danger of nightly air raids. The Old Vic, under the management of Miss Lilian Baylis, was one of the theatres that opened every night throughout the war. On the eve of the production of *King John* in 1917, when asked if the theatre would close following a week of raids, she replied, 'We'll play tomorrow. This is, unless they blow off the roof tonight'.[35] On the opening night German aircraft attempted to destroy the nearby Waterloo station whilst the performance was in progress. The audience doggedly remained in their seats and the drama proceeded. The presence of the enemy outside and above added poignancy to the lines:

> *Some airy devil hovers in the sky*
> *And pours down mischief*

Indeed any line that appeared to be topically appropriate was guaranteed to 'bring the house down', and so when Faulconbridge uttered the words:

> *This England never did and never shall*
> *Lie at the proud foot of a conqueror...*

the audience erupted into loud applause. And Shakespeare's words, as spoken by Faulconbridge, were, on the initiative of the management, 'inscribed above the proscenium arch where they remained for the duration'.[36]

Leslie Henson, the comedy actor, remembered a dangerous experience when appearing at the Gaiety in the revue *Tonight's the Night* in October 1915. During the show a Zeppelin dropped bombs so near the theatre that the door to the scene-dock was destroyed and shrapnel fell onto the stage. More tragically, the theatre's messenger boy was killed and a call boy was seriously injured.[37] The second bomb fell 'Blowing a hole in the street large enough to swallow a bus'; and at the Strand Theatre the air was filled with dust. Fred Terry, the actor-manager, in an attempt to calm the audience, ordered the conductor to play *God Save the King*, and the playgoers rose obediently but remained in their places: thus a possible panic-exodus was averted.[38] Most audiences remained in their seats when a raid was in progress; as for the artistes their 'devotion to duty', wrote Weller, 'was equalled by their indifference... with which they treated the air raids'.[39]

The actors and artistes wished to continue working regardless of air raids and the perceived dangers. The reason for wanting to do so was two-fold: first, they desperately needed the wages; and secondly, most felt they had a patriotic duty to help provide the necessary antidotal recreative diversion required by the audience, be they military or civilian. Added to the obvious risks faced by managements and audiences due to air attacks was the further problem confronting the performers; namely, the loss of jobs. Oswald Stoll had stopped paying artistes when business was suspended as a result of an air raid warning. He had, in fact, amended his contracts so that he could cancel his agreement with an artiste at any time; and considering that he ran a circuit of 20 theatres, the effects were felt by a large number of employees. Both *The Era* and the *Weekly Dispatch* suggested that the government ought to help the Theatre financially in the event of loss due to air raids. It would, it was argued, be an 'official recognition of the part they [theatres] play in keeping up the public spirit'.[40] Any financial help in the form of subsidy was not forthcoming, but in October, 1917, under the auspices of the Variety Artists' Federation, the dispute arising from Stoll's action was finally resolved by arbitration, and the rights of the artistes' were reinstated.

The total civilian casualties in Britain amounted to 5,611, of which 1,570 were fatalities; of the latter 1,413 were the result of air raids.[41] The effects of air raids may be considered very slight if compared with the daily loss of life in the trenches. Nevertheless, aerial bombardment was a new and escalating form of warfare which included civilians miles away from the warring armies: its impact was, therefore, as much psychological as it was physical. The last attack from the air took place over Kent on 17 June, 1918.

WAR LOANS AND TAXATION

In order to sustain the war effort Britain needed to borrow heavily from both home and abroad. As a result the country emerged from the Great War as a debtor nation, where before it was a creditor: the final financial outlay reached £11,325 million. A third of this prodigious cost was paid for through the ever-increasing taxation rates, and revenues raised from new taxes, such as the levy on places of amusement. The theatrical profession regarded this additional tax burden as being particularly unfair in view of the fact that its members were making strenuous efforts in voluntarily assisting the Government to raise funds via personal war loans.

Three campaigns for raising funds through war loans (the purchase of War Saving Certificates) were launched. The first was in November, 1914, the second in June, 1915 and the last in January, 1917. Once again the theatre grasped the opportunity to contribute to the war effort, and, as with the recruiting drives, it was done on an individual basis. A number of prominent theatre people subscribed to the Victory War Loan schemes. Harry Lauder was the best-known fund raiser. Lauder would, following the singing of his patriotic song *The Boys Who Fought and Won*, exhort the audience to invest what they could afford. Various theatres also supported the Loan Scheme. The Palace Theatre company, under the management of Alfred Butt, raised £20,000 and the Victoria Palace company contributed £10,000 to the Government's coffers. Charles Gulliver, the controller of 20 theatres, proposed that every member of his staff 'should pledge a portion of his future earnings… for War Loans'.[42] Whether or not this proposition was enacted cannot be ascertained.

The writers of war plays were unequivocal in their support for the war. They were constantly telling the audience to either enlist or, at the very least, financially assist by lending money to the Treasury. This was well illustrated at the Surrey Theatre in the drama *True Values*. The hero of the play, a soldier, arrives home to find his sister on strike and his girlfriend spending money on expensive clothes. In short, no female he knows is contributing to the war effort. So incensed is he by their apparent lack of understanding and misguided values that he lectures them on what they ought to be doing by proclaiming:

> … *I'll tell you. A fellow don't live out there for two years without gettin' some idea of true values… Yer don't understand this 'ere war: those as ought to know says as 'ow we must 'ave money to beat the stinking Boche, but the 'ole lot of you together 'aven't put one penny to 'elp carry on the job. The only thing my family's done is to go on strike. Yer might just as well kick me in the back, an 'ave done with it.*[43]

Inevitably the sister desists from striking and returns to work, the girlfriend and his mother resist buying a new hat and carpet respectively and instead invest the money in War Bonds. The method of debate may have been crude, but the message was abundantly clear. The writer also attempted to remind the audience that they should obey those in authority when Alf refers to 'those as ought to know...'. Indeed, any anti-authority action, such as striking, was considered unpatriotic. On a more emotive level the writer implies that the apparent selfish ignorance shown by some of those at home does positive harm to those fighting at the Front, and, furthermore, those at home do not really comprehend what it means to be in the firing line.

Propaganda messages were not confined to the spoken word. In Birmingham at the Theatre Royal in the revue *The Passing Show of 1918* the opening chorus literally sing out the message:

> *Here we are on the dear old Tank*
> > *Come along all you folk*
> *Put your money in the wartime Bank*
> > *The Bank that can't go broke*
> *By silver bullets will the war be won*
> > *That is the stuff to give the Hun.*
> *So pay – pay – don't delay*
> > *Come along, make a splash*
> *Shell out, fork out, if not walk out*
> > *What we want is cash*
> *Poor man, rich man*
> *Doesn't matter which man*
> *Roll up every rank*
> *Come along pass up*
> *Now then brass up*
> > *Put your shirt and collar*
> > *Put your bottom dollar*
> > *And some more to follar*
> > *In our beat 'em hollar – War Loan Bank*
>
> > *Roll up sport and scholar*
> > *Put your bottom dollar*
> > *In our beat 'em hollar – War Loan Bank.*[44]

It was only the affluent that could afford initially to put capital into war investment, but regulations were later eased to allow other people to purchase certificates for smaller amounts.[45] It is impossible to calculate how effective the theatre was in persuading people to invest, but this was another example of the stage's voluntary contribution to the war effort.

Additional money to meet the escalating cost of the war machine could not be found by voluntary contribution alone, and inevitably there had to be an increase in taxation. Not surprisingly, therefore, in November, 1914, Lloyd George – then Chancellor of the Exchequer

– doubled income tax. His successor, Reginald McKenna, made further demands on the taxpayer by raising taxes another 40 per cent, and widening the scope of those eligible for taxation.[46] Britain had never been engaged in such a gigantic conflict and normal means of supplementing the Government's revenue were seen to be woefully inadequate.

A hitherto untapped source of tariff return was the area of 'luxuries', and several daily newspapers had hinted in 1915 that entertainment could be considered under the heading of durable commodities. Sir George Alexander, the actor-manager, thought the idea of paying extra dues an imposition, and outlined his objection in the theatre press, saying:

> *Managers already suffer very heavily from rates and taxes, and they and the actors and actresses surely are taxed sufficiently in the way of giving their services for the war charities.*[47]

The French already had a form of theatre taxation, and those in favour cited this as a precedent; but, as pointed out in *The Stage*, the Droit de Pauvres, which was fixed at 10 per cent, only affected the theatres of Paris.[48] Furthermore the monies collected were returned in the form of grants for theatrical purposes. Unfortunately for the theatre in Britain no such system of subsidy existed, despite the continual pleas for government assistance, and the latter's public acknowledgement of the profession's valuable contribution to the war effort.

A group of music hall and theatre managers – Oswald Stoll, Alfred Butt and Arthur Bourchier being the most prominent – believed it would be folly to employ the continental idea without adopting the French system of increasing revenue by opening on Sundays.[49] Managers, and Stoll in particular, argued that the appropriation of extra income would be difficult as many of their patrons were at the Front, and that large numbers of munition workers attended theatres and music halls less often because of the unsocial hours they had to work. In addition, business was lost through closure caused by air raids, and the resultant darkened streets restricted travelling. It was even opined that a significant proportion of the public believe it inappropriate to patronize places of amusement in war time.[50]

A considerable amount of a theatre's revenue was derived from bar receipts, but this too was drastically reduced. In 1915 the Defence of the Realm Act (DORA) was amended to regulate the drink trade because it was felt that excessive drinking was interfering with the war effort; bad time-keeping in the munition factories, shipyards and transport industries was blamed on the habits of excessive drinking by the workforce. The universal practice of treating military personnel to free drinks was considered detrimental and was officially discouraged. The Act stipulated, in an effort to curb these malpractices, that licensed premises would not open in the evening until 8pm and would be closed by 10pm. This in effect cut theatre bar receipts by 50 per cent.[51] Such was the concern regarding alcohol intake that the King in 1915, in an effort to show a good example, 'took the pledge' and abstained for the duration.[52]

The delineation of the various trials and tribulations facing the industry as expressed by its leading employers and employees was to no avail; for the Chancellor of the Exchequer, Mr McKenna, on 4 April, 1916, announced a complete reappraisal of all taxes. This included the new 'proposed [tax] on admission to public amusement of all kinds'.[53] The outcome was a surcharge on tickets from a half penny to a shilling; this, it was estimated, would raise five million pounds per annum. At the imposition of the Amusement Tax it was generally envisaged that the public would bear the extra cost incurred. The public, whilst not complaining, did tend to occupy the cheaper seats. 'Many of those who formerly sat in the shilling seats' wrote a *Times* reporter 'now go to the ninepenny ones and so on down the scale. Many people, too, go less frequently'.[54] This disproportionate tax on seat prices meant, in effect, that those in the less expensive seats paid proportionally more. In some cases the management altered the ticket prices so that the patrons would not experience any change. The Piccadilly Circus Theatre management, for example, reduced the stall tickets from seven shillings and sixpence to seven shillings – this reduced the tax to sixpence. The three guinea box were reduced to two pounds twelve and six, with a five shilling surcharge: the cost was therefore well under the original price.

Managers complained of a serious decline in business. Even the critics were aggrieved as their complimentary tickets were taxed. The critics, of course, took full advantage of their access to the press and their concession was soon restored.[55] The real debate, however, concerned the method of collection. Some theatres used adhesive stamps which were destroyed when the tickets were handed-in; others used strip tickets, issued in addition to seat tickets on admission. Though, in fact, the deduction of tax on gross receipts proved to the most preferred method of collection.[56] To aggravate the problem the Government in 1917 raised the tax even higher; thus some seat prices increased by 50 per cent, and managers complained that receipts correspondingly decreased by 50 per cent.[57] And with an escalation in the cost of materials, rises in rates and rents some provincial theatres had to close.[58] The end result was a loss of work for the theatrical profession; a loss of entertainment for the public, and a loss of revenue for the Government. The anticipated revenue of £5 million was nearer £3 million and this was before the deduction of collection costs.[59]

Despite the difficulty of collecting and paying the Amusement Tax, the theatre raised extra money in the form of voluntary contributions for War Loans. Indeed it was in the field of voluntary work that the theatre provided the greatest assistance to the Government, the people and the military.

Performing for Charity

Throughout the war years the number of military service personnel incapacitated – the blind, limbless and neurasthenic – along with their dependents accumulated at an ever increasing rate; by mid-1915 military casualties in the British forces had risen to nearly 400,000.[1] The Government was, of necessity, stirred into taking action, for at the outbreak of war in 1914 the only official fund dealing with 'allowances and pensions' for servicemen was that accommodating the veterans at the Royal Hospital for Soldiers at Chelsea. The actual amount of government assistance had not been altered since the Boer War. The Government's initial inaction regarding allowances was, writes Marwick, 'marked by a last flowering of grand-scale private charity'.[2]

Ministers' main concern was with the action of fighting, and the damaging consequences of such action on individuals and their families was not thoroughly considered. Any funding for families had to come from charitable donations channelled through the Sailors' and Soldiers' Families Association and the National Relief Fund.[3] It was as a result of the deeds and promptings of these organizations – the latter in particular – that the Government increased the allowance for dependents of men on active service. The National Relief Fund was begun in response to an appeal by the Prince of Wales in August, 1914, but it was not until November, 1915, when a Naval and War Pensions Act was passed, that 'a regular system of payment was introduced'.[4]

The Government did not, or could not, cope financially with every individual need and there was ample opportunity for philanthropic provision. Collectors and donors included every trade and profession, if only indirectly. There existed, however, one professional group that was eminently adept – via its collective skills, charismatic individuals and public performances – at the task of raising money. That was, of course, the entertainment profession.

INDIVIDUAL FUND RAISERS

The ever-growing numbers of wounded men could not fail to have an effect upon the people at home. One of the most affected was Charles E Dobell, a businessman, who formed an association called the Wounded Heroes Entertainments Committee (WHE). The association was registered under the War Charities Act 1916. The entertainment that this committee provided was extremely varied. It included taking men to matinees at music halls, escorting them on Thames launch trips, and organizing garden parties. The halls visited included Collins' Music Hall (to see Marie Lloyd), the Hackney and Islington Empires, Holborn Hall and the Northampton Institute. Each member of the committee, and there were four, took responsibility for escorting small groups of wounded servicemen to the various activities. A sample of the disparate nature of the music hall fare can be judged by the 1916, Hackney Empire programme. The bill included: 'Marcelle and his unique partner... a Sea Lion; "My Four Years in Germany" [5th instalment] the Serial Extraordinary. Comprising 10 single reel Instalments produced under the personal supervision of James W. Gerard, American Ambassador to Berlin. Estell Rose, the Italian and Hebrew Dialect comedienne, and Pat Docherty, the Irish comedian and dancer'.[5]

A Launch Party, which took place on 1 August, 1918, was organized to entertain a group of limbless officers from Roehampton hospital. The party travelled to Hampton Court, stopping at Karisno Island (lent by Fred Karno, Esq.) for tea and then attended a concert in the Palm Court before returning to Westminster.

A garden party in Clissold Park, north London, had a fete atmosphere with 'Sports on the Green, quoits, Aunt Sally, hoopla, coconut shies and tug-of-war'. A police band played throughout the day. The WHE Committee managed to inveigle other people to help run entertainments, and the Ladies Day and Shop Assistants Association produced a programme in which was printed 'A Motto for the Day', which in some instances must appear, to a latter-day witness, to be perverse; for example, the Clissold Park maxim read 'More than pleased I've got a Blighty one'. But for sheer optimism it is hard to cap the motto printed in the programme for the Collins' Music Hall outing which read: 'Cheerio: it might have been worse'.[6] Nevertheless, the WHE raised £2,000 by public subscription, although the running costs amounted to £2,300; but the philanthropic Charles Dobell and his generous friends covered the outstanding costs. This altruistic group entertained 20,000 wounded servicemen in one period of eight months alone in 1918.[7]

Several individuals supported specific charities. It is not surprising to find that a musical programme to raise money for Welsh troops was held under the patronage of the prime minister, Lloyd George, on

St. David's Day in 1917.[8] A number of noted women were involved in organizing different funds. In 1915, £567 was donated by the Variety Artists' Federation to a fund organized by the wives of a Field Marshal and an Admiral of the Fleet, namely Lady French and Lady Jellicoe. This donation was a percentage of the New Year's Gift from the VAF to soldiers and sailors. A proportion of the money was spent on equipping a YMCA recreation hut for troops at Dover, and an unspecified amount was sent, via the YMCA, for recreational facilities abroad in France and Belgium. The sum was raised over a period of a few weeks, and was from donations received at charity matinee performances.[9]

Several of the more famous professional actors and performers, because of their 'pulling-power', were able to work as one-man charity organizers. The man dubbed the 'Prince of Beggars' was the popular music hall artiste, George Robey *(Figure 7)*. Robey had a talent, not only for entertaining, but for organizing special concerts. By March, 1918, he had collected £50,000. 'At one of George Robey's concerts thousands of pounds invariably changed hands – one of them, at the London Coliseum, realized the splendid total of £14,500'.[10] Other equally well-known artistes, Harry Tate and Harry Lauder, also orchestrated the raising of funds. The former by concerts and the latter by what he called his 'Million Pound Fund for Scottish Soldiers and Sailors'.[11] Frank Allen, the theatre manager, had by August, 1918, raised 'something like £75,000 by special matinees'. To this list can be added the music hall magnates Walter de Freece and Oswald Stoll, both of whom used the theatres under their control for the benefit of charity funds.[12] The Government was indebted to the show business fraternity for

Figure 7. The popular George Robey as The Queen of Hearts.

their efforts to generate money for the military casualty funds, via, for example, the Red Cross appeals. Coles Armstrong, commenting in *The Stage Year Book*, 1919, quotes Lauder, saying:

> *One can but re-echo the opinion of Mr Harry Lauder that the Government, after the tribute to the King, should pay the profession an official compliment for the splendid work it has accomplished during the great struggle...*[13]

It was, at times, extremely difficult to obtain the necessary funds for the casualties of war, not only because of the Government's seemingly meagre response, but because of the continual exhortation to give. Various ploys had to be cunningly implemented to encourage the theatre audience to attend the ever-increasing number of fundraising matinees. In 1916, at the Empire Theatre, the actor-manager, Seymour Hicks recounts a time when he was attempting to raise funds by auctioning boxes and stalls for a forthcoming charity performance. The bidding was not going well, until Hicks noticed the very attractive French artiste Gaby Deslys in the audience, and in a moment of intuitive improvisation he called her to the stage. The result was the audience immediately became more responsive. The bidding for the Royal Box had reached 300 sovereigns when Seymour Hicks had a second inspiration; he recalls:

> *... I said, 'Miss Gaby Deslys will give a kiss to the gentleman who will bid another fifty pounds'... and asked if she would oblige... 'Kiss a kind-hearted man... of course...' Up came [an] old gentleman... he received two, or three very nice kisses.., and I hope he occupied the box for which he had paid £350.*[14]

Oswald Stoll, unlike his contemporaries, did not pass on the money he accumulated to another deserving charity but used it to provide housing for disabled servicemen. The money was collected, under the auspices of The War Seal Foundation Fund, in the form of stamps or seals which the public could purchase. The trading of the seals was done through the offices of the variety artistes organization, The Grand Order of Water Rats and its Ladies Guild. The cost of each flat was £400, and by 1918 a whole block was completed and ready for occupation. The apartments, which are still occupied today, are located in the Fulham Road, West London. In 1919, in recognition, not only of his services to the stage – he built the Coliseum Theatre in 1904 and ran a very successful music hall circuit of theatres – but also in appreciation of his war time charity work, Stoll was knighted.[15] An indication of the Government's appreciation of Oswald Stoll's efforts can be seen in the letter Sir Arthur Stanley, then President of the Board of Trade, wrote to Stoll in 1918, saying:

> *I feel confident that they [the flats] will meet a real need and will bring comfort and happiness to many men who otherwise would have been separated from their families. I look upon this as... one of the best.... bits of war work that I have seen...*[16]

Fund raising and donating to charities was not the sole preserve of actors, artistes and managers: playwrights too supported the benevolent societies. As one of his contributions, George Bernard Shaw, for example, unbeknown to most people, gave £200 to the Belgian Relief Fund.[17] Another playwright, James Barrie, concerned about the conditions in which the war-stricken children in France had to survive, decided to open a refuge for them. In 1915, Elizabeth Lucas, a friend, did, without much persuasion from Barrie, leave for France to set up a home at Bettancourt. Barrie, having sought the necessary permission for the venture to go ahead, gave an initial contribution of £2,000.[18] He subsequently made several trips to the continent, and, in fact, financed the entire undertaking himself until the home closed in 1916. Its closure was due to the ill health of Elizabeth Lucas, and by this time other larger organizations were at work and, presumably, they were better equipped to perform such a task.[19] Some songwriters, such as Paul A. Rubens, gave the profits from the sale of a song to charity; in this case the proceeds from *Your King and Country Want You* went to the Queen Mary's Work for Women Fund.

ROYALTY

The employment of the theatre as a source of charity funding was apparent from the beginning of the war. Within the first month of the Declaration, Herbert Beerbohm Tree had rehearsed and presented Louis N. Parker's patriotic play *Drake* at His Majesty's Theatre. Tree, the actor-manager and the lead player, with the 'generous co-operation of his author... and his company gave all the show's profits to War Charities'.[20]

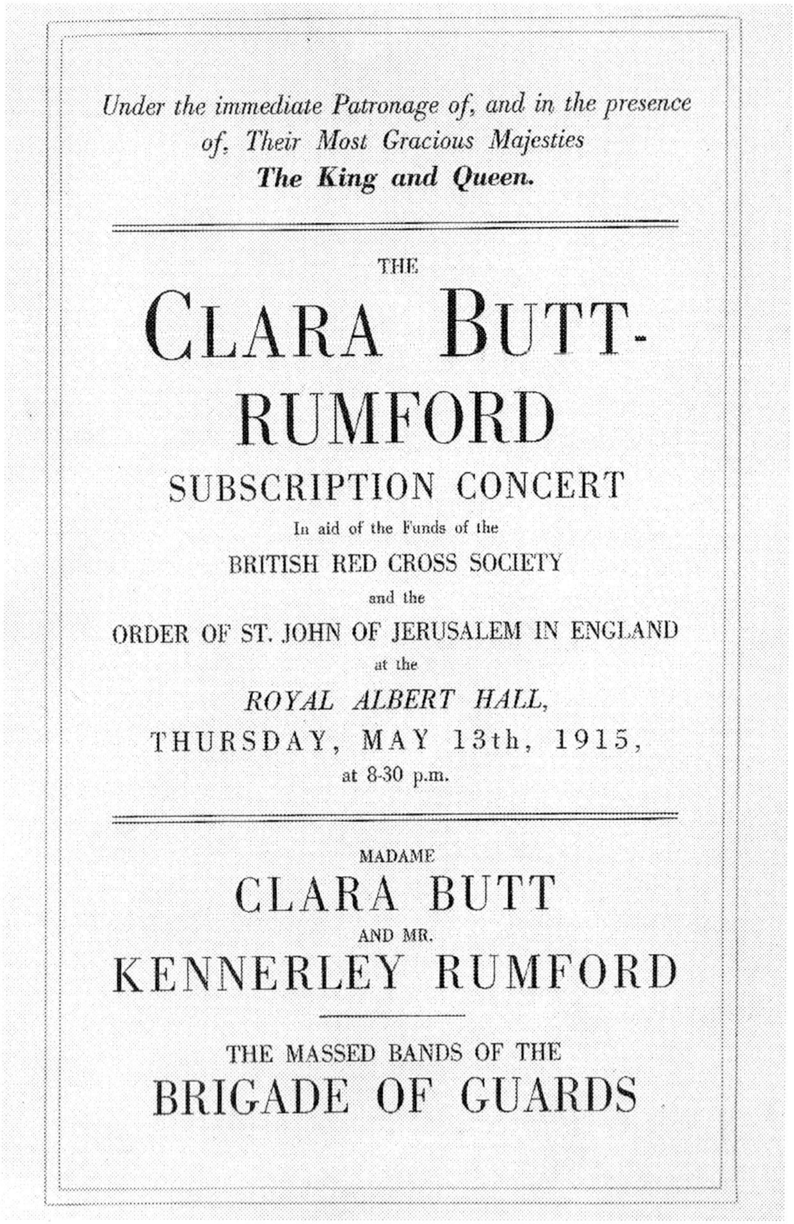

Under the immediate Patronage of, and in the presence
of, Their Most Gracious Majesties
The King and Queen.

THE

CLARA BUTT-
RUMFORD

SUBSCRIPTION CONCERT

In aid of the Funds of the

BRITISH RED CROSS SOCIETY

and the

ORDER OF ST. JOHN OF JERUSALEM IN ENGLAND

at the

ROYAL ALBERT HALL,

THURSDAY, MAY 13th, 1915,

at 8-30 p.m.

MADAME

CLARA BUTT

AND MR.

KENNERLEY RUMFORD

THE MASSED BANDS OF THE

BRIGADE OF GUARDS

Figure 8. The programme cover for the concert featuring Dame Clara Butt and Kennerley Rumford.

Despite such efforts as the Beerbohm Tree productions, 'in the autumn of 1914', wrote Sanderson, 'the theatre entered its blackest phase of the war'.[21] By September many people had ceased going to the theatre and nearly 200 touring companies had been taken off the road.[22] A large and significant proportion of the theatregoers had decided that it was inappropriate to attend places of amusement at this time – it was regarded as the height of insensitivity and bad taste. The King and Queen initially held this view, and the monarch, in September, 1914, declined a request from the Actors' Association to continue theatregoing.[23] In fact, they both attended the Shakespeare Tercentenary performance of *Julius Caesar* at Drury Lane on 2 May, 1916, and *The Dream of Gerontius* at the Queen's Hall on 10 May, 1916; neither of which were reported to have been in aid of charity. It is true, however, that only one member of the Royal Household, Queen Alexandra, attended the theatre between August, 1914 and February, 1915. That was to see a matinee performance at Covent Garden in aid of the War Emergency Arts Fund. The King and Queen attended their first charity benefit show when they went to see *School for Scandal* at Covent Garden on 2 February, 1915. From then on there was a steady flow of Royalty to the theatre.

In total, the lists in the annual *Stage Year Book* show that members of the Royal Family attended forty-three charity productions in the West End during the war. Of these, 18 were evening performances, which included: *Motherhood* at the Haymarket, and the Russian Opera Company at the London Opera House in 1915; *The Passing Show* and *Puss in Boots* at the Palace Theatre in 1916, and various others. The type of shows visited included both 'legitimate' and variety entertainment.[24] In 1918 all war time benefit shows were matinee performances. The afternoon became the usual time of day to attend the theatre for charitable as well as pleasurable reasons.

Most of the Royal Family were present at a charity matinee at some time during the war. Prince Albert (later George VI), the Prince of Wales (later Edward VIII), and Prince George (later Duke of Gloucester) paid, as would be expected, fewer visits as they were serving with the armed forces. Foreign aristocrats made occasional appearances in the royal boxes; included amongst them were King Manuel and Queen Amelia of Portugal and the Duchess George of Russia. George V (the King), Princess Maud and Princess Victoria attended between eight and fourteen benefit shows respectively, and both Queen Mary and the Princess Royal managed to attend the theatre on over twenty occasions; but for sheer love of the theatre, or perhaps an overwhelming sense of duty, Queen Alexandra (the Queen Mother) was present at forty out of the forty-three charity matinees attended by royalty.

The number of charities benefiting from donations when member(s) of the Royal Family were present is long and varied. There was just the one performance in aid of Infant Welfare Work and the Royal Free Hospital, and one performance per year for the King George Pension Fund for actors and actresses. The vast majority of shows were for the direct and indirect benefit of war-related charities. The latter included civilian hospitals in which it is supposed the largest number of patients were military personnel.

The sale of souvenirs was another method of raising funds. At the Clara Butt-Rumford concert at the Albert Hall in May, 1915, patrons could buy a 12-inch long stick mounted with a 10-inch silk pennant. The pennants were ornately embossed with coloured flags of the Allies in the centre, which are encircled with a laurel wreath. Inscribed in the silk are photographs of the King and Queen, and the names of the charities – The Red Cross and Order of St. John of Jerusalem in England – are printed on the flag. King George V and Queen Mary were both present, but Queen Alexandra, in her absence, sent a cheque for £20 towards the funds. Over £5,000 was subscribed to the fund from the sale of tickets, and the money received for the sale of boxes was described as 'remarkable'. Two boxes went for 500 guineas, nine for 100 guineas, seven for 50 guineas and another ten for 25 guineas each. One anonymous benefactor bought 'six 50-guinea boxes for wounded officers, soldiers and nurses'.[25]

Clara Butt and Kenneley Rumford *(Figure 8)* were the only soloists at the concert. Dame Clara suggested that at the end of her singing *The Home Flag* the audience should turn to the Royal box and wave the pennants as a sort of 'general Royal salute'. The soloists were supported by a choir of 250 well-known singers and artistes, which included: Angus Nicholls, Ruth Vincent, John Coates, Ben Davies, Harry Dearth and Plunket Greene. There were also 100 well-known women working as programme sellers. Amongst these many belonged to the theatrical profession; they were: Nina Boucicault, Lilian Braithwaite, Constance Collier, Lady Tree and Grace Lane. The programme included '*The Lost Chord, Abide With Me*, and *Land of Hope and Glory*, to be sung by Mme. Butt at the express wish of the Queen'.[26]

The King and Queen and show business artistes did not confine their combined charitable appearances to the theatre and concert hall. In March, 1916, a large number of wounded servicemen was invited to attend Buckingham Palace for tea and entertainments. The invitations, it was reported in the press, were sent 'chiefly to more distant hospitals, such as those at Croydon, Epsom and Greenwich, which have not benefited to the same extent from the kindness of the public as those actually in London or just outside it'. The men were first given tea and then adjourned to the riding school 'in which several well-known artistes from the music-halls will take part'.[27] In all 3,000 men, over a period of three successive days, were fed and entertained.

At each table there was a member of the Royal Family – and the waiters and waitresses under their command included no less than twenty-six aristocratic ladies and gentlemen of the Court. The entertainment was provided by: 'Du Calion on his ladder, Neil Kenyon as a golf caddie, Cornalia and Eddie as eccentric acrobats, Miss Madge Sanders and George Grossmith in *They Didn't Believe Me*, De Biero with his magic hoop, Arthur Playfair and Nelson Keys as optimistic and pessimistic guardsmen, with T.G. Graham to help them... (as Charlie Chaplin), and Miss Gladys Cooper and Gerald Du Maurier in Sir James Barrie's sketch *The Fatal Typist*... and the corps de ballet of the Palace Girls'. And there was organized community singing. The hosts – The King, Queen and Queen Alexandra – after dining at the top table took their seats in the front row for the entertainments.[28]

The second day's performance saw a change in the programme. It included a great deal more singing, and several stand-up comics and fewer visual 'turns'. The reason for this was that a large section of the audience was blinded. The audience was also more cosmopolitan, and included Australian, New Zealand and Canadian troops. The entertainment was organized by Alfred Butt – manager of several West End theatres. The chorus came from the Empire Theatre. The show also included community singing led by Dr. Walford Davies with the Temple Church Choir. It was by all accounts an enjoyable occasion; however, the most poignant moment of the event was supplied by the men themselves; as *The Times* reporter put it 'the singing of the wounded men... was far finer and more moving than anything that the stage offered for their entertainment'.[29]

In order to generate funds it was not sufficient simply to have members of the titled elite present in the theatre audience, it helped if the cast list matched their adductive power. At the Coliseum in March,

1915, a double-box contained the Queen and four other Royals, a
on stage there was an array of famous theatre actors, actresses a
music hall artistes. There were also thirty-five titled persons in t
audience. It seems that whenever the King and Queen attended the
appeared a whole entourage of socially, and presumably financia
important people. On this occasion the audience seemed to get
money's worth as the show lasted over four hours. The show includ
one-act plays and sketches performed by leading actors and actresse
The theatre notables included: Will Evans, Arthur Bourchier, Vio
Vanburgh, Charles Hawtry, Lorette Taylor and Sir George Alexand
The show was in aid of Princess Victoria of Schleswig-Holstei
Auxiliary Committee of the YMCA for providing funds for conce
for the troops at hospitals, and recreation huts in England and Fran
At the finale Miss Lena Ashwell, who organized such milita
concerts, announced that the not inconsiderable sum of £1,450 h
been raised.

On several occasions members of the Royal Family did more th
just attract people to the theatre. The King and Queen not only attend
the matinee of *The Man Who Stayed at Home* at the Palace Theatre
May in 1915, in aid of the Officers' Families Fund, but a
purchased the entire gallery, some 400 seats, for wounded soldi
from various London hospitals.[31] The intriguing question is, were
wounded soldiers officers or other ranks? If they were non-comm
sioned ranks, how did they feel about going to a show to raise mon
for the families of their superiors? Perhaps they didn't care, and w
only too pleased to get out of hospital for some free entertainme
Whatever the reason the sum of £1,330 was raised for the benefit
officers' families.[32]

What is apparent and significant about the shows for charity w
their multi-disciplinary, multi-national and multifarious format. Th
were often, as with a matinee for the Lady Arthur Paget's Fund for
Blind (1916) at the Prince of Wales' Theatre, designed to appeal
different tastes, 'high' and 'low' brow; the show was entente-cordi
in approach, and encompassed performers from different sides of
theatrical divide. There were dances from the ballet and Greek thea
classic musical solos and musical comedy and sketches.[33]

Another example of this co-operative effort was on behalf of
Blinded Heroes Fund, inaugurated by the Variety side of the professi
The idea originated from two Variety artistes, Sergeants Dick Bu
and Sam Mayo, and was administered under the aegis of the mana

Mr Allen and his Moss Empire staff. The entertainment consisted of matinee performances held throughout Britain, with those in London having the benefit of attracting royalty, which combined the talents of both branches of the industry. As a result of their efforts a cheque for £11,327 was handed to Sir Arthur Pearson at St Dunstan's Hospital for the Blinded Heroes Fund in September, 1916. In Regents Park Lord Derby, who was at the presentation, gave the vote of thanks, saying:

> *I want, through Mr Allen, to thank all those in the theatrical and music hall profession who have done so much to assist in getting this large sum together. I know of no two professions who have more cheerfully given up their leisure (and their leisure is often of a very brief description).... to amuse and, in this instance, to provide almost the livelihood of our soldiers.*[34]

By August, 1918, Mr Allen, via the special matinees, had accumulated approximately £75,000 (about two and a quarter million pounds in 1994 terms) for charitable funds.[35]

In 1915 and 1916 the number of charity matinees produced was phenomenal. It was recorded in *The Era* that in 1915 there were as many as three, sometimes four benefit matinees a week in London alone.[36] Royalty did not, could not, be expected to attend all the charity performances, and on occasions the cast list did not match the popular distinction of those present in the Royal Box; and performing in the afternoon never has quite the same cachet as an evening show. Indeed, according to a contemporary commentator the artiste's job was a far from easy one. Reporting on a particular war charity matinee in July, 1916, a critic wrote:

> *The artists find the work immensely harder, but the charity matinee was worse in this respect than any ordinary matinee.*
>
> *The audience was restrained and showed little enthusiasm. Its applause was scanty, and it was not until nearing the end of the programme that anything like warmth was shewn... The fact that these charity matinees are held in such a freezing atmosphere more than doubles the debt of gratitude the country owes to these artists who have never hesitated since the war began to support deserving charity by their services.*[37]

It can be imagined that if every time a theatregoer, on entering the portals of a theatre in an afternoon, was by exhortation urged to part with his or her hard earned cash they would, inevitably, become blasé: an attitude of 'OK, if you want my money, you're going to have to work damn hard for it!' must have, at times, prevailed. The money for charity was, therefore, not easily obtained and was certainly hard-earned, particularly when it is remembered that the shows were done in the artists' free time, and, for those that were working, between rehearsals and other performances.

CHARITY FOR FIT TROOPS AND POWS

The Government was very slow in shouldering responsibility for all the casualties of war. Indeed, the authorities displayed a remarkable 'Pontius Pilate' attitude to one category in particular, namely the prisoner-of-war. It was because of the Government's dilatoriness that the voluntary civilian Prisoner-of-War Committee was set up in 1915; in fact, the War Office did not show any official interest in British POWs until September, 1916.[38] The War Office was invited to take responsibility for the voluntary organization but declined the offer. Eventually the official Central civilian Prisoners-of-War Committee undertook the task of supplying food and clothing to the POWs, but this caused some degree of resentment among the voluntary organizers and individual donors as they wished their gifts to go to specific recipients.[39] It was, therefore, prior to September, 1916, incumbent on the voluntary bodies to supply the POWs' needs. One theatrical organization that did a great deal for the troops abroad was the Beneficient Order of Terriers. The Terriers comprised two hundred and fifty Variety artistes, about eighty of whom served with the Colours, gaining two Military Medals and one Distinguished Service Medal for gallantry. The contribution they made was in the form of food, along with 'parcels of music, stage properties, wigs, grease paint and newspapers every week to army members'.[40] Most of the Terriers' members, both in and out of uniform, also entertained their comrades in camps and hospitals.

Military units at home, acutely aware of the plight and needs of comrades abroad, also sent aid. In Scotland, for example, in September, 1918, at the Kings' Theatre, the Glasgow Anti-Aircraft Battery staged an entertainment that consisted of one-act plays. The cast comprised serving officers and professional civilian actors. The funds raised were for the purchase of necessary goods for Royal Artillery and Royal Engineers POWs.[41] Amateur drama groups and choral societies also made contributions. The Gravesend Ladies' Choir was one such that used its talent to aid charity, in this case for the benefit of the ex-mayoress' Prisoner of War Comfort Fund (*Figure 9*). As the programme shows it encompassed orchestral pieces, patriotic and humorous songs, selections from the most popular show *Chu Chin Chow*, and the almost mandatory rendition of *Land of Hope and Glory* by Elgar. If Tipperary was the popular song in the theatres and music halls, then Edward Elgar's patriotic air was a pre-requisite for almost every amateur and professional choral concert.

Charity work for the troops via entertainment was not confined to the precincts of a theatre. At the Royal Small Arms factory, at Enfield Lock, Middlesex, the workers put on short concerts during their supper hour from 10.30pm to 11.30pm. The amount of money contributed is relatively small, just £209 over a period of twenty weeks, but it was raised mainly from young lowly paid apprentices.[42]

What the troops required was money to buy goods, items that would help to make their existence more comfortable, more enjoyable. The troops did, of course, put on entertainment for themselves, but in order to do this more effectively they needed the ancillaries of theatrical production, in particular musical scores and instruments. In response to this need the Musicians' Gift Fund organized appeals for money, books on music and instruments for the amateur and professional entertainers in the 2,000 YMCA recreation huts at home, and abroad. The result of this appeal, begun in December, 1917, as recorded in the Imperial War Museum archives, was as follows:

1. £2,000 was raised in the first six months
2. 2,500 instruments were sent to every theatre of war
3. Complete music libraries were equipped in Rouen, Havre, Boulogne, Salonica, Cologne and 17 other centres of the Rhine Army and many YMCA huts in England
4. Gifts of music and instruments have been freely distributed to the camps at home and in France, North and South Russia, Salonica, Egypt, Syria, Mesopotamia, India, Constantinople etc., and the Internment camps in Germany and the Hague.[43]

TOWN HALL, GRAVESEND

(By kind permission of the Mayor).

Evening Concert

BY

The Gravesend Ladies' Choir,

KINDLY ASSISTED BY

THE VOLUNTARY ORCHESTRA

of the 1st Res. Batt. Suffolk Regiment.

Conductor - Lieut. D. G. BONHAM.

(By permission of Bt. Col. C. F. GRANTHAM.)

TO AID THE

Ex-Mayoress' PRISONERS OF WAR COMFORTS FUND.

Wednesday, March 13th, 1918,

PROGRAMME.

Accompanists:

Mr. PERCY G. HART.   Miss R. V. CRIPPS.

Conductor - - Mr. DAVID J. THOMAS.

Figure 9. Programme for Gravesend Ladies' Evening Concert in aid of Ex-Mayoress' *Prisoner of War Comfort Fund* 1918. [L.J. Collins]

The most popular instrument, because of its portability, was the mouth organ. In a *Musical News* article of 1915, it states that in the first year of the war 7,675 mouth organs were dispatched abroad; '5,675 to France, 1,000 to the Dardanelles and 1,000 to the Fleet...' The donations came from Britain and America.[44]

The military-run concert parties did not rely totally on civilian co-operation to gather funds. The *Diamond Troupe* of the 29th Division, along with other military concert parties, assisted in raising funds for the British and French Red Cross Societies; they, the military, were perhaps more aware than most fund-raisers of the true value of their efforts.[45]

ENTERTAINMENTS FOR MILITARY HOSPITAL PATIENTS

On the periphery of hospital patients' entertainments were the Royal Institute Companies of London. In 1915, on the suggestion of the Institutes' Council, the Livery companies of the city: the Skinners', Goldsmiths', Grocers' and Haberdashers', entertained wounded servicemen from the various Dominions to tea in their Company Halls, and, on occasions, 'treated' the men to theatre and music hall visits.[46] Royal Institute members may even have been among the generous benefactors who paid a one guinea subscription to the Savoy Hotel, which would have entitled them to act as host to ten soldiers, sailors or airmen for tea and a concert on the first and third Tuesday in each month. By October, 1916, some 5,000 wounded had been entertained in such a manner at the Savoy. An example of what was on offer can be seen by the programme of 3 October, 1916. On that day 370 soldiers listened to the hotel's orchestra and were kept amused by some of the most popular artists of the theatre and music hall. *The Times* reporter noted that the cast included such well-known artists as: Nelson Keys, Arthur Playfair, Violet Loraine, Arthur Roberts, George Robey, Maria Novello and Dutch Daly. They all gave their services gratuitously for the benefit of the soldiers, as did the arranger Oswald Stoll and the managers from his Coliseum Theatre, Arthur Croxton and Henry Crocker.[47] There was a multitude of smaller organizations providing either one-off or regular entertainments for the wounded. The Convalescent Committee of the South African Comfort Society was one of these lesser-known philanthropic societies, which provided tea and a concert for 600 wounded soldiers at Caxton Hall in 1916.[48]

Entertainment for wounded personnel was not, of course, confined to London. Every city and most large towns gave assistance in providing theatrical amusements. In Birmingham efforts were made in 1917 to rationalize and organize the supply of good entertainment and to distribute fairly the work among actors and artists from the professional companies. One of the problems, outlined in *The Stage*, was 'that some institutions have at times been surfeited by well-intentioned mediocre amateur performers' [49] The criticism levelled at some of the amateur groups was more than likely true, but it may also be true that the newly-formed Birmingham organization wanted to preserve jobs for its members. In February, 1917, a sub-committee of the City's Professions and General Trades Wounded Sailors and Soldiers Entertainment Fund (sanctioned and presided over by the then Lord Mayor, Neville Chamberlain) was formed to co-ordinate the supply to hospitals; the committee members came from the Royal, Grand, Alexandra and Empire Theatres, the Aston Hippodrome and the Birmingham Athletic Institute.[50] The Birmingham branch of the British Red Cross Society (which had been responsible for organizing much of the entertainment in hospitals) issued a statement in January, 1917, showing the number of visits made by the sick and wounded to theatres since August, 1914. It reads:

> *The Royal, more than 30,000; Alexandra, 5,800; Grand, 4,360; Prince of Wales's, 1,000; Repertory, 474, Royal Lemington, 200; and Aston Hippodrome, 209.*[51]

Efforts were also made to entertain the servicemen's dependents. To this end, on 16 November, 1917, nearly 3,000 children from the homes of serving men were, as in the previous two years, admitted to the pantomime at the Royal Theatre. Admission was free, but tea (and cigarettes for the men) plus transport to and from the various hospitals was provided care of the Entertainment Fund. The entertainments were enjoyed by all, but to the individual it may have been more than light relief from the monotony of hospital. According to the subsequent Director General of National Service, then Lord Mayor, Neville Chamberlain, 'it was partly psychic'. The men, he affirmed, needed to be given the opportunity to forget the experienced hardships, injuries and traumas of combat.[52]

Entertainment for the bed-bound and other in-patients in hospitals up and down the country, by both amateur and professional performers, was a regular occurrence during the First World War years. This was certainly true in the London hospitals where the majority of casualties were boarded. As reported in an *Observer* report in 1915, the 1st London General Hospital, Camberwell, had a YMCA hut in its grounds which held 400 patients, for thrice weekly concerts. The 2nd London General Hospital, Chelsea, had three to four shows each week, and the London Hospital, Whitechapel, accommodated audiences of 300 in the library twice a week through the winter months. A similar pattern of entertainment pertained at St George's, and the 3rd London Hospital at Wandsworth. At the Middlesex Hospital small parties of eight or nine wounded were taken out on day trips, and at St. Bartholomew's a Territorial Army band played at lunch time on certain days of the week. During 1915, patients at King George's received entertainment every day over the Christmas period until the middle of January. At the latter the cast included; Lady Tree, Lilian Braithwaite and George Robey. The audience of 400 were assembled in a large corridor in the basement. The programme was varied and incorporated 'songs, recitals, playlets and Shakespearean readings'.[53] The Colonial troops were, naturally, included in these rounds of entertainment. The Australian Auxiliary Hospital at Harefield Park was particularly well equipped, having a concert room with a stage which seated 500. Again there were dramatic readings, including an appearance by the tragedian H B Irving, in *A Story of Waterloo*.[54]

The visiting concert parties were seen, by the medical staff, as more than temporary diversions from the pains of suffering. Sir Frederick Mott, Commandant in charge of the Maudsley Hospital in London found that:

> ... *provided no organic trouble was present, shell shocked men could sing where they could not speak, and if words came with a tune, soon after they came without it.*[55]

Sir Bruce Porter, another hospital commandant also expressed the view that entertainment was a beneficial form of medical treatment which speeded-up the process of recovery. He wrote:

> *The opinion of my staff and myself is that these entertainments reduce the period of illness by an average of at least 5 days and in a hospital of 2,000 beds that means 10,000 days. If the duration of a patient's stay averages 30 days the concert room entertainments are equal to 300 beds... In days gone by no provision was made for this form of treatment.*[56]

Encouragement for the theatre, in a more general therapeutic sense, came as early as 1914, from the Church. The Bishop of Winchester and the Bishop of Birmingham both recommended the public support the stage.[57] The catholic Bishop of Northampton was also supportive;[58] so was Bishop Welldon of Manchester who endorsed the work of the Women's Emergency Corps who were responsible, in part, for organizing concerts for troops and munition workers.[59]

EMPLOYEES' WAGES AND FEES FOR CHARITY WORK

What the stage did for charity in London, Glasgow and Birmingham was repeated in other cities. In Manchester the theatres were opened on Sundays for charity performances. The theatres and music halls raised thousands of pounds; for example, by December 1917, the London Hippodrome company had collected £7,500.[60] So prolific was the work for charity throughout the British Isles that H. Charles Newton, the critic and dramatic author, having perused the relevant financial statements was able to report that by August 1915, that artists 'have raised more than, £1,000,000 for War Charities'.[61] However, despite this enormous effort to collect and donate funds for the less fortunate servicemen and their dependents most theatre performers, of whatever persuasion, were living on, or precariously close to, the poverty line.

It is impossible to assess the earning power of the music hall artiste or the actor. What they could earn was determined by individual contracts with specific agents and managers. The difference was that the music hall artiste might be paid per appearance, whereas the actor is more likely to have been on a weekly wage. The pay differential was, indeed still is, very wide. The 'star' artiste could, even during the war, earn a few hundred pounds a week; alternatively the jobbing actor on, say a fifteen-week tour in the provinces, would be paid £3 or less per week.[62] No one who earned less than £160 per year – lowered to £130 in 1917 – was eligible for income tax, and most theatre performers were below this financial threshold.[63] Many more workers were added to the tax-paying class during the war, particularly those employed in war-related work, but as wages rose so too did rents, food prices and the cost of travel. In many cases, unlike the workforce in general, the actor's wage did not go up: conversely or some might argue, perversely – it went down.

Theatre managers, because of the uncertainties with tours being cancelled and a number of theatres 'going dark', took precautions in order to safeguard their financial status. Touring managers, wrote MacLeod, 'told their companies, not always with justification, that if there were to be any performances at all. They [the actors] must accept reduced salaries'.[64] This cost-cutting exercise meant that wages were reduced by between 20 and 25 per cent.[65] By 1915 theatre traffic had almost reverted to the pre-war level, but managers, particularly in the provinces, were somewhat reluctant to redress the imbalance in wages. The employers were able to keep the wages artificially low by using 'semi-amateur' actors. These actors were described in *The Stage* as 'hamfits', and were people 'with some financial means and little or no ability'.[66] They were mainly to be found playing the small roles and under-studying the 'leads' in the larger touring companies. They were, according to the career actors, too incompetent for the more varied and arduous job of Stock company employment. And part of this unscrupulous use by employees and their 'payment' was the 'exacting of free service for relief funds'.[67] Sir Herbert Tree, aware of the actors' plight, suggested that a fee, no matter how small, should be exacted from every charity performance and be donated to an Actors' Emergency War Fund.[68] There is no evidence of such a fund being inaugurated. The Actors' Association did, however, set up a fund which drew its income from one performance per year in aid of actors and their dependents; this seems so minimal that help must have been meagre.

One group of stage employees who did manage to put pressure on their management and secure a pay rise was the front and back-of-house staff at Golders' Green Hippodrome. They, via their National Association, called a strike in July, 1916, and within twenty minutes their demands were met.[69] The musicians employed by Oswald Stoll, who included those at the Coliseum, Middlesex and London Opera House, were not so successful. They asked for the 3/6d payment per performance to be raised by one shilling. This was refused and they gave a two-week warning of a pending strike. The management, in what appears to have been a scurrilous attempt to discredit them, publicly point out that many of the men were eligible for the army, thereby implying that they should not be working in the theatre but doing their duty. A peculiar statement to make as national conscription was then in operation. The musicians, in their defence, replied that 'most of them are over military age, many of them are old soldiers with 21 years' service, and others have been discharged... on account of wounds received in the present war'.[70] Oswald Stoll's altruism towards charitable causes (for which he was knighted) did not, it seems, extend to his employees, as he refused to compromise and merely sacked the whole lot, and replaced them with an all-female orchestra.

The problem of reduction in wages due to a manager's thrift could not be rectified by doing charity performance, as these were done 'gratis'. Millions of pounds were raised by specific performances, many of them specially arranged on Sundays, for which money would usually have been ranked as receipts from which the artistes would have received his or her due share. It must have been quite galling to the lesser known performers to work for free for others when they were in need of charity themselves. If paid weekly, or if the contract stipulated for a certain number of performances per week, the artistes still lost out because the charity show could be included in the former and excluded from the latter. Artistes also complained of the unpalatable way in which 'well-known singers and performers were made use of by rich people to gather funds for charities'.[71] Most of the charity shows were organized by titled ladies who tended to treat the performer in a 'curt and distant manner'. To add additional insult, at a show in 1917, a lady approached an artiste, who was unpaid, and asked 'would he please take up a collection among the other artistes as the financial result of the matinee had fallen considerably short of expectations!'.[72] At the Vaudeville in 1917, at a charity matinee show where Queen Alexandra was present, the organizer's incompetence ensured that the show started late, finished early and was incomplete, but it did include a new play written by the temporary amateur producer.[73] *The Stage*, in its editorial, proposed that all charity be organized and co-ordinated on the Birmingham model, and that work, whether it be raising money or entertaining the wounded and men in training ought to be regarded as part of National Service.[74] This it was argued, would prevent overlapping of provision, and eradicate the 'abuses arising from promiscuous entertainments at the hands of amateur promoters...'[75] This, alas, was not done and charity entertainment remained unco-ordinated.

There were agencies, with specific interest in music and singing, that took the provision of their contribution more professionally; that is to say they were better organized. The problem of provision was addressed very early in the war by an influential group of people who set-up the 'Music in War-Time and After Committee'. K.C. Collis, an enthusiast, collaborated with a group of friends in September, 1914, for the purposes of providing musical entertainment and employment for artistes. In a short time he was assisted by some of the most notable composers and musicians of the day. Dr. Vaughan Williams became responsible for compiling a register of individuals and societies requiring support. Mary Paget, whose musical interests centred on the Tipperary League of Honour, Union Jack Groups and Factory Girls' Clubs, offered her services. Sir Hubert Parry offered the Royal College of Music for use as a headquarters, and eventually assumed the chairman's role. The committee expanded to include such luminaries as Sir Henry Wood and Sir Edward Elgar. In addition, Annette Hullah whose primary concern was providing 'musical distraction for Soldiers' joined the group. She was also responsible for compiling the postwar report of the Committee's work; in which the Committee's aims are stated as: first, to help artistes obtain employment; secondly, to establish and maintain a 'standard below which performances were not to fall'; thirdly, to entertain the public – particularly members of the Armed Forces; and fourthly, they saw the voluntary movement as a sort of crusade designed to 'provide opportunities of bringing music to those who do not wish for it but need it'.[76] It therefore had a musically propagandist aim which the Committee hoped would continue post-war, hence the words 'and After' contained in the full title.

In order to achieve the first aim the agency joined the Professional Classes Relief Fund, which was glad to contribute generously to the Music in War-Time expenses – particularly as the Committee was doing much of the Relief Fund's work. The Committee, according to *The Times*, received an annual £7,000 grant from the Fund which meant expenses were reduced to a minimum; thus most of the income was paid to the artistes. The work in England was directed from London, with the exception of Leeds and Manchester, 'whose needs were great enough to demand a whole colony of their own'.[77] As a result of the Committee's work, musicians and singers, unlike other branches of the entertainment industry, enjoyed a greater opportunity to get paid work, and no doubt the members of Stoll's sacked orchestras made use of these opportunities. The first groups to benefit from the share of funds were the choral and orchestral societies. One of these was a Male Voice Choir created by Dr. Walford Davies, whose objective was to 'promote music amongst the King's Forces'.[78] They performed in hospitals and camps. The succeeding beneficiaries were Instrumental Quartets; other awards went to music and orchestral societies from Woking, Skipton, Reading, Bath and Northumbria, and 'a Women's Composers' Concert.[79]

The demand for work became so great that the Committee's treasurer needed an assistant. The number of distressed artistes in the first weeks of war increased at an alarming rate. Every singer and musician, it seemed, needed help. It was therefore necessary for the Committee to weed out the 'Unsuccessful' and the 'shirker'.[80] The reasons why some were not given employment was not because of their lack of proficiency, but because of their obliviousness to the state of others and the plight of the nation: in short, to their total selfishness. In addition, some artistes had an irritating habit of falling ill at the very last moment – especially when another promoter offered a higher fee. This put the Committee in an invidious position. The officials did not want to deprive the artiste of employment, but at the same time the Committee had a duty to the envisaged audience. The problems were not all of the artistes' making. Camp Commandants could aggravate the situation as they regarded the Music in War-Time Committee as a twenty-four-hour concert clearing-house. They expected concert parties to be 'on tap', especially on public holidays. This was not withstanding the fact that, wrote Hullah:

> … *many commanding officers were alarmed at the idea of civilian concerts for their men and some directly opposed them as effeminate invasion, sentimental and unnecessary.*[81]

Even some of the hospital authorities were initially sceptical. Other problems included double-booking, and the sudden posting abroad of a regiment just hours before the concert party arrived. Two of the Committee's organizers had the supplementary task of attending as many concerts as they could in order to re-assess some of the 'sensitive artistes' who did not perform to par at audition, 'and could not be accurately placed till they were heard from the platform'. The organizers made every effort to fit the artiste to the size and type of audience. The screening process was also felt necessary because some artistes' 'sense of duty was undeveloped'.[82] They were, in other words, only concerned with the acquisition of the pay packet.

The Music in War-Time Committee also provided work for music hall artistes and a limited number of actors. The cast of a concert comprised a pianist, two other musicians (violinist or cellist), two singers and a comedian. No concert party was complete without the 'humourist'; he was, wrote Hullah, 'indispensable', as were the singers. The party could also contain a conjuror or ventriloquist, who were by all accounts popular. The same could not always be said of the actor-reciter 'who wallowed in tragedy', although 'amusing stories were popular'.[83] As an antidote to war it might be assumed, with regard to music, that people would prefer the light airs. This was not always the case. A critic from *The Observer* expressed surprise at the demand for serious music.[84] The military audiences, unlike say the concert hall or operatic audiences, were more likely to contain a greater cross-section of society, and whilst men liked the opportunity to sing-along with the popular songs, they also appreciated more reflective music.[85]

In the first five months of the war, between September, 1914 and January, 1915, the number of concerts given by the Music in War-Time parties amounted to 177; from the beginning of 1915, after the agency had become properly established, until August, 1919, the number totalled 4,690; and £25,000 was spent on performers' fees and travelling expenses. The venues included schools, munition works, military camps and hospitals; just over 50 per cent of the concerts were performed in hospitals. Nearly a third of the funding came from private subscriptions, the remainder from public relief funds such as: the Prince of Wales' relief Fund, Professional Relief Classes Council, the Red Cross and the Order of St. John.[86] There were other agencies that shared similar objectives to those of the Music in War-Time Committee, although the audiences aimed at may have differed. The War Emergency Entertainments, under the patronage of Her Majesty Queen Alexandra, concentrated entirely on military hospital entertainment; and was specifically concerned with providing help, but not charity, for those female artistes who had lost their menfolk in the war and had families to support. The money to provide this entertainment came from charity donations, and, by June 1918, the WEE had given 1,000 concerts.

The most prominent person engaged in charity concert work outside the legitimate theatre and music hall was Clara Butt, the concert singer. In October, 1914, she inaugurated the Butt-Rumford Fund for 'the assistance of artistes in difficulties owing to the war'.[88] She began by organizing 60 concerts for troops in hospitals, and the less fortunate people in workhouses and asylums. Initially any profits were divided among the various artistes. As it became clear that the war would be a protracted affair artistes were paid a fee and expenses; the principal tours lasted either a fortnight or a month, and were so successful that they payed their way, and even made a handsome profit. The work done by her concert parties also raised money for other charities.[89] Another entrepreneurial fund-raiser was Victor Beigel, an entertainer. Beigel began in 1914 by giving concerts by himself and with friends, the profits of which went to his Wounded Soldiers' Concert Fund. So successful was this venture that a subscription list was drawn-up, and enough money was forthcoming to pay expenses until 1916; after this Red Cross grants enabled the work to continue until 1918. Most of the entertainment was for the hospitalized. 'He was' wrote Hullah in her report 'one of the first to realize the medical value of music in shell-shock cases' In all he organized 523 concerts, and collected £4,000 for the Wounded Soldiers' Fund.[90] Efforts were made during the war to provide work for members of the theatre industry, but even greater efforts were made to cater for the comforts of others, often at a considerable cost to the artistes. The theatrical press launched an appeal to help ameliorate the artistes' often improvised state. The amount raised by the end of 1914, for the Actors' Benevolent Fund, plus money from the Actors' Emergency War Fund, totalled £4,826. However, from 1915 onwards, all efforts, apart from one charity benefit show per year were, not unnaturally, channelled towards more obvious war charities; and as the commentator and critic, Bernard Weller pointed out in 1916:

> ... *no actor or other artist in employment has not given his service, not once but repeatedly. That in itself means from every performer a gift of salary; and... actors, badly as they could afford it, have contributed per head to War Funds much more than the ordinary person.*[91]

There is an ironic twist to this philanthropic catalogue which concerns the Variety Artists' Benevolent Fund. 'It was computed' wrote Coles Armstrong, quoting from the Fund's annual report in 1919, 'that the variety profession has raised for... charities connected with the war upwards of £3,000,000 (£90 million in 1994 figures). Despite this the Variety Artists' Fund was struggling for the want of a mere £3,000.[92]

Raising money for military charities was not a new phenomenon. The precedent had already been set in the Boer War when matinees were put on in order to gather funds for an Actors' Hospital for the Troops.[93] What was phenomenal was the extent of charity work and the huge amount of money raised during the First World War.[94] The £3 million attribute to the altruistic efforts of the variety profession is misleading, as much of the charity entertainment was supplied by a combination of music hall artistes and actors from the dramatic branch of theatre. And this does not take into account funds raised by performances on the dramatic stage, or its individuals, such as the £25,000 accumulated by Ellaline Terriss for disabled soldiers, or the £30,000 collected by Lady Martin-Harvey for the Lord Roberts' Workshop for the Wounded.[95] The sum does not include the money donated at music concerts or the salaries forfeited by managers and artistes, or the thousands of pounds raised by amateur dramatic societies, both civilian and military. It is impossible to give a total figure, but a realistic sum, using the RPI as a guide, would today be well in excess of £100 million pounds sterling. To this end the world of entertainment more than fulfilled its role.

With regard to individuals and the profession as a whole, the provision of charity entertainment satisfied two further equally-important functions. It gave the industry and its members a public war-time role, and in so doing helped to ensure its survival. Proof of the effect of 'entertainment therapy' and its success can be gauged by the response to the hospital concert parties. The need was great. Almost 50 per cent of men who served in the war became casualties. According to Jay Winter 'over 700,000 [British] men died or were killed, and over 1,600,000 were wounded or fell ill in uniform'.[96] The Empire lost another 200,000 and many more were wounded. Those who died did not all fall on the battlefields. The hospitals, everywhere, were filled to overflowing. In this venture the stage's effort were augmented by the support of Royalty.

The amount of work the theatre did for charity cannot always be measured in monetary terms. The Women's Emergency Corps, for example, formed by the theatricals Decima and Eva Moore, Lena Ashwell and Gertrude Kingston, was the first organization to deal with Belgian refugees, send blankets to Serbia and women to France to teach French to soldiers.[97] The Little Theatre was lent to the Corps by Gertrude Kingston as a base.[98] The work the Corps did expanded to such an extent that the headquarters had to be moved to larger premises at Old Bedford College. At the college an offshoot of the Corps, the Three Arts Employment Fund, was formed and run by

Naomi Jacob (still then an actress) which provided war work for unemployed theatre people.[99] The Corps was also responsible for the administration of *The Era* Distress Fund. Decima Moore and Eva Harefield began the Women's Volunteer Reserve which preceded the official Women's Auxiliary Army Corps. Decima Moore was also later to run the Leave Club for troops in Paris. The Corps was also responsible for sending women's hospital units to France, and raised over £50,000.[100] In addition to this the Star and Garter Hotel at Richmond, Surrey, was restored for use by disabled servicemen.[101]

Government recognition of the work done by the professional entertainment bodies came in the form of individual honours. Oswald Stoll was knighted, and Decima Moore received the CBE, but perhaps the most noteworthy was Dame May Whitty who, in 1918, became the first British actress to be awarded the DBE. 'She was' records Sanderson 'the ubiquitous "Madam Chairman"'. Among the organizations she served in this capacity were: The Women's Emergency Corps, The Actresses' Franchise League, The Three Arts Women's Employment Fund, the British Women's Hospital and numerous others.[102] The honour bestowed upon her, as with Decima Moore and Stoll, was not so much for their contribution to the arts, but rather for their public service in war time.

Forces Entertainment in Britain

The mobilization of hundreds of thousands of young men and their subsequent collection into training camps posed a considerable difficulty for the military authorities. This was by far the largest potential fighting force the country had ever assembled. The immediate concerns were necessarily to do with billeting, feeding, kitting-out and training. The military mind did not foresee the additional problem of what to do with the assembled multitudes in their time-off. Military training was strenuous and could, in its repetitiveness, be tedious. Fit young men tired from the routine of military drill, exertion of route marches, cleaning weapons and performing the essential fatigues of communal military life, to say nothing of the trauma of separation from home – most for the first time – and the total absence of female company, required an outlet for their surplus energy and emotions. The local pub, assuming there was one near the encampment, provided the focal point for off-duty relaxation, but this form of recreation not unnaturally resulted in disciplinary problems concerning drunkenness and public disorder. Clearly another method of distraction was required, and here theatrical entertainment was partly to fulfil a need, although the military authorities did not formally address the problem until 1917.

In the first months of the war the entertainment industry reached its nadir in terms of provision. And the removal of a large proportion of the population to particular and often isolated military training areas merely exacerbated the theatre's plight: it meant audiences were depleted. It was therefore in the interests of both the military and the theatre that entertainment for the troops should be provided. The industry could rightly argue that there was both a new demand and a need for their services, and, of course, the military camp theatres provided a means of employment for a considerable number of artistes. Several organizations were set up, such as the Soldiers' Entertainment Fund, with the specific task of providing theatrical amusement for the vast army camps and enlarged naval establishments.

ENTERTAINMENT ORGANIZED FROM OUTSIDE
THE MILITARY

Anything resembling a theatrical diversion from the tedium of military
life came, in the first instance, from the troops themselves. It was
initially ad hoc and unorganized, and consisted of sing-songs around
a piano and possibly a comedian. Not surprisingly the troops tired of
them and hankered for contact with people from outside the confines
of the military establishments. In some camps local amateur artistes
filled the entertainment void, but as noted in a 1920 post-war report:

> ... *kindly amateurs who offered a drawing room ditty or a piano
> solo, unaware of the high-strung condition of their audience, were
> quite inadequate.*[1]

Greater variety and a higher standard was called for, and those
professionals who had connections with the military soon became
aware of the need to supply more appropriate diversions. The
entertainment supplied by professional artistes was, at the outset,
voluntary. This free gesture of goodwill could not, however, be
sustained indefinitely, as rail fares and accommodation expenses
became prohibitive. It therefore became imperative to obtain some
form of financial assistance if such provision was to continue.

Ashton Jonson, a relatively unknown but enterprising individual
entertainer, found it difficult to obtain funds, and so devised a novel
system of his own. He 'hired a trolly, put a piano on it, and with four
friends all masked... went round streets and squares [in west London]
every day for a fortnight till he raised enough to cover loss and pay a
small fee to his helpers'.[2] He also petitioned by letter hundreds of
affluent people, and gave the proceeds of any lectures he delivered to
the fund. Hence he was able to take fortnightly concert parties to a
military establishment on Eel Pie Island, and make periodic visits to
entertain troops at Fleet and Aldershot. Jonson's second objective
was to provide work for unemployed singers and musicians. He was
inundated with requests for work, and in order to sift the capable from
the less able organized auditions at his home.[3]

Entertainment provision also came from people not directly
connected with the stage. The firm Broadwood and Sons, for example,
specialized in organizing concerts in the more remote camps where
servicemen were virtually out of contact with the civilian world. The

navy was particularly devoid of professionally-provided amusement, as perforce many of its stations were in outlying coastal locations many miles from major towns. The sailors' entertainment, before the arrival of the concert party, often consisted of just a gramophone. At Harwich, however, the officers were more enterprising and set up a stage 'in an iron building' where Mr. Tennent, Broadwood's concert organizer, gave shows to men of the submarine fleet.[4] The major cost of these concerts was paid for by donations to an appeal in the *Daily Mail* newspaper; the remainder by Messrs Broadwood and Sons.[5]

Individuals from both the 'legitimate' stage and music hall performed for the troops. Ellen Terry, for example, *(Figure 10)* gave a Shakespearian recital at the Aldershot Hippodrome in 1918. It was reported in the *Aldershot News* that whilst the audience at the recital was enthusiastic the well-known actress did not attract as many people as a music hall comedian.[6] This was an unfair comparison to make as the majority of the rank and file soldiery would be more familiar with the repartee, banter and singing of the popular music hall entertainer than the sobriety of a Shakespearian recital. This is not to suggest that the military audience was unusually raucous or ill-behaved. A report in the *Daily Chronicle* stated that they were better behaved

Figure 10. Ellen Terry, who did not attract as large an audience as a comedian might have done.

than the West End patrons, but added, condescendingly, that they were less sophisticated.[7] Whether or not the military audience was always restrained and well-behaved is open to doubt. An Australian soldier related in a letter home in 1918 an incident where he, and several of his friends, ejected some drunken British conscripts from a theatre. The latter were harassing the performers and spoiling people's enjoyment.[8] There is no evidence, however, to suggest that this sort of boorish behaviour was commonplace.

Aldershot, 'the home of the British Army', had stationed in the town and its environs the largest concentration of troops in training in the United Kingdom. On Sunday there would be eighty separate church parades in the morning. The padres who conducted the services were ostensibly employed to cater for the soldier's spiritual needs, but many of them were also aware that the troops needed not only a place to pray but a place to play. As a result the ministers turned their Sunday schools into recreation centres where, wrote a *Times* reporter in 1914, 'concerts with the soldiers as the principal performers are held nightly'.[9] It was stated in the report that the philanthropic gesture on the part of the churchmen was not merely a desire to provide relief from the army routine, but that:

> *The ministers of every denomination... have also done everything in their power to relieve the monotony of military life and to combat evil influences.*[10]

The evening recreation and entertainment was also intended to be a healthy diversion from the 'dubious pleasures' of drink and sex which many of the troops would have sought when off duty in the town. It is doubtful if this means of moderating a man's behaviour could have succeeded to any significant degree.

Peer group pressure with regard to drinking, and the basic individual sexual instinct have always proved a more potent 'regulator' of a soldier's off-duty conduct; given the precariousness of life for the serviceman, it was inevitable, wrote Clephane when reviewing the sexual mores of the First World serviceman, that this was the case.[11] Medical records provide some evidence of the troops' interest in sex. In 1918 there were 60,000 British and Dominion troops receiving hospital treatment for venereal disease in France.[12] And it was estimated that 50 per cent of the 153,531 British and Dominion troops admitted to hospital with VD contracted one of the disease strains while stationed in Britain.[13] It seems that the clergy may have been successful in their first aim (the relief of boredom) but naive in the belief that they could substitute drama for drink and singing for sex.

A number of organizations that provided entertainment for the wounded and convalescent (and presumably the sexually infected) extended their field of operation to include troops in training. The Music in War-Time Committee, already providing for the hospitalized, espoused the general aim of promoting music 'among the King's Forces'.[14] Dr. Walford Davies, the noted choral conductor, singing teacher and Committee member, dedicated himself during the war to teaching soldiers to sing. He formed a choir and toured the larger military camps. Dr. Davies said that what the 'soldier-audience' lacked in manners they made up for in 'sincerity and communicativeness'.[15] In other words, they were keen but if they were bored they would do the performers 'the blunt kindness of starting a better song among themselves'.[16] The teacher's method was to divide the audience, sometimes 200 strong, into tenors, baritones and basses and get them to accompany his small choir of three or four professionals. Despite the initial reticence on the part of some members of the audience, he successfully managed to form a number of regimental choirs; he argued that 'an awakened nation will always choose to sing at its work' and thus its morale will be raised.[17] The participatory concerts were broad in the choice of musical repertoire: folk-tunes, homely ditties, rounds and sea-shanties, a 'few songs frankly solemn and even religious' but no 'patriotic effusions' were the order of the day. It was also important to include a number of light-hearted songs contributed by the audience itself.[18]

A concert put on for the troops could be quite a lively occasion. A show to raise money for the Soldiers' Entertainment Fund in 1915, was just such an event. The MC, wrote a *Morning Post* reporter, had to 'announce the turns through a megaphone and crave attention [of the 3,000 strong audience] with a whistle'.[19] Communal singing it appears was the favoured item and songs such as *Tipperary* and *John Bull's Catechism* never failed to get a response, along with *Here We are Again*, *Let'em All Come* and *Are We Down Hearted? No*. The musical director was Lyell Johnston, the writer and composer of *John Bull's Catechism*. He was the MD for all the concerts on behalf of the Soldiers' Entertainment Fund. The aim of the SEF, as for other organizations, was dual purpose, namely to promote entertainment for the troops and to provide work for performers.[20] All artistes received a small fee, but work was given, in the first instance, to those with young families and dependents. Initially, for the first six months, the SEF concentrated on providing concerts for troops in 'training camps in lonely country districts'. Later the emphasis was on entertaining the hospitalized; between February, 1915 and May, 1919, some 750 artistes were engaged and 2,000 concert parties sent out, most of them within a range of one hour's journey time from London. There was also one excursion abroad to Malta in 1916. The island was not only a naval base, but a large hospital garrison catering to the needs of the wounded and convalescent from the war on the Eastern Front. Approximately £23,000 was expended on SEF concert work, and an additional £20,000 on fees to artistes. The money was raised by public subscription, concert receipts and grants from the National Relief Fund.[21]

The size of an audience at a military concert varied, the largest recorded was a concert held at the White City sports stadium in west London on 15 December, 1914. Mrs. Julian Marshal and her orchestra, enlarged for the occasion by means of a grant from the Committee for Music in War-Time, played to a collective gathering of 8,000 Territorial soldiers.[22]

There were several providers of venues for entertainment within the camps; the armed services supplied, where they could, accommodation for recreative pursuits as did the Church Army organization.[23] The main provider, particularly in the newly-erected camps, was the YMCA. At the outset the YMCA facilities consisted of large marquees, and by the beginning of October, 1914, the YMCA had erected over 400 recreation tents in camps throughout the United Kingdom. The YMCA had also distributed over 200,000 copies of a selection of popular songs for in-house entertainment.[24] As it became clear that the war was going to continue for an indefinite period the YMCA was able, via its public appeals for funds in the press, to replace the temporary tents with large wooden huts, some of which could hold audiences of five hundred.

The military, because of the vast number of trainees, had, apart from erecting temporary accommodation, to requisition likely sites; hence a naval division was stationed at Crystal Palace, the national exhibition centre south of London. The main provider of entertainment at the Palace was the YMCA. The range of recreative provision could be called eclectic; there were shows put on for amusement, others that had an educative aim – such as an interest lecture on a topical war theme – and, of course, there were separate church services, but interestingly the entertainment and religious services were sometimes combined. Whatever the occasion a proportion of the time, albeit small, had to be for religious devotion. This was a stipulation laid down in the YMCA's manual, in which it was suggested that 'the middle of the programme is preferable to the end' for prayer.[25]

The ideal or preferred weekly programme as outlined in the YMCA handbook is as follows:

Sunday:	Sacred song-service and address
Monday:	Company or battalion concert or Lecture
Tuesday:	Camp sing-song or Games
Wednesday:	Religious service, lantern lecture or classics
Thursday:	Local concert party or Debate
Friday:	Professional concert party from headquarters
Saturday:	Games tournament, camp sing-song or Boxing.[26]

In the handbook there are useful tips on how to conduct a sing-song, and how best to utilize both the artistes and the space. The YMCA leader is reminded that each camp has servicemen with artistic talents, both professional and amateur, and that it is better when organizing a concert 'to have three good artistes on separate nights than to have nine on one particular occasion'. The objective for the YMCA leader was to have some activity on every night of the week. The handbook contained rudimentary advice on building ante-rooms on the side of the platform for the use of artistes as dressing rooms, which could, in an emergency, be used as bedrooms: advice most appropriate to those YMCA hut leaders serving in the battle zones of Europe.

An example of a programme that encompasses the recreative, educative and spiritual aims was printed in *The British Empire YMCA Weekly* in September, 1915. It is the week's programme for August 19–26, 1915 at *HMS Crystal Palace*. On Thursday 19 August, there were a conjuror and a singer; on Friday a lantern lecture on aircraft by a man from the Navy League; on Saturday the men were entertained by a comedian; on Monday there was a female cartoonist; on Tuesday the visiting popular Soldiers' Entertainment Party gave a concert; on Wednesday the Frisk Jubilee Trio played in the theatre and the large audience was addressed by the General Secretary of the

Figure 11. Cartoon from *The British Weekly YMCA* magazine, April, 1915. [YMCA Library].

YMCA, and there was singing from the choir; and on Thursday 26 August, in the Social Court there was a concert party and a choir from St Bartholomew's church.[27] Sunday 22 August, is omitted from this published social review as that day was dedicated to religious worship. It is doubtful if this is a typical YMCA evening programme. The nearness of Crystal Palace to central London meant that there would be no great difficulty in getting professional concert parties or artistes to visit; secondly, the national exhibition centre location with its vast size and more than ample space for lectures and entertainment was atypical. Nevertheless, an examination of the YMCA's handbook and its weekly journal, plus accounts in the national and theatrical press, give a picture of the considerable breadth of recreational and theatrical accommodation and service provided by the YMCA. Crystal Palace was at one extreme of provision but the humourous cartoon profile (*Figure 11*) from a 1915 YMCA weekly magazine provides evidence of what constituted a typical camp concert.

After 1915, and as a result of an encroachment agreement between commercial theatre managers and the War Office, temporary places of entertainment were constructed within or next to the grounds of military establishments.[28] It was found that despite the utilizing of the YMCA huts for ad hoc in-house entertainment and the occasional visit by outside amateur and professional concert parties, there still existed a large number of troops in outlying camps miles away from any regularly organized entertainment. In a climate of uncertainty regarding the theatre trade and the removal of a sizable proportion of potential audiences to collective sites elsewhere, it made commercial sense to the entrepreneurial managers to take the goods to the client. This they did, 'encouraged' in many cases 'by the military authorities'.[29] The commercial managers not only 'entered into arrangements with the companies and artistes to keep the supply going' vis-a-vis the actual entertainment, but they had also to make a considerable personal capital commitment towards the erection of the accommodation: The managers of the theatres were also, as with any other commercial houses, subject to the burden of the Entertainment Tax, and the rising costs of ground rents – expenses which were judged to be perniciously unfair. There were fifteen privately constructed theatre houses in Southern Command alone, and it is apparent, judging by a letter from one high-ranking officer concerning Mr Albany Ward, a manager, that the army was very appreciative of the work being done. In 1915, Lieutenant-General W Pitcairn Campbell wrote:

I am strongly of opinion, that in helping to entertain the men in the various camps round Salisbury, Mr Albany Ward is doing great work for the nation.[31]

In 1917, the AQMG (Assistant Quartermaster General) writing on instructions from the QMG, reiterates the sense and sentiments of the previous incumbent Lieutenant-General Pitcairn Campbell. The extent of the theatre work may be assessed by the fact that, according to *The Stage*, about 80,000 attended Southern Command theatres each week. Given the number of troops in training and the number of camps around the Salisbury Plain area this may be a conservative figure.[32]

PROFESSIONAL ENTERTAINMENT ORGANIZED BY MILITARY PERSONNEL

Many professional actors and music hall artistes had volunteered for military service and, from 1916, every able-bodied actor within conscription age was in the armed forces. The only ones left were those too old or too young, plus the medically unfit and those invalided out of the forces. The army and navy therefore acquired an amount of professional theatre expertise, combined with a considerable number of keen and talented amateur performers.

The instigators of much of the entertainment provided by the troops themselves were the artistes in uniform, who in their leisure time and with the permission of their commanding officers, 'worked on their own account, obtaining songs, sketches and properties... by appeals... that appear in *The Stage*'.[33] A letter from one of His Majesty's ships is typical of the numerous advertisements that appeared in the theatre press each week; it reads:

Sir – Perhaps through the agency of your paper...we can obtain some discarded theatrical gear... for our gear at present consist of two Marines' coats [less arm and buttons], bowler hat [about 1882], various pieces of canvas... a wig of oakum, picked out by an energetic 'matelot' while he was doing ten days 'cabins' [cells] for being too happy on his birthday... our greatest difficulty is in women's clothing, for it wants doing to make a 'flat foot' look like a lady.[34]

In order to organize good professional entertainment it was helpful if the producer had connections with people of importance still working on the stage, and if this influence could be augmented by high-ranking military associates then so much the better. The Women's Army Auxiliary Corps (WAAC) managed both. Arthur Croxton, the manager of the London Coliseum and his wife, Edith, an officer in the WAAC, arranged entertainments not only for the WAAC, but also for its naval and airforce equivalents. The most prestigious show was a concert held at the London Scottish Regiment's London HQ in 1918. This was attended by the Queen – who held the honorary position of Colonel-in-Chief of the Corps – and Princess Mary, Lady Ampthill and General MacDonagh. The entertainment was unusual in that it was a joint affair combining military personnel who were female only, and civilians of both sexes. The show also integrated entertainment with the more serious occasion of prize-giving; the Queen was honouring the Corps by being present at the 'distribution of a cup given by Her Majesty and other prizes to winning groups'. The professional performers from the Coliseum provided the variety acts, and the WAAC supplied folk dancers, gymnasts and singers.

Most regiments and corps did not have the luxury of calling on their Colonel-in-Chief to endorse their entertainments, or indeed of having the distinct advantage of connections with royalty, or the Stoll 'variety empire' in the form of a professional manager. The organization of entertainment, if it existed, was often left in the hands of an enthusiastic but theatrically-inexperienced officer. One such was Captain Kenney of the Royal Artillery. The captain was posted to Woolwich in the suburbs of south-east London in 1917, as assistant adjutant. On arrival the commanding officer asked him to organize a 'concert or two'. The colonel was concerned about the incidences of public disorder in the town involving his troops, and so the immediate aim of the concerts was, recorded Kenney in his diary, 'to keep the men away from Woolwich and trouble'.[36] Theatre entertainment was, once again, as in Aldershot, being employed as an instrument of social control, although in this instance for civil and disciplinary reasons and not for the 'betterment' of the men's spiritual and moral welfare.

Kenney was extremely fortunate as the brigade had an abundant supply of good musical talent. An orchestra of twenty-five first-class professional musicians was mustered and put in the charge of Lieutenant W.H. Read, who until war came was a professor at the Royal College of Music. Read acted as conductor and orchestrator, and all solo artistes were accompanied on the piano by Lieutenant Harold Croxton, the organist at St. Peter's Church, Eaton Square. No camp, and few theatres, could boast of such a collection of musical talent. What is more, it was free!

What was initially envisaged as being a small Sunday entertainment using brigade talent only, became a weekly show given by some of the best known West End actors, actresses and music hall artistes. This was due, in the main, to the efforts of the stage manager, Bombardier Ernest Benham. At the time Benham was the brigade telephonist which meant he had unlimited access to communication and was therefore able to spend time negotiating with the performers. The telephone exchange closed down at 5.30pm each evening, which also meant he could rush off to the West End to perform his 'civvy' job at the Lyric Theatre, Shaftesbury Avenue, where he 'moonlighted' as stage manager for the show *Romance* starring Doris Kean. He therefore also had personal contact with a number of performers, although much of the securing of artistes and interviewing was done by his fiancée Olive Sturgess, a concert singer.

The arrangement was for the artistes to meet Kenney and Benham at the Lyric stage door at 3pm on Sundays. They would then be taken by car – care of the volunteer drivers of the Army Service Corps – to arrive at Woolwich at 4pm. A high tea was laid on and curtain-up was at 7.30pm. Many of the professional artistes were surprised to discover that the show was not done in huts but in a large hall seating five hundred, complete with a good-size stage and a full set of footlights. What was more surprising, given the stringency of war time, was the fact that the Colonel entertained the artistes with a champagne supper after each show. This convivial repayment was in lieu of fees. Both the shows and the suppers – the latter went on until 10.30pm, although they sometimes lasted 'until 2 or 3 in the morning' – were adjudged a great success, and according to Kenney the shows 'most certainly kept hundreds of men' away from the Woolwich pubs and 'trouble'.[37] In addition to the Sunday concerts artistes also did a charity show on behalf of the Royal Artillery Benevolent Fund. This time it was the Brigade General who entertained the artistes to supper at the RA HQ Officers' Mess. The artistes were accorded the honour of being waited on by Mess servants dressed in their ceremonial garb of 'Old Time Livery: blue plush knickers, white silk stockings, black shoes with large silver buckles, and their hair powered white as of old'.[38]

The artistes included actors, singers, dancers and speciality acts. One of the more unusual was an escapologist who, at his own request, was locked-up in the cells of the guardroom. Displaying his talent, he managed to free himself and vacate the cells within two minutes of the door being secured. A list of those appearing at Woolwich included such noted performers as: Fred Emney, Bransby Williams, Leslie Henson, Nelson Keys, Doris Kean, Lily Brayton and Benham's fiancée Olive Sturgess. Captain Kenney, in return for his hospitality, was made an honorary member of the Green Room Club, and both he and the Colonel had invitations to the exclusive Garrick Club in the West End.

In the more isolated training camps the provision of recreational amusement depended on the ability and ingenuity of the troops themselves. The RAMC 80th Field Ambulance unit on Salisbury Plain was one that provided its own diversions. The concert party was started by a professional entertainer, Corporal Jack West. He was assisted by a fellow professional named Weston Drury (who ran the Drolleries troupe at Dawlish, Devon); the remainder of the cast comprised good amateurs. They entertained the troops in training and those in hospital.[39] The troupe had the full support of the officers and senior NCOs; indeed, the NCOs excused them afternoon parades so they could rehearse. The officers were even enthusiastic enough to finance them by paying their expenses; they 'bought us costumes [pierrot, cerise and grey wigs, and props, together with a property basket]' recorded West; and musical publishers sent them copies of the required songs. The troupe was jokingly named *The Splints*. The first show, planned for 15 July, 1915, was to be held on the parade ground, or if wet in one of Albany Ward's theatres at Bulford. The two professional entertainers were to continue their 'showbusiness career' throughout their time in the army. Weston Drury was later to run a very successful concert party in Salonica, while Jack West created another troupe called *The Shrapnels*, which played to servicemen in France.[40]

One method of overcoming the routine dullness of training and at the same time encouraging team spirit among the troops is to promote rivalry between units. There existed, therefore, intercompany competition in training via field exercises, drill and sport; and in 1917 the same reasoning was applied to entertainment. At Oswestry camp Captain Basil Dean, the pre-war actor-manager of Liverpool Repertory Theatre (later Liverpool Playhouse) was approached by his Colonel who suggested he arrange a concert party competition.[41] So successful was the venture that as a result a battalion entertainment unit was formed, which staged regular shows in divisional canteens. The division headquarters staff was so impressed with the results that

Figure 12. Front cover of an Oswestry programme. [L. J. Collins]

the Colonel decided to 'go professional' and ordered Dean to London 'to get some actresses, and wigs and costumes'.[42] It soon became clear that the camp canteen was not the ideal place to hold entertainment, since the main concern of the proprietors was to sell beer, and not every camp had a YMCA hut; besides which the latter could not solely be used for shows. Therefore, more appropriated accommodation was required, which had to be financed, built and staffed by the resident battalions. Money was found to be available via the President's Regimental Institute (PRI). The PRI was the repository for all regimental funds, most of which came from the profits on sales in the canteens paid by the catering contractors. Basil Dean, as a result of the successful concert competition and an equally popular weekly concert held in a local cafe, attended by all ranks, managed to persuade the camp commandant, Lieutenant-Colonel H. Worsley-Gough, CMG to allow PRI funds to be spent on erecting a purpose-built theatre.[43] War Office permission was not needed as building work was under civilian contract, and so construction went ahead without any bureaucratic hindrance. Dean devised a scheme whereby each battalion in the camp contributed towards the building and running costs. Scenery was built by the Pioneer Sergeant who 'constructed large wooden frames, and covered them with latrine canvas'.[44] The design was by George Harris, a friend of Dean's from the Liverpool Playhouse.

The opening night was judged an unqualified success despite, according to Dean, the low standard of the mixed amateur and professional performance.[45] The future of entertainment in the Command was assured when General Campbell announced that he wanted more camp theatres. The programme (*Figure 12*) indicates that the type of show provided was diverse and included plays, military band concerts, revues and later on, on one occasion, the Beecham Opera Company which gave excerpts from several operas. The programme was a busy and hectic one with twice-nightly performances seven days a week, the theatrical shows alternated with films, with two or three special concerts on Sundays.

Dean, using his connections in the world of show business, was able to elicit the help of professional designers and scenic artistes, in addition to encouraging more companies to visit Oswestry. Leslie Henson was one of the better known music hall artistes who responded to 'the call'; he brought the full Gaiety Theatre company, including David Burnaby the noted pierrot actor, and the Gaiety chorus up from London in a revue called *How's yer Father?*.[46] The army authorities were so impressed with the theatre at Oswestry that they posted Captain Dean to Western Command with specific instructions to replicate the Oswestry organization at Rhyl. This was followed by the construction of more theatres in Northern Command.

The canteen proprietors, in mid-1917 still providers of venues for shows, were continually being criticized for the unfair pricing of their goods. In order to stop this form of private profiteering the government decreed that prices should be fixed and that canteens would, in the future, be run by a central body known as the Army Canteen Committee, soon to be renamed the Navy and Army Canteen Board (NACB) – later to become the more familiar NAFFI (Navy, Army and Air Force Institute).[47] As the NACB ran the canteens, and was thus proprietor of the venues for shows, it was logical for the Board to assume the responsibility for organizing the entertainment; and who better to co-ordinate the NACB's proposed new function than the professional producer who had already been responsible for building several army theatres and organizing entertainment, namely Captain Basil Dean. In 1917, by the authority of the Army Council, the Entertainment Branch of the NACB was formed under the control of Basil Dean.[48]

The Branch was divided into separate companies each responsible for a specific type of entertainment.[49] Dean was posted to London, which had the advantage of giving the NACB Entertainment Director the opportunity to contact and employ some of the best theatrical talent. Fred Melville of the Lyceum Theatre was co-opted onto the Board in order to produce and supply the melodrama, Robert Evett of Daley's Theatre produced the musical comedies, Douglas Furber the revues and Sir Frank Benson appeared in the Shakespeare productions. George Harris, the Liverpool Playhouse designer, was seconded to the NACB, and was resident at its London HQ for the duration of the war, where he designed costumes, programmes and posters as well as stage sets.[50] The NACB provided work for professionals, and for that the theatre was grateful, but perhaps just as important, it was a public recognition by the Armed Services that diversionary off-duty entertainment had a purposeful role to play within the military during war time: indeed, the Secretary of State for War, in an official communiqué, stated that what the NACB Entertainment Branch was doing was 'important war work'.[51] The number of garrison theatres grew and by the end of 1917 the NACB ran theatres at: Oswestry, Catterick, Bramshott, Bulford, Tidworth, Blackdown, Kinmel Park,

Bordon and Ripon. These theatres were served by nine touring concert parties, which stayed between three and twelve nights.[52] The majority of touring companies – particularly in the field of light entertainment – belonged to the NACB circuit, although outside drama companies were employed. The following shows a typical autumn programme for a garrison theatre. It is the itinerary for Theatre No. 4 on circuit No. 1, for the period September 17 to December 24, 1917:

September 17 – The Official NACB Light Comedy Company with
    Peg o' My Heart *and other plays.*
September 24 – The Official NACB Vaudeville Party in their own
    entertainment.
October 1 – Messrs. Armstrong and Leigh's Company in Lucky Durham,
    Find the Woman *and* The Lion and the Mouse.
October 8 and 15 – The Official NACB Musical Comedy Company with
    The Merry Widow *and* Gipsy Love.
October 22 and 29 – The Official NACB Play Company with
    The Man Who Stayed at Home, Under Cover *and* Raffles.
November 5 – The Official NACB Melodrama Company in
    The Story of the Rosary *(second visit).*
November 12 – The Official NACB Light Opera Company in a fresh
    repertory (second visit).
November 26 – Messrs. Lewis Casson and Henry Dallas's Company in
    The Marriage Market.
December 3 – The Official NACB Vaudeville Party in a new programme
    (second visit).
December 24 – The Official NACB Play Company in Mr Wu *and*
    other plays.[53]

The programme shows the wide range of work done by and for the NACB. Theatre No. 4 opened twice nightly and operated a full-time box office. The theatre also took bookings 'for "special performances" given in addition to the foregoing'.[54]

The NACB theatres were administered by a manager and an officers' committee, and staffed backstage by soldiers. The charge for admission was at a standard rate of 3d and 6d, 'with a few rows of seats at 1/- and 2/6 at the second nightly performances for officers'.[55] The twice-nightly performances therefore served two purposes, affording more people the opportunity to see the show but also allowing for the segregation of ranks. Whether or not this was done for purely administrative reasons or as a means of maintaining the social divide is not known. Evidence shows that the division of audiences was usually along the lines of the seating arrangements – officers at the front, other ranks further back. It must be acknowledged that a social gap did exist between the officer class and the remainder, and the men may have found it inhibiting if the seating arrangements did not conform to the norms of their society. The segregation within the auditorium was therefore an extension of the demarcation that existed in society generally, and in the forces in particular as emphasized by the different messes, uniforms and as Fussell points out 'different accents and dictions and syntaxes and allusions'.[56]

The NACB Entertainment Branch under Basil Dean quickly became an efficient organization. The emergence of the NACB on the theatre circuit was not, however, to the benefit of everyone. No effort was made by the military authorities to incorporate or co-ordinate the NACB provision with the civilian theatrical catering that existed in a number of camps; despite the fact that within the parameters of the Encroachment Agreement many of the commercial theatres were built on or next to military property. Indeed, the authorities, did an 'about-turn' on the subject of civilian theatre provision. In 1915, the managers were applauded for the work they did, and Staff Officers of senior rank said that entertainment for men in training was vitally important;[57] but by 1917, following the formation of the NACB Entertainment Branch, the Army Council appeared to make every effort to oust the civilian theatre managers. First, the ground rents payable by the civilian managers were double, and in some cases trebled – these varied from £120 to £150 per annum.[58] By today's standards that equates to an annual rent of between £3,000 to £5,000 to be paid on a building that was probably little more than a large prefabricated hall with a rudimentary stage. The NACB theatres, being military-owned, paid little or no rent. In addition, demands were issued for the managers to pay two and a half per cent of gross profits and 50 per cent of net profits to a special garrison fund, and the Army Central Fund.[59] The civilian managers expected to pay their dues, but the NACB-run theatres' additional exemption from the payment of Entertainment Tax seemed especially unfair; it was alleged in *The Stage* that the NACB houses made a feature of 'no tax admissions' – which presumably kept ticket prices down.[60]

The Theatres' Alliance – an association for provincial theatre managers – petitioned the Chancellor of Exchequer and the Secretary of State of War, outlining the 'action of the Navy and Army Canteen Board in running privileged opposition to established places of entertainment'.[61] The Alliance argued that because NACB theatres were open to friends of soldiers, they were therefore public places of entertainment, and those not in uniform should pay the tax on tickets purchased. The managements of established military theatres made several requests asking that personnel in uniform be admitted free of tax to their theatres, but these requests were refused.[62]

Another area for dispute concerned labour. It was much cheaper to run an NACB-controlled theatre as backstage employees and administrative assistance was provided, free of charge, by the military. It was also argued that many of the NACB artistes were civilians and not subject to military law; but nevertheless their wages were restricted, as they saw it, by the military and 'market-rate salaries are not paid'.[63] The maximum an artiste was allowed to earn under the NACB was £10 per week.[64] The restriction would have affected very few as most provincial actors were paid considerably less than that amount. It was, however, not just wages, but availability of labour that concerned the profession. The Theatres' Alliance Association complained that the army was retaining militarily-unfit conscripted artistes for their concert parties instead of discharging them, and thereby depriving the civilian theatre of an already depleted male workforce. No mention is made of the fact that the thus-categorized artistes may have been perfectly happy to be in full employment, albeit on a reduced salary, and, at the same time, be seen to be doing their military duty. Major Towle, Deputy Chairman of the NACB Board of Management, replied to the criticism printed in the theatre press with an official statement in *The Stage* saying that is was not possible '… to pay any fancy salaries'.[65] The artistes also complained that the NACB was employing cheap labour, and paying artistes as little as £1 per week. The minimum payment, after negotiation, was later set at £3 per week. Those members of a cast receiving only £1 were not professionals, but 'are purely "local talent", who, in most cases, offer to "walk-on" for nothing', said Towle.[66] It was thought expedient to pay them something to ensure that they turned-up regularly. In a leading article in *The Era* it was argued that in order to provide entertainment at an affordable cost it was necessary to subsidize amusements via funds from the NACB.[67] A measure of agreement was soon reached between the artistes, managers and the military regarding pay; but wages was not the most contentious point.

The secretary of the Theatres' Alliance, Moverely Sharp, writing in *The Era* in 1917, refuted much of what Major Towle wrote on behalf of the NACB. Once again the Alliance secretary emphasized the unfairness of the Entertainment Tax, adding that the NACB managers were also not burdened by income tax or excess profit duty.[68] A compromise was sought and in November 1917, admittance of civilians to NACB houses was restricted to those directly connected with the military, thereby reducing to a limited degree, the unfair competition with the theatres run by outside agencies and those located in the neighbouring towns.[69] On occasions, however, dubious methods were employed to ensure the NACB's advantageous position. It was not unknown, for example, for civilian theatres to be deemed 'out-of-bounds' to military personnel. A manager, Harrison Frewin, complained of such a procedure in *The Era,* saying:

> *... the theatre I was visiting was placed 'out-of-bounds'. Had I*
> *been travelling a 'leg-show' I could have understood this action,*
> *but as I was giving grand opera, I can only assume that it was done*
> *to 'freeze me out.*[70]

Frewin said that hundreds of would-be patrons expressed their displeasure at this 'arbitrary proceeding'. A secondary, yet interesting and intriguing question is, why was Frewin seemingly prepared to understand, if not accept, that such restrictive practices could be applied to 'low-brow' leg-shows? It might be assumed that the leg-show was judged to be in direct competition with the NACB shows; it appears that the military-controlled theatre authority was determined to eradicate all forms of alternative provision.

The NACB companies were not able to visit every military establishment, and a number of the civilian-owned theatres did continue until demobilization was completed in 1920. Many units, particularly those located in the less populated and more inaccessible parts of the country, continued to produce their own shows. One unit which was isolated, although not in a rural sense, was MI5 – the military secret service. The covert organization could not invite outsiders to any entertainment that it may provide, indeed the Service had to wait until a year after the cessation of hostilities before advertising anything as overt as a concert party. In March, 1919, finally, for the first and last time, and presumably with the imminent demobilization of most of its members, MI5 celebrated with a concert which was aptly called *Hush-Hush.* The wry sense of humour of the organizers and performers can be judged by the show's play bill (*Figure 13*).

Figure 13. Programme for MI5 production, *Hush-Hush* 1919. [Imperial War Museum].

THEATRE FOR FOREIGN TROOPS AND PRISONERS

Theatrical concerts for the military were not confined to the Allied Forces. German prisoners-of-war also spent much of their time organizing in-house entertainment. At the Brocton POW camp on Cannock Chase in Staffordshire, where 6,000 German prisoners were held, there was a camp theatre. The POWs had a string orchestra and a brass band. Theatre entertainment, whether dramatic, musical or choral, was employed as a means of relieving the tedium of incarceration. To the authorities, on the other hand, attendance at the theatre was seen as a 'privilege' and was used as a means of maintaining control. And on at least one occasion, when the POWs displayed 'gross collective insubordination', the theatre, along with the canteen, was closed for two days by the Commandant, Colonel Sir Arthur Grant.[71] The same disciplinary sanction was applied at the camp for German internees at Wakefield.[72]

It was reported in *The Times* that at the POW camp at Dorchester, a neutral observer, the London editor of *Amsterdam Telegraaf* along with several American press representatives, noted that the 3,400 prisoners had organized their own entertainment. They had an orchestra – most of the instruments being sent over from Germany – and some of the rooms contained hired pianos. The Dutch observer commented perfunctorily that 'they are allowed to play, German national songs'.[73]

Like people in detention anywhere the German POWs and internees made strenuous efforts to engage in pursuits that for a variety of reasons were deemed very important. To the actors, wrote Cohen-Portheim, a scenic designer interned at Wakefield:

> the theatre was intensified for the simple reason that everyone
> there tried hard, in self-defence, to persuade himself of the real
> importance of the work.., in order to forget its inherent futility, and
> so the actors found no work too much for them.[74]

The camp at Wakefield was divided into three sites and there was rivalry between the different sectors, each having its own productions. The drama varied from one-act plays by Tagore, Strindberg, Chekhov, Andrief and Shaw, and Japanese Nôh-plays, all of which Cohen-Portheim translated into German. There was also a small orchestra. Wakefield, being a camp for internees, was slightly more relaxed than the POW camps, which meant that costumes and musical instruments could be hired from outside firms for in-house productions.[75]

Another, and perhaps better known, place for civilian imprisonment was Alexandra Palace in London, which in 1915 contained over 2,000 internees. The inmates came under military authority but as they were civilians no work was required of them. Businessmen managed to carry on their work to a limited degree, and artistes of all descriptions found themselves in an almost ideal working environment. Rooms were turned into studios with a separate room for solo artistes to rehearse. Theatre practitioners had a proper theatre, with a seating capacity of 1,500 at their disposal.[76] It was reported in *The Times* that performances were given once a week on Fridays. The producer of the shows was a well-known German professional theatre manager; the newspaper declined to print the name of the manager, or of the conductor of the camp's orchestra who was the leader of a West End orchestra before the war. Why the paper did not reveal the names is not clear, but it may be assumed that it was considered unreasonable to give prejudicial publicity to non-combatants who might wish to continue their career once the war was over. Members of the orchestra, which contained nearly 40 musicians, gave weekly Sunday concerts not in the theatre, but in a separate hall seating 600. In December 1915, it was noted in the press that the Sunday concert was being performed by a 'well-known Hungarian violinist, a Polish pianist, and an opera singer of note and that the programme is eclectic, though German composers are conspicuously absent'.[77] It will never be known whether or not the abstraction of Teutonic composers was part of a planned season's programme, or whether it was simply a ploy to appease the visiting British media reporters. Whatever the reason the internees certainly spent a great deal of their time in artistic pursuits; indeed, judging by the size of the exhibition centre with its facilities for theatre and music, it is doubtful if any prisoners, civilian or military, enjoyed such palatial surroundings in which to indulge their artistic pastimes whilst in captivity during the First World War.

Troops came from all corners of the British Empire and were made welcome. The same could not always be said of visiting Americans. The British public's sentiments regarding the latter were mixed, and the United States' initial insistence on neutrality angered many British people, although a significant number of Americans sympathized with the Allied cause; but as the historian A.J.P. Taylor said, the United States, until 6 April, 1917, 'remained virtuously aloof'.[78] The British had always maintained that it was a world war; the Americans pre-1917 saw the war as a European conflict. It was the sinking of American shipping by U-boats, and the offer of Germany to help Mexico to recover the lands of the state of New Mexico – a wholly spurious offer, for a war Mexico did not want – that prompted President Wilson to abandon his peace mission, and America to join the Allies. Prior to this the USA was sometimes the butt of music hall jokes. The public criticism of America on the stage caused the Lord Chamberlain's Office some concern. It was important, for propagandist and political reasons, not to offend the neutral. This was especially true of the USA, which was helping to finance Britain's war effort. In the revue *Cocktails* (1916) at the Marlborough Theatre, the censor warned the producer that the neutral officer, who was being given overly-preferential treatment at the expense of those doing the fighting, was not to be dressed in 'an actual uniform'.[79] By this the censor meant an identifiable, and in particular an American, uniform.

With the entry of the USA into the war in 1917 attitudes changed, and with the use of public parades and receptions much was done to welcome the American troops. The theatre was employed as a means of encouraging Anglo-American comradeship. It was decided that every Sunday at the Palace Theatre in the West End, 'a great entertainment would be given, to which American and British troops should be admitted free – and fraternize'.[80] The shows, an example of which was *Hullo America* produced by Alfred Butt were lavish affairs. The troops were entertained by some of the best music hall talent, such as Stanley Lupino, Elsie Janis and Will West. The various West End managements took it in turn to produce the shows, which were sponsored by the Ministry of Information. The management committee was run by Sir Walter de Freece, the music hall magnate, and it was he who decided whose turn it was next to stage the Sunday show. The entertainments were varied and included an evening of opera by the Beecham company, although this was not as popular as the variety shows put on by Butt, De Corville or Charlot.[81] The artistes performed free but much of the production costs, which were considerable, were met by the philanthropic Rochdale millionaire James (Jimmy) White. The shows continued throughout the latter half of 1918 until two Sundays after the signing of the Armistice in November.

On the last weekend of August, 1918, the Birmingham and District Professions and General Trades Fund in association with the Red

Cross and the Navy League organized a visit for American airmen to see Stratford-on-Avon. The Americans were greeted by the mayor at a reception in Shakespeare's House before going on a tour of the Memorial Theatre. The cultural visit was followed by a game of baseball on the Warwickshire County cricket ground, and a parade through the streets of Coventry preceded by the band of the Royal Marines. The Americans also undertook a tour of North Wales.[82]The tours and parades were ostensibly for the entertainment of wounded servicemen, although there may have been covert reasons for the public parading of the American troops; perhaps after years of satirical jibes and press criticism it was felt necessary to change the public's perception of the former neutral ally. What is recognised, however, is that by 1917 – after three years of seemingly endless war and its resultant psychological, physical, economic and material stress, the British were grateful to have the assistance of the richest nation in the world.

The Americans were not the only allies to be entertained. Troops from all countries of the British Empire passed through London and on occasions separate concerts were put on for their benefit. One such was held at His Majesty's Theatre in April, 1916. The show was for Australian soldiers. The distinguished guests included Princess Louise (Duchess of Argyll), General Birdwood and Mr Andrew Fisher the High Commissioner for Australia. The cast list was equally noteworthy and included: George Robey, Ada Crossley, Ethel Levey, Ellaline Terriss, Violet Loraine, Alfred Lester, Harry Tate and Seymour Hicks. The evening was not totally for entertainment. During the interval the High Commissioner presented Distinguished Conduct Medals to four soldiers who had fought in the Gallipoli campaign.[83]

MILITARY TROUPES IN THE WEST END

Towards the end of the war in 1918, a number of military concert parties, which until then had been performing overseas, were invited by various managements to display their talents in London. The best known, according to the critic Arthur Coles Armstrong, was *The Dumbells* of the 3rd Canadian Division, 'who achieved marked success at the Victoria Palace'.[84] Previous to the troupe's London show they had, following the signing of the Armistice, performed a full version of the *Pirates of Penzance* at Mons on the Western Front. The Victoria Palace was also the venue for a company of New

Zealand artistes, and the quartet *That* from the American flagship *USS Nevada*. At the London Coliseum, the *See Toos* of the 2nd Canadian Division also had a popular London tour. Another Allied troupe, the *Anzac Coves*, did a tour of several theatres. The British were represented at the Middlesex and Court Theatres, and by the 1st Army Headquarters concert party entitled *Les Rouges et Noirs* at the Beaver Hut (The Little) Theatre.

The jokes and sketches of the military concert parties naturally belonged to war time, but the vast number of servicemen stationed in or around London, or in transit through the capital, meant that there was no shortage of audiences ready to appreciate the nuances of Service humour. Some concert parties were honoured by the presence of distinguished guests. When the *Diamond Troupe* from the 29th Division produced their show at the Court Theatre in January, 1918, the Lord Mayor of London, Lord Derby and the famous actress Ellen Terry attended the opening matinee performance; and the programmes were sold by a number of leading actresses, Viola Tree, Gladys Cooper, Eva Moore, Renée Kelly and the American actress Doris Keane. The show ran for a week with matinee and evening perform- ances. No alterations were made to accommodate the London transfer, and the scenery, costumes and dresses designed by the troupe in the field were transported to London; as pointed out in *The Times*, 'Every item included in the programme had been performed under shell fire in France' [85] The programme included items from well known musicals plus original sketches and songs written by the members of the troupe. The military concert parties were distinguished by the absence of females in their companies, and as Coles Armstrong commented 'a feature of their performance was the excellence of their "female impersonators"' [86] The critic added that it was to the credit of the Navy and Army troupes that the audiences' appreciative response was due to 'legitimate artistic means' and not reliant on any sentimental or popular feelings for those serving in uniform.

The reason for the appearance of Military concert parties on the stage in Britain, and in particular in the West End of London, was, in most cases, the raising of funds for the various regimental and military charities. The 29th Division Concert Party gave all its profits from the week's performances to the Divisional Benevolent Fund. The money was specifically for the assistance of families of non- commissioned officers and men who had lost their lives or who had become incapacitated.

Theatre entertainment for the forces at home had a variety of functions, the aims of which depended on the recipients, and also, to a large extent, upon the needs of the providers. To the greater proportion of the audiences – the rank and file of those in training, POWs and internees – the theatre entertainment was a welcomed diversionary relief from the tedium of camp life. To the civilian actors, producers and other stage workers it was a livelihood, and particularly during 1914 when theatre entertainment was less prolific, an occupational life-line. To the performer in uniform the theatre fare provided a welcomed opportunity for the amateur to indulge his hobby and for the professional to practice his craft; and it gave both a respite, when rehearsing and performing, from some of the more mundane tasks of military existence. To the civilian and military professional artiste it was also a public way of contributing to the war effort in a manner most appropriate and satisfying to him or her, and, productively to the industry. To the authorities, both secular and clerical, entertainment was seen as an agent of social control, albeit not a completely effective one. And, perhaps most importantly to the people in the theatrical profession, it was – via the formally organized forces entertainment and the NACB – a long-awaited recognition from the military and the government of the importance of the stage in war time.

Military Provision Abroad

If the need for entertainment for the troops at home was important, it was doubly so abroad. The reason was not just the relief from the arduous task of fighting, or the chance to enjoy the therapeutic effect of laughter. The theatre reminded those serving on the Western and Eastern Fronts of home, another life.

The military theatre entertainment was far more temporary than at home but nonetheless highly organized at the more permanent rearward bases. The men, left to their own devices regarding amusements, as most units were, improvised and organized their in-house entertainment on roughly a two-tier system. First, ad hoc entertainment existed at brigade and regimental level. Secondly, at the higher divisional level, the form and structure of theatrical recreation became, given the unusual circumstances of war, remarkably sophisticated. The same can be said of theatre provision in the prisoner-of-war camps.

AD HOC ENTERTAINMENT

In mid-1914 there was little time for entertainments as the army was constantly on the move; in the initial stages, much of it in a rearward direction. However, by September, following the first battle known as the Marne, the French and British halted the German advance on Paris, although at a cost of 50,000 casualties. The opposing armies then dug in and by Christmas the entrenchment system had become well established: thus the conflict entered the first stage of a protracted and static war of attrition. During any lull in the fighting the troops, if not otherwise engaged, would amuse themselves by playing cards or dice. This proved an insufficient diversion for many, and on the initiative of one or more members of a unit impromptu 'entertainments' were held. Initially they were just sing-songs, and any accompaniment was provided on rough home-made appliances. To augment the musical backing, many soldiers wrote home requesting musical instruments. The mouth organ, being the most transportable, was the most popular choice. A sergeant serving with a Territorial regiment wrote to *The Times* in 1914 describing the response on receiving musical instruments sent from home. On their arrival the platoon immediately formed a 'band' and produced an ad hoc concert combining the acquired implements with an array of home-made sounding boards; he said:

... the big drum was an empty packing case and the drum stick an entrenching tool with a piece of sacking tied round the end; empty biscuit tins were side drums; tin whistles, squeakers and combs and paper came in as well. Candles and electric lamps gave illumination... it was funny to see this band of 30 marching round, headed by a self-appointed drum-major... in a goatskin twirling a big stick which I use in feeling my way to and from the trenches.[1]

After the initial parade the platoon formed a circle, in the centre of which successive performers did their vocal or instrumental act; 'the turns' had to be punctuated with further parading around when the troops' feet became uncomfortably cold.

An obvious location for entertainments, as in the UK, was the YMCA canteen hut. The huts were sited in depots or rest camps some five or more miles behind the Front line trenches. At one end of the hut stood the ubiquitous piano on which the player belted out comic tunes, light airs or hymns depending on the occasion. The musical range depended on the availability of artistic talent and interests of the performer. Mr E. Horning, a YMCA manager, writes of a young man, an accomplished pianist, who ordered from the rudimentary YMCA library music by Beethoven, Chopin and Schumann so that he could entertain himself, and presumably others.[2]

The 'organized' battalion canteen shows varied in quality. They were, as reported in *The Stage* in 1917, 'sometimes excellent, more often not', They appeared marginally more 'orchestrated' than the spontaneous platoon amusement already mentioned. The sing-songs were occasionally punctuated with turns by crude comedians. The task of the Master of Ceremonies at the battalion concert was undertaken, said the reporter, by '... some grey-haired old member of the permanent staff' who had a walrus moustache and 'probably sported ribbons of the Zulu campaign and the first Boer War'. His unenviable job was to try and maintain some semblance of order which he attempted to do by 'beating time with his cane, and demanding, "the best of order, please"'.[3] The 'smoker' or concert at company and, perhaps to a lesser extent, at battalion level must have resembled a rugby club booze-up with noisy and bawdy entertainment, and was 'not always of a very high order' and certainly did not compare with the concerts at Division HQ.[4]

THE DIVISION CONCERT PARTY

When troops were withdrawn to the rear they wanted, indeed required, diversionary activities and theatrical entertainment was one of the main recreational pursuits. The 'Divisional Troupe' recorded Major Cockman in his diary 'provided the best form of entertainment in the theatrical line'.[5] And a number of other records substantiate this view. The Divisional Concert Troupe, which drew men from different regiments and corps, was very soon adjudged to be of such importance that its provision almost became a statutory requirement in all base camps.

The staple diet of all concerts was the songs, especially those in which the troops had the opportunity to join in the chorus; above all the soldier needed the chance to laugh, to sing and to give vent to feelings of release from the tensions of trench life, war and death. Edmund Blunden, referring to the well-known song *Take Me Back to Dear Old Blighty,* describing the accompanying scene of collective emotional escape, wrote:

> *The barn roof ought indeed to have floated away on the paeans and warblings that rose from us... we roared inanely, and when a creditable cardboard train was jerked across the stage and performers looking out of the windows sang their chorus 'Birmingham, Leeds or Manchester', the force of illusion could no further go.[6]*

Apart from the popular song many of the familiar old tunes were parodied and then 'employed to accompany the most grotesque words, with great success.'[7]

At a Machine Gun Corps concert the comic singer gave voice to *Old King Cole.* First he sung it as it should be sung, then repeated the song in the characters of a Private, an NCO and finally an 'upper-crust' Colonel. He was encored time and again; the soldiers obviously enjoyed the sending-up of themselves and the humorous irreverence directed at the senior ranks. The renderings were widely appreciated by everyone, although four officers sitting in the front row, whose injuries necessitated their jaws being padded with gauze and fixed with pieces of wire, must have found the effort of laughing rather excruciating. They were, wrote one of the ladies from the Voluntary Aid Detachments (VADs) 'laughing and groaning at the same time'.[8]

The females in the audience, the nurses and VADs, because of the decorum expected of them, would pretend to be embarrassed by some of the crude allusions and references made by the comedians and singers, Dorothy Nicol, a VAD, referred to one comedian's song as 'frankly immoral', the chorus of which went:

> *I will have a night tonight,*
> *The missus is out of sight,*
> *The woman who lives next door to me,*
> *Her old man had gone to sea*
> *I will have a night tonight...*[9]

Despite the impropriety suggested in the lines everyone joined in the chorus 'even' wrote Nicol 'the VADs and nurses, and we were supposed to be very proper'.

Apart from the fun and noise of the mass singing there were times when the collective rendering of a song could evoke an emotional poignancy that was deeply moving. At the Corps' concert the pianist began to play and the men to sing *The Long Long Trail* in what must have been an altogether different, quieter and more reflective mood. Nicol joined in the first two lines:

> *There's a long, long trail a-winding*
> *Into the land of my dreams,*
> *Where the nightingales are singing,*
> *And the white moon beams...*[10]

The sentiments and the atmosphere could, however, make even the most war-hardened nurse's throat constrict: 'it cut you to the heart' she wrote in July, 1917. In an effort to control her whelming emotions she, and perhaps others, averted their eyes to the scene outside the windows where the convoy of motor ambulances and train full of men, guns and horses were 'going up the line'. Following the capture of Messines Ridge in June by the British and New Zealanders, the troops were moving forward to take up positions before the Third Battle of Ypres which began in July. The time spent at a concert would have been a welcomed respite for people like Nicol and other hospital orderlies, as the advance started in June did not end – although forward momentum was halted for a period due to torrential rain and the resultant quagmire – until the Australians and Canadians took Passchendaele on November 6. During the five-mile advance the Allied losses amount to 240,000 men: the costliest of all the Allied advances.

Many of the Division concert parties that performed in the YMCA huts and other venues mirrored the pierrot troupes of the pre-war years. The pierrot troupes in the UK were to be found touring towns in the smaller theatres and halls, or working at the end of the pier at the seaside resorts. The military concert parties included the pierrot musical chorus line 'potted pantomimes and potted plays' in their repertoire. The standard dress of ruffles and skull cap was thus a common feature of military concert parties during the Great War (*Figures 14 and 15*). And each troupe included a 'female' artiste. Indeed, the pierrot troupes appeared to be the rule rather than the exception.[11] There remained, of course, the problem of obtaining the requisite costumes for the pierrots. It was often the 'ex-pros' who ran the Division Concert Party and they, naturally, used their theatre connections to obtain the requisite costumes and props. One such was Cecil Parke who ran a concert party called the *Whizz-Bangs*, so named after the enemy projectile, the name of which describes its noise and effect. Parke advertised in *The Stage*, asking for pierrot costumes, black hats and 'gags and patter' for as he put it, 'After ten-and-a-half months out here one's repertory is practically "done in" '.[12]

The assembling of a cast was an additional and constant problem. It was difficult to maintain any semblance of a permanent theatre

Figure 14. A photocall for Central Stores Troupe – Tank Corps. [Imperial War Museum].

Figure 15. Canadian Concert Party – *The Maple Leaves* 1917
[Imperial War Museum]

company due to the unpredictability of war with the ever increasing casualty list; the personnel of a battalion could change 'every three or four months, and sometimes oftener' [13] The losses were not always attributable to enemy bombing though Private S. Smith a member of *The Crumps* troupe and the BEF band noted in his diary that a fire in one of the huts deprived the band of its viola player the latter being one of three soldiers burnt to death.[14] On another occasion the concert party organizer was relieved to hear that the baritone had been released from 'clink' in time to do the show

Apart from the constant transition of casts was the additional problem of finding enough performers with talent and someone with the expertise to manage and produce shows. This was an area of concern where the professional and experienced amateur proved invaluable. One such was a professional Shakespearian actor Arthur Whitby. He was, according to his Colonel, 'one of the unsung heroes of the war'.[15] No senior officer had taken notice of him until after the Battle of the Somme when the Colonel decided to form a concert party. The Shakespearian actor was a short, over-aged, over-weight Captain in the South Staffordshire Regiment. He appeared to be an unlikely person to manage any sort of party, let alone a concert party in France in 1915. He suffered shellshock and occasional loss of memory due to being buried by debris from a shell that exploded near him when previously serving in Gallipoli. However, with the running of the division concerts he had, within the theatre of war, found his metier. He had a high standard of theatre discipline and the divisional theatre company benefited from his expertise. Unfortunately, for the army, due to the recurring effects of his injuries he was invalided home late in 1915 – where he later resumed his career in the West End theatre.

The concert party initiated by Colonel Nicholson belonged to the 17th Division and was known as *The Duds*. They performed at a variety of venues. The shows were sometimes in the open-air and at other times in a converted barn or hall. The standard of accommodation varied considerably and was often, whether inside or out, adversely affected by the weather. The temperature inside the makeshift theatres could be either stiflingly hot or bitterly cold, and when the roof leaked, uncomfortably wet.[16] The major problem for the producer came when the Division had to move. There always existed the difficulty of obtaining transport; needless to say, the moving of theatre props, costumes, seating and rudimentary scenery was not a priority in a battle zone. On arrival at a new location an anxious search would ensue for an appropriate site, and a great deal of reconstruction was usually necessary before a premises could be properly utilized. The costumes, particularly the dresses, were the best available, 'since' wrote the Colonel 'the whole performance depended at least in part on these adjuncts... We had pink and grey silk curtains, grey pierrot kits with pink bobs, and endless selections of dresses and clothes'. The producer and his cast were determined to take the illusion of reality, indeed pure theatre, to its limits: hence the emphasis on female attire. *The Duds* seemed to be better equipped than most comparable concert parties due, in no small measure, to the interest and enthusiasm of Colonel Nicholson and the support of the staff officers.[17]

The desire to perform on stage may have been motivated by a variety of factors; not least of all, it offered a momentary chance to get away from the routine of soldiering. At Division level auditions were held and naturally the best were selected. At the shows the audiences listened intently to the musicians, sang loudly when accompanying the singers, laughed uproariously at the comedians, but when the female impersonator came on stage they whistled, stomped and bawled their encouragement in no uncertain fashion. 'We loved the manner' wrote a Signaller 'in which the female impersonators primped around the stage, doing a "Mae West" before Mae

West was even thought of'.[18] Obtaining a good female impersonator was difficult, so when a young soldier from the Highland Light Infantry, who had worked professionally as a female impersonator, presented himself to the adjudicators he was immediately drafted into the theatre company. A problem arose later when the 17th Division had to be restationed. The impersonator, Private Connel, belonged to the 32nd Division – both units shared the same encampment. The 32nd Division, although remaining at the base, did not intend to take up the option of continuing the theatre vacated by the 17th, and, what is more, would not 'hear of lending, loaning or transferring the female impersonator'. The management of the 17th, anxious to keep the 'star' performer, offered to exchange 'her' for 'two radial machine-gun mountings' along with the theatre decorations, but the 32nd Division representatives 'were sniffy' in their response. To this the senior 17th Division Commander merely remarked, 'If the girl [sic] comes along with us, it will be unfortunate; but what can we do?'.[19] Needless to say feelings between the two Divisional Commanders became strained. The problem of the abduction was finally solved when the Army Commander and his staff was invited to dinner and a concert; during the show it was pointed out to the visiting high-ranking guests that it was pointless to waste such talent, to which they agreed. Hence the 'girl' became, with the Army's consent, a gunner with the 17th Division.

Another female impersonator, also a member of the adjoining 32nd Division, was recruited in a similar fashion to Connel; that is to say, he was abducted. This additional 'female' was talent-spotted in a casualty collecting station, only this time, instead of inviting the Army Commander to endorse the transfer, he was 'unfortunately lost'. The newest theatrical recruit became an accomplished 'actress' and made 'a most attractive flapper', but success evidently turned to conceit as he became slovenly, then too vulgar and finally over-indulgent in performance. He was a novice amateur and perhaps, therefore, unused to such approbation and acclaim. Connel, on the other hand, treated a show and the applause with a professional's aplomb. The good female impersonator was therefore a highly prized commodity in an all-male concert party *(Figure 16)*.

Some of the less experienced performers may well have learnt the rudiments of stagecraft and the discipline of remaining in character while on stage during their stay in the armed forces. On his second visit to one revue an officer in the Coldstream Guards wrote that he

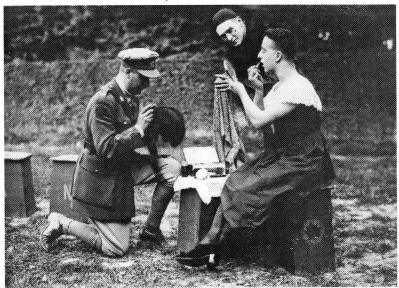

Figure 16. Female impersonator artiste – *The Maple Leaves* 1917 [Imperial War Museum]

Figure 17. The Ugly Sisters in Cinderella RFC production 1918 [Imperial War Museum]

Figure 18. Prince Charming, Buttons and Cinderella – RFC production 1918. [Imperial War Museum]

'was glad to see that Cinderella had learnt to refrain from the horrible act of taking off her wig to sing the National Anthem'.[20]

The 1st Canadian Division concert party, *The Volatiles* gave a show that wrote Major Cockman in his diary, 'was very nearly as good as a London performance'. Like many of the troupes it was managed and directed by an actor who had many years of professional experience The company included the usual array of diverse artistes including an excellent "knut" [man-about-town] and three first rate girls [sic] one of whom was truly the most amazing success'.[21] 'She' was called Kitty O'Hara and sang with a soft Irish accent and danced with consummate art'. The young female impersonator must have looked younger than his twenty years and had an air of Aphrodite about him, for 'even when dressed in boys' clothes 'she still looked more of a girl than a boy'. 'It was' wrote the Major impossible to think of her as anything else but a delightful flapper' The whole illusion and performance appeared incredible considering the 'flapper' had been 'over the top' nine times 'without receiving more injuries than such as were caused by being blown about by shells on three different occasions'.[22]

Some of the Division theatre companies had fixed dates for changes of programme. *The Balmorals* programme mainly comprised

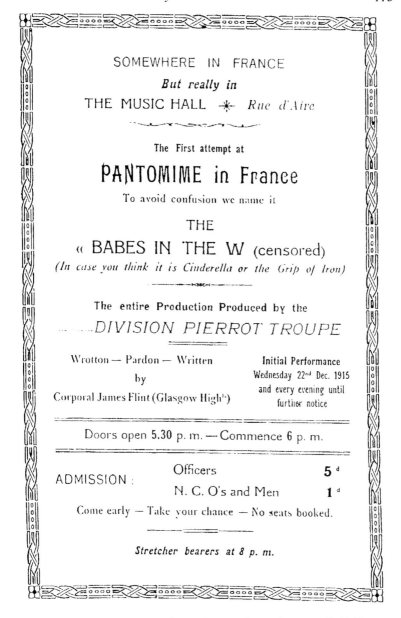

SOMEWHERE IN FRANCE
But really in
THE MUSIC HALL ✳ *Rue d'Aire*

The First attempt at

PANTOMIME in France

To avoid confusion we name it

THE

« BABES IN THE W (censored)

(In case you think it is Cinderella or the Grip of Iron)

The entire Production Produced by the

DIVISION PIERROT TROUPE

Wrotton — Pardon — Written
by
Corporal James Flint (Glasgow High¹ˢ)

Initial Performance
Wednesday 22ⁿᵈ Dec. 1915
and every evening until
further notice

Doors open 5.30 p. m. — Commence 6 p. m.

ADMISSION :

Officers	5 ᵈ
N. C. O's and Men	1 ᵈ

Come early — Take your chance — No seats booked.

Stretcher bearers at 8 p. m.

Figure 19. Programme cover for *Babes in the W (censored)* 1915. [Imperial War Museum].

songs which as the run progressed became broader in delivery and content, and by the end of a week bore little resemblance to the initial rendering.[23] Other companies combined the pierrot with the music hall turns; the first half of the programme featured the pierrots, the latter half, individual music hall performances with occasional playlets. *The Duds,* on the other hand, had pierrot turns with sketches in the first half and songs in the second; 'but the feature of the whole performance was a musical sketch or an occasional farce while most of the songs were successfully welded into the sketches'.[24] A programme's content really depended on the interests and availability of talent within the units. A number of companies veered towards music hall, others towards the drama. At Mons a Canadian Division put on the operetta *HMS Pinafore.* As in many of the music hall sketches, the female impersonators played a leading part. Barry Findon, writing in the *Play Pictorial,* commenting on one of the performances, said that 'The men who played the ladies' parts were good' but that 'Certain innovations, however, would have had W.S. Gilbert's hair stand on end'.[25] Although he did not specify what the changes were, it is safe to assume – judging by the content of other shows – that topical references and personalities must have been hinted at, if not inserted, in the original dialogue.

No high-ranking personality was excluded from the jests and jibes of the comic performers. In February, 1918, the Commander-in-Chief, Sir Douglas Haig, visited Colonel Nicholson's division and was invited to a concert given by *The Balmorals.* On entry to the converted barn/theatre he received a great ovation; a warm response he must have needed for it was noted he looked 'old and careworn'. Nevertheless, this did not stop the delivery of occasional jibes directed at the C-in-C 'all of which were cheered to the echo'. The show also included a sketch entitled 'A Peep into the Future'. It depicted the last British and last German soldier. They were using the same parapet, the Tommy was entrenched on one side, Fritz on the other, and Fritz was shown using the bayonet periscope held up by the Tommy as a shaving mirror. The exact interpretation of the sketch is not known, but Nicholson concluded that there was 'No intentional reflection on the Commander-in-Chief'.[26] It may be assumed, however, that the irony, following nearly four years of war and its millions of casualties, was not lost on Field Marshal Sir Douglas Haig.

The theatre productions followed the British tradition and so at Christmas there were pantomimes (*Figures 17 and 18*). The panto with it melodramatic victims and heroes provided the script writers and actors with ample opportunity to adapt both scene and dialogue to fit the times. A glance at the 1915 programme cover (*Figure 19*) indicates a way in which the panto was adapted to fit the wry humour of the soldier at the Front.

The seating capacity of each division's theatre varied, but an audience of between four and five hundred appeared to be the norm. Whatever the show the theatre was always full, and it was not unusual to turn people away because the house was packed hours before 'curtain up'. The theatres generated considerable income, the profits of which served two purposes, one recreational and divisional, the other national. First, the money could be used to pay for the running of the theatre and future productions, and a percentage was sometimes used to pay for free hand-outs of cigarettes and chocolates for the troops. Secondly, money was on occasions donated to regimental and national charities to help alleviate the sufferings of the bereaved relatives or maimed servicemen In some divisions the money collected from the theatre, cinema and canteen was pooled before being divided for the various purposes There did exist different prices; the officers' seats were more expensive and in some places this was further divided between officers, senior NCOs and junior ranks. The cost of mounting a production depended on the props required and the need for building and reconstruction work. The Canadian concert, referred to by Cockman cost £300 to put on (in today's terms, £9,000): a large expense considering there were no wages to be paid.[27]

One of the aims of the concert was to provide a means whereby a combatant could escape from the tribulations of reality, albeit temporarily but this did not always stop at the conclusion of the final song. At the end of some shows the illusion of normality was extended to include the presentation of 'bouquets and boxes of cigars and cigarettes on the last night, when there was a scene of great enthusiasm'.[28]

Until 1918 all personnel involved in producing shows for the British Army in France and Belgium were fighting men; their entertainment duties were in addition to their main function, that of soldiering. The proliferation of concert parties and the effort put in by the soldiers involved underlined the importance of theatre entertainment, and there was a growing realization by those in authority that recreation was a necessary and integral part of the convalescent process, both for the physically injured and the battle-wary serviceman. As mentioned, the maintenance of a theatre company was a constant problem; the next logical step, therefore, was to form a concert party consisting of soldiers whose specific task was to entertain the fighting troops. In 1918 Leslie Henson – the musical comedy artiste – was employed to form such a company.

General Sir Hubert Gough, the Commander of the Fifth Army, had read in a paper that Henson was to be posted to France, and thought Henson would be ideally suited for the role of Entertainments Officer. And subsequently, on the order of General Gough, in March, 1918, Henson was commissioned and posted to Nestlé with the given purpose of forming the required theatre company. He called his troupe *The Gaieties*. It numbered twelve in total, and included Bert Errol, the noted female impersonator, and two other professional artistes – Tolly Brightman, then serving with the Artists' Rifles, and Rob Currie.[29] The remainder were selected amateurs. They acted, like most of the other concert parties, in pierrot costume. Unlike the divisional troupes, however, *The Gaieties* was a touring unit; it was thus given the luxury of a permanent means of transport to convey themselves, the props and the lighting set from venue to venue. Many of the shows were for one night only. The company performed in any available space, but on one occasion they had the rare distinction of having a theatre built for them. The Chinese Labour Battalion, under the direction of the Tank Corps, constructed an entire theatre in twenty-four hours. The Chinese workmen 'even provided stalls, made of wood and canvas, perfectly fitted and finished, in which one sank back at ease'.[30]

Following the German evacuation of Lille on 17 October, 1918, the Allies, accompanied by Henson's concert party, re-entered the town. Henson's first objective was to locate the theatre. It was sited in the main square and was by far the grandest venue the company had played in. The theatre was larger than the London Opera House, being built just prior to the war, but not completed due to its seizure by the Germans in 1914. The occupying forces finished the job of construction and made use of the facilities. The indigenous inhabitants of the town had not been inside the building for four years, vowing not to use the place until the Germans had left. Henson's troupe discovered that upon withdrawal the Germans had smashed the entire electrical plant, and the lighting board was broken beyond repair. The problem was overcome by the acquisition of two Australian lorries carrying a complete lighting plant; the vehicles were parked in a narrow street outside and cables were run, via the rear windows, up two floors to the stage. The lifts, which carried the artistes to the stage, were obviously out of order and the scenery 'appeared very over-powering... since it was chiefly Wagnerian stuff and none of it stood less than 40 feet in height'.[31]

The backstage crew worked day and night ensuring that the theatre was operational within a week. Footlights, battens and side lights were fixed, and in the absence of limes, searchlights were installed. The Germans had erected a Royal Box in the centre of the Dress Circle for the use of the Kaiser and Hindenburg. According to Henson the Royal Box, with its drapes of purple and black with gold stripes, appeared rather kitsch. Nevertheless, it was put to good use when His Majesty King George V, the Prince of Wales and the Duke of York visited Lille theatre later in the year.[32]

The first show in Lille was a revue which included two prominently-billed French artistes, a violinist and a vocalist. Any attempt at entente cordial always delighted the Anglo-French audience, whether it were the inclusion of French artistes or the policeman dressed as a gendarme in an English sketch.[33] As the 'liberation' of the Opera House was an auspicious occasion it was attended by the Mayor and his Corporation suitably attired in evening dress; the importance of the event was not lost on the British Army Commander and his staff who arrived resplendent in khaki service dress and medals.

The show, although billed as a revue, was more reminiscent of a masque with patriotic scenes. It depicted the story of the war, and in particular the Allies' struggle against the invading Hun. The opening, called *1914 – The Angelus,* showed a tranquil scene with a man and a woman working peacefully in a field. It is likely that this was a representation of Jean Francois Millet's famous painting *The Angelus.* The reference would not, it is presumed, have been lost on the French audience. The idyllic life of the scene was disrupted by a bugler playing *Fall-in.* The woman appeared terrified, the man, of course, took heed of the call. The next, inevitable, picture was of the peasant, now the Poilu, preparing to leave for the Front while a girl buttons his coat, and nearby a widow sits weeping. There followed a scene, accompanied by the storm music from *William Tell,* called *The Enemy,* showing the consequences of occupation; the girl, in the custody of a German officer, was being abused whilst being chained by the ankles and wrists. There ensued further harassment by a German sentry while she was still manacled and unable to defend herself. The Germans were, as expected, graphically depicted as the arch-villains; the French as the long-suffering and brave underdog; the British and Dominion forces as the heroic saviours. And to the strains of *Tipperary* a British Tommy rushed on the stage and rescued the girl. At the conclusion of the *Liberation* scene the stage lights came full on revealing 100 children who began to sing the *Marseillaise*. 'The whole audience' recounted Henson 'rose to their feet, and stood in awed silence'. The final effect was the producer's coup de grace: from three floors below the stage in a distant scene dock the swirl of a Scottish pipe band could be heard. As they neared the stage the music grew louder and the atmosphere more emotionally charged. Hence, when they finally stepped on the stage the audience's response was excitedly tumultuous. The curtains up-stage centre then parted to reveal a girl (although in reality the female impersonator) draped in a huge French flag with an Amazonian helmet on 'her' head. 'She' paraded triumphantly down stage through the choir of children flanked on either side by a British Tommy and a Poilu: the finale included the combined musical offering of the orchestra, the pipes and the choir in 'one triumphant chorus'. The audience joined in as two hundred flags floated down from the flies.[34] The opening night at Lille with its patriotic offering, occurring as it did before the pending armistice, captured the expectant mood of victory and relief felt by both the French citizenry and the Allied troops.

Leslie Henson was not the only thespian-soldier to be employed full-time by the British Army. Lieutenant Charles E. Bovill of the Coldstream Guards, and author of several plays including *The Dancing Viennese* (1912) and *The Gay Lothario* (1913) was also given the job of Entertainments Officer. Bovill was commissioned in 1916 and saw active duty but was eventually classified as unfit for service in the trenches, although he remained at the Front where he wrote and directed shows put on by the soldiers. It is not known what shows he was directing, but it is believed his death in 1918 was due to the effects of a shell bursting nearby while he was rehearsing a party of soldiers in a revue written by himself.[35]

Most of the military shows on the Western Front catered for the recreational needs of the troops in the line, but those in hospital were not forgotten – although the latter were catered for, in the main, by the civilian concert parties. At the rear of the line there were the less-publicized units, such as the Labour Battalions; units which consisted of men too old to fight, who did not carry arms but were enlisted to carry out much of the manual work necessary to keep an army in the field. They also required entertainment.[36] The fare was the same: pierrot troupes, farces, pantomimes and sketches with their plagiarized songs. A popular example of the latter was Raymond Hickock's song. The first line reads 'When you're all dressed up and no place to go', which in the troops' version became 'When you're all fed up and no place to go'.[37]

The majority of the British Empire forces shared a common language but, as in the case of the Maoris, those who did not translated the most popular songs to fit their own tongue. It must have seemed quite incongruous to hear the following lines sung on the march or in the theatre:

> *He roa te wa ki Tipirere,*
> *He tino mamao,*
> *He roa te wa ki Tipirere,*
> *Ki taku kotiro,*
> *E noho pikatiri,*
> *Hei knoa rehita koea,*
> *He mamao rawa Tipirere*
> *Ka tae ahua.*[38]

The first line indicates that it was a rendering of the most popular and widely-sung chorus known to both civilian and serviceman. The non-English speaking colonial servicemen, as any member of a division, had the opportunity to attend shows; what they made of the humour is not recorded, but presumably the shared experience of an audience and the portrayal of figures such as the 'fierce sergeant', 'idle private' and 'Colonel Blimp' would be familiar and funny to any serviceman. Entertainment was not confined to Variety Turns and light comedy sketches. Works of Shakespeare were played but not in their entirety. At the Remount Depot in Rouen in 1915, scenes from *Hamlet* were performed. The costumes were hired from a local firm and, according to a *Times* correspondent, 'Horatio looked more like Henry VIII'.[39] Such incongruity was unavoidable and judged not too significant; what was important was the brilliance of colour on display – anything to get away from the drabness of khaki. The company learnt their lines from two books in the spare time allowed in three days. The four scenes chosen were: the Ghost scene; the room in the castle where Hamlet decides on revenge; the famous soliloquy 'To be, or not to be: that is the question', and the graveyard scene. The parts of Horatio and the Ghost were doubled by Trooper C. Howard of the Life Guards, better known professionally as Noel Phelps. The other ex-pro, who played Hamlet and produced the show, was Lance-Corporal

Herbert E. Maude of the Army Service Corps. The finale was not, however, a scene from *Hamlet,* rather a speech from *Henry V* – the one delivered before the battlement of Harfleur, the famous patriotic and rousing speech which begins:

> *Once more unto the breach, dear friends, once more*
> *Or close the wall up with our English dead...*

Interestingly this was delivered in 1915 to an audience of cavalry men. The effect, wrote *The Times* reporter, 'was electric'. The cavalry had seen very little action, added to which conscription had not yet been introduced. The response by the pragmatic, conscripted and cynical infantryman, sapper, medic, gunner and field signaller who had seen action at, say, the battles of the Marne and at Ypres, might have engendered a more muted reaction.

PRISONERS-OF-WAR

The casualties from Mons, Le Cateau, the Marne and the Aisne hospitalized in neutral Switzerland were, in effect, POWs. They included British, Canadian, French and Indian troops; and like their counterparts in the battle zones organized their own entertainments, although the theatre shows were not regular events. The shows, with their comic songs, conjuring, Scottish dancing and communal singing, were open to local Swiss residents and the proceeds, in gratitude for the care and attention given to the soldiers, went towards building a chalet-house 'for the delicate children of the place'.[40]

There is little evidence available regarding recreative amusements in the POW camps in Germany. It is known that at Cottbus, a camp some seventy miles southeast of Berlin, theatre entertainment did occur. In 1916 the camp held some three thousand British, French and Russian prisoners. The Cottbus Kriegsgefangenelager consisted of very large wooden huts divided into two rooms, each accommodating two hundred and fifty men in two-tier bunks. There was also a YMCA hut which was the focal point for religious, social and recreative gatherings.[41]

Photographic evidence suggests that the theatre was a lively and thriving activity. Each nationality had its own theatre troupe complete with the inevitable 'grand dame' impersonators. The British theatre company, in the absence of pierrot costumes, adopted a type of uniformed sailors' outfit (*Figure 20*). Music for the shows was supplied by an international orchestra which also provided more universally-known classical music concerts.

There was a similar international orchestra at Stendal POW camp in Germany, which housed both French and British soldiers. Stendal, judging by photographs and theatre programmes kept by Sergeant Furse, a Royal Marine, who was held prisoner from 1914 to 1918, was a camp specifically for non-commissioned officers. The curious difference between Cottbus and Stendal was the fact that the latter combined sporting events with theatrical shows. At the Christmas concert in 1915 the programme was divided into two parts. Part I was exclusively for songs, rag-time, comic and sentimental. Part II consisted of a turn involving comic acrobats and a boxing exhibition with three different 'matches', followed by a selection of musical pieces from the orchestra. The entertainment was done with 'Permission of the Red Cross of the Camp', who also benefited by receiving the proceeds. The popular choral singing was led by a 'barbershop quartet' known as the *Interned Coons,* who as their name implies dressed as blacked-up minstrels.

How much liaison there was between the French and British at Stendal cannot be known. There were certainly international football

Figure 20. Cottbus POW camp concert troupe – English Theatre [Imperial War Musuem].

matches. Judging by the Tyrolean costumes (*Figure 21*) worn by the theatricals, which do not appear to have been 'run-up' by the prisoners, there was considerable collusion between the German authorities and the internees. There must have been a lot of time and effort spent on the productions as the costumes and scenery for shows like the 1916 presentation of the pantomime *Dick Whittington* were relatively lavish (*Figure 22*)

The POW camp for civilians at Ruhleben was located on a disused oval track near Berlin The camp was for British and British Colonial internees. It held approximately 3,000 prisoners, and served the same function as its counterpart at Alexandra Palace in London. The accommodation included wooden stables which were converted into barrack blocks The lower portion of the grandstands, of which there were three, provided storage space and offices while the raked seating above served as lecture theatre space for the camp school. It also provided an ideal auditorium for summertime promenade concerts. The music was supplied courtesy of the prisoners' orchestra.

Reports regarding the treatment of prisoners at Ruhleben are conflicting, but life for the civilian internees was less severe than that experienced by military prisoners. The Lager Commandant Rittmeister Von Brocken, and the overall Commandant Baron Von

Figure 21. The chorus of a British concert troupe at Stendal POW camp [Captain A. Furse].

Figure 22. The Pantomime *Dick Whittington* at Stendal POW camp in 1916 [Captain A. Furse].

Taube and his wife, according to a report in *The Era* mixed freely with the inmates.[42] The comments in the 1919 Ruhleben Exhibition Souvenir Album are less flattering and it appears that the guards were not always so friendly.[43] The internees were however, more or less left to manage themselves. The camp was a society in microcosm. Thus sporting, educational and artistic pursuits were catered for. In the artistic field there were rooms for painting and arts and crafts. There was a madrigal choir, an orchestra, and theatre for both music hall and drama. The theatre was considered important because, apart for the most obvious reasons, it was a money-making institution.

The repertoire of the Ruhleben Dramatic Society was catholic in its scope. It began in early 1915 with Shaw's *Androcles and the Lion,* there followed a revue *Legs and the Woman* and in April a production of Galsworthy's *Strife. (Figure 23)* In June the drama society became more ambitious and the forest scenes from *As You Like It* were performed; and by 1917 the society was enacting Sheridan's *School for Scandal.* The year before it was *Twelfth Night* and *Othello.* They were performed as a way of celebrating the tercentenary marking Shakespeare's death. The *Othello* production evidently suffered by having a not very good Desdemona; as a result the society refrained from putting on any of the tragedies in the future, but *Twelfth Night* 'was a triumph'.[44] There were also variety shows put on by professional artistes, and a 'girl' chorus line began to appear which 'captivated the audience'. There was a musical comedy in German, *Der Fidele Bauer* and as a result of its success the Ruhleben Society for German Drama and Literature joined the group of dramatic clubs, along with the Société Dramatique Française de Ruhleben.[45] In total the theatre housed 128 different productions during the war years.

With the use of the arts and crafts workshop the dramatic societies were able to mount relatively extravagant productions. The arts flourished to such an extent that one branch of the arts, the Orchestral Society, actually formed a trade union to protect its members, such was the demand for their services: the conflict arose between 'duty and inclination'. Concerts were planned for all year round, 'with almost daily rehearsals and much private practice, but theatrical producers expected an overture and interludes at each of the five weekly performances'. The musicians, it seems, were being over-worked![46] The orchestra comprised nearly sixty in total, the madrigal choir about forty and the theatre company more than forty.[47] The reason for the success of the artistic endeavours was that per capita there was more artistic expertise at Ruhleben than at any military camp. A number of professional actors and musicians (the latter complete with their instruments) were stranded, or chose to remain, on the Continent in 1914. The result was they were collected, incarcerated and concentrated all in one place. This allowed the theatre to operate without hindrance on a repertory basis, and a new production was mounted practically every week.[48]

By October 1918, shortly before the Armistice, the Ruhleben lager was closed and the prisoners moved to The Hague in Holland. There they awaited repatriation, which was to take several months. In the interim a British theatre was set up in the town. This was run on similar lines to the one at the previous venue. The internees required some assistance in the Hague venture as they now had few resources. According to an article written in *The Review,* the interned theatricals thought they should receive some help from the British Government. This was not forthcoming, as the magazine writer commented 'since the Ministry of Information had definitely decided not to make use of drama and music in propaganda, there [was] no... organisation to deal with the matter';[49] besides which the temporary plight of a small number of civilians would be low on the Government's priority list at this time of mass demobilization.

Figure 23. Two of the ambitious Ruhleben productions: *Top. The School for Scandal, Below. The Merry Wives of Windsor.*

ENTERTAINMENT ON THE EASTERN FRONT

Most of the British and many of the Dominion troops stationed in Macedonia and the Balkans had, following basic training in the UK, seen action in France. As a result they had already sampled army-style concert recreation. Those who had experience in running shows elsewhere were recruited to continue the work out East.

Corporal Weston Drury of the RAMC, a professional artiste, had already been responsible for entertainment while stationed at Warminster, where he hit on the novel idea of cadging props or costumes from the 'stars' so as to promote his shows; the programme could thus read, 'Private Blank will sing a Scotch [sic] song in a kilt once worn by Harry Lauder'.[50] Drury had a keen eye for publicity. Later, in Macedonia, he even produced postcard-size bills of himself which depicted the character he was playing at the time. In Macedonia in 1917 he directed a two-act pantomime, *Bluebeard*, and later wrote, and played a major part in, a revue entitled *Delightful*. This meant he was also responsible for casting, although with regard to the script there was 'strict censorship and every fresh line had to be submitted to the Colonel'.[51]

The concert party's headquarters was the Gaiety Theatre at Kalinova. By all accounts it was a well-managed and permanent set-up. The theatre was built by the Pioneer regiment. It seated 200 and contained an orchestra pit, raked seating, dressing room and even a Green room for the actors. The theatre company comprised, in the main, members of the Royal Army Medical Corps (RAMC) and was sardonically known as *The Splints*. There was an enthusiastic manager, Captain Thompson, whose additional duties included entertaining visiting Staff Officers. The Captain's clerk, Lance-Corporal Mather (who wrote an informative diary) also acted as interpreter when any French flying officers came to visit. Within the army-built complex there was an officers' lounge and other ranks' canteen, and at a later date 'a pukka restaurant was built nearby, where dinner before and supper after the show was provided'. This was staffed by four chefs and six waiters all of whom had been professionally engaged in the catering business before the war. Needless to say this additional social luxury was the preserve of the officers who would entertain the nursing sisters from the Hospital in Salonika.[52]

In the winter of 1917 the pantomime cast, which combined the talents of artistes from all units, counted sixty; by the end of the run it had expanded to one hundred. It was, however, not an entirely happy social mix. The differences were not based on regimental lines; rather, the snobbish element that pervaded the company was reminiscent of the worse amateur dramatic society. It was not helped by the fact that against normal military practice the actors and orchestra were billeted separately from the back-stage, and canteen staff. Indeed, if any of the 'latter party [was] able to wangle "promotion" to the other camp it [was] considered "un grand succes"'.[53] The performers obviously harboured delusions of grandeur and considered themselves more important than the backup teams.

The show was performed once nightly for the first month, and four nights a week thereafter. The female impersonators were the chief attraction. There were three principals and seven chorus 'girls'. The FIs assumed an exaggerated importance in the socially-artificial environment. Although there were a number of nurses and VADs at the Base Hospital, the vast majority of servicemen did not come into contact with females for months, sometimes two years on end. Even brothels, although provided for troops of other nations, were not part of the British Army's official provisions.[54] At one level the sight of 'girls' was a nostalgic reminder of better times at home, but it also underlined what was fundamentally missing from the soldier's precarious existence. Within the theatre company and its deceptive actuality the place of FIs could cause friction. 'Those who took the male parts' wrote Mather 'had their special "pets" and jealousy amongst the 'ladies' was, in consequence, rampant'. One particular 'girl' incurred the resentment of some of the cast because of 'her' penchant for upstaging others by 'flirting' with the audience while on stage. This delighted some of the patrons. The French officers who frequented the shows would, unlike the more socially-constrained and phlegmatic British, bring 'exotic gifts for their "girl friends"', but in hindsight, Mather thought it did not stop at that'.[55] To what extent this seemingly homosexual behaviour pervaded that particular concert party, or indeed the theatre scene *per se*, is impossible to determine. It may be that the donning of female attire within a legitimized context gave some men the opportunity overtly to display their feminine inclinations, and the reciprocal reaction of some others may be construed as a form of apparent homosexuality. Homosexuality is a punishable offence in the British Armed Forces, and any such behaviour would of necessity have been covert, and difficult to define. The fact that a degree of homosexuality occurred, outside the theatrical existence of the FI, would be hard to deny, considering that during the war nearly 5 million British men were in uniform; perforce a percentage must have been homosexual by inclination.

The Theatre continued to flourish throughout 1917 and, records Lance Corporal Mather, men would tramp up to four miles from the trenches to see the concert party. The shows lasted for three hours, ending at 11 pm. After the show the beer ration was issued. Attempts were initially made to give out the alcohol before the show with, wrote Mather, fatal results.[56] Apart from being administratively disruptive, it meant that a potentially enthusiastic audience could well turn into an uncontrollably vociferous one. However, in September 1918 the theatre was closed, due, firstly, to the sweeping 'flu epidemic and, secondly, troops being recalled to the Front for action in the battle of Monastir-Dorian, in which the Bulgarians were defeated by the combined efforts of the British, French and Greeks. Finally, an Armistice was signed on 30 September, 1918.

Facilities for concerts on the Eastern Front varied and not all soldiers were within walking distance of Division HQ and its theatre. As early as Christmas, 1915 the 85th Field Ambulance unit solved the first problem – the provision of an adequately-furnished theatre. It was impossible to build a wooden stage as all timber stock was required for the erecting of dug-outs. The 85th's solution was to put up three large marquees in the shape of the letter T. The horizontal one became the stage, the other two the auditorium. The floor of the auditorium was then dug out and the excavated earth used to raise both the level of the stage and bank the rear of the auditorium to provide a form of raked seating. The majority of the audience sat on the ground, but stalls were fashioned for the officers by digging out three rows of trenches, and then lining them with sandbags half-filled with straw.[57]

The 85th's ensuing 1916 production of *Dick Whittington* was by all accounts a resounding success. This was due to the hard work of the production team led by Frank Ketchington – a professional actor – and the enthusiasm and support of Major-General C. J. Briggs CB, General Officer Commanding the Division. The General was so impressed with the show that he decided that it ought to go on tour.[58] The theatre company visited three brigades which included twenty-one different gunner and infantry regiments, and other front-line support units. Inside the transportable canvas theatre the stage was encircled by army blankets, which allowed for entrances to be made from either wing and from up-stage. The curtains consisted of blankets attached to a pulley system. The stage lighting was a combination of three acetylene operating-lamps, a headlight from the motor ambulances in either wing, and 'two in the auditorium serving admirably as limelights'. The footlights, which acted as reflectors, were twenty-five jam tins with one side cut away.[59] The costumes were cleverly manufactured out of army kit; 'The gorgeous tights of the "principle boy" being merely army pants transformed'; an officer's overcoat turned inside out served as a fur coat for the prosperous Alderman Fitzwarren, and obsolete army forms cut into long strips and strung together became an Elizabethan ruff.[60]

Private Ketchington scripted the pantomime in less than two weeks. All the characters and situations were, naturally, adapted to reflect the military setting. Hence Dick Whittington first got promoted to Sergeant, and finally ends up becoming, not the Lord Mayor of London, but a 'proud full-blown ADMS' (Assistant Director Army Medical Services – in effect, a General). The chief villains were Count Maconochie and Sir Joseph Paxton. The former stood for a certain army ration, the latter was the well-known manufacturer of jam issued to the army. Alderman Fitzwarren was depicted as a dubious government official. Dick Whittington, of course, marries Alice – Fitzwarren's daughter – but the cat dies in extreme agony having consumed army rations supplied by Maconochie. The pantomime, because it was re-written by a soldier for soldiers had, as reported in *The Times* 'jokes you can make in Salonika which must not be reported in the London Press'.[61] Great efforts were made to make the show as 'professional' as possible and a souvenir programme with script was published in 1916.

Wheresoever the soldier went so did the theatre, and the same type of concert parties could be seen in India and Egypt, as were witnessed in France and Salonika. Gunner Vines, a professional artiste and conscript, managed to continue his 'career engagements' in Egypt following a successful tour in France. While stationed in the Middle East he rehearsed his songs and comic patter routines most days and, when not performing in the evening, went to other concerts given by the British and Australian troops. The main aim was to glean material for his own act. The YMCA hut was, as usual, the focal point for theatrical activity. The daily schedule, according to his diary, was for the concert members to work until mid-afternoon, then rehearse at 4pm before curtain-up at 7.15pm. The theatre appeared well organized,

and was publicized with photographs of the cast in costume a▮
write-ups in the local army press.[62] Further indication of the growi▮
importance of the theatre was the fact that Vines' pending draft
September, 1917 was stopped, because he was deemed to be t▮
important an integral part of the concert party.[63]

The concerts were not just a bright hiatus in the ennui of camp li▮
they helped to remind the military personnel, both male and fema▮
of home, better times, another world. At Kantara, Egypt, in 191▮
Siegfried Sassoon wrote an ode to a concert party. The second ver▮
outlines one of the main functions of the theatre; namely, that
collective nostalgia. In the poem Sassoon vividly describes t▮
'draw' of the concert party, and it is worth quoting in full:

CONCERT PARTY

They are gathering round...
Out of the twilight; over the grey-blue sand,
Shoals of low-jargoning men drift inward to the sound —
The jangle and throb of a piano... tum-ti-tum...
Drawn by a lamp, they come
Out of the glimmering lines of their tents,
                              over the shuffling sand.
O sing us the songs, the songs of our own land,
You warbling ladies in white.
Dimness conceals the hunger in our faces,
This wall of faces risen out of the night,
So long beyond their sight.
Jaded and gay, the ladies sing; and the chap in brown
Tilts his grey hat; jaunty and lean and pale,
He rattles the keys... some actor-bloke from town...
God send you home; and then A long, long trail;
I hear you calling me; and Dixieland...
Sing slowly... now the chorus... one by one
We hear them, drink them; till the concert's done.
Silent, I watch the shadowy mass of soldiers stand.
Silent, they drift away, over the glimmering sand.[64]

The female auxiliary members of the armed forces – the nurses ▮
VADs – attended the concerts but rarely participated. The ov▮
reason can be attributed to the fact that the soldiers, like actors, co▮

experience periods of relative idleness punctuated by times of intense hyper-activity. Unlike the actor, however, it was the periods of rest that allowed them time to engage in theatrical business. The women employed in the hospitals worked continuous shifts and there were no block-release periods for training or rest, hence no time for rehearsing shows. The nurses' contribution was often confined to running up dresses for the female impersonators.[65] And, of course, the nearer the concert was to the front-line the less likelihood there was of finding women in the vicinity. Evidence suggests that the women who had the opportunity of seeing the Base Camp shows enjoyed them, despite the crudeness of some of the songs and jokes. If the latter became too broad they could always do, as Miss Aldridge, a nurse in an Indian hospital did, pretend not to comprehend.[66] Not all the shows were coarse. The recognized plays were not, and yet females rarely took part. A more covert reason for this non-participation was that female medical staff could not be seen to socialize with the rank and file, and, apart from the individual young male subaltern, the cast of the shows was formed almost exclusively from the non-commissioned ranks. When women did participate, as in concerts aboard *HMS Britannic*, a hospital ship, they did so in sketches that contained only female characters. Occasionally a nurse or VAD would perform a song solo, or give a pianoforte selection, but always there were officers present in the cast. There was even a rigid line of distinction between the sister (the professional) and the VAD (the amateur), added to which the VAD was often a daughter from an upper or upper middle-class family; this separated them further from the working-class rating, soldier or airman. Within the social framework, still rigidly Edwardian during the war years, there was little room for transgression across the cultural divide, and certainly not in the armed forces – a highly formalized, structured society based, as it was, in large measure, on social distinction.

THE FUNCTION OF ENTERTAINMENT IN THE WAR ZONE

Entertainment, on both Fronts, helped to provide an antidote to the drabness, hardship and misery of soldiering; an unforgettable misery brought on not solely as a result of the killing and the dying, but also the appalling living conditions. On the Western Front there were the vermin-infested trenches; and the rain-filled bomb craters which formed deep, interlocking scallops of water in which the injured and the unwary could drown. Edmund Blunden, describing the onset of a storm, vividly conveyed the mood of depression accompanying its arrival. 'Another storm' he wrote 'and a more serious and incontestable one, was now creeping miserably with grey vapours of rain over the whole field…'[67] The weather could be as deadly as the enemy. Trench-foot and pneumonia were only two of the incapacitating results of living in water-logged conditions for weeks or months on end. The wind with its laden clouds of chlorine gas fired by the enemy could also be lethal. In fact, due to the capriciousness of the wind, the effects of gas cylinders launched by the Allies could be just as deadly. At Loos in 1915 the wind changed direction with devastating effect. As a result the attack was eventually abandoned after eleven days, but not before another 60,000 casualties were inflicted, a significant number from 'friendly gas'. Any diversion from these horrors of battle and its consequences was important to the mind of the individual and the collective morale of the troops. E. Scullen, a private in 1916 who was later commissioned, summed up the importance of theatre in his diary. He wrote '…there is a chance to forget there's a war on now and again. What a blessing these concert parties are'.[68] T.P.C. Wilson, who was killed in action in March 1917, underlined the psychological need to release the tension and trauma of war by light entertainment in his poem *Magpies in Picardy:*

> *And still we laughed in Amiens,*
> *As dead men laughed a week ago.*
> *What cared we if in Delville Wood*
> *The splintered shells saw hell below?*
> *We cared… we cared… but laughter runs*
> *The cleanest stream a man may know*
> *To rinse him from the taint of guns.*

As early as January, 1915, and before many of the newly-arrived drafts from the UK had experienced battle, the theatre had a role to play. Men would remain in the transit camps for some time, either completing training or doing endless fatigues before being moved to the Front. An army chaplain reported that there was much mud and that 'the atmosphere [was] not inspiring'. Some soldiers, not unnaturally, felt homesick, and the ever increasing lists of killed and wounded could not have inspired confidence, or raised the morale of the volunteers. 'It is evident' wrote the padre 'that they stand in need of some enlivening influence'.[69] Such an influence, he concluded, was provided by the large marquees erected to house the diversionary entertainments. The theatre provision was both popular and productive. According to the padre it afforded a measure of 'well being' and made the army more effective, and 'from a chaplain's point of view it is most satisfactory'.[70]

As in the garrison in Aldershot, the religious authorities saw entertainment as a method of persuading men to stay in camp and away from the sinful temptations of the flesh. Much of the entertainment was conducted in YMCA huts, and the YMCA, being a Christian organization, was concerned with the spiritual needs of the troops; the huts were also used as places of worship. Whilst the YMCA helped to satisfy some of the temporal requirements its message and role were clearly moral, and was spelt out in an article in *The Times* in 1915:

> ... *if soldiers are to be kept away from the* estaminets *and the company of women, they must have as many opportunities as possible of going to places where they can amuse and occupy themselves in a wholesome manner.*[71]

There was some censoring as to content of shows. It is doubtful, however, if this was done for security reasons as the shows were, in the main, for military personnel. On the occasions that the padre was 'detailed' to produce the show, the censoring was for a different reason. The padre, wrote Major Cockman, 'Would be liable to turn down the most effective and popular items if these were at all on the doubtful side'.[72] This is to say, if they appeared too risqué. The way in which the cast circumvented this mode of restriction was to 'smuggle' songs into the repertoire by including them in any encore, thus leaving the puritanical, or prudish padre no time to object effectively.[73]

The inclusion of some sketches clearly gave the serviceman a platform on which his grievances about the food, conditions, sergeants and the officers were aired. From this point of view the shows provided a safety valve, or at least a 'public' forum for a shared and sympathetic grumble. Cynicism and pessimism, not to mention ironic humour, could not be excluded from a military concert: the forces' humour, given the precarious existence of the military – especially in war time was, and still is, 'black' in tone. The pessimistic feelings of those in the Front line in 1917 were reflected in a revue in France, in

THE

SOMME-TIMES.

WITH WHICH ARE INCORPORATED

The Wipers Times, The "New Church" Times &
The Kemmel Times.

No 1. Vol 1.   Monday. 31st July, 1916.   PRICE 1 FRANC.

THE CONTALMAISON OPERA HOUSE.

—o–o–o–o—

THIS WEEK,

The Great Spectacular Drama, Entitled :

"THERE'S ONE MORE RIVER TO CROSS."

INTRODUCING THE CELEBRATED MALE IMPERSONATOR,

LITTLE WILLIE.

—o—o—o—o—

THE THREE LORELEI

IN THEIR SONG SCENA. ENTITLED :

"OH WILLIE COME HOME BEFORE YOU GET HURT."

—o—o—o–o—

The Original Bottle-nosed Comedian,

FRITZ

IN HIS NEW SKETCH

"I'VE HAD SOMME."

—o–o–o–o—

PRICES AS USUAL.   BOOK EARLY.

Figure 24. Front page of *The Somme Times* 31 July, 1916. [Imperial War
Musuem].

which Scene III was called 'In the Trenches, 1967'.[74] The irony of the scene-title speaks for itself.

Paul Fussell writes about the way in which the war was conceived in theatrical terms.[75] He writes of the facetious advertisements in *The Wipers Times,* a forces' newspaper in which war is described in the language of the farcical music hall sketch. The paper was later incorporated in *The Somme-Times.* The front page of the first edition of the latter, printed on 31 July, 1916, provides a vivid example of the ironic humour, and the place of music hall in the thinking of the soldiers (*Figure 24*). The final advert displays the 'blackest' humour:

FRITZ

in his new sketch

'I'VE HAD SOMME'

The last line is the cruelest joke of all. The paper was sold when the Somme offensive was only a month old; when the British casualty list was already over 100,000. But within ten weeks and after an Allied advance of only seven miles the British rota of dead and wounded had grown to 418,000, the French to 195,000. On 18 November the Battle of the Somme ended and the 'joke' died with it; by this time the 'joke' had gone too far. Nevertheless, collective comment, either in scripted or journalistic form, and through the language of show-business, provided the fighting man with a mode of expression.

The music hall revues put on by the military and civilian concert parties provided, writes Fussell, an interesting ironic analogy; for whenever 'they emerge from the show... in the distance another "show" [was] in progress, with its own music, jokes and dancing'.[76] The ironic parallel is perhaps nowhere better expressed than in the poem *The Concert Party: Busseboom* by Edmund Blunden:

> *The stage was set, the house was packed,*
> *The famous troop began;*
> *Our laughter thundered, act by act;*
> *Time light as sunbeams ran.*
>
> *Dance sprang and spun and neared and fled,*
> *Jest chirped at gayest pitch,*
> *Rhythm dazzled, action sped*
> *Most comically rich.*

With generals and lame private both
Such charms worked wonders, till
The show was over: lagging loth
We faced the sunset chill;

And standing on the sandy way,
With the cracked church peering past,
We heard another matinee,
We heard the maniac blast

Of barrage south of Saint Eloi,
And the red lights flaming there
Called madness: come, my bonny boy,
And dance the latest air.

To this new concert, white we stood;
Cold certainty held our breath;
While men in the tunnels below Larch Wood
Were kicking men to death.

The analogy between the theatre of war and the stage is not hard to find, going as it does beyond the semantic jingle. The connections are illustrated by the training, constant rehearsal, attention to detail, opening night with the accompanying illuminations, anticipation and adrenalin and resultant heightened emotion. The soldier talks of the 'show', the 'party' and the actor of 'going over the top', 'dying on stage'; some of the language is inter-changeable. The Great War and the concert party thus provided the poet with a rich and useful literary mode of expression. Such was the importance of therapeutic laughter and the need for diversionary recreation that men were assigned, even before the inception of the soldier-thespian such as Basil Dean and Leslie Henson, to full-time theatre duties. William Erskine, a bandsman with the Sherwood Foresters regiment, is a good example. Apart from his periodic military pursuits such as guarding POWs in transit, or the more onerous tasks of burying dead men and horses, Erskine played his musical instruments. He was an accomplished performer with the oboe, violin and clarinet, and was part of a small orchestra that occasionally entertained the officers and sergeants in their respective Messes. He also worked as scene-painter, sign-writer and musician with the *Wunny Wuns*, the 11th Division Concert party.[77] The military have, for a very long time, had full-time entertainers in the form of musicians, but it was not until the First World War that this type of war-time military employment was expanded to include actors, music hall artistes and theatre producers.

The reason for the reported high standard of many of the concert parties was the inclusion of the professional. The 11th Division, for example, had, apart from trained musicians, a professional stage manager in Lieutenant Cecil Field – formally of the Hammersmith Palace – and a female impersonator in Corporal Philpotts (stage name, Percy St. Clair) who had 'worn petticoats professionally for ten years'.[78] It was, in fact, the inclusion of the latter that distinguished the vast majority of concert parties abroad from those in the United Kingdom. That is not to say there were no FIs in the home-based companies, but clearly their need to 'improvise females' was not a necessity.

As in Britain both Christmas and New Year were celebrated in part by going to a pantomime. And the military concert parties made every effort to maintain this tradition. Indeed, efforts were also made in some quarters to celebrate the Tercentenary of England's most extolled writer, namely Shakespeare. In the Kinema Hut No. 1, on 2 and 3 May, 1916, scenes from *Twelfth Night* and *Henry* V were performed along with Shakespearian songs.[79] Interestingly the Tercentenary programme at the civilian POW camp in Ruhleben the programme was printed in German, which suggests that not only were the Germans invited but that a degree of amicable co-operation existed between captors and captive. The introduction to the programme was written in English and did, however, serve to remind the internees of their important and shared heritage:

> *This festival is offered... as a tercentenary commemoration that cannot be without a special significance to all who reverence the ideals that... live in the English tongue.*[80]

By 1917 each division (an organization of about 10,000 men) had at least one military theatre company.[81] The concert parties filled a variety of functions, and for the troops who lived in a world of drabness, death and destruction the theatre's part was more than just a cameo role providing light relief.

Civilian Theatre Provision in the War Zones

The inclusion of theatre entertainment by civilians in the war zones of Europe, the Balkans and the Middle East initially augmented, then greatly enhanced, the theatrical fare on offer to the troops. The structure of this entertainment can loosely be divided into three categories: tours by individuals; one-off performances and short tours by independent companies; and tours organized by Lena Ashwell – the actress and former proprietor of the Kingsway Theatre.

VISITS BY BRITISH THEATRE NOTABLES TO FRANCE

There were few visits by individuals to the battlefield of Europe. The problem of getting permission from the War Office, and the requisite transport, could only be surmounted by those with connections in the corridors of power. Interestingly, those that managed to travel came from different theatre backgrounds and for a variety of reasons. Harry Lauder derived great satisfaction from combining his job of being Britain's best-known music hall artiste with that of recruiter and propagandist, and like many patriots he felt and wrote with pride about his only son John, who was an officer in the Argyll and Sutherland Highlanders. It was, however, in December, 1916, that Harry Lauder felt the full impact of war when he received the terse telegram from the War Office; it read:

CAPTAIN JOHN LAUDER KILLED IN ACTION
DECEMBER 28. OFFICIAL. WAR OFFICE[1]

After a period of private grief and mourning at his son's death Lauder, with feelings of retribution, attempted for the second time to join the army in order to fight. Understandably, he decided it was both impossible and inappropriate for him to carry on his theatrical career. The idea of trying to make people laugh seemed, at the time, anathema; besides which he was still only forty-six and within the revised age limit for Front line duty. His absence from the stage was short lived. People of influence from the world of theatre and politics persuaded him, as they did before, that he was more use to the country as a recruiter, propagandist and entertainer. Furthermore, he felt he had a duty to the remainder of the large cast in the London show. The revue *Three Cheers* at the Shaftesbury Theatre had been dark for three days following Lauder's departure home to Scotland. On his return he received a standing ovation, for everyone knew of his plight and no doubt many in the audience shared his sad experience. At the climax of the final act Lauder had to sing his patriotic song *The Laddie that Fought and Won*. Lauder records that all went well until he came to sing the two lines of the refrain:

> *When we all gather round the old fireside*
> *And the fond mother kisses her son...* [2]

The poignancy and immediate relevance of the lines proved too much; however, his grief was covered by the chorus of Scots Guardsmen who sang for him. At the end of the show and at the conclusion of the National Anthem, the feelings of emotion generated were so overbearing that Lauder fainted.

Lauder's desire to don uniform and actually fight had not left him, and when the curtain finally came down at the end of the show's run he renewed his efforts to enlist; but again he was told his duty lay elsewhere. Since he was denied the opportunity to fight, the next and obvious step was for him to apply to the War Office for permission to entertain the troops in France – this he did. It was to the more dangerous Front line where he wanted to go, and not just to the base camps. He also wanted to see where his son died and was buried. [3]

In May, 1917 permission came from the War Office for Lauder to go to France to entertain the troops, and in particular the Scottish regiments which included the Argyll and Sutherland Highlanders, the Gordon Highlanders and the Highland Light Infantry. He was not to go alone. Two other people, both politicians, were to accompany him. One was James Hogge, a Member of Parliament for an Edinburgh constituency, who was known for his work on behalf of war widows and orphans. The other was the Reverend George Adams, an official in the Munitions Ministry. [4]

His first concert was held in early June, 1917 at the Boulogne Base Hospital, once the Boulogne Casino. The programme consisted entirely of songs. 'Best of all they liked the love songs, and the old songs of Scotland' and not, he wrote, the 'sad lugubrious songs'. [5] Lauder tells of how one 'great actor' recited to bed-bound soldiers

Longfellow's *The Wreck of the Hesperus*. The patients' reaction was governed by their training and they 'went to cover'. The orator was thus left reciting to mounds of shaking bedclothes.

Many of the travelling music hall artiste's 'concerts' were alfresco, impromptu sing-alongs at the side of roads to passing troops who had stopped for a brief respite. Once into their singing the break in marching could become quite a prolonged affair, lasting longer than Lauder or the officer-in-charge anticipated.

In his autobiographical account of his travel through France in 1917, Lauder admits to his hatred for the enemy. His understandable taste for malevolent revenge was temporarily satisfied when he was afforded the opportunity to fire one of the artillery guns sited on Vimy Ridge.[6] The main task in hand, however, was to entertain the troops and this he did in an almost perfectly made amphitheatre, which turned out to be a large bomb crater. It was, he recorded, 'a superb theatre'. Lauder, referring to the crater, asked the Battery Commander how often they received such a near hit. The man replied with apparent aplomb that had he come the day before they would have had to find an alternative location for this concert.[7]

Figure 25. Harry Lauder with staff officers at 1st Army HQ Ranchicourt, 5 September, 1918. [Imperial War Musuem]

Lauder and his travelling companions had decided on a set format for their programme. Proceedings were opened by James Hogge, MP who talked to the men about pensions, and the Reverend Adams spoke about war loans and food conservation at home. In essence, the two men tried to reassure the troops and let them know that everything possible was being done for them and their families; and what was just as important, they attempted to describe how the people at home were supporting them: in short, it was an exercise in boosting morale. The third and major part of the programme was given over to Lauder and his one-man show, which invariably began with a rendering of his song *Roamin' in the Gloamin'*.[8] The locations varied from shell-holes to rest camps, dug-outs, old chateaux and barns, and audiences could number a hundred or a couple of thousand.[9] Thus the music hall artiste had satisfied his desire to visit the Front and sing 'under fire'. On one occasion a concert had to be abandoned as the trench came under bombardment from missiles known as 'whizz bangs', so called because of the noise they made, and their effect was that of a large and deadly fire cracker. Towards the end of the tour at the end of June, Lauder's main wish was granted. The party took the road to the military cemetery at Orvilliers to visit his son's grave. It was, of course, a sad and painful moment for Harry Lauder, although it did not stop him returning to the war zone again a year later (*Figure 25*).

As a result of what he had seen in France, Lauder decided, on his return home, to set up a fund for the crippled and the maimed. His target was one million pounds. Lauder appears to have had considerable connections, if not influence, in the corridors of power for he persuaded the Earl of Rosebery – the former Liberal Prime Minister – to become Honorary President of the Fund, and Lord Balfour of Burleigh to be its treasurer. Later in the year the artiste travelled to America in order to raise money for his fund. His concerts and pleas for funds were not always well received in the USA, particularly in those cities where the German-American population was strong.[10] Lauder, a practiced propagandist had, however, managed to win a considerable amount of support. His efforts were augmented by the song which he wrote called *Marching with the President*. This appealed to the American people. He even managed to meet and play golf with President Roosevelt. Thus with the help of American money his fund grew.

In 1918, just after the conclusion of the war, Lauder set sail for Australia, and on his arrival received unexpected but pleasant news.

He heard that he had been awarded a knighthood for his war-time exploits as recruiter, propagandist, fund-raiser and entertainer of many years standing.

Frank Benson was a famous Shakespearian actor, and like Lauder, used his professional skills for the purposes of recruitment. The similarity persisted in that he too had a son in the army. Benson's son was an officer in the King's Royal Rifle Corps, and to the pride of his family became the youngest Lieutenant-Colonel in the British army; and what is more, he had been awarded the Military Cross for bravery. However, in September, 1916, Eric Benson defied the doctor and left hospital early so he could lead his advancing regiment in an attack. This proved a fatal decision as he was mortally wounded.[11]

Frank Benson, unlike Lauder, did not hurry across the channel but continued his war work at home, embarking on a music hall tour in an act entitled *Shakespeare War Cry*. This was a propagandist piece which served its purpose well in 1914, but in 1917, and following the debacle of the Somme offensive, was adjudged not a success and his contract was not renewed. Most members of an audience had suffered a loss, and any rallying nationalistic hype' must, it is assumed, have run the danger of being received with the utmost cynicism. In 1917, Benson resigned his position as Festival Director at Stratford-on-Avon Theatre and embarked for France, declaring that 'my services, however small, are needed elsewhere than in the theatre. I should have studied Shakespeare in vain if I thought otherwise'.[12] His work in the war zone was not as an entertainer but as an ambulance driver for

Figure 26. The famous Shakespearian actor Frank Benson, who became an ambulance driver.

the Red Cross. The fifty-five year old actor did not go alone but was accompanied by his actress wife, Constance Featherstonehaugh. She was to take charge of a *cantine de eclopes* – a type of convalescent camp for wounded *poilus*.[13] When the work ceased later in the year they reluctantly returned to England. At home he and Constance went on a short but unsuccessful music hall tour, playing scenes from *Macbeth* and *Taming of the Shrew*. The audiences' response was, according to J.C. Trewin the critic, 'tepid, though at Barrow an audience rallied to throw... cabbages'.[14] Benson then toured with the NACB and did the round of garrison theatres. In 1918, he again quit the stage and returned to France. He drove a French ambulance and worked, wrote a *Times* reporter 'in the high temper with which a knight of old rescued maidens from... Savage men'.[15] The metaphor was apt as Benson had been knighted for his services to the theatre in 1916. In France he served under the most dangerous conditions, rescuing soldiers under fire and, to his everlasting pride, was awarded the Croix de Guerre for his bravery.[16] It could not, of course, compensate for the loss of his son and Benson did not act again until 1920, some two years after the war ended.

In 1917 another actor, propagandist and recruiter, John Martin-Harvey, realized his wish to visit the Front line; but, unlike Benson, he wished to continue his craft and give recitals to the troops. His desire to 'confront the war' was not based on feelings of tragic loss or enmity as felt by Lauder, or a sense of inappropriateness of his profession as expressed by Benson; although like the latter he did experience a disturbing sense of inadequacy. In his autobiography Martin-Harvey *(Figure 27)* recalled an incident on a London underground train which engendered in him feelings of 'pain, of wonder and of humiliation'.[17] On one particular journey he remembered the carriage being filled with about thirty soldiers who were evidently returning to the Front. On entry, after settling themselves down with their equipment, they began to sing 'soldier choruses' in a plaintive, quiet 'almost ghostly manner'. It was not just their demeanour or the unfamiliar words that the actor found both strange and compelling, but it was their air of total detachment. They acted as if they were in a world apart. 'They had' wrote Martin-Harvey 'no eyes for us wretched civilians. There was no contempt; we simply did not exist!'.[18] Martin-Harvey had been an unofficial recruiter for two years and had visited the wounded in hospital, but always it was as a man talking, lecturing or reciting to others. It appears that for the first time he realized that he was on the outside looking in – excluded from the real war by lack of experience. In the carriage the roles were reversed. The actor was part of an audience watching a scene he did not fully understand, and it unnerved him. He added:

> ... *their eyes [were] far away in a world of which we who sat by their side knew nothing.* [19]

In July, as a result of the 'railway carriage experience' and with the help of Lena Ashwell (Lady Simson) who organized concerts abroad, the fifty-year-old John Martin-Harvey left for France. He was clad in the khaki uniform of the YMCA and was engaged as one of their helpers, although his main aim and function was to entertain the troops.

The first lecture-cum-recital delivered by Martin-Harvey was to a group of Australian soldiers. He expected a 'respectful hearing', and that was precisely all he got. He recalled 'My remarks about war-weariness, about the worthwhileness of their sacrifice, fell flat'.[20] The response to Shakespeare's stirring speeches from Henry V was more encouraging. The actor appeared slow to learn for he tried the same format again before another Australian audience; the reaction was again respectful, but muted. It then occurred to him that the last thing the combat soldier needed to hear about was the 'worthwhileness' of it all; particularly if those words of 'encouragement' happened to be uttered by a non-combatant. There was only one course of action left; he ditched the lecture and concentrated on the recitations. He still continued to recite Shakespeare. The famed speech from Henry V

(Figure 27). The actor Sir John Martin-Harvey, who learned from the troops.

'Once more unto the breach dear friends, once more... was delivered near Harfleur; the Crispin speech within a couple of miles of Agincourt. To these he added speeches from *The Only Way* based on *A Tale of Two Cities*, and other Dickensian Christmas stories. The latter, he said, were very popular.[21] The recitals were given in YMCA huts and, on occasions, in the open air, and he experienced, as did all entertainers, the rude interruptions of audible shellfire during performance. At the end of July, 1917 he returned home a satisfied, and presumably a wiser man.

The year 1917 witnessed not only the appearance at the Front line of a music hall star and two famous classical actors, but also a noted playwright. This was George Bernard Shaw.

At the beginning of the year Shaw was guiding rehearsals of his playlet, *Augustus Does His Bit*, a satire on bureaucracy and officialdom. The playlet was written, noted Holroyd, in response to a Government appeal 'to dramatists and theatre managers for didactic pieces inculcating war savings'.[22] The main character, dressed as a colonel, Lord Augustus Hardcastle, does his duty with abundant enthusiasm, but the result of his 'highborn' efforts are totally ruinous. This one-act piece was to strike a chord with anyone who had to deal with mandarins employed in positions of power. It was, therefore, a little ironic that Shaw should receive an invitation to visit the Front from an actual panjandrum; namely, Field Marshal Sir Douglas Haig. Shaw's initial response, writes Weintraub, was suspiciously wary. GBS assumed that all he would be allowed to see were the areas designated for official visitors, and he was disinclined to be a pawn in a public-relations exercise. Nevertheless, he decided, after some prompting from his wife, to accept the invitation.[23] Throughout his dealings with the War Office administration Shaw was treated in a courteous manner. Whether this irony had anything to do with the opening of *Augustus Does His Bit* at the Court Theatre is open to conjecture. Certainly many had suffered at the hands of an 'Augustus' who was judged a 'well-meaning, brave, patriotic, but obstructively fussy, self-important, imbecile and dangerous' bureaucrat.[24]

At the end of January, 1917, Shaw crossed the channel to France. On his arrival at Boulogne he was afforded the VIP treatment, being met by a staff captain in a private car, in which he was transported direct to Field Marshal Haig's HQ. This was near St. Omer in a large estate containing three chateaux: one for the C-in-C and his staff, the second for accredited war correspondents; the third for important visitors. These included, apparently at the same time, Harry Lauder, Members of Parliament, the writer Arthur Conan Doyle, Japanese Royalty and a delegation of Welsh miners.[25] The scene at St. Omer, some sixty miles behind the front lines, was in complete contrast to the reality of the trenches. The staff had obviously done their homework, for even Shaw's dietary needs were catered for – he was a vegetarian.

Shaw visited most of the notable battlefields: Ypres, Arras, the Somme Front and Vimy Ridge. On his guided tours the Shavian humour was often lost on his audience. At Arras Shaw commented that the shelling of the town had been partially beneficial as the cathedral, 'a copy of a copy, looked better as a ruin than when it was intact'. This wry and observant humour may have appeared in bad taste, but nevertheless it was reported as being beyond the comprehension of his companions.[26]

Shaw was even taken by Sir Douglas Haig to see a demonstration of experimental weapons. His most pleasing visit was, however, to 40 Squadron RFC at Trezennes where he met his long-time friend and actor, then Major, Robert Loraine MC. Shaw spent several days at the small airfield with the Royal Flying Corps, and whilst there attended the dress rehearsal of his playlets *The Inca of Perusalem*, performed by the rank and file, and *O'Flaherty VC*, acted by the officers (a class distinction still observed in some though not all the troops' in-house shows, possibly for no more significant reason than the convenience of organization).

The purpose of *O'Flaherty VC*, written in 1915, was, said Holroyd, twofold. First, it was intended 'to help the resources of the Irish Players at the Abbey Theatre', and secondly, 'to serve as an Irish recruiting poster in disguise'.[27] Shaw had been asked by Sir Matthew Nathan, Under-Secretary of State for Ireland, to help boost the disappointing recruiting figures. The responding Shavian reply was prompted by the reported exploits of a Private Michael O'Leary who had killed eight German soldiers, and captured fifteen others single-handed. Twenty years earlier Shaw had campaigned for pensions to be paid to holders of the Victoria Cross and, writes Holroyd, this may have been an additional motivating factor when considering the material. O'Flaherty sees the war as a means of escape from the boredom of living in Ireland; a way of getting away from the dominance of his mother, and the opportunity to 'have a French wife'. Despite his heroic success O'Flaherty considers war morally wrong: 'No war is right' he concludes. Shaw understood how war could be a liberating influence for some individuals, and warns through the voice of O'Flaherty – as he did in his political tracts – of the dangers of blind patriotic fervour. These sentiments troubled Sir Matthew Nathan, and after he consulted with his immediate successor General Sir John French, Commander-in-Chief of Home Forces, the production was postponed.[28] Thus the first performance of *O'Flaherty VC* occurred on 17 February, 1917, in a Royal Flying Corps camp at the Front in Belgium actually the world premiere, a fact not previously noted. Shaw's friend, Major Robert Loraine, who nominated the playwright as his next-of-kin, almost ended his acting career in France. He had already lost a lung and was later in the year to suffer a shattered knee cap. The doctor wanted to amputate but Loraine demurred, preferring to seek Shaw's advice first. Shaw's reply was typically humourous, yet indirectly helpful. He wrote:

> *I don't know what to say about your leg. If you lose it, an artificial leg of the best sort will carry you to victory as Henry V. If you don't and are lame, it means a lifetime of Richard III, unless I write a play entitled 'Byron'.*[29]

Loraine decided against amputation, recovered and later resumed a successful career on the West End stage.

On his return to England Shaw penned three articles for the *Daily Chronicle*. Those who regarded Shaw as a complete pacifist and pro-German – though he was neither – would have been surprised by his reports. He still thought war an offence to humanity but concluded that 'it is too late to consider it when the sword is drawn. You cannot vindicate outraged morality by surrendering or allowing yourself to be beaten'.[30] He did not dwell on the wastage of human life, but emphasized the economic cost. He argued that the public should produce more in order to augment provisions, thus helping to hasten the end of destruction.

There were questions in the House of Commons regarding Shaw's visit to the Front. Given the reaction to his earlier pamphlets criticizing the politicians and war-mongers, this was hardly surprising. Weintraub concludes by saying that if permission to allow Shaw, who was thought by many to be a gadfly, 'to have a first-hand look at the war had been a calculated risk, it had paid off'.[31] The aim of the newspaper articles was to help to console those at home who had relatives and friends in the trenches. He realized there was nothing to be gained by attacking those in authority, or deepening the hurt of the people at home. Contrary to the reports in the paper, he admitted privately that his visit to the Front had been 'a most demoralizing experience'.[32] Shaw must have felt aggrieved when, a few days after getting home, he heard that the Prime Minister, Lloyd George, had erased his name from the 'list of persons with ideas'. This was a list of people who were to form the Reconstruction Committee, their task being to advise on post-war social problems.[33] Despite this socio-political set-back there was a resurgence of interest in his plays both at home and abroad; clearly he was no longer viewed as the arch-villain by everyone, although as Holroyd points out 'he was still an outsider'.[34]

Bernard Shaw and Harry Lauder's party were afforded the VIP treatment which means that the War Office were aware of their importance and effect. Both had a political resonance: the latter because it contained two politicians, and an artiste who had influence on the national stage; the former because the author had access via his artistic renown to the world's 'political stage' through his polemic writings. The theatre, or rather certain people within it, could not be ignored, although the extent of their influence is impossible to gauge. What was certain in this war of attrition and high losses was that bad press and criticism from people in the public-eye were not welcomed by either the political or military authorities.

FIRST CONCERT PARTY TO VISIT THE FRONT

In August, 1914 Seymour Hicks, like other leading actors, volunteered for military service but to his great disappointment was refused entry on grounds of age – he was too old. Hicks, along with his actress wife, Ellaline Terriss, was appearing at the Lyric Theatre in *The Earl and the Girl*, but during the day they entertained the wounded

(Figure 28). Seymour Hicks who organised the first civilian concert.

in hospitals and at matinees in the theatre. They also raised funds for war charities via bazaars and sang recruiting songs.[35] Despite this war work they were looking to do more, so when the opportunity came to visit the Front, they grasped it with enthusiasm. The idea of going to France came from a wounded soldier in a London hospital. Ellaline Terriss had finished singing in a ward when one of the invalids remarked 'How the fellows at the Front would enjoy such a treat'.[36] Seymour Hicks thought it a good idea and approached the *Daily Telegraph* newspaper proprietor, Lord Burnham. The chance to be involved in the enterprise was accepted with alacrity; and the newspaper, no doubt with the best philanthropic intentions and not wanting to miss a good opportunity for publicity, underwrote the costs. On the suggestion of Lord Burnham an approach was made to Field Marshal Lord Kitchener who readily gave his approval, and told Hicks to contact General Sir John French. The General said that it was, at that time, impossible for them to entertain the troops in the Line. Permission, however, was granted for a party to visit and entertain those troops behind the lines in training and rest camps, and the hospitals at Le Havre, Rouen, Abbeville and Boulogne.

The military authorities, whilst welcoming the concert party, said they could not take any responsibility for them or provide the necessary transport. The initial task, before concerning themselves with the logistics, was for the theatre couple to gather together a good and varied cast. This posed no problem. The party comprised: Gladys Cooper – regarded as the most beautiful actress in England; Ben Davies the famous tenor; Will Van Allen, a noted comedian; Ivy St. Helier, comedy artiste and pianist; Willie Frame, a Scottish comic singer; Eli, Olga and Elgar Hudson, a variety turn; and, of course, Seymour Hicks and Ellaline

(Figure 29) The beautiful Gladys Cooper, who entertained the troops.

Terriss. All artistes cancelled their engagements for a period of two weeks. The complicated problem of organizing the tour fell on the shoulders of Mr. Boardman, the then manager of the Hippodrome Theatre, Brighton. The entire entourage, including press representatives from the *Daily Telegraph* and *Daily Mail* numbered twenty in total.

A playbill was produced and sent ahead of the concert party to be posted on every available noticed board. It was headed 'The NATIONAL THEATRE at "AT THE FRONT"'. The language and tenor of the playbill script with its phrases, such as: 'You will confer a favour on us by letting us work for you' and 'The Price of Admission is OUR GRATITUDE TO YOU', may appear by today's standards, to be overly patronizing and ingratiating; but it must be remembered that these were extraordinary times.[37] Britain, indeed the world, had never been involved in a conflict on this scale. In Britain it affected practically every family; and never before had a complete concert party, with nationally known names, which combined both theatre and music hall artistes, been organized to go to a battlefront. This mode of production and entertainment was to become the norm over the next four years, and thus the advertising hype of the initial playbill was not to be needed subsequently.

This, the first concert party to leave England, departed from London – along with a considerable amount of luggage and equipment, which included two pianos and six cars – in December, 1914. The party landed at Boulogne to a great reception, and like so many others to follow, gave their first performance within an hour of arrival in the local casino, by then converted into a hospital. Everyone was touched by the enthusiastic response they received; Ellaline Terriss found the grateful humility of the staff a quite humbling experience, for she felt the nurses' contribution far outweighed the party's seemingly pathetic efforts. After the first performance Ellaline Terriss was asked to visit a very young soldier who was unable to attend the concert. He, in fact, had little time to live. His bed was segregated off behind a screen in a dimly-lit ward. She took his hand and at his request – and doubtless with great effort – sang *The Honeysuckle and the Bee*.[38] Such moments of poignant pathos proved emotionally hard to bear for members of the concert party. The actress recalled another occasion when she was particularly moved emotionally. This was when Ben Davies sang *Land of My Fathers* to a Welsh regiment. The audience, five hundred men clad in full service marching order, were standing in ranks in the pouring rain one night waiting to be entrained for the journey to the Front. The Colonel, Lord Ninon Crichton Stuart, called the men to attention and Ben Davies began to sing the national hymn in Welsh. They took-up the refrain. Within a week the colonel, along with many others, lay dead on the battlefield.[39]

The concert party was not without its personal mishaps. Most of them fell ill. The strain of touring in war time was considerable, particularly for Willie Frame who was over sixty years of age. Only Ivy St. Helier and Gladys Cooper remained fit, and the latter was pregnant with her first child. There were times when they had to give the whole show by themselves; Ivy St. Helier sang and played the piano, and Gladys Cooper recited well-known pieces, one of which was Kipling's *Gunga Din*.[40] The most debilitating case of ill-health was suffered by Seymour Hicks who was invalided home, suffering from a serious bout of pneumonia. In January, 1915, on their return, the party gave a repeat performance in a London theatre. The profit from this was donated to charitable causes, half going to theatrical charities, and the remainder to the fund for procuring waterproof shelters for the troops in training.[41]

Two factors became important for anyone, or any concert party, wishing to travel abroad. First, was the necessity of obtaining permission and support of those in the very highest positions of military authority; secondly, was the relative closeness of the war to home. Indeed, so close was the war in mainland Europe that it was possible for artistes to make weekend visits to the Front. In 1916, for example, a concert party consisting of Leslie Henson, George Grossmith, Henri Leoni, Henry Ainley and Lieutenant Arthur Price travelled to France on Saturday night, gave a concert for 600 soldiers at the Front on Sunday, and was back in London for their respective West End curtain-ups on the Monday evening.[42]

Not all the civilian entertainments were done by professionals. In the more permanent rearward locations, such as the English canteen in Paris – run by the Women's Emergency Corps – volunteers from the British and American colony ran entertainments for the troops on leave. Every Sunday the volunteers offered a programme of semi-classical music. Once the entertainments got going and 'after a period of respectful listening' the men took control of the concert. They limbered-up on the ubiquitous *Tipperary*, and then followed with old sentimental favourites such as *Killarney*, and *Loch Lomond*.[43]

Ad hoc, individual contributions, weekend theatrical sorties and short tours were very welcome to the troops; but in a static and protracted conflict such as the Great War there was a need, and a scope, for wider and more permanent theatrical provision. The organization of this was to be the prerogative of one person – Miss Lena Ashwell.

LENA ASHWELL AND THE ORGANIZATION OF ENTERTAINMENT ABROAD

In answer to the Clarion Call in 1914 many women volunteered their services for King and country. The most evident were those who donned the uniform of the nurse and the VAD; many undertook unfamiliar employment in the factories, fields and increasingly in the armed services. With some adjustment others used their skills in charitable ventures for the benefit – directly or indirectly – of the war machine. The theatrical profession, via its recruiting, propaganda work and fund raising, was one industry that quickly accommodated itself to the changed times. Within the theatre there existed organizations that, with a judicious realignment of aims and function, swiftly put themselves on a war-footing. The Actresses' Franchise League was one branch of the womens' theatre movement that, wrote Sanderson, 'temporarily set aside its suffrage intentions and concentrated on war work'.[44] This apparent about-turn regarding Government support on behalf of many suffragettes was, according to Marwick 'one of the most interesting psychological phenomena of the war'.[45] Within two days of war being declared several leading figures in the Actresses' Franchise League felt moved to set up an additional organization specifically designed to relocate women and place them in posts necessary for helping the war effort. The new organization was called the Women's Emergency Corps. Its founders were the actresses Decima and Eva Moore, and the actress-managers Gertrude Kingston and Lena Ashwell *(Figure 30)*. Both the Actresses' Franchise League and Women's Emergency Corps complimented each other by taking responsibility for the administration and raising of funds for different war charities. It was as a member of the Womens' Emergency Corps that Lena Ashwell attempted to get entertainment for the troops organized on a national basis. The aim was twofold: first, to provide entertainment for troops at home bases, and secondly, to provide work for members of the Corps. In 1914 the War Office was concentrating all its efforts on providing adequate training and accommodation for the ever-increasing numbers and hence she 'met with a blank refusal'.[46] As recorded it was left up to the army itself, under the aegis of Captain Basil Dean via the NACB, to provide entertainment in the training depots. In November, 1914, the President of the Womens' Auxiliary Committee of the YMCA, Princess Helena Victoria of Schleswig-Holstein, gave Lena Ashwell an unexpected opportunity by inviting her to organize concerts for troops in France.[47] The precedent had, as mentioned, been set by Seymour Hicks and his concert party, added to which royal patronage obviously carried more influence with the War Office than the enthusiastic ideas of an actress; and the YMCA already had entrée to the military via its religious and recreational work in their huts at the base camps. In effect the YMCA was already equipped, albeit in a basic way, to cater for concert parties.

The 'Concert at the Front' campaign, as the move to take civilian entertainment to France and Belgium became known, was the result of the combined effort of three people. The initiator was Annette Hullah, a member of the Music in War-Time Committee. Miss Hullah and her Committee were aware, by 1915, that concerts were 'badly needed in France' and she subsequently outlined a scheme for such provision, but her organization did not have sufficient funds for such a venture and the plans were submitted to Princess Helena Victoria and the Committee had to be content with recommending suitable artistes to the Ladies' Committee of the YMCA – in effect to Princess Helena Victoria and Lena Ashwell. The organizations, although not

(Figure 30). Lena Ashwell, who did so much to organise entertainment during the First World War, with C.M. Hallard in *Diana of Dobson's*.

actually working together, remained in sympathy. Whilst Annette Hullah was the originator of the 'Concerts at the Front' scheme, Princess Helena Victoria was its catalyst, and Lena Ashwell the architect and planner.[48]

The first concert party Lena Ashwell organized disembarked in France on 18 February, 1915. It was a two-week tour of Base camps and hospitals. There was no subsidy or sponsorship and so it was privately funded by Lena Ashwell – most of the money being donated by friends. Initially the YMCA, wrote Barry Findon in the *Play Pictorial* 'regarded the experiment as a risky one'; but it was judged an overwhelming success by every recipient, be they private or general, doctor or chaplain.'[49] It was, therefore, as a result of the initial reception and the subsequent demand that she became the permanent honorary organizer of the 'Concerts at the Front'. Lena Ashwell continued her acting and management career at home, but finally, due to the ever-increasing overseas commitments, she relinquished her managerial post at the Kingsway Theatre in December, 1916, and confined her acting to selected roles in plays performed in France.

The Music in War-Time Committee submitted only the names of those musicians and singers who were of a good standard; likewise Lena Ashwell restricted employment to actors and artistes of comparable ability. The musical offerings were broad and included classical pieces, selections from operas, ballads, old folk songs and the new rag-time.

The party normally consisted of seven or eight artistes and reflected a wide range of tastes. There would be a soprano, contralto, bass and tenor singer, a violinist or 'cellist, a pianist and accompanist, with a conjuror or ventriloquist, and a comedian or someone to recite. As was the norm, the men enjoyed a chorus song which allowed them to participate, but they equally appreciated good instrumental music be it a piece of Bach, Handel or Beethoven.[50] Lena Ashwell, in her own account, wrote that 'The last movement of the Mendelssohn Concerto, the Intermezzo of the Cavalleria Rusticana, and Handel's "Largo", were always much loved by those in hospitals'.[51] When the Westminster Singers toured France in September, 1916, they agreed that the taste of the soldiers was 'extraordinarily good'. The soldiers were always eager to sing *Annie Laurie*, but they also appreciated the old English songs such as the two-hundred-year-old *Would You Know My Celia's charms?* Above all, according to two of the group's singers, Carrie Tubb and Phyllis Lett, *Drink to me Only With Thine Eyes* was the most popular.[52]

Lena Ashwell had strict control from the start. Conditions of service with her concert parties meant 'No advertisement, no making use of the war to aggrandise one's professional popularity'.[53] However, the programmes reveal that Lena Ashwell made certain that she got top-billing and that her name was printed in a larger and bolder type; and given the amount of general press coverage concerning 'The Concerts at the Front', her career in no way suffered by taking time out to play in productions not usually covered by the critics in the national newspapers. Although both she and Princess Helena Victoria were responsible for the artistes' professional and social conduct, the YMCA organized the venues, timings, billeting and feeding. This, in fact, was the most sensible and logical way to administer such an operation. It meant that the army was free from the day-to-day minutiae of management, but, of course, nothing could be accomplished without the total co-operation of the military. This allowed Lena Ashwell the freedom to direct operations on the English side of the Channel, and to act in particular productions.

REMEDIAL AND EDUCATIONAL WORK

One-third of the entertainment work was done in military and Red Cross hospitals. The sick and wounded who were mobile were gathered in the largest ward, hall or tent for the main performance, after which the artistes would individually visit the more serious cases.[54] Apart from the diversionary and palliative effect of entertainment, the visit of a civilian concert party reminded the wounded man that there was an alternative and happier existence to which he could one day return. Or as one soldier put it 'I was fighting for no one until that cheery party came along. I can even now fancy I can hear the sweet notes of the violin'.[55] Those words were written before the second battle of Ypres in 1915: the battle in which, for the first time, the lethal chlorine gas was used. The Germans fired the deadly canisters at the British and Canadian forces. The end result was 60,000 British and Allied losses. And during the battle the young soldier who was revitalized on hearing the 'sweet notes of the violin' was wounded four times, in addition to being gassed.[56]

Entertainments were a benefit to many, probably most of the hospitalized servicemen, but not to all of them. Ada Ward, an entertainer and lecturer with one of the concert parties, writing in the *Bradford Weekly Telegraph*, explained the problems facing some of the men:

Of the scenes in the hospital... Oh, it is terrible to see some of them.
Some without limbs, some still gasping with gas fumes, some whose
eyes have looked into hell and will never forget it. Even our sweetest
music and merriest jokes failed to awake a smile...[57]

The concert party was not the only mode of entertainment for the
troops. Lena Ashwell organized a group of enthusiastic instructresses
to go to France and teach the soldiers to dance; not of course, ballroom dancing, but old English folk-dancing. 'The country dances of
"Merrie England" proved enormously popular' wrote Barry Findon.[58]
How popular is difficult to assess, but judging by the numbers there
were certainly enough participants to make the venture worthwhile.
There was both a recreative and a serious side to the dancing. The
dancing classes in the convalescent camps 'secured the cordial
approval of the Army medical authorities' because they provided the
men with remedial exercise which aided their recovery.[59] And for
those suffering from shellshock the folk and country dancing was the
only exercise they were allowed to take.[60] Classes were taken at three
depots, and as each depot contained between three and five thousand
men there was no shortage of volunteers. In the afternoon the female
teachers gave occasional classes for the Army Gymnastic Staff. This
meant that the latter could assist the teachers on the morning parades,
which catered for between 60 and 200 men dancing on the parade
ground, accompanied by the regimental fife band.[61]

Photographic evidence indicates that country dancing had, on
occasions, an extra attraction as females working in the hospitals and the
YMCA also participated. Therefore, apart from the obvious remedial
benefits for the wounded, the country dances could be a social event
for everyone. The officers commanding the convalescent depots
would have been aware of the beneficial effects of the classes, and
hence they became an integral part of the soldiers' remedial training.
By 1918, there were fifteen civilian dance teachers serving in France.[62]

In 1916, Lena Ashwell was requested to send lecturers to France.
Some people in authority at the War Office, although it is not clear
who, felt that the soldier needed intellectual stimulation. There may
have been a more covert reason for the inclusion of educational
lectures, as it was noted that 'the few that were thinking at all seemed
to be studying Karl Marx and little else, and for all real progress it is
necessary to strike a balance'.[63] It was reported in the *Daily News* in
1916 that the YMCA intended to form a strong committee of educa-

tionists for this purpose.[64] There had been, via the YMCA and Lena Ashwell, 'conversational' discussion classes on the works of Shakespeare, but now the committee intended to widen the programme. A list of subjects deemed appropriate by the committee contained the following: the Napoleonic Wars; history of high explosives; the Balkan situation; regimental history; and astronomy.[65]

The sample of topics may appear odd, particularly the inclusion of the 'history of high explosives'. Whether those troops subjected to heavy bombardment attended this lecture cannot be known. But the most perverse subject proposed was a lecture on *Air and Water, showing the necessity of avoiding stray pools and puddles as thirst assuagers.*[66] The soldiers must have been more than aware of the dangers of such hazards, given that the battlefield was pitted with deep, interlocking, water-filled bomb craters. There is no record of this lecture being delivered, but if it was the reaction of the cynical battle-hardened soldier can only be imagined!

The most notable theatre lecturer to tour France, who wore the uniform of the YMCA, was John Drinkwater – the poet, playwright and manager of Birmingham Repertory Theatre. He did a five-week tour of base camps. The audiences were 'intensely responsive' wrote the critic in *The Stage* in 1918. The size of audiences varied from 50 to 400. Drinkwater's style was not to perform poems like a dramatic actor, but rather to sit at a table, 'and read [them] simply'.[67]

The YMCA Educational Committee's project did not start until 1918 when the War Office set up a branch to deal with education. Headquarters for this purpose were located at Lille, to which volunteer lecturers were sent. It occurred to the War Office that with the cessation of hostilities in Europe in November, 1918, the soldier might become overly bored and apathetic; therefore he was in need, not only of sport and entertainment, but also education. One of the lecturers was the *Play Pictorial* editor, Barry Findon. Findon's abiding interest was theatre and this is what he talked about to the soldiers.[68]

The lecturer had to be adaptable, particularly the one who did not have the advantage of lantern slides, but relied solely on entertaining rhetoric. The educational and social make up of an audience varied considerably, and if the speaker, wrote Findon, had 'a few hundred men who are not interested over-much in drama, it is useless to hurl at them eloquent periods, and, therefore, some of one's most cherished phrases must go by the board'.[69] The orator, like the entertainer, was subjected to the vagaries of war; an audience could disappear at a moment's notice on the command of a superior, and the conditions could be equally as capricious. At one lecture in a hall which possessed neither windows nor electric light, the single lamp that was suspended from the ceiling went dark within the first ten minutes. Findon was left, in the presence of 300 men from the Gordon Highlanders and the Black Watch Regiment, with a candle and his note book. They were, he said 'a tough audience' and the gloom of 'the hall was only relieved periodically by a cough, a match being struck or a more welcome sound of applause'.[70] If the majority of the Scottish soldiers' experience and knowledge of theatre was based on music hall, and less on the orator's middle-class esoteric interests, and given the disadvantage of the venue, it can be imagined that the phrase 'a tough audience' was an English understatement.

CONCERT PARTIES

The first concert parties sent out by Lena Ashwell in February, 1915 gave 35 concerts in fifteen days. The debut performance was at Camp No. 15 in the Harfleur Valley. As it was winter the conditions were not ideal. The whole valley was a quagmire through which people picked their way on duckboards. This was in complete contrast to the hot, smoke-filled YMCA hut. The 'auditorium' was packed to overflowing with all ranks, and the artistes had to sit on the stage as there was no room for 'entrances' and 'exits'. 'The concert' wrote Lena Ashwell 'had to be fairly short – two hours at the most'.[71] The most notable member of the party was Ivor Novello who had written the song *Till the Boys Come Home*, later re-named *Keep the Home Fires Burning*.[72] The men greatly enjoyed the song. They readily took up the chorus, and no doubt the thought of 'the Home Fires' meant a great deal to them. Ivor Novello 'admits [the song] was not a master piece... But it had an instantaneous appeal to the emotion'.[73] In fact the song was to prove just as popular in the Second World War. Novello went to sing in France on more than one occasion and performed in seventy concerts abroad before applying for, and receiving, a commission in the Royal Naval Air Service. This first party gave concerts at a variety of venues, including the casino at Boulogne, a railway station on the quay at Le Havre, and at a race course. At the latter 'a tarpaulin was stretched over the front [of the stand] to keep out some of the weather; it was bitterly cold. A huge coke brazier was put at one end of the stand, where artistes kept warming their fingers. The artistes were cold enough, but what the audience felt like, one cannot guess. But not one of those boys in blue moved until the end' wrote Ashwell.[74] The 'boys in blue' refers to men from the hospital – a blue jacket being the statutory hospital garb.

Ivor Novello wrote other patriotic ballads, such as *Laddie in Khaki* and *When the Great Day Comes*, but none was to be as successful as *Keep the Home Fires Burning*.[75] An indication of the song's popularity with the British public – it was also sung in America – is the fact that 'no less than twenty-four famous pantomime principal boys made it the theme song of their shows' in 1915.[76]

The conditions in the war-zone of continental Europe varied; obviously the nearer the Front the greater the danger. This necessitated the sending out of two different types of concert party. There were touring parties and permanent parties. The Front line touring parties consisted of males only and did their shows as near to the actual fighting as the authorities would allow. A pre-requisite for selection of such a party was that the individual be exempt from military service on the grounds of age or medical fitness. Clearly it would have been undiplomatic, not to say insensitive, to send a young militarily-eligible male to the front line. Indeed, such a person, unless he was attested and therefore waiting to be called-up, would not be selected given the immense pressure at home for young men to enlist. Female artistes were not, from 1915 to 1917, allowed to perform with the touring parties as it was considered to be too dangerous.

The length of duty with a touring party lasted between four and six weeks. One reason for these short tours, concluded Lena Ashwell, was that the work was very exhausting for the over-age and the not-so-fit artistes. The rough journeys, long hours and the strain of over seventy performances meant that many performers were totally fatigued at the end of the run. To cut down on the travelling the concert parties were based in one of three sectors; the first sector party operated from Le Havre and Rouen; the second from Boulogne and Calais; and the third company from Aimes, Dieppe and Le Tréport. The number of parties increased as more men were posted to France and Belgium and consequently more bases were opened. There were soon five concert parties leaving Britain every month. The War Office obviously approved of the work being done, because contrary to normal practice, the touring concert parties had extended permits which allowed them to stay in the Line for a month or more.[77] Nelson Jackson, a concert performer, gives a first-hand account of what it was like to be a member of a Front line troupe during 1916, in *The Stage* and *The Stage Year Book*, 1917. His role in a party which called itself *The Firing Liners* was that of comedian, writer and master-of-ceremonies. The remainder of the party consisted of Walter Hyde – tenor, Percy Sharman – violinist, Charles Tree – baritone, and Arthur Fagge – pianist. In a joint letter, all members of the troupe expressed their thanks to Lena Ashwell for, as they put it: 'The opportunity [the concerts] gave five men over military age to be of some service within sound of the guns'.[78]

The small company gave three concerts at base camps before moving into billets about four miles from the Front. The attic billet for Jackson and Hyde was by 'courtesy' of a local inhabitant on the command of the military authorities. It cost one franc a night; cheap enough to warrant the exclusion of carpets, pillowcases, soap and towel. This was in complete contrast to the 'high profile' treatment enjoyed by Harry Lauder. Transport was a small delivery van which carried the five performers, the driver, and a piano which had neither legs nor pedal. The van and the piano were supplied by the army.[79] The party did three concerts a day – the largest was to an audience of fifteen hundred. Each concert lasted an hour and a half. Touring near the Front was a hazardous business as there was always the danger of being shelled, but on a more mundane level there was the problem of the weather. Nelson Jackson described some of the effects of the weather in his report, saying:

> *Long distances separated the pitches, the roads were vile, and the weather worse than vile... The concerts were given in... huts, leaky barns, flapping tents, in the open air, and in the mud. Chiefly in the mud! He [the soldier] will pack into a YMCA hut and get in twice as many as the hut will hold, and stand with a fog of steam rising from his dripping garments.*[80]

One of the most unusual venues was a Trappist Monastery which was used as a rest station. *The Firing Liners* appeared in the refectory to perform before 400 battle-fatigued soldiers newly out of the line. Nelson Jackson described the scene:

They all had the 'trench-look' in their eyes – the strained look of men who have been at grips with death for days and weeks. It is quite indescribable, but one is conscious of it. They seem to be listening. Though what they are listening for after the awful continuation of guns seems to be a mystery. Perhaps they are listening for silence.[81]

The concert party afforded the men some relief, at least for an hour and a half, from the stresses of war. The party's reception, once the show got under way, astonished the artistes. The soldiers, recorded Nelson Jackson:

Seized on every song, violin solo and jape as though they were children at a Christmas party... The following day the officers told us that the bracing effect of our concert had... Men... take a fresh interest in life.[82]

The concert party on this occasion was obviously in exactly the right place at the right time, and the vital remedial effects of laughter was clear to see. All doctors and medical officials were of the same opinion when referring to the concert parties: they unanimously agreed, as one commanding officer put it, that concerts 'act as a tonic and uplift to us, which does not wear off in a hurry'.[83] This applied to both staff and patient. War is a cruel process and inevitably the soldier, and the nurse, must at times don an emotionally cynically veneer – if for no other reason than for personal survival. The death of a man would affect his comrades, his family and his regiment but not the army, or the nation. There was, however, one exception. When Field-Marshal Lord Kitchener was drowned at sea in July, 1916, the British nation, and in particular the army, mourned his loss. At the time Kitchener was Secretary of State for War, and according to other members of the Cabinet, not the most efficient manager, but to many, including the historian, A.J.P. Taylor he was regarded as an 'outstanding military figure'.[84] The news of his death was initially received with incredulous derision, reported Jackson in *The Stage*, 'But as the dreaded truth became known the whole atmosphere changed. It was a worse blow than any inflicted by the enemy'.[85] Kitchener was a popular national hero.

Services commemorating the dead hero were held in various sectors of the Front. There was a small memorial service in the town where *The Firing Liners* concert party was staying, and their assistance was requested. The music was supplied by the party's pianist, Arthur Fagge, and violinist, Percy Sharman. The party's organizer recalls that:

The piano was not of the best, but the exquisite simplicity of the service and the greatness of the dead, gave the 'Death March' a new solemnity, and the wailing bugles thrilling [sic] the 'Last Post' broke all the barriers of emotion, and grief had its full sway.[86]

It is reported that the men would go to extraordinary lengths to hear a concert. Lena Ashwell writes of times when the hut was so crowded that the men '… climbed on the roof and tore off the slates, making holes through which they could see and hear'.[87] Even allowing for a degree of exaggeration, and the fact that there may have been attractive female artistes in the more rear-ward concert parties, it does not detract from the fact that men were desperate for entertainment, or at the very least a diversion from the gruesomeness of war. It was not uncommon for a touring party to find the marquee full and a thousand or more men waiting outside.

It was necessary, for reasons of concealment, to move troops during the hours of darkness. This meant that most of the concerts in the Line were done in the afternoons. The noises of war, as mentioned, presented problems for the artiste, but aerial bombardment was an actual danger, and at time concerts had to be abandoned. All the Front line parties petered out by February, 1917. The reason was, wrote Ashwell, that:

We could not continue this part of the work owing to the impossibility of getting men. There were no longer any men over age.[88]

Conscription age had been raised to fifty, and most men who were not in uniform were engaged in work covered by the terms of National Service.

In March, 1918 all concerts were suspended because, as Lena Ashwell put it, of 'the big battle'. Although the battle was not specified, it was, in fact, the Second Battle of the Somme. This was the biggest offensive by the Germans. It began on 21 March following a bombardment of the Allies' lines by 6,000 guns and a sustained gas attack. The Germans almost succeeded in breaking through. The Allies were handicapped by having a divided command and there was a breakdown in communications, but this problem was rectified when Marshal Foch was appointed General-in-Chief. The Germans had made notable progress and advanced 38 miles. The Allies did even-tually, after 16 days of heavy fighting, stop the advance but at a cost of

230,000 casualties, and the first battle of the German's final offensive ended on 6 April. This was immediately followed by a second assault against the sparsely-controlled British lines in Flanders. The centre of this sector was held temporarily, but an attack on the Portuguese Division which occupied the central position proved successful for the enemy. The Belgians, with British and Australian re-inforcements, slowed down the enemy's advance, and finally on 21 April Marshal Foch sent French reinforcements. This helped to offset the great German numerical superiority and the final enemy attack was repulsed. The battle ended on 27 April. Allied losses, nine-tenths of which were British, amounted to 305,000.

When battles were not actually in progress entertainment became limited to visits to the Front by a few single-handed entertainers – men who 'were able to get about more easily and be able to give an hour's programme on their own'.[89] However, the shortage of men became so acute that by late 1917 touring parties of women were allowed to tour in a number of sectors; and despite reservations felt by some in authority – who presumably thought the venture too hazardous – there was no alternative. The all-female concert parties were very successful because, as Lena Ashwell noted 'one can realize that it was an instant joy, as one man said... "to see a pair of slippers"... '.[90] The female touring parties comprised mainly musicians and singers, with some music hall turns. The Permanent Parties, on the other hand, were larger both in numbers and in their 'brief', that is they had additional functions.

PERMANENT PARTIES

The Permanent Parties – so called because they were located in a specific area, and did not tour the Front line sectors – were set up in the second year of the war. The first Permanent concert party started work in December, 1915, and was based at Le Havre. Each company consisted of 'four or five girls, an accompanist, instrumentalist, singers and humorist'.[91] The girls, it is assumed, although nowhere specified, acted in short sketches, as well as dancing and singing in the chorus. The tour for such parties lasted three months – three times as long as the Firing Line parties. The fact that they remained in one area for an extended period meant that the artiste had a more personal and knowledgeable relationship with the troops. They undertook the additional function of organizing concerts among the men themselves. They started theatre clubs for soldiers, 'and in some cases got up orchestras and choirs'.[92] The parties' location at Base camps meant they had access to the hospitals and hence most of their work was for the wounded and convalescent. The time spent after a show was as important as, if not more so than, the actual concert. Many Permanent Parties were managed by women, such as Sara Silvers who ran the Calais company. While there she wrote music to many of the 'stirring poems of Fox Smith and sang ballads'.[93] Considering the shortage of material, it was essential that producers should be both inventive and flexible in their programming of theatre entertainment. There were, however, restrictions on who could work in France. Any artiste who had a German relation, no matter how distant, was regarded as a security risk and was banned from the war-torn continent. In the case of Ada Ward, a lecturer and humorist, her tour was foreshortened, not because of an alien relative, but for the fact that her husband – who was a soldier – was posted to France. Perhaps it was considered unfair to other serving men whose spouses were at home; it might also divert a man's mind from the vital task of fighting.

The Permanent Parties, although located in areas of relative safety, were not totally immune to the perils of war. They could be, and were, at times bombarded. There is no record of civilian artistes being killed by shell fire, but there were other dangers. There was the precarious need to travel about at night across pock-marked battlefields. In February, 1918, it was reported in the *Daily Mirror* that Vincent Taylor, 'a young baritone of great promise' and Emily Pickford, a singer, were drowned in the Somme river when their car slid over an icy bank in the dark. The driver was also killed. The two singers were part of a Lena Ashwell concert party.[94]

The concert party visits arranged by Lena Ashwell were, wrote H.L. Hoare, a YMCA worker, in *The Englishwoman*, 'immensely appreciated; each party was enthusiastically received'.[95] Any criticism of the entertainments was reserved for military concert parties. The latter were, of course, at a definite disadvantage as there were no females in their cast, and the quality of performance varied considerably – from the very good 'ex-pro' to the enthusiastic but obviously amateur. The all-professional civilian party could also sing the latest songs, whereas the military troupes had to rely on the old and known favourites. H.L. Hoare seemed surprised that 'most of the songs [sung by soldiers] were about children dying young, and a man's best friend was his mother'. They were often sung unaccompanied and, Hoare commented:

... were very depressing to listen to, but the men loved them. The choicest one had a refrain which went – 'I've seen many children, but never one younger, that seemed so depressed at the loss of his dad' [96]

The civilian concert party's function was to bring laughter and remind the men of what life used to be (and could be) like. Some of the soldier entertainers, alternatively, seized the opportunity to express their cynicism publicly through song; the pathos of the words of the 'depressing song' was a form of ironic humour well understood by the soldier, but totally lost on H.L. Hoare. It was the derisive, black humour and seeming insensitivity of the soldiers' wit that helped them maintain a public 'brave face'. It would have been totally inappropriate for the non-combatant and female entertainer to do likewise. The Front line soldiers in their 'private' concerts were, like those witnessed by John Martin-Harvey on the tube train in London, inhabitants of a world divorced from that of the civilian – and in particular women – and this was reflected in their amusements: the jokes were 'broader', the sketches more risqué and the songs more cynical. The YMCA worker added, in his article, that the men 'in our camp were rather a rough class', and was consequently surprised that Dickens was the preferred author of the books the men borrowed from the hut library. This apparently patronizing attitude of the 'do-good' middle-class civilian towards the rank and file soldier was echoed in the choice of subjects by some lecturers, and by the likes of Martin-Harvey in his speeches of the 'worthwhileness of it all'. The same uncomprehending, some might say naive, view was forthcoming from Lady Smith-Dorrien, wife of General Sir H. Smith-Dorrien, who said in 1916 when referring to the type of dramatic entertainment she thought appropriate for the soldier:

> *He wants more plot... there is no need to encourage vicious thinking. The soldiers want nice, exciting plays with no harm in them, not thin, poor stuff that has to fall back on nastiness to get any snap at all. The Old Whip at Drury Lane, or such pieces as White Heather, are things they would love... Pieces with pretty music, charming scenes and nothing at all to stir unworthy passions.* [97]

It is true they wanted fantasy with colour, but what Lady Smith-Dorrien was advocating was frivolity; and evidence shows that the soldier was also ready for Shakespeare with all his 'unworthy passions'.

By the end of the war there existed eleven Permanent Concert Parties on the Western Front. The value of the work done by these concert parties was spelt out in a letter from Colonel Crawley to Lena Ashwell in 1916. It read:

> *You must have realized yourself the intense enjoyment that these concerts give to the men... you know what a grand service you and your artists have rendered them...* [98]

REPERTORY COMPANIES

The dramatic side of the entertainment work increased gradually. The servicemen had become used to the music hall style, and this had become the accepted norm, but in 1915 Lena Ashwell, in consultation with Gertrude Jennings – the actress and playwright – decided to increase the scope of entertainment on offer. The latter produced the first one-act play to be done at the Front. Gertrude Jennings took the opportunity to produce and act in one-act plays that she herself had written; they included: *Five Birds in a Cage*, *The Bathroom Door*, *No Servants*, *Waiting for the Bus*, and *In the Fog*. Jennings' theatrical group comprised three musicians who also doubled as actors, although it was still, ostensibly, a concert party and not a drama company.[99] It was not until 1916 that the first repertory company was formed. The subsequent development was inevitably the production of full-length plays and the introduction of more serious drama.

Initially there appeared to be some feelings of apprehension regarding the inclusion of classical drama. Who from, it is not known, but in 1916 Penelope Wheeler – an actress – went to France at the invitation of the YMCA to perform Greek plays. At first she invited a Sergeants' Mess to hear her read a Greek tragedy, the *Electra of Euripides*, and to the astonishment of Lena Ashwell – who was one of the initial sceptics – the soldiers not only understood the play, but asked to hear more serious drama played. The first play Penelope Wheeler produced was an old miracle play *The Three Shepherds*, at the Central YMCA at Le Havre.

By 1917 Penelope Wheeler was producing a new (short) play every week, and it seems that she was making every attempt to reach a new audience, in two senses of the word, for as organizer Lena Ashwell noted:

... every week [the company] play in different camps, but every Wednesday and Friday they played at the Central, and the seats were entirely for the men; officers were only admitted if there was room... There were a great number of men to whom the theatre was an absolute new experience.[100]

There was also a special matinee every Saturday for the convalescents. Eric Patterson, Professor of Economics and Literature at Oxford, was the Director of the Central YMCA at Le Havre, and considering his interests it is likely that Penelope Wheeler had his co-operation in her efforts to widen the dramatic repertoire.

The second dramatic party went out in March 1916. They took: *The Bathroom Door*, *In the Fog*, *Mother o'Pearl* and *The Lady in Black*, although this time they went to different venues at Dieppe, Etaples and Le Tréport.[101] The plays were often performed in the open air, and with the minimum of props. Performing in the open meant that, besides the obvious difficulties associated with acting in a war zone, there remained the technical challenge of projecting to a large audience in an open space; added to which the vagaries of the weather could spoil the show. In 1916, a performance of *The Bathroom Door* and James Barrie's *The Twelve Pound Look*, both one-act plays, were done, for the most part, in 'torrential rain'. The whole audience at this hospital venue, wrote Lena Ashwell, 'was bed-bound with no cover'.[102] The troops made every effort to accommodate the players, and none more so than the men at the horses' hospital at Forges Les Faux. In an effort to make the area as theatrical as possible the men surrounded the stage with a ring of flowers instead of footlights, and for a backcloth they draped a huge Union Jack. The play to be performed on this occasion was Sheridan's *The School for Scandal*. In the Base camps, where there was a more mixed audience, props could be scrounged from the soldiers, airmen, nurses, and even civilians. Those supplying the theatrical props naturally received reciprocal payment in kind, and got the best seats. [103]

As with the touring and permanent parties, the repertory companies suffered from a shortage of male actors. The deficit was, in part, overcome by the inclusion of amateurs, and professional actors serving with the armed forces, although the latter could cause acute problems as they were liable to be moved elsewhere at any time.[104] On occasions a repertory company was lucky enough to be able to call on the services of an experienced and well-known actor. Cicely Hamilton, who was in-charge of the 2nd Repertory Company at Abbeville was, for example, particularly fortunate in having Leslie Banks – a seasoned 27-year-old repertory actor – as leading man. This was when he was free from his duties as gas officer.[105] Leslie Banks served from 1914 to 1918 as a member of the Essex Regiment before continuing his career in repertory and later in the West End.

It was not easy persuading the dwindling number of eligible actors to tour France. Some felt that a lack of professional exposure at home due to working abroad would damage their careers, and hence Lena Ashwell employed, at varying times, two amateurs: Frank Macey (a builder) and Paget Bowman (a solicitor). The latter was to become a director of the National Opera Company.[106]

Following the success of Gertrude Jennings and others, Lena Ashwell toured with one of Jennings's plays, *The Bathroom Door*, in which she and the authoress acted; although it was Lena Ashwell who had star billing. Included in the programme was J.M. Barrie's *The Twelve Pound Look*, and scenes from *Macbeth*. Interestingly, the programme also included songs, one of which, *Friend O'Mine*, was sung by the noted singer George Burrows. In the company were the two amateurs and Ben Field, a professional actor who was past the enlistment age. The scene-changes and resultant alterations in mood were indicated by Theodore Flint at the piano, and during the intermission the depot band provided the music. The company was billed as the London Party.[107]

The idea of including Shakespeare came from the soldiers. They, or at least a considerable number of them, wanted more than the light escapism of the one-act comedies. Referring to the scenes from *Macbeth*, a reporter in the *Yorkshire Observer* in 1916 stated:

> *Anyone who said that the masses wanted the lowest class of amusement and did not want education is a liar.*[108]

Under the direction of Cicely Hamilton the repertory company at Abbeville widened its programme to include: *The School for Scandal, Quality Street, Just to get Married, His Excellency the Governor, Much Ado about Nothing* and *The Taming of the Shrew*. Lena Ashwell attempted to raise a full cast, but the ubiquitous problem concerning lack of male actors meant the Sheridan comedy, like the Shakespearian dramas, had to be acted in scenes rather than in full. *The School for Scandal* was first performed in a ward, 'with a backdrop of flags'. Whether all the men enjoyed the production cannot be known, but women in brightly coloured costumes must have been a very welcome sight.[109]

The repertory companies gave as many as three performances a day; one in the afternoon for the hospitalized, and another two in the evenings in the camp/hut theatre. The London Party that produced the two one-act plays and *Macbeth* did seventy shows in the course of one month in 1916.[110] The different venues had their own particular problems. In the hospitals many, if not most, of the audience would be bed-ridden, and therefore not always in a position to see what was being acted. The difficulty was surmounted by the actors showing themselves, prior to the show, 'to the wounded who were lying in beds outside the hut, so that when they could hear the dialogue they would know what the actors looked like'.[111] The theatre companies and the audience were not always restricted to makeshift provision. Occasionally the French citizens were considerate enough to allow the company to use the local theatre, but permission to do this had in any case to be sought from the British Base Commander. This imposed formality was, naturally, thought of as an imposition by the French, and, as a result entente cordiale became strained as 'feelings ran a little high' at times.[112]

The greatest achievement by the company at Rouen was the staging of the operetta *The Mikado* in March, 1919. It was a notable production because it was done in its entirety and with a mixed company; males and females, military and civilian personnel, professionals and amateurs. The show was produced by Mary Barton and the musical director was Llewelyn Bevan. The orchestra was composed of British and Canadian military bandsmen, and the cast came from every contingent in the Base camp. It is also worth noting that the company included both officers and other ranks. The producer was amused during rehearsals when watching the men in their heavy boots, manipulating their tiny Japanese fans; however, she said 'because of the severe drill they had been through, they were much quicker in picking up movements than the women, and much less conscious of themselves'.[113] Permission was sought and given by the Base Commander and the Matron in charge of the nurses for their respective personnel to be in the show. This reinforces the fact that those in authority were not only in favour, but also supportive of entertainment.

Much, if not most, of the secular entertainment was done in the YMCA theatres, but the organization was very conscious of its religious

WITH BRITISH EXPEDITIONARY FORCES

Lena Ashwell Concerts at the Front

THÉATRE-DES-ARTS

TUESDAY, MARCH 4th, 1919
WEDNESDAY, MARCH 5th, 1919
THURSDAY, MARCH 6th, 1919

7.45 p.m.

THE MIKADO

By W.S. Gilbert and Arthur Sullivan.

PERFORMED BY

Officers, N.C.O.'s and men of H.M. Expeditionary Forces
Administrators and Workers of Q.M.A.A.C.
Workers of Y.M.C.A. and U.A.E
Stationed in the Rouen Area

BY PERMISSION OF

Major-Gen. Sir Edward Graham, K.C.B.
Brig.-Gen. L.F. Phillps, C.M.G. D.S.O. (Base Commandant)
Miss Deputran, D.C.Q.M.A.A.C.

PROGRAMME :- 30 CMS.

Special Notice.

The Y.M.C.A. desires to express regret that through oversight
these performances should clash with the commencement of the
Lenten season. While it is the purpose of the Y.M.C.A. to give free
expression to all that is best in social life, even more it desires to
observe and promote the religious interests of men, and the
arrangements of the Christian Church to this end. The date of Ash
Wednesday was overlooked. As all seats had been sold it was thus
too late to change the date of the programme.

Figure 31. The programme for the Lena Ashwell production of *The Mikado* 1917 [L.J. Collins]

function. The opening of *The Mikado* clashed with the start of the Christian observance of Lent, which included the holy day of Ash Wednesday. The YMCA management, not wishing to disappoint the theatre company or spoil the troops' pleasure, did not cancel the show – besides which all the tickets had been sold. But the YMCA director felt obliged publicly to distance, if not exonerate the YMCA from sinful blame, by including a Special Notice in the programme which explained the YMCA's action (*Figure 31*).

Civilian repertory companies were established at Le Havre, Rouen, Abbeville, Etaples, Dieppe, Trouville and Paris. The more dangerous venues, were, of course, the preserve of the concert parties, but the repertory companies were not immune. At Abbeville in 1918, the town was continually subjected to air raids by German Gothas for a period of two months. Most of the billets were damaged or demolished so the theatre party sought refuge in tents in the nearby forest of Crecy. The town was reasonably safe during the day time, and so at 8 o'clock each morning the artistes caught the train back to town in time to rehearse and perform in the afternoon and early evening shows.[114]

The repertory theatre in Paris was opened on 29 June, 1918, at the Theatre Albert in the presence of Lord Derby and the Corps Diplomatique. The arrangements were again by courtesy of the YMCA, and in particular a Mr Worthington whose job it was to organize trips for men to the capital; approximately 3,000 British and Empire troops a day arrived on leave or were departing from the city: there was no shortage of audiences. Theatre rents were high in Paris but the Comédie Française helped by allowing the company to rehearse at their premises, and even invited them to give some matinee shows.

Following the Armistice in November, 1918, the men were naturally anxious to get home as soon as possible, but it was to take some time before all the conscripts could be demobbed. 'Demobilization' wrote A.J.P. Taylor 'threatened to provoke violent disturbance' as men were not prepared to go back to the old pre-war conditions.[115] They had had enough of life that relied on unquestioning obedience to an all-powerful authority. There was a mutiny at Calais and Folkestone. The War Office had devised a scheme for discharging the men most required by industry, but this often meant that those were the last to have been called up. At home 3,000 men marched in protest from Victoria station and occupied Horse Guards Parade. The government felt they could not respond by relying on other soldiers to disperse them. Winston Churchill, then Secretary of State for War, seeing the danger, took the initiative and scrapped the War Office scheme by immediately introducing the simple formula of 'first in, first out'. This expedient action appeased most of the men. By September, 1919, four out of five men had been released from the Services, but as there was still a large number in uniform entertainment for the troops was to continue until late in 1919.

Entertainment was, in one way, more necessary as troops became increasingly bored with the relative inactivity, and, of course, they now had the time to show any resentment they may have had towards the bureaucratic military and political machine that held them against their will. At Harfleur valley the men demonstrated their discontent, only this time it was over food rationing. Put simply, as there was no fighting, there was less food: the result was a riot. There was, recorded Lena Ashwell, a great deal of trouble over the hard-tack biscuits given to British troops to eat – particularly for those with no teeth. The men complained several times through the official channel, but to no avail. They finally, in total frustration, broke into the canteen and stole the bread that was destined to be sold to them. Lena Ashwell comments on the incident in her autobiography, and on the part played later by the repertory company. She wrote:

> *The outbreak was instantaneous. They [the soldiers] burnt the canteen and other huts. The riot lasted all night and there was some shooting.*[116]

In an effort to pacify the men, emotionally calm them down and hence control them, the repertory company was called for; they came, and all other engagements were cancelled. The only play ready for production was *Candida* by Bernard Shaw. The atmosphere in the theatre was very tense, but 'Gradually the men grew interested and the evil spell was broken'.[117] In the play the young rebellious Marchbanks does not succeed in gaining the love of Candida. The status quo is maintained when she reaffirms her devotion to her clergyman husband, Morell. The play is one of anti-climax in which the rebel is ousted and the old order is maintained. Thus the play, it could be said, mirrored the men's position ironically.

Civilian theatre on the Western Front took several forms, and the professional directors and producers were called upon to work with both the civilian and military companies. Penelope Wheeler, for example, apart from managing a professional civilian troupe, had, in 1917, seven soldier theatre companies to run. The first play the soldiers chose to perform at Le Havre was *A Night at the Inn* by Lord Dunsany, a one-act play which contains three murders and four deaths.[118] The work done by the enterprising stage managers in France and Belgium was prodigious considering the abnormal conditions in which they worked. The known list of managers-cum-directors included: Cicely Hamilton, Penelope Wheeler, Gertrude Jennings, Mary Barton, Marie Ault and Messes Oswald Marshal and H. Lomas.

CONCERT PARTIES ON THE EASTERN FRONT

In 1916, the parameters of the civilian concert parties extended to include entertaining those fighting in Turkey, the Mediterranean, the Balkans and Palestine. The first concert party to venture eastwards bound for Malta left London on 12 February, 1916. It went at the request of Lady Methuen, wife of Admiral Lord Methuen. Its specific task was to entertain the sick and wounded soldiers from Gallipoli and Salonika, as well as the sailors who fought at Suvla Bay and the Dardanelles.

Malta had become not only a strategic naval port and stores depot, but also a very large hospital base. Venues were diverse enough for the concert party to include, beside the hospitals, a large hall called Australia Hall – built by the ANZACS – which held fifteen hundred people, the ballroom at Government House, and the Opera House. Concerts were also held on board various classes of warship. The concert party was not confined to the Mediterranean base as invitations from the Navy meant trips to Italy to entertain the Adriatic Fleet. It was, by all accounts, an exhausting tour as the schedule included two, sometimes three, shows a day at venues that were some considerable distance apart. A number of the performers found it tiring as the 'usual practice was for each artiste to sing four songs consecutively, and do it twice in each show'; on this evidence it does not seem too punishing a schedule, but without details of the precise distances travelled, living conditions, or war-related dangers it is impossible to judge.[119] The first party was on tour for five months, and included more classical fare in its programme than that which was offered on the Western Front. Lena Ashwell outlined a 'Specimen programme' which included the following:

Handel's *Largo*
Adagio from *Concerto in G Minor* from Mendelssohn
'She alone Charmeth my Sadness' by Gounod
Violin Solo 'Romance' by Svendsen
Prelude and *Allegro* by Pugnami Kreisler
Aria from *Tosca* by Puccini
Una Boce Poco Fa by Rossini.[120]

Occasionally the professional performers were able to relax when they in turn were entertained by military concert parties. Two more parties, due to the demand, left the UK some few weeks later. The second and third concert parties to disembark at Malta were not under the customary authority of the YMCA, but the Red Cross. The latter acted as their sponsors and undertook the financial responsibility.[121] This affiliation to the Red Cross was further recognition of the valuable medical-related work the entertainers were doing. In a minute to the Director of Medical Services for the Armed Forces, Admiral Lord Methuen wrote in March, 1916:

> *I attribute the orderly conduct of the patients in a great measure to the concerts and other amusements so admirably organized in the different hospitals and camps.*[122]

It was the Admiral who asked for the additional second and third parties to be sent to cater for the recreational needs of the 60,000 or so patients in the hospitals.

The war on the Gallipoli Peninsula and the Dardanelles waterway had begun on 3 November, 1914, when the Turkish ports were bombarded by Allied squadrons. The abortive landings began on 25 April, 1915, but a withdrawal – the only successful operation of the campaign – took place on the 9 and 10 January, 1916. The bungling inefficiency of General Hamilton and the delaying apathy of General Stopford led to a casualty list totalling 250,000. Those who survived would have stayed for varying periods of time at Malta before being transported back to Britain. The concerts were needed for some time in Malta as the island did not cease to be a hospital staging-post until 1918.

The first concert party to visit the island returned to the UK for a short period of recuperation before being re-formed and departing again on 30 September, 1916, only this time bound for Egypt. The intention was to stay in Egypt for six months, but due to the dangers of sea travel, they were prohibited from returning home. In the event they did not arrive back in Britain until after the Armistice some two years later. The party was under the direction of Theodore Flint who had already seen 'theatrical service' in France, and had been in charge of the first Malta party.[123]

The concert party gave shows in the by-now familiar venues: hospital ships, army camps, local Opera House (Cairo) and theatres constructed or converted by the military (Alhambra, Alexandra). The party spent Christmas, 1917 in the Libyan desert before accompanying the British and Colonial forces into the Sinai, then following General Allenby, after the defeat of the Turks, into Palestine. Once there they gave concerts in Jerusalem. One of the shows was for a very mixed audience which included British and Indian military personnel, nurses and priests of different religions. It is recorded that the Military Governor wrote a letter expressing his appreciation and gratitude, saying that the concert was politically as well as socially beneficial.[124] Two of the party departed – after the Armistice – to get married, which left the remaining four performers to give concerts to audiences of up to 5,000 men. The army, along with the Military Governor, was also very appreciative as a letter from General Dobell to the YMCA Auxiliary Committee indicated. An indication of the party's importance can, said the General, be judged by the fact that they were allow to go where 'no civilians in any circumstances had previously been allowed to go'.[125] It is possible that the concerts gained an added importance as the men on the Eastern Front were further from home, unlikely to get to see their families as often and, compared with those fighting in Europe, may have felt forgotten; the sight of civilian and female artistes singing familiar songs must have been a tremendous morale boost.

RAISING OF FUNDS

The Auxiliary Committee of the YMCA had three primary concerns: the selection and hiring of artistes; the administrative arrangements of concert parties; and the raising of large sums of money. The organization of civilian concert parties abroad became a major operation, and all that was achieved could not have been done without vital private funding.

Many of the professional artistes worked for nothing, which was a great saving, but those who did receive payment were not – as was the case in the commercial theatre – remunerated in accordance to their artistic status, or their money-making potential. Fees covered only their out-of-pocket expenses 'which would go on at home while they were abroad' and ranged from one guinea per week [£1.05p] to £7-10s per week [£7.50].[126] Billeting and travel were free but the mandatory YMCA uniform (with its slightly different cut and concert badge) had to be paid for from funds raised from the public.

Over the period from August, 1914 to November, 1918, the theatrical profession raised £100,000 (over £3,000,000 in 1994 terms) for 'Concerts at the Front'. The money came mainly from matinee receipts. The first of the matinee fund-raising shows was performed in the presence of Royalty at the Coliseum on 25 March, 1915. Those present included: Queen Mary, Queen Alexandra, Princess Mary, Princess Victoria, Princess Helena Victoria and Princess Alexandra of Teck. The money collected amounted to £1,500. The raising of cash was not limited to London venues. The Prince of Wales Theatre at Birmingham, with the aid of the D'Oyly Carte Repertory Opera Company, gave a show in June, 1917 with the specific purpose of raising funds for this cause. The collection of cash via matinee shows for the Concerts Fund was a feature in theatres all over Britain.

It was the task of Miss Olga Hartley (journalist, minor novelist and Lena Ashwell's press secretary) to write to the newspapers requesting financial help, and as a result of her efforts a sum of £1,000 was added to the coffers in 1915. But by 1917 the public had become tired of the endless charity matinees for the variety of 'good causes' – many of which were below par in quality – and the numerous begging letters in the press. Different means were, therefore, required to induce the public to part with their money. In 1917, a novel bazaar was held at the Royal Albert Hall. The additional and main attraction at the event was a lottery, in which the first prize was a freehold piece of land on the Chiltern Hills. The donor of the gift, and possessor of such unusual largess, was Baroness d'Erlanger. The demand for tickets was very high and the organizers had to operate a night shift in order to cope. Other prizes included: 'a bathroom with porcelain bath, beautiful dresses from London dressmakers, pedigree puppies', and perhaps most fantastic of all, 'a pedigree bull'. The amount of profit accruing from the bazaar is unknown, but whatever the amount, it was certainly a welcomed benefit to the Concerts' appeal fund. Tombola tickets for the Albert Hall bazaar were sold as far afield as Liverpool, and a further £1,000 was raised.

In Liverpool, the city's Lord Mayor, having had the experience of seeing the shell-shocked and neurasthenic cases and the beneficial effect of recuperative entertainment provided by the concert parties, began his own fund. The Lord Mayor's Khaki Fund, as it was called, advertised in the local press and thus raised the considerable sum of £6,207 for the 'Concerts at the Front' appeal. The need for such entertainments and its funding was emphasized by Field-Marshal Sir Douglas Haig who publicized his support in the *Liverpool Daily Post* in November, 1917.[127]

Others, amongst them Lena Ashwell, made personal appearances in different cities throughout Britain where they addressed a variety of institutions. Lena Ashwell spoke to the Cardiff Dock Exchange, and subsequently received a donation for £1,500. She noted in her autobiography that it was often the poorer areas that gave proportionally the most money.

The efforts of the Ladies Committee of the YMCA to finance the concerts were usually but not always successful. They were not welcomed in Edinburgh. This was due, in the main, to a vociferous attack launched at Lena Ashwell and her committee in *The Thistle*, a Scottish Patriotic Magazine, in which she was referred to as a pirouetting 'English heroine who has at last subdued Scotland and placed it under her heel'.[128] The perpetrator of this attack was Sir Robert K. Inches, ex-Lord Provost of the city. He objected to the fact that Scotland would not be allowed to send independent concert parties to France, and that any arrangements had to be via the YMCA Committee. He also did not accept the fact that Lena Ashwell was the national organizer, and as such had the final say regarding selection of artistes; in effect, he totally disregarded her professional expertise on the grounds that she was a foreigner. In *The Thistle* of December, 1916, under the heading 'Scandalous Insult to Scotland', Sir Robert wrote vehemently about the three leading female YMCA Committee members, saying:

> *What have these people to do with Scottish Songs and Scottish Singers...*
> *and who are the Princess Victoria of Schleswig-Holstein, and her hench-*
> *woman, Miss Ashwell... Apparently this "Ladies' Auxiliary Committee"*
> *has resolved itself into a committee of three – a Patroness, a dictatrix,*
> *and a treasurer. The first, a German Princess; the second, a theatrical*
> *damsel of a very aggressive type and an official recorder of the ordinary*
> *character... 'The Ladies' Committee' seems to be in reality an 'Anglo-*
> *German Committee' of two, whose aim is to insult and mutilate Scotland!*[129]

It may be that he felt his status as Chairman of the Scottish Edinburgh Committee was being undermined, as he believed it was his job to organize such entertainments. Lena Ashwell, by all accounts, appears to have been a strong-willed and dominant character, but how much this contributed to the ex-Lord Provost's reaction is not known. It cannot be denied, though, that she had the necessary professional experience to do the job, and over a period of two years had gained the confidence and support of the military authorities.

In the other great Scottish city, Glasgow, the response was quite different. The Glasgow authorities were much more amenable, and financially generous. A visit was later arranged for a special 'firing-line' concert party from the city to tour the Front in 1917 – by, of course, the Ladies' Auxiliary Committee!

There were over 800 civilian artistes contracted to work in the Western and Eastern war zones. And in total the concert parties and theatre companies gave, between 1915 and 1919, over 14,000 performances a year.[130]

It was the civilian concert parties that were the main providers of entertainment for the hospitalized and those convalescing; and it would seem that the civilian rather than the military was the best suited for such work. The civilian concert party had a greater range of musical skills (and possibly instruments) and were able to provide more appropriate and soothing music for the sick and dying. The civilian, particularly the female artistes, offered a link, albeit an ephemeral one, with home, and evidence suggests that the time spent talking to individual patients was as important as the actual concert. Some entertainers had the time to work with the men suffering from shell-shock, and a number of patients attended rehearsals for military concert parties run by a civilian producer. It is unlikely that theatrical participation was always effectively therapeutic, but it certainly provided a psychological release for some, and could be a comfort to others.

There is no doubt entertainment in all its forms was very popular, although J G Fuller, quoting a regimental officer, implies that enter-tainment 'flourished rather upon its own initiative than due to the ordination of the General Staff'.[132] In the first months of the war this may have been true, as the minds of those in charge were focussed on the enormity of the task ahead; but very soon the General Staff became aware of the vital contribution made by entertainers, both military and civilian. This is made clear by the numerous letters from staff officers from Field-Marshal Lord Haig down. If the General Staff did not actually ordain theatre entertainment, they certainly endorsed it; indeed, without the Staff's permission it could not have gone ahead.

What percentage of the entertainment was military, and what civilian, is now impossible to determine. According to Fuller, 'Civilian troupes were rarely seen by the front-line soldiers';[133] but a greater proportion of a fighting soldier's time was spent in billets and rest camps. By the end of the war there were 25 civilian concert parties touring the war zones, and most of them were stationed at Base camps. Evidence, therefore, indicates that most, if not all, soldiers had the opportunity to see civilian troupes performing.

The first civilian concert party left England in 1914 with the simple but expressed purpose of giving the fighting men some light relief from the mental and physical strains of war. By 1918, the scope of entertainment had broadened, become highly organized and relatively sophisticated. Its overall success, despite the inappropriateness of some of the offerings, was due to the complicity of the General Staff, the structure and facilities of the YMCA, the enthusiasm of the artistes and producers, and the organizational ability of the YMCA Ladies' Auxiliary Committee under the leadership of Lena Ashwell. In recognition of the function and value of the theatrical work done, Lena Ashwell was awarded the Order of the British Empire medal for her unique contribution.

War Plays

G.T. Watts, a war-time critic writing in 1916, was of the opinion that 'legitimate' theatre had all but disappeared.[1] That no new plays now universally acclaimed were staged in Britain during the Great War is indisputable; although as Allardyce Nicoll points out, 'It would be... foolish to deny that... the London playhouses for the most part sank into becoming the purveyors of the cheapest entertainment'.[2] Both Watts and later Nicoll, whilst appearing to disagree about the extent, do in effect dismiss the period. Watts, in fact, totally disregarded the classical productions performed during the war years. The Old Vic Theatre, under the control of Lilian Baylis, continued to produce the Bard's work throughout the conflict; and in 1916 there were many productions of Shakespeare in celebration of his tercentenary. Nicoll, while acknowledging that not all drama was of the popularized kind, mentions only the more successful shows such as *Chu Chin Chow* and ignores the plethora of war plays. This selective view of theatre overlooks the socio-political needs of the time, and therefore rejects, albeit unwittingly, the contemporary psychological and propagandist function of the theatre. In the *Revel's History of Drama in English* Vol VIII, the authors proclaim that 'It was not only problem plays that were swept off the board, but nearly all plays of quality'.[3] The *Revel's History* devotes two pages to the theatre of 1914–18 (not much, but a great deal more than most historical accounts); and within this summary the effects of the war on the stage are likened to the closing of the theatres in 1642.

The most obvious, and it could be argued beneficial, role for the commercial theatre was that of providing antidotal entertainment during a time of universal stress. The desire for popular diversionary amusement was, understandably, great; but the function of theatre went beyond the utilitarian advantages of comical revue and musical comedy. The war play and the war-related productions served other discernible roles.

The war plays can be categorized in two ways. First, there were those that dealt with specific issues regarding the war – the vast majority of which were concerned with spying. Secondly, there are the war-related plays which, if stripped of their war setting, could be classified as the usual melodramas or farce. The latter are included in the definition of war plays because they often incorporated a secondary function; that is, they could be both patriotic and propagandist in content as well as, say, romantic and farcically comic. The war plays accounted for a very large proportion of theatre output. Research shows that within the first twelve months of conflict nearly 120 war plays were passed by the Lord Chamberlain's Office for subsequent production. The second twelve months saw a reduction in number to just over ninety. Despite the reduction such a volume of theatrical processing cannot be dismissed entirely, no matter how low in literary regard many of the productions may have been judged.

RECRUITMENT AND PATRIOTISM

In the first two years enthusiasm for the war was almost unanimous but with the absence of any decisive victories, and the dearth of good plays, managers looked to historical figures to provide the models of the British fighting-spirit. Thus it was suggested in *The Era* that Sir Herbert Tree should use the drama *Henry V* 'with its magnificent appeal to the patriotism of the nation spoken by the King in Act III, Sc 1', for the purposes of recruiting. It was, as noted, Frank Benson, and not Tree who put on *Henry V* at the Shaftesbury Theatre on Boxing Day, 1914. And, of course, feelings of nationalistic excitement ran high in that first year of the war. Benson's emotional performance was marked by 'an unwonton [sic] fervour... He evidently, felt himself to be not merely playing the stage-part, but delivering a solemn message' wrote *The Times* reporter.[4]

The most ingenious use of Shakespeare and his characters was seen in a 'One act Extravaganza' by Mary Packington, entitled *Shakespeare for Merrie England*. It was produced at the Theatre Royal, Worcester in April, 1915. The drama concerns a German professor who has the preposterous idea of decorating a bust of Shakespeare with a wreath inscribed 'To the Divine Teuton Wilhelm the Third'.[5] The play takes place in the professor's sub-conscious as he dreams of the meetings he has with Shakespeare's heroines, all of whom are indignant at his claim of national relationship. Beatrice goads him; Lady Macbeth, in more aggressive mood, threatens him; while Rosalind chaffs him in rhyme. Portia argues with him and finally Titania ends up placing an ass's head on his shoulders. Satire was a favourite form of attack, particularly in the one-act plays and sketches, and naturally the Germans were the focus of much ridicule.

More recent historical figures and the depiction of their military victories via revivals, such as *Drake* at His Majesty's Theatre in August, 1914, helped promote feelings of patriotic fervour and further entice young men to enlist. So enthusiastic were the patrons at the showing of *Drake* that during one of the intervals the entire audience stood and sang the national anthems of the Allied Forces, and, not unexpectedly, they also joined the company in singing *God Save the King* at the culmination of the scene of Drake's final triumph.[6] It is doubtful if the singing of the Allied Forces' anthems was spontaneous as it is unlikely that most people would have known the words. It is assumed that the audience were given song sheets, or more likely conducted whilst following an enlarged communal song board displayed on the stage. Another revival was *The Dynasts* by Thomas Hardy, produced by the stage's most noted director Granville Barker, at the Kingsway Theatre in November, 1914. The play harked back to the days of Wellington and Nelson. Any reminder of Britain's 'glorious past' had powerful sentimental value and was a well-used ploy in the effort to engender patriotic sentience, and for some it probably acted as a 'call to arms'. The theatre, via its plays and public assemblage, was an ideal vehicle for the transmission of such historically-linked sentimentalism.

The many new plays dealing with the current conflict were written and produced in haste, and it is difficult, if not impossible, to separate recruitment from patriotism as the former is dependent on the latter. Clearly, not everyone witnessing a war play was eligible for recruitment into the armed forces. The plays were not, however, necessarily directed just at the younger men. The women too were urged to do their duty; whether that meant doing war work – nursing or working in a munitions factory – or, at the very least, ensuring that the menfolk went into uniform.

A theatrical entertainment also provided the circumstances where large, and often socially disparate collections of people could, and would, give voice to their emotion. This could manifest itself in spontaneous vocalization, or contrived communal singing – as in the Drake production. The theatre, therefore, provided a perfect setting for engineering a corporate sense of patriotic identity. It also meant, because of the social diversity of the audience, that a play's message(s) must appeal to the different social classes. An example of employing a broad appeal can be seen in the play *Home To Tipperary* produced at the Court Theatre in December, 1914.[7] In the first scene Sir Dennis, a landlord, and Patsy a peasant, enlist – much to the chagrin of their womenfolk. The end result is that, after having braved great danger and being believed by everyone to have been killed, they return heroes. Following a stirring speech by Sir Dennis all the men in the village enlist. The universality of 'the cause' was also strongly underlined in *The Man Who Wouldn't* at the Kilburn Empire in April, 1915. The man is characterized as a selfish, middle-aged solicitor who is vehemently against any of his class enlisting. He jeers at a friend for joining the National Volunteer Forces and forbids his daughter's fiancé to enlist. The solicitor, displaying a seemingly arrogant, pompous and ignorant manner, derides the working class; saying:

> *... there are plenty of men who haven't much to give up... who haven't got a house, or a profession, and good prospects. Let them go and fight.*

The lawyer's arguments and views are opposed by his clerk, who retorts:

> *No, Sir... the man who's lucky enough to have a successful career to look forward to is the chap who ought to be first to enlist. He's got something to fight for.*[8]

Inevitably the solicitor recants and completely changes his stance. His conversion comes during a dream in which he visualizes the possible effects of an enemy occupation of his home.

The message was that the war affected everyone and that social differences were an irrelevant factor, and that 'King and Country' came before self and family. To men this meant actually donning military uniform, or answering the call in the form of National Service. The latter also applied to women, although their contribution was usually voluntary; even knitting socks for soldiers was regarded as a patriotic duty. Teenagers, too, were not exempt as service in any sort of uniform was considered patriotic. The number of youngsters in organizations such as the British National Cadet Association (Army Cadets), Boys and Girls Brigades, Scouts and Girl Guides expanded considerably, and service in any uniformed youth organization was regarded highly. Community and family involvement was exemplified in *A Bit of Khaki*, a musical sketch at the Empress Theatre,

Brixton in May, 1915. In the sketch a father objects to his daughter's engagement, but when her fiancé appears in khaki and the daughter in a Girl Guides' uniform, he relents and decides to do his duty by joining the Special Constabulary.[9] A similar scene occurred at the York Empire in the play *One o'Kitchener's*, in September, 1915.[10]

If every character in a play joined the armed forces at the sight of a uniform then not only would this have been totally unrealistic, it would have robbed the drama of one of its essential ingredients, that is, conflict. Besides which, some men could not join the forces no matter how much they desired to do so, so both the conflict and a compromise had to be sought. In *Listing for a Sojar* (sic) at the Hippodrome, Oldham in 1914, an answer was forthcoming. In the play a wife sneers at her husband's intention to enlist, but then becomes distressed when she realizes it is not an idle threat. Meantime he is adjudged to be medically unfit. The couple eventually settle their differences and vow to do their patriotic duty by taking in two Belgian refugee children.[11] The play, apart from stressing the need for individual and national patriotic effort, was particularly topical as Belgian refugees were still crossing the channel to seek refuge in Britain following the German advance. In fact, before the play opened in September, 1914, Britain had agreed to take 100,000 such refugees.[12]

The conflict between husband and wife, boy and girlfriend was a recurring theme in the recruiting plays. Occasionally the woman tried to dissuade the man from enlisting, but more often the reverse was true. In *The Sportsman* in 1915, the wife berates her husband for not enlisting and calls him a coward, but changes her mind when she finds he is unfit for service.[13] In *The Way to Win*, also in 1915, a Frenchwoman tells her English boyfriend, a sculptor who is dissatisfied with a statue of victory he is carving, that he can only properly comprehend the full meaning of his artistic expression by seeing things as a man: in short, by enlisting.[14] The goading of a man by a woman on stage was designed to pierce a young man's image of himself by attacking his ego. Those characters that enlisted were lauded as heroes whereas those who could but didn't were branded uncompromisingly as cowards. Nowhere was this expressed more strongly than by a woman in a speech to her future husband in *The Call* at the Tivoli Theatre, Manchester, in 1915. The woman is unequivocal towards him, his duty and their relationship, saying:

Don't touch me. Or I'll go mad... You've no place here... I loved you –
but that's done with. Love goes with respect. I don't respect you, now...
How can I trust myself to you? You can't stand the test.... Don't touch me.
The man that stayed at home![15]

On stage, duty and patriotism were often portrayed as more than
answering the nation's call. It was personalized and given added
urgency and emphasis by stressing the basic emotional bonds of trust,
respect and love that ought to exist between a man and a woman. This
pressure, both social and psychological, brought to bear on the man
in particular, was not confined to the stage. The playwrights acted,
initially, as an unsolicited 'pressure group' which helped to fuel the
fires of patriotism set alight by the media. Pressure also came from
the Government, a person's peer group, his work place and for some
from the young girls with their white feathers.

In the plays dealing specifically with middle-class characters, as
in *The Man Who Wouldn't* the concept of sacrifice was stressed. The
loss of material wealth, career and professional success were viewed
as being almost as important as family separation. This is well illustrated in the aptly titled *Supreme Sacrifice*. This drama concerns a
young, newly-married couple, the husband of which has just been
offered a partnership in his firm. He wrestles with the thoughts of
domestic and business prosperity while, at the same time, he feels
bound to take the honourable course when his wife asks 'Have we
any right to be thinking of ourselves – our own business – when others
are thinking of their country?'[16] The theme of sacrifice persists in J.M.
Barrie's *The New World*. Although the play deals mainly with the
self-conscious relationship between a father and son, the author refers
to the sacrifice of the mother; namely, the departure of an only son to
war. To emphasize the point the mother talks of an older child who,
had he lived, would have been aged twenty-one in 1915. And on seeing
her remaining son in uniform she says 'I wouldn't have had one of
you stay at home, though I had had a dozen'.[17]

The portrayal of war in drama had to show, if it was to have any
credence, that the burden of sacrifice must be shared. The days of
localized campaigns in far-flung corners of an Empire with volunteer
armies were over. This was total conflict on a scale that affected
practically every household and, therefore, universal support was
necessary. The role of the parent, the spouse and the girlfriend
became an integral part of the recruiting process and hence the war

play. Even in the late summer of 1916, nearly three months after the inception of compulsory conscription, the theatre audiences were still being exhorted to subjugate their own profit and family interests in the name of national hour and sacrifice. In *Howard and Son* at the London Coliseum in August, 1916 the leading character, a merchant, has the opportunity of saving his ailing business by selling goods via a neutral country to Germany. The offer was very tempting, especially as the final destination of the goods would be well camouflaged; but at the last moment, despite hearing of his son's death, he reaffirms the need for parental sacrifice and national honour.[18]

The role of the theatre, via the war plays, as an agent for recruitment and its effect is impossible to judge precisely. There were at least twenty-five new plays written for the direct purpose of recruiting, although the Lord Chamberlain's collection contains many more in which the aim of recruitment was part of the sub-text. Certainly the war plays that contain a recruiting element, combined with the efforts of individual artistes and the jingoistic choral stirrings of the music halls, provided the government with a vast amount of free propagandist support.

The recruiting campaign undertaken by the stage, although not officially supported by the government, was not ignored by the military. Indeed, at times there was a discernible degree of co-operation with the recruiting personnel being present in the theatres. In *A Call to Arms* at the Golders Green Hippodrome in 1914, the company enacted a sketch which parodied the efforts of a recruiting sergeant to persuade the 'laggards' to join the army. The censor commented that the sergeant's 'sound arguments are backed up by the self-denying spirit of a wife and sweetheart'; underlying, once again, the supportive role of women in the fight. The recruiter delivers a stirring speech outlining the reasons why a man should enlist, saying:

> *The Army is fighting... to defend the weak and the old and the helpless, the little children who are to be the men and women of tomorrow. It's to uphold the name... of one of the greatest nations the world has ever seen. It's to prove that a man must be true to his friend and keep his word of honour, even if it's only written on a scrap of paper...*

The denouément of the piece is the turning of fiction into fact when the 'recruiting sergeant' turns to the audience and makes the following announcement:

Gentlemen, I am asked by the Authorities to state that a Recruiting
Officer is in attendance in the vestibule of the building. Is there any man
here tonight who can and will help his country in her hour of need?[19]

It is not known whether or not recruiting officers were present at other 'recruiting plays' of 1914 such as: *England Expects* (London Opera House); *The King's Men* (Royalty Theatre, Soho); *John Shannon Reservist* (Empire Theatre, Shoreditch); *Your Country Needs You* (Tivoli Theatre, Manchester); *The Hem of The Flag* (Hippodrome Theatre, Woolwich) and many others.[20] The fact that the recruiting authorities attended any place where crowds gathered suggests that they may well have been present. A blue-print for the writing and production of these recruiting plays was set prior to the war in 1912, with the revival of Major Guy du Maurier's play *An Englishman's Home*. The producer was the author's well-known actor and brother Gerald. Apart from boosting recruiting figures for the Territorials, it also dealt with the themes of invasion and heroism; however, with the Conscription Act of 1916 and the subsequent demise of the recruiting sergeant, the playwrights had to concentrate on the latter themes.

PROPAGANDA

The stirring of patriotic emotions, and constant reminders of why Britain was at war, were not enough to sustain the public's support over a very long period. Lasswell in his analysis of propaganda in the Great War, stated that it was essential that the first objective of strategic propaganda be adhered to, namely 'The mobilization of hatred against the enemy'.[21] The tide of euphoric patriotic enthusiasm that swept the country in 1914 meant that initially no great effort was required. As the war continued into the next year the enormity of the task, and the time it might take, became apparent and it was necessary for the government to re-double its propaganda campaign. To this end the authorities had the theatre's continued backing.

Almost the first, and by far the largest, genre of war drama was the spy play. The reasons, although never stated, appear twofold. First, the playwrights may have had little or no knowledge of fighting at the Front, and so any depiction of actual battle scenes was beyond their ken. A few playwrights did attempt to write scenes of 'life in the trenches', but they were few in number and such plays did not run for very long and therefore must be judged failures. Secondly, the locale for a spy could be home-based and involve everyone, military and civilian alike. The spy drama could therefore appear more relevant and engaging to the home audience. Evidence of the popularity of spy plays can be measured by the number of productions. There were fifty plays concerning spies submitted to the Lord Chamberlain's Office during the first two-and-a-half years of war – all of which were produced. During 1917 and 1918 a further forty-three spy dramas were performed. In fact nearly 100 plays, many of which were one-act dramas involving espionage, were produced in Britain between September, 1914 and November, 1918. The spy play helped augment the propagandist's aims by instilling a distrust of anything German. In the early plays the enemy was often referred to as an Ulhan or Prussian, but soon, as the public's sense of abhorrence and outrage became more widespread, the feelings of hatred encompassed all Germans.

The spy could, of course, not only be in military or civilian guise but might be male or female, and of any nationality; and the spy could be placed in any situation. The villain or saviour sometimes had a romantic link either with the adversary or the rescuer. The spy play thus provided, as in *In Time of War* (1914), the setting for what in reality was a conventional romance.[22] In the one-act sketch *War, Wine and – a Woman!* (1915), which was written in the same style, the heroine was shown to be a member of the British Intelligence Department. The censor took exception to the latter and insisted that any reference to British Intelligence be removed but conceded that 'we [the British] do have female spies at times'.[23] As long as the enemy spy had some Teutonic blood in his or her veins the drama was acceptable to the censor. In *Inside the Lines* (1917), the spy was shown, not to be of Teutonic extraction, but an Indian servant with a grudge against the English. The censor thought the idea too insensitive both to the Indians and other Colonials who were fighting on the side of the Allies; thus, on the 'advice' of the censor, this was changed and a character of non-determinate nationality was inserted.[24] Whether or not the spy play was a convenient vehicle for what, in essence, was often a romantic drama is perhaps of secondary importance. What is significant is that the audience was continually reminded of the possible enemy threat. In November, 1918, when the war was coming to an end, audiences who saw the four-act play *Beware German*, were still being told to be suspicious of not only Germans but all aliens.[25] It was suggested, via the play, that although the Germans were beaten they could still exert a destructive influence on the British economy by instigating strikes. The theme was continued in *Lest We Forget*, performed in 1919. In the latter it is argued that the Germans would seek revenge for the indemnity imposed by the Allies. The method employed would be the infiltration of British industry for the purposes of profit and disruption.[26] Thus the play helped to maintain any feelings of hatred at the forefront of some people's minds.

Spies were characterized as being not only treacherous, but also brutal. The greatest atrocities were attributed to the depraved antics of the German soldiery. This included the killing of mothers, beating of children and rape of young girls, the latter being the most common. In order to incite deeper feelings of animosity the dramatists ensured that the crimes perpetrated were against the most innocent. The cruelty in *In the Hands of the Hun* (1915), is a good illustration of this point. In the play Count Otto, a German officer, wants to burn down a nunnery and then give the women to his men.[27] And in *For Those in Peril* (1916), the German naval captain echoes the same threats, saying 'And when this... is over; why! the lovely convent – it will be a prize for my men'.[28] The play *Armageddon* (1915) veers from the poetic to sheer melodrama, but is one of the better war plays in terms of plot and dialogue; that apart, German brutality is still evident in a superior officer's speech to his colleagues in which he says:

> *Be deaf then to the wail of women, blind*
> *To children's blood; the cause demands of you*
> *That you shall lie and burn, betray and snare!*
> *Remember Attila! The great ruthless Hun!*[29]

Armageddon contained almost all the ingredients present in a typical war play, wrote a *Times* reviewer. There were, 'pictures of German barbarity and "frightfulness" – prisoners shot, women insulted, interceding priests mocked, and so forth... German sentiments about world-power declaimed'.[30] And there was the almost statutory scene concerning the anticipation of victory. The leading actor was Sir John Martin-Harvey who played the roles of Satan, a leading Abbé and a British Commander. Nevertheless, it failed in the West End much to the disappointment of its star, its writer Stephen Phillips and the producer Sir Charles Wyndham. It seems that the war play format had, according to the critic, been literally over-played as the resultant outcome of any such drama was so predictable as to be boring.

The censors did not automatically give their stamp of approval to every submission that denigrated the Germans. Indeed, there was a considerable amount of inconsistency. In *A Daughter of England* (1915), the censor took exception to the suggestion that a Prussian officer would treat the burning of a house containing a prisoner as a joke; although he concluded that it was 'no worse than incidents passed', and the play was recommended for production.[31] On the other hand, the stripping to the waist of a Mother Superior, and her subsequent whipping in *In the Hands of the Hun* (1915), proved just too much; but in the same play Count Otto could say:

> *... but a red hot iron applied judiciously may make you change your mind... don't be squeamish, burn her eyes out one by one unless she tells us what we want to know.*[32]

This was not cut as it was 'done off' [stage]. For outrageous violence that went beyond any human decency see *War, Red War* (1915), in which the German Colonel calls for a baby to have its brains knocked out on a doorpost, and for the infant to be thrown on the fire. This, judging, by the censor's blue mark (there was no comment) was cut.[33] Although the Lord Chamberlain's Office managed to curtail some of the more grotesque excesses of the zealous playwrights, it also reflected society's general hatred of the enemy by offering subjective opinions when the Germans were thought to be getting off too lightly. J.M. Barrie's play *Der Tag* (1914), came in for some such criticism.[34] In *Marie Oldie* (1915), the author, Edward Knoblauch, states that any reference to Germany will be omitted and that the 'war, soldiers and country be made indefinite': to which the censor opined:

> *I conjecture his reason must be that the soldiers are made so much more decent than the actual German soldiers in this war...* [35]

It could be argued that the censor's comments were uncommonly subjective and appeared as gratuitous as the depicted violence.

It is difficult to assess what the public thought of the propagandist war plays with their excessive violence and unlikely plots. The fact that so many were produced throughout the war suggests that they were popular. The response of the critics in the 'quality' press was somewhat taciturn. The latter presumably felt it undiplomatic to criticize the stage's patriotic offerings. Reviewing *The Day Before the*

Day (1915), a melodrama at St James's Theatre, the *Times'* critic neatly side-stepped the problem of outright criticism saying:

> *Whether romantic fiction is profitably employed upon the tremendous facts which we are all of us 'up against' is a question... We prefer not to discuss, but merely record that the performance last night appeared to give a great many people a good deal of gratification.*[36]

A year later, in the same paper, the critic reviewing *Kultur at Home* at the Court Theatre, outlined the dilemma facing the public; he wrote:

> *There are playgoers who delight in war plays, And there are playgoers for whom war plays exasperate, whose patriotism is not cheered but offended by a calculated appeal, who feel... that any actuality of the moment... is too heavy a burden for art to carry.*[37]

In the main it was the Germans who were vilified: in comparison the other Central Powers – Austria-Hungary, Bulgaria and Turkey – received scant recognition on the British stage.

ALLIES AND NEUTRALS

In December, 1914, at the Manchester Hippodrome, there was a three-act play produced called *Kulture*. It was billed as 'A propaganda, a Military Spectacular Aqua-Drama', and was purported to be based on actual incidents.[38] The production was in the tradition of the patriotic spectacles mounted during the time of the Crimea War.[39] The inclusion of water in the drama was, however, left until the end. The denouement arrived with the opening of sluice gates which sent horses and cannon into the water, and houses collapsed under the cascading deluge. Thus the German army was pictured as being drowned. The remaining image was of a group of soldiers standing on a level below a Red Cross nurse who proffered a wreath of peace, and above her head there hung an illuminated halo under a collage of Allied Flags. The play had all the hallmarks of the typical propagandist production as it depicted the combined efforts of the Allies in the over-whelming defeat of the enemy. The finale not only showed the triumph of good over evil but suggested, with the inclusion of the illuminated halo, that God was on the side of the Allies. It was a strengthening, or re-affirmation, of the idea that the cause must be a just one.

On a smaller scale use was made of the patriotic tableaux, and to a lesser extent the masque. Tableaux were constructed to form appropriate backdrops for numerous patriotic singing concerts. At the Middlesex Theatre a show, put on the day after war was declared, incorporating a 'tableau representing France bearing the Triple Entente' behind which were displayed the British and Russian flags.[40] As an initial method of stirring the nationalistic pride the tableau was appropriate because it was both visually and, combined with the singing, emotionally evocative. It was also easily constructed and filled the gap, so to speak, between the announcement of war and the time taken for the numerous playwrights to put pen to paper. Any communication, whether it was a vocal pronouncement or visual display, that supported and demonstrated the country's respect for friendly powers fulfilled one of the propagandist's major objectives: namely, the preservation of concord with one's Allies.[41]

Co-operation between the Allies on the stage took many forms, and was often used in the sentimental romantic dramas. The French hero was more often than not in love with a British Red Cross nurse, or alternatively the British Tommy would – at the last moment – save the Belgian waif from the marauding Hun. The clearest evidence of mutual support can be seen in the revues. In the revue *The Pedlar of Dreams* at the Vaudeville in December, 1915, each country and its contribution to the war – including Germany's – is referred to in the song *Everybody's Chasing William*.[42] The verse concerning Belgium emphasizes the dependence of one state upon another:

> *I'm little Belgium*
> *They've ground me to the dust*
> *They've taken everything I had*
> *It really was unjust.*
> *But now the Allies fight for me*
> *In them I put my trust.*
> *They're sure to win, they're bound to win.*
> *I know they'll win – they must!*

The final verse optimistically refers to peace and implies that not only will the individual gain his just reward, but that Britain will again have 'pride of place'.

John MacKenzie writing about the Victorian music hall concluded that its entertainment 'reflected the dominant imperial ethos of the day in topical and chauvinistic songs, royal fervour, and patriotic tableaux'.[43] These forms of expressing popular patriotism continued throughout the Edwardian period and the First World War. Indeed, the fact that so many colonial troops were sent to fight in Europe was not just welcomed but expected. In the pantomime *Red Riding Hood* (1916) at the Theatre Royal, Edinburgh, the chorus sung the song *There's no Land like the Old Land* the words of which extol the virtues of the colonies, but at the same time it is clear that the various imperial dependencies are, in effect, repaying a debt to Britain. The words of the second verse spell this out:

> *What an Empire these Sons have cemented*
> *With the blood of the brave and free;*
> *There's Canada and Australia*
> *Twin brothers they be:*
> *While India and Africa and Egypt*
> *Play a part which Time alone will have to tell*
> *Yet tho' they fret,*
> *If the Mother tries to check,*
> *Still they never forget the debt*
> *To the land they love so well.*[44]

What the battle-weary Maori, indigenous Indian and African member of an audience hearing such jingoism thought cannot be known, but the native British audience were used to such fare, and would have thought the sentiments patriotic rather than patronizing. The pantomime was the favourite vehicle for the expression of jingoistic hyperbole. In *Sinbad the Sailor* (1916) at the Palace Theatre, Tottenham, the same sentiments were expressed in the song *I Love My Mother land*.[45]

At the collective level the Allies were shown, at least on the stage, to form a homogeneous collective in pursuit of a great patriotic crusade, and any country not a member of this 'holy alliance' was open to ridicule. Hence, until April, 1917, America came in for some satirical and indignant criticism via the stage. In the show *The Pedlar of Dreams* Henry Ford, the US car manufacturer, is ridiculed for trying to convene a Peace Conference.[46] In the revue *Joyland* (1915) at the London Hippodrome it is intimated that the only reason Mr Ford wants peace is so that his business will flourish.[47] Another example of an attempt to shame the Americans into the action came in the masque *The War Men-Agerie* (1915) at the Scala Theatre. In the production each country or notable was introduced as an animal, and was accompanied by a chorus with appropriate words recited in rhyming couplets. As the words show, criticism of the United States was very thinly veiled indeed:

> *Enter the Neutral*
> *The Neutral has an artful eye*
> *swift any danger to espy;*
> *a very amphibian he,*
> *preserving strict neut-rality.*
> *His pattern is peculiar too,*
> *with stripes of variegated hue;*
> *and when he's marked with stars as well*
> *there is no need his name to tell.*[48]

Criticism of America on the stage was sporadic rather than universal. It would appear, in hindsight anyway, inevitable that America would join the Allies in the struggle. Most of the allied countries had historical connections with the US, although Germany, too, had a sizable number of former nationals living in America; to say nothing of the sympathies of the Irish who at the time were engaged in a struggle against the British. Britain, however, had the benefit of direct cable communications with the USA, which gave her a political and strategic advantage. In theatrical terms there was a shared heritage; more Americans read Shakespeare than Göethe; New York and the West End still maintained an interchange of artistes and entertainment, and, therefore, ideas and sympathies. And because of the literary and artistic links the modus operandi of propaganda could be more easily accessible, and subtle in approach. British and American artistes and their companies still crossed the Atlantic despite the war.

SOCIALISM AND CRITICISM

The criticism of the USA was relatively muted compared with the vociferous attacks on British-based war critics and dissidents. Apart from stating that the war was a fight for freedom, few playwrights actually debated the issue publicly; perhaps the dramatists thought it unnecessary as the cause of the war and the country's involvement were discussed at length in the national press. The question of whether or not Britain should fight 'reflected the view' wrote A.J.P.

Taylor '[that] war was an act of state... with which ordinary citizens had little to do'.[49] When it was discussed it was on an individual level, and looked at in terms of personal sacrifice. As the war continued into its second year, and the casualty figures inexorably mounted to unheard-of proportions, it was even less likely that a voice of dissent would be heard in the theatres – it would have appeared grossly unsympathetic and anti-patriotic.

The major voice of public opposition came from members of the Labour Party, most notably from Ramsay MacDonald, Keir Hardie and from some of the revolutionary shop stewards – especially those on Clydeside.[50] The war, wrote Stevenson, 'utterly disrupted the more militant sections of the Labour movement. Plans laid by the Second International (Congress) for an international general strike in the event of a European war were swept aside by the tidal wave of Patriotism';[51] although, ironically, the centres of greatest industrial discontent 'provided the highest proportion in the country of recruits for the army'.[52] Those in two minds about going to war were convinced, following Germany's invasion of Belgium, that there was no alternative course of action. Given the rolling wave of patriotism, and growing German xenophobia, it was not surprising that any drama supporting socialist ideas, or indeed any views that were not pro-government, would be seen as anti-patriotic.

'The Governments of Western Europe' wrote Lasswell 'can never be perfectly certain that a class-conscious proletariat within the borders of their authority will rally to the clarion of war'.[53] In Britain, following the industrial unrest in the years 1912–13, there was the possibility that mobilization would be hampered by a general strike, and 'that social revolution might raise its ominous head'.[54] It never came about, but the major advocates of social reform were seen by some as deserving malevolent denunciation on the public stage. The chief subject for such public ridicule was Keir Hardie, the Scottish miner and founder of the Independent Labour Party. Hardie incurred disfavour by addressing a Labour demonstration against the war in 1914. The ensuing anti-war assemblage in Glasgow after the Declaration further increased his unpopularity with the war zealots. In the revues and sketches he was referred to as that 'Cur Hardie'. The suggestion as to his 'deserved' fate was unequivocal in the refrain of a song in *The Passing Show* of 1915: the inference is that he should be hanged.[55] Hardie was regarded in some quarters as an ally of Germany, therefore, ipso facto, a traitor. In the show *Good*

Evening in 1915, the song *The German's Hymn of Love* emphasizes Hardie's supposed German affiliation.[56]

In the revue *Push & Go* at the Hippodrome (1915), Hardie is linked with the playwright George Bernard Shaw, and the Labour politician Ramsay MacDonald. Shaw added to his unpopularity when in his essay *Common Sense about the War* he suggested that the rank and file of both Britain and Germany should shoot their officers and go home. In several articles Shaw stated that the war was not about a fight for freedom, but was first and foremost an imperialist power struggle.

Shaw's article caused great controversy. The reaction was for libraries and bookshops to remove his works from their shelves. His ironic and satirical sense of expression was not viewed with objective discernment, and many read what he wrote about the war with a literal blinkeredness. Granville Barker warned that, as a result of his article, even some of his friends were turning against him. Michael Holroyd, commenting on the reaction to his tract in America, wrote that President Roosevelt referred to Shaw as a 'blue-rumped ape' and 'lumped him with "the unhung traitor Keir Hardie" among a "venomous herd of socialists"'.[58] Shaw was against war *per se* but he was pragmatic, and realistic enough to know that once war had started the Allies had no option but to pursue the struggle to the end. Unbeknown to most people Shaw contributed £200 to the Belgian refugees fund, and £20,000 to the British War Loan (£6,000 and £600,000 in today's terms). According to Holroyd, Shaw kept quiet about this partly because 'it was a matter of self-respect, and partly that of out-manoeuvering those who wished to surround him with obloquy'.[59]

Whilst the war had a homogenizing effect on the ambitions of most of the populace there were pockets of social discontent, particularly in 'Red Clydeside'. A few of the politically hard-left advocates believed that the war was a manifestation of the errors of capitalism, and it was therefore to be avoided. They also saw the war as presenting the opportunity for the workers to bargain for their long-term prosperity, and hopefully gain control. In South Wales the miners rejected the coal-owners' offer of a war bonus, the agreement of which meant that any monetary advantage would be terminated on the cessation of war; the miners wanted permanent improvement regarding their wages. A strike was called on 14 July, 1915. It was not syndicalism and the desire of labour to gain control through universal action that caused disruption, but the disagreement over the payment of war bonuses. The belief and dilemma facing the malcontents was aired in the drama *John Feeney – Socialist* which played, appropriately, at the Pavilion Theatre, Glasgow in June, 1915. In the play John Feeney is a miner who takes the Marxist view of the capitalist war. He argues his case with a middle-class lady, Mrs MacDonald, who counters with the accusation that he is a murderer; saying:

> *Mrs MacDonald:*... *is a time of war a time to haggle over an extra wage? And you would jeopardize the fate of your Empire for a paltry penny? You would murder those who take your place in the trenches and laugh – laugh – to see them cut down by bullets!...*
>
> *John Feeney:* *You don't understand it – you speak from your own side. The fault lies, not with labour but with capital. If we, the labourers live on murder, then them as is capitalists, live on carrion. Look at your munition factories. Their turnover is millions. And what does the worker get out of it?... The offer of a bonus...*

Feeney then continues putting the same argument as the Welsh miners, stating that it is a decent wage that they want and not a bonus that can be stopped. Mrs MacDonald changes tack and raises the question of Belgium and the fate of its people. Feeney's retort appears heartless when he says:

> *... it is for the sake of Belgium as a buffer and not Belgium as a people that we are in this war. It is not a question of neutrality at all; it is merely geographical position. What do we care for Belgium as Belgians?.*[60]

The Belgian refugees were, at first, welcomed with open arms but attitudes changed as 'their competition was feared on the labour market'.[61] The refugees' accounts of the German invasion and the stories of the enemy's heinous atrocities were widely believed. 'Very soon the invasion of Belgium became in the popular mind a chronicle of murder, rape, pillage, arson and wanton destruction'.[62] In the play a

Belgian refugee bursts onto the scene and, in hysterical fashion, tells of how her parents were shot before her eyes. She then related more tales of German maniacal behaviour. Feeney thus relents. His conversion is complete and he enlists.

The question of coal-mining being a form of National Service and therefore indispensable to the war effort, and the fact that coal profits, by 1916, were treble those of the 'average of the five pre-war years' were ignored.[63] The play is a classical example of propagandist hype. The argument against the war and its proponent is set up in order to be debunked and belittled. The importance of supporting an ally is again stressed. At the same time the feelings of an audience are stirred with emotional incitement by reference to the enemy's unacceptable behaviour. Finally, it is a call to duty, and can therefore be viewed as a recruiting play. It is, of course, also a debate – albeit naive – of two opposing political ideologies. The playwright began by taking the chance of presenting a logical argument, but it was finally lost in a welter of emotional subjectivity, sentimentality, and moral blackmail.

The problem of obtaining skilled workers was an acute one, and it was necessary to use 'diluted' labour – unskilled, semi-skilled or female workers. The unions eventually agreed to do this following a meeting between their leaders and government representatives, provided that it was for the duration of the war only. The workers in the munition factories also agreed not to strike. The Government, for its part, was to ensure that unions' standards were maintained. The question of upholding the rights and justices of the unions, exploitation of labour and the use of non-union employees, plus the moral issue of whether to strike, was addressed in the play *War Mates* in 1915. The protagonist argues that not only are they – the munition workers – 'doing their bit' but they are also protecting the rights of their absent war mates. The employers, on the other hand, are said to be taking an unfair advantage – knowing that many workers would find it morally repugnant to strike while the war is on – and it is assumed that what concessions the employers gained would be continued in peace time. A soldier (Wilfred) returning from the Front is appalled at the idea of a strike. In an effort to avert the damaging effects of such action he tells a sympathizer (John, a munition worker) how an attack failed through lack of ammunition, and that the man's son had to be left wounded on the battlefield. The story was a total fabrication, but it had the desired result and the strike was averted. Any ruse was permissible as long as it supported the government's views. The opinion of the censor is illuminating in that he conceded that there may be objection to Wilfred's fraudulent arguments, but concludes that 'they are certainly what the men in the trenches are really saying, and I think can do nothing but good in being repeated here'.[64] A study of shows sent to the Lord Chamberlain's Office indicated that anyone considering writing a play which was critical of the government, and the war, would not submit the play for license knowing that it would be rejected without a second thought.

Socialist themes and the possibility of strike action is returned to in *Boys of the Old Brigade*. An ex-soldier, now reservist, is visited by his old Colonel, and they debate the rights and wrongs of a probable strike. Graham, the reservist, states the workers' case. The Colonel counters by casting aspersion on anything remotely suggestive of being anti-patriotic and therefore, to him, socialist in form, saying:

> ... *but this is all damned socialistic nonsense you know, simply ruining the country it is. Ex-soldiers always have a good chance to get employment through the soldiers Employment Agency...*

From Graham comes the curt, realistic and stinging reply:

> *No one employs a cripple.*[65]

The instigator of the strike is discovered to be a German spy. And true to the war-time dramatic form Graham – in the words of the censor, 'an honest, misguided man, on the elements of patriotism', realizes his folly and knows his duty lies elsewhere. Graham's and the socialist case is forcefully argued, and if it were not for the insertion of a German spy, would sound more convincing than that of the military patriot. An equally cogent, plausible counter-argument could have been written for the part of the Colonel but it was not, and once again theatrical subjectivity decided the outcome; or, as the censor concluded, the play was acceptable as patriotism wins out in the end.

Censorship via the Lord Chamberlain's Office had been in operation since 1737, and certainly since the abolition of the patent system in 1843 any impersonation of political and royal figures was discouraged on the stage.[66] This was definitely true during the early years of the war, and included not only allusion to allied neutrals but also to the Kaiser himself. It is difficult to see how the censor could monitor all shows, and the temptation to ape the Kaiser would it is thought, have been irresistible. Nevertheless, in the show *Somewhere in France* (1915), the censor reminded the producers that the rule must be observed.[67] There was, however, some inconsistency. In *The War Men-Agerie*, the masque produced at the Scala Theatre, Leachcombe in Cheshire in 1915, the censor relaxed the rules and allowed the recognizable notables to be displayed as there was no dialogue, and the depictions were 'merely equivalent to pictures on a screen'.[68] This mode of deference and protection did not, as previously noted, extend to non-conservative people such as Ramsay MacDonald. G.S. Street, one of the Lord Chamberlain's readers, reviewing *By Jingo, If We Do* (1914), stated that 'no country can be denied the satisfaction of vilifying its enemies in war time'[69]

The ban upon the portrayal of members of the royal family was vigorously imposed. Not only were the King and Government inviolate, so too was the King's uniform. With so many plays containing military characters in khaki and navy blue it was almost a prerequisite costume for every theatre's wardrobe. The manner in which the uniformed character behaved was of abiding interest to the Lord Chamberlain's Office. No hint of impropriety or anti-patriotic stage business went undetected in a censor's report. It was also important to the military authorities that a character should not act in such a ridiculous fashion as to bring discredit on the Service or the King's uniform. This would have been considered as being in the worst possible taste when men were dying in their thousands. The line between ridiculousness and comedy is, of course, a fine one and must perforce be based on taste. Apart from which, as the censor pointed out in the notes to *For England, Home and Beauty* (1915), 'the comic relief man generally enlists and continues to be comic relief'.[70] The problem was further compounded when the playwright attempted to draw the character with an air of realism. This was highlighted in *A Day in a Dugout* (1916), and *Mother's Sailor Boy* (1916). In the former an army private is a burglar, but the censor justifies his inclusion thus:

> *I don't think there is any harm in one of the privates being a burglar – there are several in the Army – as it is not taken seriously and only put in for contrast.*[71]

Through the genre of comedy it was assumed, perhaps naively, that characters are far enough removed from reality not to pose a threat to an audience's perceptions. In the latter naval play, *Mother's*

Sailor Boy, a serving mariner is introduced who is in a 'hopelessly drunken state'. This, on the insistence of the censor, had to be removed.[72] It is hard to imagine that a thief was more acceptable than a drunk, but presumably a drunk looks more ridiculous, and so was deemed to be more offensive. The fact that the 'drunken sailor' is a proverbial figure, and has been on stage for two hundred years at least, seemed to have escaped the notice of the censor. Further inconsistency is found in the 1916 production of *Diddled*. In the play a naval lieutenant, who is in an impecunious state, attempts in various ways to avoid paying his boarding-house rent. The writer was ordered to change the character to a civilian.[73] The implication is that it was alright for a private to be a thief, but an officer must be beyond reproach. The more elevated the social and authoritative position of the character the more unimpeachable he became. The difference between officers and other ranks in the forces had an important disciplinary function. The theory was, indeed still is, that social distance aids respect and enhances discipline. As Fussell points out, there existed unambiguous distinctions in behaviour and dress in the armed forces. In London, for example, 'an officer was forbidden to carry a parcel or ride on a bus, and even in mufti – dark suit, white collar, bowler, stick – he looked identifiably different from his men'.[74] The censor ensured that the behavioural differences of fictional characters as portrayed on stage maintained this social divide; and whatever the rank, the King's uniform was to be treated as sacrosanct. This respect for sartorial symbolism was, at times, taken to absurd lengths. In one of the scenes of the musical farce *Water Birds* (1916), a soldier refuses to leave a swimming bath and eventually falls in the water. This was regarded as highly objectionable by the censor and the producer was told that the man should not be in uniform.[75] The sensitivity that the censors displayed towards military dress and etiquette seems, at times, to have been a little excessive. In *Airs and Graces*, a revue in two acts at the Palace Theatre in 1917, the censor cut a whole scene because an Army Provost Marshal is shown to do all the things an officer should not do: dance in public; smoke a pipe while in uniform; and when in mufti, put his arm around a girl's waist; wear trousers with turn-ups when wearing shoes; and wear gaudy coloured socks. Theatrical initiative was suppressed because the censor believed it would offend the War Office.[76] Clearly, the censor had never been to a military concert where the aim of the entertainment was to extract laughter from the audience at the expense of the caricatured depictions on stage.

The conscientious objector was a target of fun, but the military tribunal could not be held up to ridicule. In the one-act play *The Conscienceless Objector* (1916) at the Hippodrome, a man claims exemption from military service on the grounds that he has six pretty daughters to look after. The Committee assure the man that the country will look after his children, and the Chairman adds... if the country doesn't the Committee *will*'. This innuendo was too much for the censor who wrote, '[this] seems to be dubious... while the insincere "conscientious objector" is fair game it is not desirable that too much fun should be made of the tribunals themselves'.[77]

CHANGE OF ATTITUDES AND CONTENT

The prohibition regarding the thinly veiled disguises of the Kaiser on stage lasted until August, 1915. What made the Lord Chamberlain change his mind is not clear. The fact that any arch-villain on stage that spoke with a German accent was assumed to be the Kaiser, coupled with the almost daily lampooning of the German Emperor in newspaper cartoons, meant that stage restrictions were pointless. Thus in the 1915 production of the one-man-show *Gott Strafe England* – written and performed by Edmund Frobisher – in which the Kaiser is clearly identified, the censor finally, and inevitably, waived the prohibitive rule.[78]

Zara Steiner, in discussing the origins of the First World War, concluded that 'in Britain a real effort was made to teach boys that success in war depended upon the patriotism and military spirit of the nation and that preparation for war would strengthen 'manly virtues' and 'patriotic ardour'.[79] This theme was re-iterated time and again in the war plays. Some playwrights went even further by intimating that war was an adventure, and could even be fun. In *The Man They Wouldn't Pass*, a man's wife, who is a nurse, suggests they give everything up and go to war because, 'It would be so lovely to be in it all'.[80] A month later in April, 1915, in *Up Boys and at 'Em*, Sir Gilbert Weston persuades two young men to enlist, declaring that it would be 'thrilling' to go to war.[81] The same sentiments are echoed in *Twixt Love and Duty* or *The Call to Arms* at Bedford Music Hall in August, 1915.[82] However, as the war progressed and the horrors became more apparent views began to change.

Songs extolling the virtues of war and the adventures of Tommy Atkins and Jolly Jack Tar must, come 1916, have seemed misplaced, or at least inappropriate. The year 1916 was a watershed; with the introduction of conscription due to the ever-extending casualty lists it became obvious that the fight was no longer the preserve of the enthusiast, the volunteer. War was now on a scale in size and horror unheard of or experienced. The neurasthentic, the maimed and the blind were everywhere to be seen. The war was no longer, either on or off the stage, referred to as fun, an exciting venture. People were afraid – they were not all heroes – and they were not frightened to say so. In the song *Life in a Trench* (1916), in the show *Somewhere in France* at the Chiswick Empire, the reality of trench warfare is expressed in the following extract:

> *Living in the trenches we've been*
> *Germans may be heard but seldom seen,*
> *You go out on patrol in the dickens of a funk,*
> *And lie in a hole where a shell has sunk,*
> *You think about a tale to tell the boss,*
> *Consider you deserve the Military Cross,*
> *You say you've cut the evening's wire*
> *And everybody says, 'What a blinking liar!'*
>
> *Sniped all the day and sniped all night,*
> *Bombs on the left and bombs on the right*
> *But nobody seems to care a damn*
> *So long as we get our Tickler's jam;*
> *Lovely iron rations for our grub,*
> *Dug-outs in the evening for our pub,*
> *The sergeants love to pinch our tot of rum,*
> *Strafe 'em all to Hallelujah Kingdom Come!*[83]

The mocking tone of the words and the admittance of being in a 'funk'; the inadequacy of the rations; and the sergeants stealing the rum would not have been lost on the majority of the audience, and was a far cry from the heroic sentiments expressed in the songs of 1914 and 1915. By 1916 the servicemen's thoughts were directed not towards the battlefield and glory, but in the opposite direction. To the haven of home, as voiced in the song *The Home Road*:

> *There's a road that leads to glory,*
> *There's a road that leads to gain;*
> *And... sometimes you will wander*

In the road that leads to pain...
Sometimes there is a pathway,
With the branches over grown
But there's roses all a-blowing
In the road that leads back home.[84]

The patriotic songs did not cease altogether, but there were fewer of them, and increasingly the songs became comically ironic in content. Perhaps the best known is *Oh! It's a Lovely War*, sung in 1918 in the show *Jack in the Box*. The ironical humour is evident from the first verse:

Up to your waist in water, up to your eyes in slush,
Using the kind of language that makes the Sergeants blush.
Who wouldn't join the army? That's what we all enquire.
Don't we pity the poor civilians,
Sitting beside the fire.[85]

It would be incorrect to say that the playwrights became more critical. If not in dialogue, at least in song, the realities of war, post 1916, were being aired; but even if the playwrights did attempt to bring a greater degree of realism into the play the censor would often sanitize the action, and if it appeared too 'real' it was cut altogether. A number of plays included Zeppelin raids and bomb attacks, each of which was subjected to the modifying stroke of the censor's blue crayon. In *Britain's Guests* (1917) at the Empire Theatre, Mile End, the Zeppelin raid had to be cut as the censor thought it might alarm the audience;[86] likewise the gun fire in *By Pigeon Post* at the Garrick Theatre a year later.[87] The Zeppelin raid was also excluded from *When Joy Bells are Ringing* (1918) at the Elephant and Castle Theatre.[88] The censorial knife was used twice for the play *Over the Lines* (1918) at the Baths Hall Theatre in East London. First, the air raid scenes were cut, and secondly the censor banned the scene showing wounded men on stretchers. The reason he gave was, 'There is always a risk that this sort of play may reproduce horrors too vividly...'.[89] The producer of *Home Service* (1918) had to give a written undertaking that the bomb explosion would be done by the means of a big drum.[90] It seems that any dramatic reproduction coming too near to reality was in danger of being omitted. The comments penned at the bottom of *The Angels of Mons* (1916) at the Coliseum, illustrates the censor's sensitivity; it reads:

[The Play] is infinitely more painful than the silly trash on the subject that we usually get, and it offends me, just because it is lifelike, that a dying soldier should be in a show.[91]

Whilst it is possible to have some sympathy with the censor regarding Zeppelin raids, it looks as though people were denied the opportunity to experience a greater sense of what might happen at the Front merely because of the censor's 'delicate' and prejudicial discrimination. Nevertheless, evidence suggests that with a creeping reluctance the Lord Chamberlain's employees, Messrs G.S. Street and E.A. Bendall, had, by the second half of the war, gradually eased the restrictions and allowed some more realism on stage.

The censor's office notwithstanding, the playwrights shied away from the more contentious problems created by the war; for example, what was to be done with the crippled and the maimed? There were nearly two million still alive, many of whom suffered grievous mutilation. In the very few plays dealing with the blind – there were none to be found in the Lord Chamberlain's Collection mentioning anyone suffering from the effects of gas – the unfortunate soldiers thus impaired usually made a miraculous recovery at the end of each play. An example of this can be seen in *British to the Backbone*.[92] There are two exceptions to this. First, in the *Black Widows* (1918) at the Savoy Theatre, the pain of a soldier's blindness is made more palatable by the love and compassion of his girlfriend.[93] The injured on stage are treated as heroes rather than the victims of war. In the other play, *The Grousers* (1917) at the Ardwick Empire, Manchester, a middle-aged man complains of the inconveniences imposed by the war: dark streets, drinking restrictions, tobacco up in price and an increase in the cost of food. He is put to shame by two maimed soldiers – one has lost an arm, the other is blind. The soldiers are portrayed as two individuals who bravely and cheerfully bear their injuries with a remarkable stoicism.[94] This reminds both the middle-aged character and the audience that they really have little to complain about; although what any actual amputee or blind member of an audience thought cannot be known. It is perhaps not surprising that this subject was not really debated in dramatic form – it may have been considered too indelicate to do so.

Feelings towards the United States of America did a complete U-turn once President Wilson had, finally, announced his country's intention to fight against Germany and her allies. This necessitated the hurried modification of any scripts criticizing the Americans, and the deletion of jokes referring to 'President Will-soon' as in the revue *Cheep* at the Vaudeville Theatre in April, 1917.[95] Songs with lyrics that were critical of America's neutral stance were shelved, and new Anglo-American verses of patriotic praise were written and sung, or recited in pageants and plays: an example of the latter can be read in *Pageant of Fair Women* in May, 1917:

Hold!
What were your firmament without my stars?
No more I stand aloof! The old world's scars
Are now the New World's wounds. With you I fight
To crush the tyrant and uphold the Right.
We'll win together everlasting Peace.
By waging ceaseless war till War shall cease![96]

The recitation was repeated a year later in *Pageant of Freedom* at the same Queen's Hall venue in London.[97]

ADDITIONAL FUNCTIONS OF THE THEATRE

The presentation of military events on the British stage was not a new phenomenon. In fact, 'it was' wrote MacKenzie 'the rapid translation of military and naval news to the stage that became the principal excitement of nineteenth-century theatre';[98] and to this end certain theatres specialized in either nautical or military spectacles. In 1913 two playwrights, Cecil Raleigh and Henry Hamilton, produced a play about German spies called *Sealed Orders*. The precedent for war plays, including spy plays, had therefore already been set prior to August, 1914.

War can engender extremes of emotion and encompasses many of the essential components integral to the essence of drama: conflict, sentiment, romance and heroes. The difficulty for the playwrights was not, therefore, content, but rather its mode of presentation. The playwright should, advised *The Era*'s Leader writer in August, 1914:

Avoid boastfulness and brag, and... preserve a tone of quiet confidence
and reliance. The public will resent flippancy and chauvinism as much
as weakness.[99]

The writer concluded by suggesting that people may, as an antidote to the strain of the time, 'go and see a funny or sensational piece: not a military one'.

The playwrights, those writing war plays, ignored the counsel proffered in *The Era*. It would be unfair to say that the playwrights were flippant, but they were certainly chauvinistic; although it must be admitted that the line between chauvinism and patriotism is a thin one, and it is difficult, at times, to judge where national pride ends and jingoistic militarism begins. The playgoers, at least in London, may not have found the editor's advice helpful, as many of the theatres in August, 1914 were closed for the summer recess. The majority of the clientele had dispersed to their summer retreats. There were only half a dozen plays that had an extended run into the autumn; and come December, 1914, only two, *Potash and Perlmutter* and *When Knights were Bold* continued to be produced.[100]

There was naturally some nervousness regarding what the public wanted and, according to E.A. Baughan writing in *The Stage Year Book*, 1915 this was one of the reasons why the managements decided to 'play safe', and revert to known successes. There was also the question of cost. Few of the revivals – there were twenty-one in total – required remounting. The plays that were re-run (excluding Shakespeare) can be described as intellectually light. The musical comedy, *A Country Girl* at Daly's Theatre is a good example. The stage recovered fairly quickly from the war's initial reverberations, and adjusted itself to the new restrictions concerning transport, printing limitations, air raids, lighting restrictions, and later the imposition of Amusement Tax, and finally the problems incurred via National Service commitments. By the first Christmas there were twenty-six theatres open compared with twenty-nine in the previous year.[102] The most popular form of entertainment was the revue. The revue had two advantages over the other forms of light entertainment – musical comedy, melodrama and plays of farce. First, wrote Baughan, 'audiences like comedy to have a serious satirical or symbolic interest' and the revue was ideally suited for this sort of treatment.[103] Secondly, many of the musical comedies were written by 'enemy' composers and for that reason they would not be performed: to produce them would have appeared an anti-patriotic gesture. The show *The Cinema Star* came to a premature end in early September, 1914, for just that reason. The original version was by the German writers Georg Okonkowski and Julius Freud, and the music by Jean Gilbert who, in spite of his name, was also German.[104]

The role of the music hall with its revues can be viewed in antithetical light. In a show, two seemingly contrasting functions could be seen to operate. On the one hand, there were the innocuous sentimental songs and melodramatic farcical sketches which had no connection with the war, but interspersed with this recreational amusement were patriotic songs, and propagandist one-act plays. Some of the music hall shows may have been non-political. Examination of over 400 manuscripts passed by the Lord Chamberlain's Office show that the majority of shows had a wide programme which embraced most facets of life. Therefore, the advice from *The Era* journalist for the theatregoer to seek non-war escapist entertainment to the exclusion of political (in the main military) drama was hard, if not almost impossible to follow.

The war was all-pervasive. It dominated every aspect of life in Britain, and this included theatre. People could find some refuge from the war in some of the plays of the 'legitimate' theatre, but in the socio-political entertainment of the music hall there was no escape. The pantomime, like the revue, had certainly since the second half of the nineteenth century, been one of the most topically-responsive forms of amusement and the war time writers and producers used the pantomime as another platform for jingoistic, patriotic flag-waving. The pantomime *The Babes in the Wood* (1917) at the Opera House, Middlesbrough was an excuse for putting on different war sketches, such as one called *At the Front*.[105] All pantomimes included the popular songs of the day and predominantly this meant the rendition of *Tipperary* and *Take Me Back to Dear Old Blighty*, both included in *Babes in the Wood* (1916) at Gateshead Hippodrome.[106] In *Bo-Peep* at the Coliseum, Glasgow, in the same year, Boy Blue in answer to the question 'What can a poor starving peasant do?' replies:

I'll join the Navy, and will bravely fight.
Our ships are splendid, and our men are right.

And Bo-Peep, who is in love with Boy Blue, encores:

He'll don khaki, and he'll face the foe.
For Britain's honour. He will strike a blow.
For enemies he'll neither fear nor care
When he is wanted, you will find him there.

Why Bo-Peep said he would be a soldier when he clearly stated a preference for the navy seems odd unless it was the cue for some comic stage-business, but, as expected, the wicked Baron was made-up to look like a Hun.[107]

As the war moved inexorably into its third and fourth year there was little change. 'From a high, artistic point of view' wrote Baughan in *The Stage Year Book*, 'the drama of 1916 had been, no doubt, of no great moment'.[108] Again, a year later, he came to the same conclusion.[109] Baughan was referring to non-war plays. In light entertainment it was no different, but a handful of shows were better than most and stood the test of time. The farce *A Little Bit of Fluff* was moving into its second year, and in August, 1916, Oscar Asche's *Chu Chin Chow* was to begin its five-year run. The latter was kept alive by its popular light operatic music, bright colours, chorus line and ever changing scenes. It was constantly being adapted with the insertion of new material, but the process did not change its overall shape. 'It is easy' wrote Lynton Hudson the critic 'to be "superior" about *Chu Chin Chow*, but the audiences who attended its 2,238 performances were not composed of morons... It had charming light operatic music... in Courtice Pounds... a singer who had not only a delightful well-trained tenor voice but also a genuine comedic gift, and in Oscar Asche and Lily Brayton accomplished Shakespearean performers'.[110] The show was part pantomime, part farce, part musical comedy and shaped like a revue. In short, it was, in both senses of the word, variety. A very large proportion of the audience was clad in khaki and navy blue, and no doubt what most of them wanted was gaiety, girls and colour, and a release from the monotony of military training, to say nothing of the horrors of war: in this, the light musical and comedy shows were the perfect antidote.

Many people, especially servicemen, faced with the uncertainties caused by war sought release via hedonistic pastimes, one of which was going to the theatre or music hall – a seemingly innocent enough interest, but one which elicited criticism from some quarters. In *The Stage* in 1916, theatres, according to General Sir Horace Smith-Dorrien, were on a par with immoral night clubs with their 'exhibition of scantily dressed girls and songs of doubtful character'.[111] The General sent an accusing letter to *The Morning Post* and *The Stage* in which he said theatres, and music halls in particular, produced shows of 'low tone, specially... for the younger members of our forces'.[112]

The accusation caused considerable furore at the time. And of course, it was good copy for the press, although the charges set out by Sir Horace were found to be random and unsubstantiated hearsay. Indeed, the General admitted that he did not go to the theatre himself during the war. In November, 1916, at about the same time, the Bishop of London joined in the moral condemnation of the theatres, complaining that plays could be regarded as 'slimy and lecherous'. The bishop later qualified the remark in a letter to the Secretary of the Incorporated Society of Authors, Playwrights and Composers, saying that he was, in fact, referring to the music hall sketches.[113] An examination of the plays submitted to the Lord Chamberlain's Office shows that the censorial comments of his employees demonstrate that any hint of impropriety, actual or inferred, was instantly removed. The General and the Bishop had no case. At the insistence of the Society of Authors and of Oswald Stoll, the music hall proprietor, the Bishop withdrew his allegations.[114]

It was not the plays or sketches that were responsible for the licentiousness of the music hall; the objectors may have also been protesting about the practice of promenading. The antecedence of the music hall lies in the public house, and many of the customs of the pub still prevailed in some of the halls: drinking, smoking and soliciting by prostitutes. It was, in an earlier era, David Garrick who abolished the footman's free gallery, which had 'through its brawling become a nuisance', and it was Macready who did away with the promenade at Drury Lane. And in July, 1916, Alfred Butt, the manager, finally stopped the promenade at the Empire Theatre.[115] The Theatre and Music Hall Committee of the London County Council, at their meeting in November, 1916, refused to renew the licences of a number of halls, and in addition had inserted in the rules governing licences 'that no part of the said house shall be used by prostitutes for the exercise of their calling'.[116] The quality of the evening's programmes aside, the extra activity of promenading may account, in part, for the added attraction of the music hall, particularly for the large numbers of servicemen stationed in the transit camps in London.

There were others who found the actual entertainment not necessarily sinful or sexually explicit, but too frivolous and futile. Writing in *The Times* in 1916, Mr Sidney Lee, who served with the ANZAC Department of the YMCA as a tour guide for overseas soldiers, reported that the colonial soldier was dissatisfied with the West End theatre, and that:

> *The better-educated naively expected the playhouses of the Imperial*
> *capital to offer them sound and exhilarating music and drama,*
> *something far better than they were familiar with in Melbourne...*
> *or Wellington.*[117]

Sidney Lee was publicly supported, at least on one occasion, by an Australian sergeant who wrote in *The Times*:

> *There is a very real need and demand for something other than drivel*
> *and frivolity and coarse vaudeville.*[118]

Mr Lee ended his report by reminding readers that classical drama and opera was available at The Royal Victoria Hall (The Old Vic), which at the time was playing Shakespeare's *Henry VIII*. The theatre was about to embark on a twenty-week run of alternative shows, one Shakespeare the other an opera.

The spy play was still, in 1918, the main theme of war plays. Through 1917 and 1918 there was, however, a discernible lessening of jingoistic and exuberant patriotic cant declaimed on the stage; 'Hun bashing' and heroism had became passé. With regards to actors, this must have been a relief. Hall Caine, the novelist and dramatist, in an address to the American Luncheon Club in March, 1916, outlined the dilemma facing the actor when he said 'Most actors have a dislike to appearing on the stage to spout cheap patriotism as a khaki hero...'.[119] Following the Somme Offensive which began three months later in June, with its horrendous casualty lists, the job of spouting 'cheap patriotism' must have been even more embarrassingly difficult.

People were tired and war-weary by 1918. The restrictions, particularly regarding food, had become irksome. A few plays reflected the public's frustrations. Although the hoarder is castigated in the play *Mrs Pusheen: the Hoarder* at the Alexandra Theatre, Stoke Newington, there is a detectable sympathy in the lines of the song *I'm a Hoarder*:

First Verse
I'm shivering with fear, I am
I'm in an awful state.
And all because I do my best
To fill my little plate.
Suppose Lord Rhodda hears of me.

Or calls round at my place
It's ten to one I'll figure in
a nasty p'lice court case.[120]

The same sympathy is echoed in *Rations*, a play with songs, at the Hippodrome, Colchester, where a little girl quizzes her mother asking:

Little Girl: Mummy, what are those people standing there for?
Mother: They're want for meat [sic].
Little Girl: Meat, Mummy, what's meat?[121]

Whilst most people could identify with the hoarder, the same could not be said for the profiteer. The latter was the butt of many a comedian's joke. The profiteer figured as a character in several plays, although in two of them, *When Our Lads Come Marching Home* and *Illegal Gains*, both produced in February, 1918, the profiteer becomes, following his moral reformation, a hero.[122] The theatre, especially the music hall revues, served the function of giving voice to the frustrations of people who, perhaps, needed to laugh at their plight, and at the same time object to the more minor personal dis-advantages imposed on them by the war.

A number of the better military concert parties were invited, on their return in 1918, to give shows in the West End. The Victoria Palace Theatre played host to, among others, '*The Dumbells*' of the 3rd Canadian Division, a New Zealand troupe, and '*That*' quartet composed of American sailors from Admiral Sim's flagship *U.S.S. Nevada*. The British 1st Army headquarter's concert party, '*Les Rouges et Noirs*', were at the Beaver Hut Theatre (The Little). 'The Dumbells' also appeared at the London Coliseum, and the '*Anzac Coves*' visited several other houses. The entertainment was primarily for servicemen, nevertheless 'it was to their credit', wrote Arthur Coles Armstrong in 1919 'that their applause was invariably gained by legitimate artistic means'.[123] The troupes were composed of men only and, naturally, the female impersonator figured prominently, and by all accounts they were excellent. The military entertainers, like their civilian counterparts, employed the stage as a kind of soap box to voice their criticism of the government, and air their grievance regard-ing the problem of re-employment; an example of this can be seen in the song written by the minor novelist Valentine and partner L.D. Scott, called *Demobilization* (*Figure 32*).

"DEMOBILIZATION."

The war is all over now you all know,
Back to our homes we would all of us go;
The Government's doing their best to assist,
But there is something they seem to have missed.
            Refrain.
        Demobilization!
That's the stuff for the nation,
Old Dally and Dilly are driving us silly
        Down Whitehall way,
Oh! What a sensation – tons of procrastination,
They promise a heap – then they fall asleep
        On Demoblization.
                2.
A cabinet minister, so they say,
Had a most horrible dream yesterday,
Woke up and noticed a bogey, it's said,
Grinning at him from the foot of his bed.
            Refrain.
        Demobilization!
Oh! Whata sensation,
Although he pooh-poohed it and even got rude it
        Refused to go.
Then in desperation got a fine inspiration,
He slumbered again, and dreamed he had slain
        Demoblization.
                3.
Daisy and Reggie were having a spoon
Close on the sofa the whole afternoon,
When Daisy's pa comes and catches the two,
What is it both of them naturally do?
            Refrain.
        Demobilization!
There is no hesitation,
All of a muddle they quickly uncuddle
        In record time.
Oh what consternation– there is no explanation,
Reggie feels sick – when he gets a kick and his
        Demoblization.
                4.
Back again, that is what you like the most
Find in your absence they've filled up your post,
Questioned all day by your kiddie (aged four)
"Daddy, what *did* you do in the great war?"
            Refrain.
        Demobilization!
Back you go with elation,
You look with enjoyment to finding employment
        Without delay.
Oh what consternation– you can't get occupation
In Labour Bureaus – why nobody knows
        Demoblization.
                    Valentine and L.D. Scott.

Figure 32. Songsheet for *Demobilization* by Valentine & Scott 1919.
[L.J. Collins]

The war play was soon to vanish from the West End theatre after the Armistice, although in early 1919 it was still going strong in the provinces. It is interesting to note that the villainous-hun character who appeared in the musical by Oscar Asche and Dornford Yates, *Eastward Ho!* that was submitted to the Lord Chamberlain's Office in August, 1919, had, in the October version, suffered re-casting. He became a Bolshevik. The war plays were quite naturally to die out as people and playwrights turned their minds to the problems, and more pleasurable pursuits, of peace. 'The real war play' wrote the editor of *The Era* in January, 1919 'will come after the war'.[124] The implication was that war was too fresh in peoples' minds to be properly and objectively dramatized. 'And when it comes it will probably not only set the whole country talking – it will very likely pay'. The editor was right, but it was ten years until such a drama was presented: it was R. C. Sherriff's *Journey's End*.

Conclusions

It was rumoured early in the war, wrote George Grossmith –'Gaiety' actor, minor dramatic author and in 1916 Lieutenant in the RNVR – that Field-Marshal Lord Kitchener, the Secretary of State for War, was going to close all the theatres. The order, thankfully for the profession, the theatre-going public, and the military, was not promulgated. Lord French, Commander-in-Chief of the BEF and later Home Forces, remarked to Grossmith that, 'To have closed the places of entertainment would have been a great error'.[1] There was early recognition, not just from Lord French but many other people, and in particular those involved with the stage, that the theatre still had a role to play. This was nothing new. The provision of diversionary amusement is an integral function of the theatre, whether it be war time or not. What was new was the scale of need for 'light entertainment', and the psychologically, if not sociologically, homogeneous make-up of the audiences. Almost everyone needed an avenue of release from the anguish of war, and the theatre with its various forms of entertainment was one means of affording people a temporary escape; although this was not considered by the British government to be a good enough reason for allowing the theatre any financial or manpower relief, despite the difficulties of war-time production.

Evidence points to the fact that theatre had more specific functions, which could be summarized under five headings. First, there was the individual function: theatre work provided a role – be it as recruiter, propagandist or fund raiser – for actors who were too old, infirm or invalided out of the forces. Within the armed forces entertainment allowed the professional to continue his craft and the amateur his hobby; and it supplied the individual performer, especially the better-known artiste, with a public justification for continuing his or her work. Some realized, however, that no matter how laudable their efforts, they still felt somewhat inadequate. Willie Frame, an old music hall entertainer who went to France with the first civilian concert party in 1914, was reported in *The Era* as saying 'This gives one a feeling of gratitude and humiliation; gratitude for being allowed to do what we have done, and humiliation because we can do so little'.[2]

Secondly, within the armed services the function of theatre entertainment can be divided into two sub-categories. For personnel stationed in Britain, and under training, the theatre provided relief from the tedium of military existence. It was also, although without much success, employed as a mode of social control, as in the Sunday concerts at the Woolwich Garrison and the nightly entertainments at Aldershot. To the troops in the fighting areas, on the other hand, entertainment was much more than just a release from the ennui of trench life. To both the servicemen in training at home, and personnel abroad, the theatre helped to maintain morale, but to the fighting soldier, sailor and airman who had not seen his family for months, and in some cases years, the theatre assumed a position of added importance. The sight of a pretty girl in a civilian concert party dressed in a colourful frock reminded him of another world, another time. So desirous of this other peaceful, happier and brighter place were the soldiers, that they tried to recreate a theatrical vision of home and 'normality' by attempting in their own shows to imitate the familiar – even to the point of dressing men up as women. The temporary illusion and the opportunity to sing and laugh was, as recognized by the highest military authorities, an important means of maintaining morale. The theatrical productions also gave all ranks, and in particular the lower ranks, a legitimate opportunity to voice corporate feelings of dissent: the theatre was, in more ways than one, a valued psychological safety-valve. The extent to which entertainment in the military was considered important can be judged not only by the references in private letters and diaries but by the fact that it was encouraged, if not initiated, by the highest-ranked officers. Theatre in the British and Dominion forces received authoritative sanction when the military, under the aegis of the NACB, set up its own entertainment organization.

Outside the military the function of theatre was not controlled, nonetheless its purpose became obvious. The theatre had, thirdly, an unofficial government-supportive role. It helped to rally men to the flag, that is the theatre acted as a recruiting agent for the authorities. The recruiter could be aiming his or her patter at any man young enough to be in the army, navy or air force, or it could be in the form of a song directed at a particular section of the male populace; for example, the recruiting song for the Bantams, which was for the 'benefit' of men under five foot three inches in height. It was written by Stephen West in 1915; the last verse reads:

So what does it matter what the height may be?
If it's five foot one or five foot ten?
If a Briton's heart beats right.
And he's longing for a fight,
And the Dear Old Country calls out now for Men?[3]

There were other songs, not necessarily specifically to do with recruiting, that extolled the 'virtues' of a sailor or soldier. It was part of the propagandist hype, as were the war plays that encouraged hatred of the enemy, and constantly reminded people of the largely imagined threat of foreign spies. The moral basis of these functions is open to question. The same, however, cannot be said for other government assistance provided by the theatre, which raised millions of pounds for the lengthy list of charities caring for the families of dead servicemen; for the sailors, soldiers and airmen, and their dependents; and for the employment of the civilian concert parties that went round the hospitals giving comfort and, according to the medical officers, aiding the recovery of the injured. In addition to the money raised for these purposes, the theatre also helped the British Government by encouraging people to purchase War Saving Bonds. The Government acknowledged the contribution the theatre made through the profession's war-work by bestowing honours on certain individuals.

Money and manpower assistance for the Government was not always on a voluntary basis. The fourth category of functions is the one imposed by the Government: the employment of men for National Service and the paying of Amusement Tax. The former was short-lived and relatively ineffectual as most men not serving in the armed forces were either too old or infirm. The latter, taxation, apart from the lack of manpower, was probably the greatest burden the theatre business had to endure, and was felt by some to be counter-productive. The financial cost was considered so great that a number of managers went out of business and theatres closed, thereby depriving some people of work, others of needed entertainment, and the Government of revenue.

Music hall had always provided a platform for two contrasting concepts – conformity and patriotism, criticism and dissent. Evidence from late-Victorian and Edwardian autobiographies and memoirs, writes MacKenzie, shows that anyone displaying unpatriotic ideas or socialist tendencies was 'mocked';[4] and not surprisingly, in a period of nationally-shared crisis, any dissenter would be even more likely to be subjected to public ridicule in the press and on stage. The theatre, therefore, served a fifth function when a considerable number of playwrights used the stage as a platform for airing their ardently propagandist, and chauvinistically bellicose, views. This was done with the knowledge, if not the artistic support, of the Lord Chamberlain's Office.

The war-time stage, whether inside or outside the forces, witnessed an unusual degree of co-operation between amateur and professional performers. Within the serving units it was obviously necessary, given the precariousness of the soldier's job and the paucity of trained performers, to utilize whatever talent there was available. In the civilian theatre the sharing of the stage by amateur and professional actors was confined, in the main, to charity shows, although some local amateurs were engaged on a low wage for minor parts when, argued the manager, there was a shortage of professionals. When members of the armed forces appeared on the commercial stage as a company the question of amateur or professional status did not arise, as the performances were for charity – the profits usually being donated to a particular regimental benevolent society.

The British military troupes, along with the 1st Army HQ concert party, that were known to have had runs in a London theatre in 1918 were: the (58th Division) concert party '*The Goods*' at the Middlesex Theatre; the officers of the 5th Battalion, the Middlesex Regiment at the Court Theatre in *Le Courrier De Lyon* (an adaptation of *The Lyons Mail*); and in the provinces, the revue *Excuses; Or, Why They Were Late*, presented by the Summerdown Convalescent Camp at the Pier Theatre, Eastbourne; and *Alice in Sunder-land*, a musical farce, at Hylton Castle Camp. They were all unpaid despite the inclusion of any pre-war professional artistes a company might have.[5] It was not the practice of stage employees to cross the barrier between the professional and amateur, but given the war-time circumstances the opportunity to do so was taken, and this co-operation became a consequence of the main function of providing entertainment during the war years.

As the war dragged on criticism and dissent began to be heard on the stage. It was criticism, not only of those with 'left-wing' views and the pacifists, but also of the exploiters the hoarders and the profiteers. The Government was not openly criticized, except by servicemen and entertainers in the military, who were overtly hostile towards the national demobilization policy. The fact that military concert parties were still able to perform publicly after the war ended may be due, in part, to the Government's method of releasing both volunteers and conscripts. Those who once had a job considered to be of national importance went first, the remainder would have to wait.[6] This method of selective discharge meant that a large number of soldiers, who had served only a few weeks, were released first. Under this system actors would be one of the last category of soldier to be discharged. It was not surprising that the veteran, be he actor or otherwise, who had been serving since 1914, marched to London's Whitehall and forced the Government to change its demobilization plans.

One section of society that had no problem regarding employment was the aristocracy, and like everyone else they played a part during the war. Those who could not go to the Front did 'good works' at home, much of it connected with the theatre and charities. It would not be inaccurate to say that the theatre provided Royalty and other aristocratic notables with a war-time function. It did, after all, offer them a ready-made opportunity to contribute in a public way to the war-effort, and at the same time, let people see that they were attempting to 'do their bit'.

The year 1916 was significant in military terms for the Battle of the Somme, and was a low-point for the British and Dominion armies, but it was also Shakespeare's Tercentenary. Britain needed something to celebrate, and perhaps it was a little ironic that whilst many families were lamenting the death of a soldier-relative, time was taken to commemorate the death of an English playwright. The Tercentenary was celebrated in churches, in Westminster Abbey, in theatres and in the most appropriately theatrical way of all when F.R. Benson was knighted by the King at Drury Lane Theatre, whilst still clad in the robes of Julius Caesar. Celebrations were obviously muted, but occasions of remembrance were held in different countries, at the Front and in P.O.W. camps. The anniversary of the death of Britain's greatest playwright came at an opportune moment, a time when the country desperately required something to celebrate.

Whilst the country commemorated the achievements of Shakespeare the contemporary British playwrights were extra-ordinarily quiet. Somerset Maugham was not, of course, in a position to write as he was serving in the army. Henry Arthur Jones had only one full-length piece, *The Pacifists*, produced; it lasted only twenty performances. A.W. Pinero was marginally more successful with his play *The Freaks* in 1918; it lasted fifty-one nights. John Galsworthy wrote nothing of note, but like J.M. Barrie was seconded to the Foreign Office News Department at Wellington House as part of the government propaganda machine. Barrie was more productive than the other recognized playwrights, writing *A Kiss for Cinderella* in 1916, and *Dear Brutus* in 1917. George Bernard Shaw was busy writing polemic pamphlets about war, which, as in the case of *Common Sense about the War*, caused a storm of abuse, although by 1917 he was to say 'my bolt is shot as to writing about the war'. He did, however, in 1916 write *Heartbreak House*, and was at work on *Back to Methuselah*, but they were not produced until after the war. Art could, concluded Shaw, 'only be carried out by the deaf. A fellow Fabian, Rebecca West, concurred, and added 'the artiste who, like Shaw, abandons it, at least shows that he had good hearing and is listening to the world'.[7]

The critic Arthur Coles Armstrong re-iterated the criticism of the stage and its product when he wrote:

> *In an artistic and productive sense the variety world, like the theatrical world, may be said to have been marking time during 1918.*[8]

He could have made the same comment about the preceding four years. If the theatre failed artistically it was, however, rarely more popular or, given the limitations of the time, productively more prosperous.[9]

One fact that did emerge from the operation of theatre in the First World War was the knowledge that the stage can be used and misused with the blessing, if not the connivance, of the Government for both the benefit and the deception of the public, although, judging by the short runs of the crude, jingoistic and overtly propaganda plays, the public were not totally deceived. The popularity of the theatre with the public generally, and the forces in particular, showed that entertainment can be beneficial in three distinct ways: first, materially for those in its employ; secondly, psychologically to the population at large; thirdly, and more specifically, to those servicemen undergoing physical rehabilitation.

An acknowledgement of the work done by the theatre came from the monarch. Three days after the Armistice was signed the King, Queen and Princess Mary went to see the revue *The Bing Boys* on Broadway, starring George Robey and Violet Lorraine at the Alhambra Theatre in the West End. At the conclusion of the show the King expressed his gratitude for the work the variety theatre had done during the war, when he said to Oswald Stoll:

> *I felt anxious to show my personal appreciation of the handsome way in which a popular entertainment industry has helped in the war with great sums of money, untiring service, and many sad sacrifices.*[10]

An indication of the integral and consequent role of the theatre during the First World War can be gauged by the measures taken to replicate its function(s) some twenty years later. In 1938, when the likelihood of a second world conflict looked increasingly inevitable the concept of ENSA (Entertainments National Service Association) was formulated. This was as a result of a meeting between Godfrey Tearle, Owen Nares, Leslie Henson and Basil Dean; and it was almost inevitable that Basil Dean, the former organizer of entertainment via the NACB, would become the overall co-ordinator of the new 1939–45 organization. The continuation of entertainments during the Second World War in the British and Dominion forces, via ENSA, was made possible because of the precedent set in the war of 1914–18, and because entertainments under the auspices of the NAAFI continued after 1919, albeit on an *ad hoc* basis, at special functions and 'summer canvas camps'.[11] The distance in time was not long between the two world wars and many people remembered the effect theatre had during the Great War, and they thought that theatre had, once again, an important role to play. The British Government, however, had a rather shorter memory and as soon as war was declared in 1939 theatres were ordered to close, but due to pressure from all quarters, and especially from the King's former secretary Lord Wigram, the ban was lifted within a week. Many of the lessons learnt in 1914–18 were put into practice during 1939–45. This time the authorities, once they had overcome the panic reaction of the first week, sanctioned the deferment of some artistes so that theatres could get replacements or companies finish their run, and later, actors – including Laurence Olivier and Ralph Richardson – were taken out of the armed forces, and instead served with ENSA. It was realized that the maintenance of morale through diversionary amusements such as theatre was a necessary part of the war effort.

Today the theatre of the First World War is often remembered for the satirically patriotic songs included in the 1960s musical *Oh, What a Lovely War*, produced by Joan Littlewood at the Stratford Royal

Theatre in East London. It is equally remembered for songs that were still popular in the Second World War, such as *Pack up Your Troubles in Your Old Kit Bag*, Ivor Novello's *Keep the Home Fires Burning*, George Robey's *If You Were the Only Girl in the World*, and, of course, Jack Judge's evergreen *Tipperary*.

To examine the role and function of theatre in terms of popular song only is as limiting as viewing the theatre as simply a purveyor of 'intellectual' or 'esoteric' drama. The theatre in the Great War of 1914–18 had a multiplicity of inter-related functions. It served the individual, the armed forces, the profession and the general public. For the sake of its corporate economic survival and the individual's moral peace-of-mind, the theatre had to be seen to be purposeful and relevant. In doing so it became a voluntary instrument of both the military and the government. However, what is equally important is the fact that theatre, in all its guises, not only survived but was in great demand. The lesson was learnt that entertainment is vitally important for everyone, and can be much more than a provider of ephemeral amusement, especially in times of war.

Notes

Abbreviations: Imperial War Museum – IWM; British Library – BL

INTRODUCTION

1. J.C. Kemp *The British Repertory Theatre* [Birmingham: Cornish, 1943] p.2.
2. Ibid., p. 4.
3. C.B. Purdom *Harley Granville Barker* [London: Rockliff 1955] p. 26.
4. G. Rowell and A. Jackson *The Repertory Movement* [Cambridge: CUP, 1984], p. 47.
5. Rex Pogson *Miss Horniman and the Gaiety Theatre, Manchester* [London: Rockliff, 1952] pp. 22–38.
6. Arthur Marwick *The Deluge – British Society and the First World War* [Basingstoke: Macmillan, 1965] pp. 125–127.
7. Ibid., p. 140.
8. Phyllis Hartnoll *A Concise History of the Theatre* [Norwich: Thames and Hudson, 1968] pp. 186–239.
9. Allardyce Nicoll *English Drama 1900–1930* [Cambridge: CUP, 1973] and *British Drama* [London: Harrap, 1925].
10. Hugh Hunt *The Revels History of Drama in English* [London: Methuen, 1978] T. W. Craik (gen. ed.) pp. 29–31.
11. J.C. Trewin *The Edwardian Theatre* [London: Dakers, 1976] and *Theatre in the Twenties* [London: Dakers, 1958].
12. Ernest Short *Sixty Years of Theatre* [London: Eyre and Spottiswoode, 1951], pp. 152–161.
13. W Macqueen-Pope *Ghosts and Greasepaint* [London: Hale, 1951], pp. 295–308.
14. Lynton Hudson *The English Stage 1850-1950* [London: Harrap, 1951] p. 169.
15. Arthur Marwick, op. cit., p. 144.
16. G.T. Watts 'The Tradition of Theatre' *The Englishwoman* November, 1916, in M. Sanderson *From Irving to Olivier* [London: Athlone, 1984] p. 163.
17. Central Statistical Office (HMSO) *Retail Prices 1914–1990* [prices rose enormously during the First World War; in 1915 the Retail Price Index doubled to 41. To give some indication of today's values all monetary sums should be multiplied by 30].

CHAPTER 1 RECRUITMENT AND EMPLOYMENT

1. A. Ponsonby *Falsehood in War Time* [London: Allen & Unwin, 1928], pp. 84–7.
2. A.J.P. Taylor *English History 1914–15* [London: OUP, 1965], p. 12.
3. Paul Fussell *The Great War and Modern Memory* [Oxford: OUP, 1975], p.9.
4. B. Weller 'The Theatrical Year' *The Stage Year Book, 1915* p. 11.
5. *The Era* 5 August, 1914.
6. Ibid.
7. *The Era* 17 January, 1917.
8. *The Era* 27 January, 1915.
9. *The Era* 2 September, 1914.
10. Sir John Martin-Harvey *Autobiography* [London: Samson & Low, 1933] pp. 448–9.
11. Michael Sanderson *From Irving to Olivier* [London: Athlone, 1984] p. 172.
12. Harry Lauder *A Minstrel in France* [London: Melrose, 1918] p. 44.
13. *The Era* 9 February, 1916.
14. *The Times* 15 January, 1915.
15. John M. MacKenzie *Propaganda and Empire* [Manchester: MUP 1984], p. 30.
16. *The Era* 28 October, 1914.
17. Ibid.
18. Song Sheet, IWM Collection, 1914.
19. C. Pulling *They Were Singing and What They Sang About* [London: Harrap, 1952] p. 81.
20. *The Era* 16 September, 1914.
21. *The Era* 28 October, 1914.
22. Penny Summerfield 'Patriotism and Empire' in *Imperialism and Popular Culture* J.M. MacKenzie (ed.) [Manchester: MUP, 1986] p.38.
23. Ibid.
24. Ibid.
25. *The Era* 9 February, 1916.
26. *The Era* 16 January, 1915.
27. Ibid.
28. Colin Walsh *Mud, Songs and Blighty* [London: Hutchinson, 1975] p.21.
29. Ibid.
30. *The Era* 20 January, 1915.
31. *The Stage* 22 December, 1914.
32. Colonel H.A.R. May, CB *Memories of the Artists' Rifles* [London: Howlett, 1929] p. 8.
33. Artists' Rifles *Roll of Honour* [London: Howlett, 1922] p. vii.

34. B. A. Young *The Artists and the SAS* [London: (Artists) TA, 1960] p. 19.
35. Artists' Rifles Concert programme 1915 No. 3/41 IWM.
36. B. A. Young, op. cit., p. 20.
37. Edward Potton (ed.) *A Record of the United Arts Rifles* [London: Moring, 1920] p. 3.
38. Ibid.
39. Ibid.
40. *The Stage* 17 September, 1914.
41. *The Stage* 24 September, 1914.
42. Robert Graves *Goodbye To All That* [London: Cape, 1929] p. 189.
43. Leslie Henson *Yours Faithfully* [London: Long, 1948] p. 56.
44. *The Era* 13 January, 1915.
45. Ibid.
46. Ibid.
47. *The Era* 30 June, 1915.
48. *The Stage* 28 October, 1915.
49. *The Stage* 7 October, 1915.
50. *The Era* 26 May, 1915.
51. *The Era* 30 June, 1915.
52. B. Weller 'The War and The Stage' *The Stage Year Book*,1916. p. 14.
53. Arthur Marwick *The Deluge – British Society and the First World War* [Basingstoke: Macmillan, 1965] p. 76.
54. A.J.P. Taylor, op. cit., p. 53.
55. *The Stage* 16 December, 1915.
56. Ibid.
57. *The Era* 5 January, 1916.
58. Ibid.
59. *The Stage* 18 May, 1916.
60. *The Era* 18 May, 1916.
61. *The Stage* 18 May, 1916.
62. *The Era* 11 May, 1916.
63. Ibid.
64. *The Stage* 11 May, 1916.
65. *The Era* 31 May, 1916.
66. *The Era* 24 May, 1916.
67. Ibid.
68. *The Stage* 15 June, 1916.
69. *The Stage* 20 July, 1916.
70. *The Stage* 15 June, 1916.
71. *The Stage* 7 September, 1916.
72. Ibid.
73. *The Stage* 16 August, 1917.
74. *The Times* 1 October, 1914.
75. *The Times* 12 September, 1916.
76. Ibid.

77. Ibid.
78. *The Times* 13 September, 1916.
79. Titled photographs 'Actors and The War' *The Stage Year Book*, 1916. pp. 16–18.
80. Frank Pettingell *We Cannot All Be Soldiers*. Music and programme in IWM, File 54 (41) 3.39.
81. H. Wolfe *Labour Supply & Regulations* 1923 in Arthur Marwick, op. cit., p.57.
82. Theatre programme for *Vivian*, Prince of Wales' Theatre, Birmingham 1915. Private collection.
83. B. Weller 'The Stage in War Time' *The Stage Year Book, 1917* p. 17.

CHAPTER 2 EFFECTS OF WAR ON THEATRICAL PRODUCTION

1. B. Weller, 'The War Time Stage' *The Stage Year Book, 1918*, p. 12.
2. *The Stage* 1 March, 1917.
3. *The Stage* 8 March, 1917.
4. Ibid.
5. Ibid.
6. J.C. Trewin *The Birmingham Repertory Theatre* [Birmingham: Cornish, 1943] p. 36.
7. Cyril Maud *Behind the Scenes* [London: Murray, 1927] p. 246.
8. B. Weller, op. cit., p. 13.
9. J.A. Fairlie *British War Administration* [New York: OUP, 1919] p. 254.
10. *The Stage* 15 March, 1917.
11. Ibid.
12. *The Times History of the War* Vol. VI. 1914–19 [London: Times, 1920] pp. 183—4.
13. B. Weller, 'The Theatrical Year' *The Stage Year Book, 1915* p. 11.
14. E. M. Sansom 'The Variety Year' *The Stage Year Book, 1915* p. 25.
15. A.J.P. Taylor *English History 1914–45* [London: OUP, 1965], p. 5.
16. *The Stage* 27 January, 1916.
17. *The Era* 3 January, 1917.
18. A Coles Armstrong 'The Variety Year' *The Stage Year Book, 1918* p. 28.
19. *The Era* 3 January, 1917.
20. A.J.P. Taylor, op. cit., 47.
21. Ibid. p. 43.
22. H. Pelling *Modern Britain 1885–1955* [London: Cardinal, 1974] p. 77.
23. *The Stage* 16 March, 1916.
24. *The Stage* 26 October, 1916.
25. B. Weller 'The War-Time Stage' *The Stage Year Book, 1919* p. 26.
26. *The Times* 26 December, 1914.
27. *The Stage* 17 February, 1916.
28. Ibid.

29. Michael Sanderson *From Irving to Olivier* [London: Athlone, 1984], p. 164.
30. B. Weller, op. cit., [1919] p. 25.
31. Ibid. p. 25.
32. Michael Sanderson, op. cit., p. 164.
33. *The Stage* 27 September, 1917.
34. Ibid.
35. Lilian Baylis and Cicely Hamilton *The Old Vic* [London: Cape, 1926] p. 210.
36. Ibid. p. 211.
37. Leslie Henson *Yours Faithfully* [London: Long, 1948], p. 53.
38. Marguerite Steen *A Pride of Terrys* [London: Longmans, 1926]
39. B. Weller, op. cit. [1918] p. 15.
40. *The Era* 31 October, 1917.
41. *The Observer* 12 January, 1919.
42. *The Era* 7 February, 1917.
43. Harold Holland *True Values* Surrey Theatre [April: 1918] MS 1494, Vol. 6. BL.
44. Laurie Wylie *The Passing Show of 1918* Theatre Royal, Birmingham [July: 1918] MS 1652, Vol. 12. BL.
45. *National War Savings Report*, pp. 1917–18, XVIII Cd 8516, p. 1.
46. Arthur Marwick *The Deluge – British Society and the First World War* [Basingstoke: Macmillan, 1965] p. 129.
47. *The Era* 22 September, 1915.
48. *The Stage* 3 February, 1916.
49. *The Era* 9 February, 1916.
50. *The Stage* 10 February 1916.
51. *The Stage* 9 March, 1916.
52. *The Observer* 11 April, 1915.
53. *The Era* 12 April, 1916.
54. *The Times* 15 August, 1916.
55. *The Stage* 19 July, 1917.
56. *The Era* 21 November, 1917.
57. *The Stage* 31 May, 1917.
58. *The Era* 21 November, 1917.
59. *The Stage*, 31 May, 1917.

CHAPTER 3 PERFORMING FOR CHARITY

1. John Stevenson *British Society 1914–45* [Harmondsworth: Pelican, 1984] p. 61.
2. Arthur Marwick *The Deluge – British Society and the First World War* [Basingstoke: Macmillan, 1965] p. 42.
3. Ibid. pp. 42–3.
4. John Stevenson, op. cit., p. 60.

5. 'Wounded Heroes Entertainment Committee Report' 25 April 1919 *Benevolent Organizations* File 7/12 IWM.
6. Ibid.
7. Ibid.
8. Musical Programme 1917. Ref: 9. 12 IWM.
9. E. M. Sansom 'The Variety Year' *The Stage Year Book, 1916* p. 28.
10. Arthur Coles Armstrong 'The Variety Year' *The Stage Year Book, 1919*, p. 32.
11. Ibid.
12. Ibid.
13. Ibid.
14. Seymour Hicks *Between Ourselves* [London: Cassell, 1930] p. 148.
15. Coles Armstrong, op. cit., p. 32.
16. Ibid. p. 33.
17. Michael Holroyd *The Pursuit of Power 1898–1918* [London: Hodder 1989] Vol. 2. p. 360.
18. Denis Mackail *The Story of J.M.B.* [London: Davies, 1941] p. 161.
19. Ibid. p. 498.
20. Max Beerbohm *Herbert Beerbohm Tree* [London: Hutchinson, 1917] p. 485.
21. Michael Sanderson *From Irving to Olivier* [London: Athlone, 1984], p. 161.
22. Eva Moore *Exits and Entrances* [London: Chapman & Hall, 1923] p. 80.
23. *The Era* 9 September, 1914.
24. 'Royalty at the Theatre' *The Stage Year Book, 1915* p. 20; *The Stage Year Book, 1916* p. 35; *The Stage Year Book, 1917* p. 8A; *The Stage Year Book, 1918* p. 22; *The Stage Year Book, 1919* p. 111.
25. *The Times* 12 May, 1915.
26. Ibid.
27. *The Times* 22 May, 1916.
28. Ibid.
29. *The Times* 23 March, 1916.
30. *The Times* 26 March, 1915.
31. *The Times* 5 May, 1915.
32. *The Times* 12 May, 1915.
33. *Jean Nougues matinee* Prince of Wales' Theatre programme. 30 June, 1916. Private collection.
34. Arthur Coles Armstrong 'The Variety Theatre' *The Stage Year Book, 1917* p. 27.
35. Ibid.
36. *The Era* 27 October, 1915.
37 Memo: Book, *Stage* Chapter. Files B07 15/17. IWM.
38. Arthur Marwick, op. cit., p. 136.
39. *The Organization and Methods of the Central Prisoners of War Committee* pp. 1917–18, XVIII, Cd. 8615, pp. 2–6.

40. 'Beneficient Order of Terriers' 21 June, 1919. Letter to sub-committee *Benevolent Organisations* Files 6/1, 8/18 [1920] IWM.

41. King's Theatre, Glasgow, programme. 26 September, 1918. Private collection.

42. 'Royal Small Arms Committee Report' March to November, 1918 *Benevolent Organisations* Files 6/1, 8/18 [1920] IWM.

43. 'YMCA Music Section' *Benevolent Organisations* Files 6/1, 8/18 [1920] IWM.

44. *Musical News*, 28 August, 1915.

45. Theatre Programme. Ref 86/26/1. IWM.

46. *The Times* 30 December, 1915.

47. *The Times* 4 October, 1916.

48. Ibid.

49. *The Stage* 1 February, 1917.

50. Ibid.

51. Ibid.

52. Ibid.

53. *The Observer* 28 November, 1915.

54. Ibid.

55. Annette Hullah 'Record of Music in War Time Committee' *Musical News* August/September [1920]; Entertainments Record *Benevolent Organisations* Files 6/1, 8/18 [1920] IWM

56. Ibid.

57. *The Stage* 15 October, 1914.

58. *The Times* 1 August, 1916.

59. *The Era* 25 November, 1914.

60. *The Era* 26 December, 1917.

61. *The Era* 25 August, 1915.

62. *The Stage* 29 July, 1915.

63. Arthur Marwick, op. cit., p. 21.

64. *The Stage* 3 September, 1914, in Joseph MacLeod *The Actor's Right to Act* [London: Lawrence & Wishart, 1981] p. 115.

65. *The Stage* 23 September, 1915.

66. Ibid.

67. Joseph MacLeod, op. cit., p. 115.

68. *The Stage* 23 July, 1915.

69. *The Stage* 27 July, 1916.

70. *The Times* 16 October, 1916.

71. *The Stage* 14 June, 1917.

72. *The Stage* 19 July, 1917.

73. Ibid.

74. *The Stage* 14 June, 1917.

75. *The Stage* 19 July, 1917.

76. Annette Hullah, op. cit., Files 6/1, 8/18.

77. *The Times* 23 November, 1918.

78. *The Daily Telegraph* 4 September, 1915.
79. Annette Hullah, op. cit., Files 6/1, 8/18.
80. Ibid.
81. Ibid.
82. Ibid.
83. Ibid.
84. *The Observer* 12 December, 1918.
85. Annette Hullah, op. cit., Files 6/1, 8/18.
86. Ibid.
87. *The Daily Telegraph* 4 September, 1915 and *Benevolent Organisations* Files 6/1, 8/18 [1920] IWM.
88. 'Entertainments Record' in 'Women at Work' *Benevolent Organisations* Files 6/1, 8/18 [1920] IWM.
89. Ibid.
90. Ibid.
91. B. Weller 'The War and the Stage' *The Stage Year Book, 1915*, p. 13.
92. Arthur Coles Armstrong 'The Variety Year' *The Stage Year Book, 1919* p. 35.
93. Gertrude Kingston *Curtsey While You're Thinking* [London: Williams & Norgate 1937] pp. 169–70.
94. Retail Price Index tables in Accountancy 1984. Journal of Chartered Accountant of England & Wales.
95. Sir John Martin-Harvey *Autobiography* [London: Samson & Low, 1933] pp. 449–51.
96. Jay Winter 'Army and society; the demographic context' in Ian Beckett and Keith Simpson [eds.] *A Nation in Arms* [Manchester: MUP, 1985] p. 201.
97. Lena Ashwell *Myself a Player* [London: Gyldendal, 1936] p. 183.
98. Naomi Jacob *Me* [London: Hutchinson, 1933] pp. 117–9.
99. Ibid.
100. Eva Moore, op.cit., p. 80.
101. Margaret Webster *The Same Only Different* [London: Gollancz, 1969] pp. 252–3.
102. Michael Sanderson, op. cit., p. 166.

CHAPTER 4 FORCES ENTERTAINMENT IN BRITAIN

1. 'Entertainment Record' *Benevolent Organisations* Files 6/1, 8/18 [1920] IWM.
2. Ibid.
3. Ibid.
4. Ibid.
5. Ibid.
6. *Aldershot News* 1 November, 1918.
7. *Daily Chronicle* 2 February, 1915.
8. Gilbert Mant [ed.] *Soldier Boy*. Letters and memoirs of Gunner W. J. Duffell 1915–18 [Stevenage: Spa, 1992] pp. 130–31.

9. *The Times* 9 October, 1914.
10. Ibid.
11. I. Clephane *Towards Sex Freedom* [London: Lane, 1936] p. 137.
12. T. J. Mitchell and G. M. Smith *Medical Service: Casualties and Medical Statistics of the Great War* [London: HMSO, 1931] pp. 164 and p. 174.
13. Peter Simkins 'Soldiers and civilians: billeting in Britain and France' in *A Nation in Arms* Ian Beckett and Keith Simpson [eds.] [Manchester: MUP, 1985] pp. 185–6.
14. *The Daily Telegraph* 4 September, 1915.
15. *The Times* 3 July, 1915.
16. Ibid.
17. *The Times* 17 February, 1916.
18. *The Times* 3 July, 1915.
19. *The Morning Post* 17 February, 1915
20. Soldiers Entertainment Fund' *Benevolent Organisations* Files 6/1, 8/18 [1920] IWM.
21. Ibid.
22. *Musical Times* August/September, 1920.
23. *The Times* 8 October, 1914.
24. Ibid.
25. YMCA *The Red Triangle Handbook* [London: YMCA Library, 1915] pp. 111–116.
26. Ibid.
27. *The British Empire YMCA Weekly* 31 September, 1915.
28. *The Stage* 4 October, 1917.
29. B. Weller 'The War Time Stage' *The Stage Year Book, 1918* p. 16.
30. *The Stage* 4 October, 1917.
31. Ibid.
32. Ibid.
33. B. Weller, op. cit., pp. 16–17.
34. *The Stage* 22 July, 1915.
35. Arthur Croxton *Crowded Nights and Days* [London: Sampson, Low & Marston, 1924] pp. 378–9.
36. Captain L. A. Kenny, MBE, RA *Extracts from Diaries of 1919* File 14, D/14 CB4. IWM.
37. Ibid.
38. Ibid.
39. *The Stage* 15 July, 1915.
40. *The Stage* 10 August, 1916.
41. Basil Dean *The Theatre at War* [London: Harrap, 1956] p. 22.
42. Ibid., p. 23.
43. Ibid., p. 25.
44. Ibid., p. 23.
45. Ibid., p. 25.
46. Ibid., p. 26.

47. Basil Dean *Seven Ages – An Autobiography 1888–1927* [London: Hutchinson, 1970] p. 126.
48. Ibid.,p. 127.
49. *The Stage* 20 September, 1917.
50. Basil Dean *Seven Ages*, op. cit., p. 217.
51. *The Stage* 16 October, 1917.
52. B. Weller, op. cit., pp. 16–17.
53. *The Stage* 20 September, 1917.
54. Ibid.
55. Ibid.
56. Paul Fussell *The Great War and Modern Memory* [Oxford: OUP, 1975], p. 82.
57. *The Stage* 4 October, 1917.
58. Ibid.
59. *The Stage* 20 September, 1917.
60. Ibid.
61. *The Stage* 27 September, 1917.
62. Ibid.
63. *The Stage* 20 September, 1917.
64. Ibid.
65. *The Stage* 4 October, 1917.
66. *The Era* 9 January, 1918.
67. Ibid.
68. *The Era* 17 October, 1917.
69. *The Era* 21 November, 1917.
70. *The Era* 17 October, 1917.
71. *Report on Brocton Camp Complaints 1917–19* Files: W/W/1, 78/31/1 [1920] IWM.
72. Paul Cohen-Portheim *Time Stood Still: My Internment in England, 1914–1918* [London: Duckworth, 1932] p. 91.
73. *The Times* 20 December, 1915.
74. P. Cohen-Portheim, op. cit., p. 147.
75. Ibid., p. 153.
76. *The Times* 20 December, 1915.
77. Ibid.
78. A.J.P. Taylor *The First World War* [London: Hamilton, 1963] pp. 36–37.
79. Chris Davis *Cocktails* Marlborough Theatre, Holloway [June, 1916] MS Vol 113. BL.
80. W. Macqueen-Pope *Ghosts and Greasepaint* [London: Hale, 1951] pp. 297–99.
81. Ibid.
82. *Benevolent Organisations* Files 6/1, 8/18 [1920] IWM.
83. *The Times* 26 April, 1916.
84. A. Coles Armstrong 'The Variety Year' *The Stage Year Book, 1919* p. 35.
85. *The Times* 21 January, 1918.
86. A. Coles Armstrong, op. cit., 35.

CHAPTER 5 MILITARY PROVISION ABROAD

1. *The Times* 4 February, 1915.
2. E. W. Hornung *Notes on a Camp-follower on the Western Front* [London: Constable, 1919] p. 188.
3. *The Stage* 30 August, 1917.
4. Major R. S. Cockman, MC *Diary 1916–1918* RSC/l ref: 258 p. 115 IWM.
5. Ibid.,p. 115.
6. Edmund Blunden *Undertones of War* [Harmondsworth: Pelican, 1937] p. 128.
7. R. S. Cockman, op. cit., p. 115.
8. Dorothy Nicol in *Roses of No Man's Land* compiled by Lyn MacDonald [Basingstoke: Macmillan, 1980] p. 209.
9. Ibid., p. 210.
10. Ibid., p. 210.
11. *The Tatler* 29 November, 1916.
12. *The Stage* 9 September, 1915.
13. R. S. Cockman, op. cit.,p. 115.
14. Private S. Smith *Personal Diary* 1920 88/3/1 IWM.
15. Colonel W. N. Nicholson, CMG, DSO *Behind the Lines* [London: Cape, 1939], p. 157.
16. Ibid., p. 254.
17. Ibid., p. 250.
18. Bert Chaney 'A Lad Goes to War' in M. Moynihan [ed.] *People at War 1914–1918* [Newton Abbot: David & Charles, 1973] pp. 122 – 3.
19. W. N. Nicholson, op. cit., p. 252.
20. William St Leger 'Death Wish in No Man's Land' in M. Moynihan, op. cit., p. 50.
21. R. S. Cockman, op. cit., p. 117.
22. Ibid.,p. 117.
23. W. N. Nicholson, op. cit., p. 225.
24. Ibid., p. 255.
25. Barry Findon, *The Play Pictorial* (Supplement) No. 200, Vol. XXXIII January, 1919.
26. W. N. Nicholson, op. cit., p. 225.
27. R. S. Cockman, op. cit., p. 117.
28. Ibid.,p. 117.
29. Leslie Henson *Yours Faithfully* [London: Hodder & Staunton, 1948] p. 67.
30. Leslie Henson *My Laugh Story* [London: Long, 1926] p. 234.
31. Ibid., p. 244.
32. Ibid., p. 242 and *The Times* 7 September, 1915.
33. *The Era* 14 July, 1915.
34. L. Henson *My Laugh Story*, op. cit., p. 249.
35. 'Roll of Honour–Killed in the War' *The Stage Year Book, 1919* p. 118.

36. *The Times* 30 December, 1915.
37. *The Stage* 20 July, 1916.
38. *The Times* 1 August, 1916.
39. *The Times* 24 August, 1915.
40. *The Times* 21 September, 1916.
41. Parliamentary Papers. Command Document 9106. 1916.
42. *The Era* 22 September, 1915.
43. Souvenir Album *Ruhleben Exhibition* 1919 private collection.
44. J. Davidson Ketchum *Ruhleben – A Prison Camp Society* [Oxford; OUP, 1965] p. 318.
45. Ibid., p. 202.
46. Ibid., p. 224.
47. *Ruhleben Exhibition* 1919, op. cit.
48. *The Review of Reviews* magazine. October, 1918.
49. Ibid.
50. *The Stage* 9 September, 1915.
51. W.M.D. Mather, MA *A Life with the British Salonika Forces 1917–1919* [1974] p. 160 IWM.
52. Ibid., p. 168.
53. Ibid., p. 166.
54. Ibid., p. 168.
55. Ibid., p. 168.
56. Ibid., p. 169.
57. Frank Ketchington *Dick Whittington* 356.1 61098 [1916] IWM.
58. Programme *Dick Whittington* [1916] private collection.
59. Ibid.
60. Ibid.
61. *The Times* I5 July, 1916.
62. Gunner E. Vines RA 'Personal Diary' 85/7/1 [1917] IWM.
63. Ibid.
64. Siegfried Sasson 'Concert Party' in *The War Poems* arranged by Rupert Hart-Davies [London: Faber & Faber, 1983] p. 120.
65. Miss M.A.A. Swynnerton (VAD in India) 'Private Letters' p. 5. [1917] IWM.
66. Ibid., p. 28.
67. Edmund Blunden, op. cit., p. 200.
68. E. Scullen *First World War Memories 1914–1919* pp/Mor/137 p. 130. IWM.
69. *The Times* I4 January, 1915.
70. Ibid.
71. *The Times* 21 September, 1915.
72. R. S. Cockman, op. cit., p. 115.
73. Ibid.,p. 115.
74. Sergeant J. W. Nevill, '… *and Halifax*' Pantomime Review G. 27 [1917] IWM.

75. Paul Fussell *The Great War and Modern Memory* [Oxford: OUP, 1975] p. 194.
76. Ibid., p. 200.
77. Daphne Jones *Bullets and Bandsmen* [Salisbury: Owl Press, 1992] p.47.
78. Ibid.,p. 117.
79. 'The Shakespeare Tercentenary' *The Stage Year Book, 1917* p. 55.
80. Programme *Tercentenary Shakespeare Festival* Ruhleben Camp. 356 (41) K5083 [1916] IWM.
81. *The Stage* 30 August, 1917.

CHAPTER 6 CIVILIAN THEATRE PROVISION IN THE WAR ZONES

1. Harry Lauder *A Minstrel in France* [London: Melrose, 1918] p. 72.
2. Sir Harry Lauder *Roamin' in the Gloamin'* [London: Hutchinson, 1928] p.186.
3. Ibid., p. 188.
4. H. Lauder, op. cit., p. 116.
5. Sir H. Lauder, op. cit., p. 139.
6. H. Lauder, op. cit., p. 168.
7. Ibid., p. 207.
8. Ibid., p. 203.
9. Sir H. Lauder, op. cit., p. 190.
10. Ibid., p. 219.
11. J. C. Trewin *Benson and the Bensonians* [London: Berrie & Rockcliff 1960], p. 218.
12. Ibid., p. 219.
13. Constance Benson *Mainly Players* [London: Butterworth, 1926] p. 292.
14. J. C. Trewin, op. cit., p. 210.
15. *The Times* 16 January, 1920.
16. J. C. Trewin, op. cit., p. 221.
17. Sir John Martin-Harvey *Autobiography* [London: Samson & Low, 1933], p. 481.
18. Ibid., p. 481.
19. Ibid., p. 481.
20. Ibid., p. 483.
21. Ibid., p. 483.
22. Michael Holroyd *Bernard Shaw–The Pursuit of Power Vol. 2 1889–1918* [London: Hodder, 1989] p. 378.
23. Stanley Weintraub *Bernard S/mw 1914–1918* [London: RKP, 1973] p. 213.
24. Ibid., p. 213.
25. Ibid., p. 214.
26. Ibid., p. 218.

27. M. Holroyd, op. cit., p. 374.
28. Ibid., p. 381.
29. Winifred Loraine *Robert Loraine, Actor, Soldier, Airman* [London: Collins, 1938] p. 237.
30. 5. Weintraub, op. cit., p. 227.
31. Ibid., p. 229.
32. M. Holroyd, op. cit., p. 371.
33. Ibid., p. 374.
34. Ibid., p. 374.
35. Ellaline Terriss *Ellaline Terriss by Herself and with others* [London: Cassell, 1928] p. 212.
36. *The Times* 23 December, 1914.
37. *The Era* 30 December, 1914.
38. E. Terriss, op. cit., 218.
39. Ibid., p. 220.
40. Sewell Stokes *Without Veils* [London: Davies, 1953] p. 65.
41. *The Era* 30 December, 1914.
42. *The Times* 25 January, 1916.
43. *The Era* 20 March, 1918.
44. Michael Sanderson *From Irving to Olivier* [London: Athlone, 1984], p. 164.
45. Arthur Marwick *The Deluge – British Society and the First World War* [Basingstoke: Macmillan, 1965] p. 87.
46. M. Sanderson, op. cit., p. 166.
47. Lena Ashwell *Modern Troubadours* [London: Gyldendal, 1922] p. 6 (Princess Helena Victoria – daughter of Queen Victoria and husband of Prince Christian head of Danish/German Oldenburg).
48. Annette Hullah 'Record of the Music in War Time Committee 1914– 20' in *Musical News* August/September [1920].
49. Barry Findon 'War-Time Music and Drama at the Front', in *Play Pictorial* Supplement No. 200 Vol. XXXIII,January 1919.
50. Ibid.
51. L. Ashwell, op. cit., p. 25.
52. Ibid., p. 27.
53. Ibid., p. 26.
54. 'Concerts and Plays at the Front', *The Stage Year Book, 1919* (author anonymous) p. 20.
55. Ibid., p. 20.
56. Ibid., p. 20.
57. *Bradford Weekly Telegraph* 6 September, 1915.
58. B. Findon, op. cit.
59. *Weekly Despatch* 1 December, 1918.
60. B. Findon, op. cit.
61. Helen Kennedy 'Folk Dancing in France' in *The Vote* 28 February, 1919.
62. L. Ashwell, op. cit., p. 18.
63. Ibid., p. 57.

64. *Daily News* 3 December, 1916.
65. Ibid.
66. Ibid.
67. *The Stage*, 7 February, 1918.
68. B. Findon, op. cit.
69. Ibid.
70. Ibid.
71. L. Ashwell, op. cit., p. 10.
72. Peter Noble *Ivor Novello – Man of the Theatre* [London: Falcon, 1951], p. 58—59.
73. Ibid., p. 58.
74. L. Ashwell, op. cit., p. 11.
75. P. Noble, op. cit., p. 59.
76. Ibid., p. 65.
77. L. Ashwell, op. cit., p. 35.
78. *The Stage* July, 1916 and Nelson Jackson 'The Firing Liners' in *The Stage Year Book, 1917*, pp. 57–60.
79. Ibid.
80. N. Jackson, op. cit.
81. Ibid.
82. *The Stage*, 27 July, 1916.
83. L. Ashwell, op. cit., p. 153.
84. A.J.P. Taylor *The First World War* [London: Hamilton, 1963] p.115.
85. *The Stage*, 27 July, 1916
86. N. Jackson, op. cit.
87. L. Ashwell, op. cit., p. 15.
88. Ibid., p. 16.
89. Ibid., p. 167.
90. Ibid., p. 36.
91. Ibid., p. 60.
92. Ibid., p. 60.
93. Ibid., p. 61.
94. *Daily Mirror*, 12 February, 1918.
95. H. L. Hoare 'With the YMCA in France' in *The Englishwoman* August, 1916, p. 42–44.
96. Ibid.
97. Editor 'What Fighting Men Would Enjoy' in *Lady's Pictorial* 14 October, 1916.
98. L. Ashwell, op. cit., p. 30.
99. Ibid., p. 175.
100. Ibid.,p. 176.
101. Ibid.,p.45.
102. Ibid., p. 49.
103. *Daily Chronicle*, December, 1917.
104. Ibid.
105. M. Anderson, op. cit., p. 168.

106. L. Ashwell, op. cit., p. 39.
107. Ibid., p. 48.
108. *Yorkshire Observer*, 25 October, 1916.
109. 'Concerts and Plays at the Front' *The Stage Year Book, 1919* (author anonymous) p. 21.
110. *The Times*, 18 September, 1916.
111. L. Ashwell, op. cit., p. 45.
112. Ibid., p. 44.
113. Ibid., p. 186.
114. B. Findon, op. cit.
115. A.J.P. Taylor, *English History 1914–45* [London: OUP, 1965], p. 138.
116. L. Ashwell, op. cit., p. 180.
117. Ibid., p. 180.
118. Ibid., p. 176.
119. Ibid., p. 73.
120. Ibid., p. 91.
121. Ibid., p. 77.
122. Ibid., p. 92.
123. Ibid., p. 92.
124. 'Concerts and Plays at the Front' *The Stage Year Book, 1919* (author anonymous) p. 21.
125. L. Ashwell, op. cit., p. 103.
126. Ibid., p. 37.
127. *Liverpool Daily Post*, 19 November, 1917.
128. L. Ashwell, op. cit., p. 112.
129. *The Thistle*, 'A Scottish Patriotic Magazine' Vol. VIII, No. 101, December, 1916.
130. 'Concerts and Plays at the Front' *The Stage Year Book, 1919* (author anonymous) p. 21.
131. L. Ashwell, op. cit., p. 183.
132. J. G. Fuller *Troop Morale and Popular Culture in the British and Dominion Armies 1914–1918* [Oxford: OUP, 1990], p. 115.
133. Ibid.,p. 104.

CHAPTER 7 WAR PLAYS

[Theatres in West End unless otherwise stated]
1. G. T. Watts, 'The Tradition of the Theatre' in *The Englishwoman* 1916, in M. Sanderson *From Irving to Olivier* (London: Athlone, 1984), p. 163.
2. Allardyce Nicol *English Drama 1900–1930* (Cambridge: CUP 1973), p.3.
3. T. W. Craik [ed.] *The Revels History of Drama in English* (London: Methuen 1978), Vol. III, p. 31.
4. *The Times* 28 December, 1914.
5. Mary Packington *Shakespeare for Merrie England*, Theatre Royal, Worcester (April: 1915) MS 3303, Vol. 8. BL.
6. *The Era* 26 August, 1914.

7. *Home to Tipperary* by a Tipperary woman, Court Theatre (December: 1914) MS 3088, Vol. 36. BL.

8. J.E. McManus *The Man Who Wouldn't*, Kilburn Empire (April: 1915), MS 3317, Vol. 9. BL.

9. Arthur Cleveland *A Bit of Khaki*, Empress Theatre, Brixton (May: 1915), MS 3388, Vol. 11. BL.

10. C. Hickman and Mary Ransome *One o'Kitchener's*, Empire Theatre, York (September: 1915) MS 3697, Vol. 23. BL.

11. J.J. Wild *Listing for a Sojar*, Hippodrome Theatre, Oldham (September: 1914) MS 3055, Vol. 35. BL.

12. PP., 1914–16, VII, Cd. 7750, p. 4. XXV, Cd. 7763 in A. Marwick *The Deluge* (Basingstoke: MacMillan 1986), pp. 43–44.

13. Keble Howard *The Sportsman*, Vaudeville Theatre (June: 1915) MS 3521, Vol. 16. BL.

14. Edward Knoblauch *The Way to Win*, Coliseum Theatre (June: 1915) MS 3491, Vol. 14. BL.

15. P. Kinsey, *The Call*, Tivoli Theatre, Manchester (May: 1915) MS 3425, Vol. 13. BL.

16. William Moore *Supreme Sacrifice*, Empire Theatre, Camberwell (November: 1914) MS 3050, Vol. 35. BL.

17. J.M. Barrie, *The New World*, Duke of York Theatre (March: 1915) MS 3224, Vol. 5. BL.

18. J.D. Beresford and K. Richmond *Howard and Son*, Coliseum Theatre (August: 1916) MS 343, Vol. 16. BL.

19. Bertrand Davis *A Call to Arms*, Golders Green Hippodrome Theatre (September: 1914) MS 2926, Vol. 28. BL.

20. Seymour Hicks and Edward Knoblauch, *England Expects*, London Opera House (September: 1914) MS 2941, Vol. 29. BL. G.E. Jennings *The King's Men*, Royalty Theatre (September: 1914) MS 2949, Vol. 29. BL. Jeannette Sherwin *John Shannon, Reservist*, Empire Theatre, Shoreditch (September: 1914) MS 2919, Vol. 29. BL. Arthur Dande *Your Country Needs You*, Tivoli Theatre, Manchester (September: 1914) MS 2959, Vol. 29. BL.
    K. Foss *The Hem of the Flag*, Hippodrome Theatre, Woolwich (September: 1914) MS 2934, Vol. 29. BL.

21. Harold D. Lasswell *Propaganda Techniques in the World War* (London: Kegan Paul, 1927), p. 196.

22. C. W. Mill, *In Time of War*, Theatre Royal, South Shields (September: 1914) MS 2928, Vol. 28. BL.

23. Victor Grayson *War, Wine, and – a Woman!*, Camberwell Empire Theatre (March: 1915) MS 3228, Vol. 5. BL.

24. Earl Derr Biggers *Inside the Lines*, Apollo Theatre (May: 1917) MS 952, Vol. 9. BL.

25. A. Myddleton-Myles, *Beware German*, Palace Theatre, Battersea (November: 1918) MS 1828, Vol. 18. BL.

26. Clifford Rean *Lest We Forget*, King's Theatre, Gainsborough January: 1919) MS 1971, Vol. 1. BL.
27. Dorothy Mullord *In the Hands of the Hun*, Hippodrome Theatre, Willesden (April: 1915) MS 3342, Vol. 10. BL.
28. John Brandon *For Those in Peril*, Collins Music Hall (February: 1916) MS 28, Vol. 2. BL.
29. Stephen Phillips *Armageddon*, New Theatre (June: 1915) MS 3411, Vol. 12. BL.
30. *The Times* 2 June, 1915.
31. Percy Barrow and Jose Levy *A Daughter of England*, Garrick Theatre (January: 1915) MS 3131, Vol. 1. BL.
32. Dorothy Mullord, op. cit.
33. Author anonymous *War, Red War*, Foresters Theatre (May: 1915) MS 3664, Vol. 14. BL.
34. J.M. Barrie *Der Tag*, Coliseum Theatre (December: 1914) MS 3077, Vol. 36. BL.
35. Edward Knoblauch *Marie Oldie*, His Majesty's Theatre (June: 1915) MS 3493, Vol. 14. BL.
36. *The Times* 20 May, 1915.
37. *The Times* 13 March, 1916.
38. L.E. Durrell *Kulture*, Hippodrome Theatre, Manchester (December: 1914) MS 3112, Vol. 37. BL.
39. J.S. Bratton 'Theatre at War, the Crimea on the London Stage 1854–5' in David Bradbury [ed.] *Performance and Politics in Popular Drama* (Cambridge: CUP 1980), p. 135.
40. *The Era* 5 August, 1914.
41. H. D. Lasswell, op. cit., 196.
42. Author anonymous *The Pedlar of Dreams*, Vaudeville Theatre (December: 1915) MS 3923, Vol. 34. BL.
43. John MacKenzie *Propaganda and Empire* (Manchester: MAP 1984), p. 40.
44. Author anonymous *Red Riding Hood*, Theatre Royal, Edinburgh (December: 1916) MS 670, Vol. 32. BL.
45. Author anonymous *Sinbad the Sailor*, Palace Theatre, Tottenham (December: 1916) MS 651, Vol. 31. BL.
46. *The Pedlar of Dreams*, op. cit.
47. Author anonymous *Joyland*, Hippodrome (December: 1915) MS 3935, Vol. 34. BL.
48. St. John Hamund *The War Men-Agerie*, Scala Theatre (March: 1915) MS 3280, Vol. 7. BL.
49. A.J.P. Taylor, *English History 1914–45* (London: OUP 1965), p. 4.
50. Arthur Marwick *The Deluge – British Society and the First World War* (Basingstoke: Macmillan 1965), p. 71.
51. John Stevenson, *British Society 1914–45* (Harmondsworth: Pelican 1984), p. 55.
52. A.J.P. Taylor, op. cit., p. 39.
53. H.D. Lasswell, op. cit., p. 47.

54. Ibid.

55. Author anonymous *The Passing Show*, Palace Theatre (March: 1915) MS 3221, Vol. 17. BL.

56. Author anonymous *Good Evening*, Palace Theatre, Hammersmith July: 1915) MS 3543, Vol. 11. BL.

57. P. de Corville and E W. Mark, *Push & Go*, London Hippodrome (May: 1915) MS 3372, Vol. ll.BL.

58. Michael Holroyd *The Pursuit of Power 1898–1918*, (London: Hopper 1989), p. 354.

59. Ibid., p. 360.

60. Dreda Boyd *John Feeny – Socialist*, Pavilion Theatre, Glasgow June: 1915) MS 3474, Vol. 14. BL.

61. A.J.P. Taylor, op. cit., p. 19.

62. Peter Buitenhuis *The Great War of Words* (London: Barsford 1989), p. 12.

63. *Report of Coal Industry Commission*, Vol. 1; PP., XII, Cd. 359, p. 4 quoted in A. Marwick, op. cit., p. 124.

64. Eille Norwood, *War Mates*, Victoria Palace, (November: 1915) MS 3820, Vol. 29. BL.

65. James Sexton *Boys of the Old Brigade*, Lyric Theatre, Liverpool (March: 1916) MS 96, Vol. 4. BL.

66. J.M. MacKenzie, op. cit., p. 42.

67. Herbert Sidney *Somewhere in France*, Scala Theatre Leachombe, Cheshire (April: 1915) MS 3284, Vol. 7. BL.

68. St. John Hamund, op. cit.

69. A. Wimperis and H. Carrick *By Jingo, If We Do*, Empire Theatre (October: 1914) MS 2981, Vol. 31. BL.

70. A. Emen *For England, Home and Beauty*, Prince Theatre (May: 1915) MS 3392, Vol. 12. BL.

71. S. Collins *A Day in a Dugout*, Empire Theatre, Liverpool (August: 1916) MS 402, Vol. 19. BL.

72. Author anonymous *Mother's Sailor Boy*, Hippodrome, Salford (September: 1916) MS 438, Vol. 21. BL.

73. K. Edwards *Diddled*, Empire Theatre, Durham (December: 1916) MS 543, Vol. 26. BL.

74. Paul Fussell *The Great War and Modern Memory* (Oxford: OUP 1977) p. 82.

75. Herbert Sargent *Water Birds*, Middlesex Music Hall (December: 1916) MS 5588, Vol. 26. BL.

76. Author anonymous *Airs and Graces*, Palace Theatre (June: 1917) MS 1012, Vol. 13. BL.

77. Sewell Collins, *The Conscienceless Objector* at Hippodrome (March: 1916) MS 124, Vol. 5. BL.

78. Edmund Frobisher *Gott Strafe England*, Hawick Pavilion Theatre (August: 1915) MS 3685, Vol. 23. BL.

79. Zara A Steiner, 'Britain and the Origins of the First World War' 1977, quoted in J. M. MacKenzie, op. cit., p. 50.
80. Keeble Howard, *The Man They Wouldn't Pass* (February: 1915) MS 3186, Vol. 3. BL.
81. Sheila Walsh *Up Boys and at'Em*, Metropole Theatre, Manchester (April: 1915) MS 3271, Vol. 7. BL.
82. H. Stanton, *Twixt Love and Duty or The Call to Arms*, Bedford Music Hall (August: 1915) MS 3613, Vol. 20. BL.
83. *Life in a Trench* words by D.S. Parsons, music by Paul Rubens. Performed in *Somewhere in France*, Chiswick Empire Theatre (July: 1916) MS 387, Vol. 19. BL.
84. *The Home Road* lyrics by Lena Guilbert Ford, music by Jean Nougues in *Somewhere in France*, ibid.
85. *Oh! It's a Lovely War* in *Jack in the Box*, Empire Theatre, Nottingham (April: 1918) MS 1505, Vol. 7. BL.
86. Alec D. Saville *Britain's Guests*, Mile End Empire Theatre, (November: 1917) MS 1205, Vol. 21. BL
87. Austin Page *By Pigeon Post*, Garrick Theatre (March: 1918) MS 1445, Vol. 5. BL.
88. Clifford Rean *When Joy Bells are Ringing*, Elephant and Castle Theatre (April: 1918) MS 1486, Vol. 6. BL.
89. Author anonymous *Over the Lines*, Baths Hall, Barking (April: 1918) MS 1487, Vol. 6. BL.
90. C. F. Armstrong, *Home Service*, Devonshire Park Theatre, Eastbourne (April: 1918) MS 1487, Vol. 7. BL.
91. Harold Owens & Alfred Turner, *The Angels of Mons*, London Coliseum Theatre (March: 1916) MS 95, Vol. 3. BL.
92. A. Shirley *British to the Backbone*, Hippodrome, Richmond (November: 1917) MS 1237, Vol. 22. BL.
93. Odette Teherine *Black Widows*, Savoy Theatre (January: 1918) MS 1331, Vol. 1. BL.
94. Sir John Foster Fraser [adapted for stage by Hugh C. Buckler] *The Grousers*, Ardwick Empire, Manchester (November: 1917) MS 1211, Vol. 21. BL
95. Author anonymous *Cheep*, Vaudeville Theatre (April: 1917) MS 905, Vol. 8. BL.
96. Louis N. Parker, *Pageant of Fair Women*, Queen's Hall (May: 1918) MS 939, Vol. 8. BL.
97. Louis N. Parker *Pageant of Freedom*, Queen's Hall (May: 1918) MS 1541, Vol. 8. BL.
98. J.M. MacKenzie, op. cit., p. 46.
99. *The Era* 20 August, 1914.
100. E. A. Baughan 'Drama of the Year' *The Stage Year Book, 1915*, p. 1.
101. Ibid., p. 1.
102. B. Weller, 'The War and the Stage' *The Stage Year Book, 1915*, p. 2.
103. E. A. Baughan, op. cit., p. 9.
104. Ibid., p. 8.

105. Author anonymous *The Babes in the Wood* Opera House, Middlesbrough [January: 1915] MS 750, Vol. 2. BL.
106. Author anonymous *Babes in the Wood* Hippodrome Theatre, Gates-head [December: 1916] MS 667, Vol. 32. BL.
107. Martin Byam *Bo-Peep* Coliseum Theatre, Glasgow [December: 1916] MS 650, Vol. 31. BL.
108. E. A. Baughan, 'Drama of the Year', *The Stage Year Book, 1917*, p. 1.
109. E. A. Baughan, 'Drama of the Year' *The Stage Year Book, 1918*, p. 1.
110. Lynton Hudson, *The English Stage 1850–1950* [London: Harrap, 1951] p. 164.
111. *The Stage* 7 September, 1916.
112. *The Stage* 2 November, 1916.
113. *The Times* 29 November, 1916.
114. Bernard Weller, 'The Stage in War Time' *The Stage Year Book, 1917*, p. 19.
115. *The Era* 16 July, 1916.
116. *The Times* 3 November, 1916.
117. *The Times* 3 October and 30 October, 1916.
118. *The Times* 1 November, 1916.
119. *The Era* 8 March, 1916.
120. Author anonymous *Mrs Pusheen: the Hoarder* Alexandra Theatre, Stoke Newington. [March: 1918] MS 1446, Vol. 5. BL.
121. Bert Lee and R. P. Weston *Rations* Hippodrome Theatre, Colchester [April: 1918] MS 1493, Vol. 6. BL.
122. Sheila Walsh *When Our Lads Come Marching Home* Theatre Royal, South Shields [February: 1918] MS 1399, Vol. 3. BL.
123. Arthur Coles Armstrong 'The Variety Year' *The Stage Year Book, 1919*, p. 35.
124. *The Era* 9 January, 1919.

CONCLUSIONS

1. George Grossmith *G.G.* [London: Hutchinson, 1933], p. 108.
2. *The Era* 17 March, 1915.
3. Sidney Allison *The Bantams* [London: Baker, 1981] p. 62.
4. John M. MacKenzie [ed.] *Imperialism and Popular Culture* [Manchester: MUP, 1986], p. 5.
5. 'Plays of the Year' *The Stage Year Book, 1919* pp. 79–107.
6. *Demobilization* HMSO, pp. 1–4, 1918.
7. Michael Holroyd *Bernard Shaw – The Pursuit of Power 1898–1918*, Vol. 2,1989, p. 336.
8. Arthur Coles Armstrong 'The Variety Year' *The Stage Year Book, 1919*, p. 31.
9. Ibid., p. 31.
10. Ibid., p. 31.
11. Basil Dean *The Theatre at War* [London: Harrap 1956], pp. 21, 19 and 34.

Bibliography

All articles, pamphlets and books published in London unless otherwise stated. Other Abbreviations: P. P. (Parliamentary Papers), HMSO (His Majesty's Stationery Office).

CONTEMPORARY NEWSPAPERS AND PERIODICALS

National Press
Daily Chronicle
Daily News
Daily Mirror
Morning Post
The Economist
The Observer
The Times
The Thistle
Weekly Despatch

Regional Press
Aldershot News
Bradford Weekly Telegraph
Evening News
The Standard
Leeds Mercury
Liverpool Daily Post
Yorkshire Observer

Arts Press
Musical News
The Era
The Play Pictorial
The Review of Reviews
The Stage

Other Journals
Lady's Pictorial
The Englishwoman
The Garden
The Tatler
The British Empire YMCA Weekly
The Fifth Gloster Gazette
The Vote
Wipers Times

PARLIAMENTARY PAPERS AND OFFICIAL PUBLICATIONS

1. P. P. *National War Savings Report* 1917–18 XVIII Cd. 8516.
2. P. P. *The Organization and Methods of the Central Prisoners of War Committee* 1917–18 XVIII Cd. 8615.
3. P. P. *Command Document* 1916, 9106.
4. P. P. *Report of Coal Industry Commission* 1919 XII Cd. 359 Vol. I.
5. P. P. *War Refugees' Committee Report*, 1914–16 VII Cd. 7750 and XXV Cd. 7763.
6. *Labour Conditions and Adult Education* Ministry of Reconstruction 1919.
7. *Demobilization* Z 10. Ministry of War 1918.
8. *Report on Brocton Camp Complaints, 1917–19* IWM Files: W/W/ 1 78/31 /1, 1920.
9. T.J. Mitchell and G. M. Smith *Medical Services: Casualties and Medical Statistics of the Great War* 1931.

10. YMCA *The Red Triangle Handbook* 1915. YMCA Library, Walthamstow, London.
11. Retail Price Index Tables, published in *Accountancy*. Journal of Institute of Chartered Accountants of England and Wales, 1994.
12. Report of the Committee on *Alleged German Outrages* President – Viscount Bryce, GM, 1915 HMSO.
13. *Principal Events 1914–18* Compiled by The Historical Section of the Committee of Imperial Defence, 1922 HMSO.

UNPUBLISHED LETTERS, DIARIES AND REPORTS

There is a selection of diaries, letters and reports in the Department of Documents at the Imperial War Museum, London. Many of the reports, particularly those dealing with charities, are on microfilm, and were compiled by Annette Hullah in the years 1919–20. They are included under the general heading of *Benevolent Societies*. Annette Hullah was the Secretary of the Music in War-Time Committee.

ANNUAL REVIEWS, MAGAZINES AND NEWSPAPERS

A collection of *The Stage Year Books* can be seen in both the Theatre Museum Library, Covent Garden, London and the Westminster Library, London. In each volume can be found annual reviews for both the 'legitimate' theatres and the Variety music halls.

Newspapers and magazines, including the theatrical press – *The Era* and *The Stage* – are housed at the National Newspaper Library in Colindale, north London.

PLAYS AND SCRIPTS

The contemporary scripts that were submitted for approval by the Lord Chamberlain are kept in the Manuscript Department of the British Library, London. There is a catalogue of plays, music hall revues and one-act sketches. These are listed by year and month of submission.

BIOGRAPHY, AUTOBIOGRAPHY AND MEMOIR

Ashwell, Lena *Modern Troubadours* [London: Glydendal, 1922].
Ashwell, Lena *Myself a Player* [London: Glydendal, 1936].
Baylis, Lilian and Hamilton, Cicely *The Old Vic* [London: Cape, 1926].
Bancroft, Squire *Myself a Player* [London: Murray, 1925].
Beecham, T. *A Mingled Chime* [London: Hutchinson, 1944].
Beerbohm, Max *Herbert Beerbohm Tree* [London: Hutchinson, 1917].
Benson, Sir Frank *My Memories* [London: Ernest Ben, 1930].
Benson, Constance *Mainly Players* [London: Butterworth, 1926].
Blunden, Edmund *Undertones of War* [Harmondsworth: Penguin, 1928].

Brereton, Austen *H. B. and Laurence Irving* [London: Richards, 1922].

Cohen-Portheim, Paul *Time Stood Still: My Internment in England, 1914–18* [London: Duckworth, 1932].

Collier, Constance *Harlequinade, the Story of My Life* [London: Lane, 1929].

Cooper, Dame Gladys *Gladys Cooper* [London: Hutchinson, 1931]

Croxton, Arthur *Crowded Nights and Days* [London: Sampson & Marston, 1934]

Dean, Basil *The Theatre at War* [London: Harrap 1956].

Dean, Basil *Seven Ages – An Autobiography 1888–1927* [London: Hutchinson, 1970.

Davidson Ketchum, J. *Ruhleben – A Prison Camp Society* [Oxford: OUP, 1965].

Drinkwater, John *Inheritance* [London: Benn, 1931].

Forbes-Robertson, Diana *Maxine* [London: Hamilton, 1964].

Forbes-Robertson, Sir Johnston *A Player under Three Reigns* [London: Unwin, 1925].

Graves, Robert *Goodbye To All That* [London: Cape, 1929].

Glover, Michael [ed.] *The Fateful Battle Line* [London: Cooper, 1993].

Grossmith, George *G.G.* [London: Hutchinson, 1933].

Hardwick, Sir Cedric *Let's Pretend* [London: Grayson, 1932].

Henson, Leslie *My Laugh Story* [London: Hodder & Staunton, 1926].

Henson, Leslie *Yours Faithfully* [London: Long, 1948].

Hicks, Seymour *Between Ourselves* [London: Cassell, 1930].

Holroyd, Michael *Bernard Shaw – The Pursuit of Power* [London: Hodder, 1989].

Hornung, E. W. *Notes on a Camp-follower on the Western Front* [London: Constable, 1919].

Jacob, Naomi *Me* [London: Hutchinson, 1933].

Jones, Daphne *Bullets and Bandsmen* [Salisbury: Owl Press, 1992].

Kingstone, Gertrude *Curtsey While You're Thinking* [London: William & Norgate, 1937].

Lauder, Harry *A Minstrel in France* [London: Melrose, 1918].

Lauder, Sir Harry *Roamin' in the Gloamin'* [London: Hutchinson, 1928].

Loraine, Winifred *Robert Loraine Actor, Soldier, Airman* [London: Collins, 1938.

Macdonald, Lyn *The Roses of No Man's Land* [Basingstoke: Macmillan, 1980].

Mackail, Denis *The Story of J. M. B.* [London: Davies, 1941].

Mant, Gilbert [ed.] *Soldier Boy* [Stevenage: Spa Books, 1992].

Martin-Harvey, Sir John *Autobiography* [London: Samson & Low, 1933].

Maud, Cyril *Behind the Scenes* [London: Murray, 1927].

May, H. A. *Memories of the Artists' Rifles* [London: Howlett, 1929].

Moore, Eva *Exits and Entrances* [London: Chapman & Hall, 1923].

Moynihan M. [ed.] *People at War* [Newton Abbot: David & Charles, 1973].

Nicholson W. N. *Behind the Lines* [London: Cape, 1939].

Noble, Peter *Ivor Novello – Man of the Theatre* [London: Falcon, 1951].

Pearson, Hesketh *Bernard Shaw* [London: Collins, 1932].

Pogson, Rex *Miss Horniman and the Gaiety Theatre Manchester* [London: Rockliff, 1952].

Potton, Edward [ed.] *A Record of the United Arts Rifles* [London: Moring, 1920].

Purdom, C.B. *Harley Granville Barker* [London: Rockliff, 1955].

Steen, Marguerite *A Pride of Terrys* [London: Longmans, 1962].

Stokes, Sewell *Without Veils* [London: Davies, 1953].

Terriss, Ellaline *Ellaline Terriss by Herself and with Others* [London: Cassell, 1928].

Trewin,J.C. *Benson and the Bensonians* [London: David & Charles, 1960].

Vanbrugh, Violet *Dare to be Wise* [London: Hodder & Stoughton, 1925].

Walbrook H.M. *J.M Barrie and the Theatre* [London: White, 1922].

Webster, Margaret *The Same Only Different* [London: Gollancz, 1969].

Weintraub, Stanley *Bernard Shaw 1914–1918* [New York: RKP, 1969].

Wilson, A.E. *Prime Minister of Mirth* [London: Odhams, 1956].

Other Books

Agate, James *A Short View of the English Stage* [London: Jenkins, 1926].

Barker, Kathleen *Bristol at Play* [Bradford-on-Avon: Moonraker, 1976].

Beckett, Ian and Simpson, Keith (eds.) *A Nation in Arms* [London: Donovan, 1985].

Belling, Henry *Modern Britain 1885–1955* [London: Cardinal, 1974].

Bruce, George *The Paladin Dictionary of Battles* [London: Paladin, 1986].

Buchan, John *A History of the First World War* [Moffat: Lochar, 1991].

Buitenhuis, Peter *The Great War of Words* [London: Batsford, 1989].

Cochran, Charles *Secrets of a Showman* [London: Heinemann, 1925].

Cohen, Joseph *Journey to the Trenches* [London: Robson, 1975].

Craik, T.W. (gen. ed.) *The Revels History of Drama in English* [London: Methuen, 1978].

Dakers, Caroline *The Countryside at War* [London: Constable, 1987].

Dent, Edward *A Theatre for Everyone* [London: Boardman, 1945].

Eksteins, Modris *Rites of Spring* [London: Black Swan, 1989].

Fairlie, J.A. *British War Administration* [New York: OUP, 1919].

Fuller, J.G. *Troop Morale and Popular Culture in the British and Dominion Armies 1914–1918* [Oxford: Clarendon, 1990].

Fussell, Paul *The Great War and Modern Memory* [London: OUP, 1990].

Goldie, Grace Wyndham *The Liverpool Repertory Theatre* [London: Hodder & Stoughton, 1935].

Hammerton, J.A. *Wrack of War* [London: Murray, 1918].

Hart, Liddell *History of the First World War* [London: Faber & Faber 1970].

Hartnoll, Phyllis (ed.) *A Concise History of the Theatre* [Norwich: Thames & Hudson, 1968].

Hudson, Lynton *The English Stage 1850–1950* [London: Harrap, 1951].

Hynes, Samuel *The Edwardian Turn of Mind* [London: Pimlico, 1968].

Hynes, Samuel *A War Imagined* [London: Bodley Head, 1990].

Kemp, T, C. *The Birmingham Repertory Theatre* [Birmingham: Cornish, 1943].

Lenham, John *The English Poets of the First World War* [London: Thames & Hudson, 1982].

Liddle, Peter *Voices of War* [London: Cooper, 1988].

Macdonald, Lyn *Somme* [Basingstoke: Macmillan, 1983].

MacKenzie, John M. *Propaganda and Empire* [Manchester: MUP, 1984].

MacKenzie, John M. *Imperialism and Popular Culture* [Manchester: MUP, 1986].

Macleod Joseph *The Actor's Right to Act* [London: Wishart, 1981].

Macqueen-Pope, W. *Ghosts and Greasepaint* [London: Hale, 1951].

Marwick, Arthur *The Deluge – British Society and the First World War* [Basingstoke: Macmillan, 1965].

Miles, Bernard *The British Theatre* [London: Collins, 1958].

Nicol, Allardyce *British Drama* [London: CUP, 1925].

Nicol, Allardyce *English Drama 1900–1930* [London: Harrap, 1973].

Pankhurst, E. Sylvia *The Home Front* [London: Cressett, 1932].

Pelling, H. *Modern Britain 1885–1955* [London: Cardinal, 1974].

Pick, John *The West End* [Eastbourne: Offord, 1983].

Ponsonby, A. *Falsehood in War Time* [London: Allen & Unwin, 1926].

Priestly, J.B. *Literature and Western Man* [London: Book Club, 1960].

Rowell, George and Jackson, Anthony *The Repertory Movement* [Cambridge: CUP, 1984].

Sanderson, Michael *From Irving to Olivier* [London: Athlone, 1985].

Short, Ernest *Theatrical Cavalcade* [London: Eyre & Spottiswoode, 1942].

Short, Ernest *Sixty Years of Theatre* [London: Eyre & Spottiswoode, 1951].

Taylor, A.J.P. *The First World War* [London: Hamilton, 1963].

Taylor, A.J.P. *English History 1914–45* [Oxford: Clarendon, 1965].

Trewin, J.C. *The Theatre since 1900* [London: Dakers, 1951].

Trewin, J.C. *The Edwardian Theatre* [London: Dakers, 1976].

Vansittart, Peter *Voices of the Great War* [London: Cape, 1981].

Walsh, Colin *Mud, Songs and Blighty* [London: Hutchinson, 1975].

Winter, J. *Socialism and the Challenge of War* [London: RKP, 1974].

Index